RED TIDE

RED TIDE

THE WINDS OF WAR

WILLIAM C. DIETZ

This book is dedicated to all members of the United States Navy past and present. Thank you for your service.

TABLE OF CONTENTS

ACKNOWLEDGEMENTS

I would like to thank the people and organizations without whom this book wouldn't have been possible:

Mark Bebar

Mark Bebar received a B.S. degree in Naval Architecture and Marine Engineering from Webb Institute of Naval Architecture in 1970 and a M.S. degree in Ocean Engineering from Massachusetts Institute of Technology in 1973.

Mark has over 48 years of experience with a focus on total surface ship system research and development, design and acquisition support.

Mr. Bebar began his career with the U.S. Navy Department – Naval Ship Engineering Center in 1970 and by 1971, was assigned to the concept/ feasibility study effort which led to the Patrol Hydrofoil – Missile (PHM) Class.

He was Design Integration Manager for PHM, a member of the Navy design team through lead ship testing, technical issue resolution with Boeing Marine Systems (BMS) and collaborative development of PHM-3 Series follow ship specifications.

In 1978, Mark was assigned to the PHM Program Office (PMS-303) at Naval Sea Systems Command HQ during the early stages of follow ship detailed design and construction.

Martin Grimm

Martin Grimm studied Naval Architecture in Sydney in the late 1980s and spent his career as a naval architect in the Australian Department of Defense in the field of Ship Hydrodynamics. Martin's university thesis project had been a numerical simulation of the motions of surface piercing hydrofoils in waves.

Eliot James

Eliot James is an entrepreneur who, with fellow adventurers Bill and Bob Meinhardt, purchased the *Aires* when the government put her up for sale and subsequently, with the help of his wife Diana James, founded the USS *Aries* Hydrofoil Museum.

Eliot also served as a technical advisor, and was kind enough to coordinate input from other subject matter experts during the writing of this book.

Captain Carl Weiscopf USN (ret.)

Captain Weiscopf graduated from the United States Naval Academy and was commissioned as an Ensign in 1970. After serving on the USS Waddell (DDG 24) during the Vietnam war and other ships thereafter, he was named commanding officer of the USS *Aries* (PHM 5), patrol, hydrofoil, missile ship, which served as the model for the PHMs depicted in this book.

Expertise was garnered from the men and women who invented, built and supported the PHM fleet and the experimental hydrofoils that came before.

Those individuals include John Myer, Marylin Martin, John Monk, Vern Salisbury, Sumi Arima, Harry Larson, Ray Vallinga, Martinn Mandles and countless others—as well as former PHM crew members; Chuck Shannon, Dennis "Mac" McCarthy, Mark "Buz" Buzby, Jan Downing, and Robert "Buzz" Borries.

Many thanks to the following organizations as well:

The USS *Aries* Hydrofoil Museum, located in Gasconade, Missouri: https://www.ussaries.org

The International Hydrofoil Society (IHS): https://www.foils.org

The Historic Naval Ships Association https://www.hnsa.org

CHAPTER ONE

Yulin Harbor, Hainan Island, China

Because of the Yulin navy base, the neighboring city of Sanya was subject to a 2100 curfew and blackout. So, when the ships left the harbor at 0100, there was no fanfare.

The ships were mostly dark, their engines thrumming, as the vessels proceeded single file toward the temporary gap in the closely guarded breakwater. A tug was waiting to pull the sub net back into place.

The carrier strike group's code name was *Nan Feng* (South Wind), and it consisted of six ships. A pilot boat led the way, followed by the destroyers *Changchun,* and *Macau.* The aircraft carrier *Henan* came next. Once the carrier slid past the bomb-proof sub pen, the attack submarines *Changzheng* (Long March) *401,* and the *Changzheng* (Long March) *706,* slipped out to join the nearly invisible procession.

The subs were followed by something new to the Chinese navy, and to the entire world for that matter. And that was the semi-submersible cruiser Hailong (*Sea Dragon*).

She was 667 feet long, powered by a nuclear reactor, and shaped like a submarine with two conning towers. One was located forward, and the other aft, providing redundancy in the case of battle damage.

But what made the *Sea Dragon* so dangerous was her cutting-edge design. Thanks to the cruiser's sleek hull she could travel semi-submerged, so as to reduce drag, and keep pace with a fast-moving naval strike group. Or, the *Dragon* could fight while almost entirely submerged, thereby reducing her radar cross section. What the enemy couldn't see, it couldn't hit.

Of even greater importance however was the semi submersible's total throw weight. Thanks to the *Sea Dragon's* automated systems, and relatively small crew, most of her length was devoted to offensive and defensive weaponry. That included the popup railgun located forward of Conning Tower One, as well as rows of internal launchers that could fire two hundred missiles, at a rate of one every eight seconds.

None of which impressed Vice Admiral Jinhai Wen who, along with key members of his staff, were present on the *Henan's* bridge. Wen had been in the navy for thirty-two years: first as a pilot, then as a surface warfare officer, and later as a senior staff officer.

Now Wen had what he'd always wanted, and that was command of a carrier battle group. And the situation would have been perfect if it weren't for what Wen often referred to as "the barge." Wen pretended to scan a nav screen. "Where's the *Sea Snake*?" he sneered. "Did it sink? Get Ko on the horn. Tell him to fire a flare."

The officers laughed but the enlisted men didn't. They weren't allowed to. Jokes were reserved for officers.

***

Aboard the Sea Dragon

The *Sea Dragon* was divided into six compartments from bow to stern: The Gunnery compartment, Operations Department One, the Missile Compartment, the Reactor Compartment, the Engine Room, and Operations Department Two.

And that was where Lieutenant Junior Grade Jev Jing's duty station was located. He was the ship's third ranking Communications Officer, and responsible for all incoming and outgoing radio traffic during his watch.

The com center was located adjacent to the larger and more complex Combat Information Center, or CIC, which processed all information related to command and control. But because Senior Captain Ko was forward in Ops One, the second CIC was on standby.

Jing liked the arrangement because it meant that the heat, if any, was on Com officers One and Two, who were forward. That left him free to listen in on the radio traffic between ships, and if he was lucky, eavesdrop on one of Admiral Wen's famous rants. The latest of which was directed at the *Macau's* captain: "What's wrong, Pang? Is your helmsman drunk? Order the bastard to steer a straight course."

Jing's radio operator could hear such exchanges too, but was careful to keep a mostly straight face, as the officer chuckled.

"What's so funny?" a third person demanded. "Stand to attention."

Jing knew the voice belonged to the ship's political officer, Lieutenant Commander Bohai Ang. A man who knew very little about the navy, but had connections, and delighted in exercising his power over those of lesser rank.

Jing stood, did a neat about face, and was careful to focus his eyes on a point six inches above Ang's head. "Now," Ang growled. "You were laughing. Please share the joke with me. I would like to laugh too."

"Sir, yes sir. I was thinking about a joke I heard earlier today. A married couple went out to dinner. Suddenly, the wife exclaimed, 'I forgot to turn the gas off! There could be a fire.'

"Then, in an attempt to comfort her, the husband said, 'Don't worry. I forgot to turn the water off.'"

Ang frowned. "And you think that's funny?"

"Sir, yes sir. Because if a fire starts the water will…"

"I know what the water will do," Ang replied. "What is the third principle?"

"That is the principle of upholding the communist party's leadership, sir."

Ang nodded. "Correct. Now sit down and focus on your duties."

Jing performed another about face and sat. And, thanks to Jing's excellent peripheral vision, he saw Ang leave the compartment. *Cao ni.* (Fuck you.)

***

The South China Sea welcomed the carrier strike group with negligible two-foot waves and a southerly breeze. Orders called for the vessels to sail east, around the north end of Luzon, and into the Philippine Sea.

That would have been dangerous had the Philippines been part of the Alliance that included the United States, Great Britain, France, Germany, Israel, Australia, Saudi Arabia, India, Japan, Australia and New Zealand, among others.

But President Antonio Costas and his government had chosen to declare the Philippines as a neutral country. That made practical sense, given the country's proximity to China. As did the rest of the president's pro-Chinese policies.

There was a price to pay however. Many Filipinos were sympathetic to the Alliance, hated Costas, and wanted to overthrow their government. Something they weren't likely to accomplish so long as China continued to provide Costas with the money and weapons his secret police used to keep the populace under his thumb.

It had been a long day for Captain Ko. And once the *Sea Dragon* was well clear of land, he felt comfortable turning the ship over to his executive officer (XO) Commander Shi. The relationship between the men was good. That meant Ko felt free to speak more openly than he usually did. "Let me know if the Admiral gets his shorts in a knot. But I suspect he's well into his third glass of *Huangjiu* (yellow wine) by now."

Shi smiled. "Don't worry, sir ... I'll let you know if a storm starts to blow."

After departing Operations One, Ko made his way into officer country. His cabin was 12 feet long and 6 feet wide. Not a large compartment by civilian standards, but huge aboard the *Sea Dragon*, and nearly the size of the officer's mess.

Most of the space was occupied by his desk, standing locker, and a metal framed bed. The adjoining head (bathroom) consisted of a sink, marine toilet, and a shower. That's where Ko went first. To cleanse his body, and to some extent, his spirit.

The shower lasted exactly two minutes and not a second more. That was the length of time allotted to sailors, so that was the amount of time that Ko allowed himself—for to consume more than his share would be dishonorable.

Ko toweled off, entered the cabin naked, and made his way to the far end of the compartment where, rather than the couch naval architects had planned for, an altar to the goddess Tianfei, the "Princess of Heaven," was waiting for him.

Tianfei had many other names as well, including Ma-tsu, Ah-Ma' Linghui Furen, and Linghui Fei. But regardless of which name worshipers chose to call her, they knew the goddess to be the deity of all seafarers.

A two-foot-tall statue of Tianfei occupied the center of the altar. The likeness was carved from white alabaster. Her hair was pulled back into a bun, her head turned slightly to the right, her eyes downcast. One hand was extended as if to convey a blessing.

And there, rising to break around her gown, were waves of beautifully sculpted stone. The flowers Ko had brought aboard were displayed in permanent containers to either side of the goddess; all of them were blue like the endless sky and ocean.

To approach Tianfei naked was to proclaim Ko's humility. And that was important because Tianfei cared nothing for rank or wealth. Her favors were, and had always been, for common sailors.

Ko knelt in front of Tianfei and bowed. His eyes were focused on the deck. "I am a sailor. I ask your blessing upon my ship and crew.

"We are setting forth on a journey which, if we're fortunate, will further the war effort. And that is a matter of great importance because, just as China shaped the past, so must China shape the future—and eventually the planet. May your eyes see us, may your ears hear our prayers, and may your divine powers protect us from harm."

After completing his devotional Ko donned fresh underwear, brushed his teeth, and prepared a uniform for the next watch. It was the same routine Ko had followed for twenty-eight years. First as a common sailor. Then rising step-by-step to the lofty position of senior captain. A process which, combined with Ko's decision to be celibate, left no room for a wife or children.

Finally, it was time to slip between cool sheets and grant himself permission to sleep. A state which, after decades in the navy, Ko could enter within seconds, making the most of the opportunity to rest. Ko drifted away.

When the phone rang Ko awoke quickly with all of his senses alert. A glance at his bedside clock informed him that he'd been asleep for three hours and forty-two minutes. He lifted the handset. "Yes."

"Shi, sir. You are to participate in a command call eighteen minutes from now. According to the Strategic Support Force (SSF), an American carrier strike group is approximately 200 miles east of Luzon, and headed our way. Admiral Wen has orders to attack and destroy that force."

Thanks to his many years in the navy, Ko could listen to Shi's summary, and guess what was taking place in Beijing. The Allies had sent groups into the Philippine Sea before. And so long as they stayed east of Luzon the Central Military Commission (CMC) had been satisfied to fire threats rather than missiles at the enemy.

So, what had changed? The answer was obvious. On orders from President Enlai, the People's Liberation Army (PLA) had dispatched thousands of troops into India as part of the much ballyhooed "Big Push." An initiative intended to conqueror all of India and establish a link with ally Pakistan.

But now, rather than occupying India, the army was fighting to hold onto the long, north-south slice of the country they'd been able to seize earlier. A failure which reflected poorly on both Enlai and the CMC. Viewed through that prism the Allied strike group was a gift from *Tian* (heaven). A quick and decisive victory over the Allies would go a long way toward repairing Enlai's image as China's infallible leader. "Thank you," Ko said. "I will join you in Operations One for the call."

"Yes, sir."

"And Shi…"

"Sir?"

"Sound battle stations."

***

Aboard the aircraft carrier *USS Concord*, east of Luzon

Carrier Strike Group 6 (CCSG 6) consisted of the aircraft carrier *USS Concord*, the frigate *Trevor Jones*, the destroyers *Lyndon B. Johnson* and *Herman Cady*, the fast combat support ship *Bridge*, and the submarines *Washington* and *Utah*. All of which were taking part in a search and rescue operation in the area east of Luzon. The trick was to carry out that mission without engaging the Chinese fleet lurking to the west.

But the American ships were 200 miles off Luzon. That gave Hoyer some pad, and he was determined to take advantage of it. A US navy transport plane carrying eleven people had crashed in the Philippine Sea the previous day. Eight people had been rescued and transferred to the *Concord* for medical evaluation. But three were missing.

By searching all night, the strike force's ships and aircraft had covered more than 370 square miles of ocean by sunrise. Hoyer knew the chances of finding the remaining passengers was slim, but he wasn't about to give up. Not until forced to do so.

Hoyer was on the *Concord's* bridge, ploughing through the administrative crap the Pentagon had dropped on him during the night, when Captain George Danby dropped into the chair beside him. The two men went way back, all the way to Annapolis, where Danby had been a year behind Hoyer. "We've got a problem, Will," Danby said. "According to the latest from the National Recognizance Office (NRO), a Chinese strike force put to sea from Yulin."

Hoyer looked up and frowned. "Because of *us*? Or just for the hell of it?"

Danby shrugged. "The spooks don't know."

"Shit, shit, shit," Hoyer said, as he put his laptop aside. "Break the search off. Order the *Bridge* to execute a one-eighty and run like hell. Send the remaining C-2 transport to the emergency strip on Palau. Bring the planes back and refuel them. Fighters first, Hawkeyes second. I want one in the air at all times. Pull the COs together for a conference call, ten from now. Got it?"

Danby stood. "Got it. Shall I send the crew to battle stations?"

"Yes," Hoyer replied. "You should."

***

Aboard the Chinese aircraft carrier *Henan*, west of Luzon

Lieutenant Junior Grade Jev Jing was required to monitor the command conference to ensure that there weren't any technical glitches, but would have done so anyway, just out of curiosity. All of the *Sea Dragon's* personnel were at battle stations. *Why?*

Was a battle in the offing? Or, was Admiral Wen putting the strike group through yet another training exercise? Jing assumed the latter.

But Jing was wrong—as became apparent once the call was underway. Wen came right to the point. "An American carrier strike group is approaching Luzon from the east. We have orders to attack the *Gweilos* (westerners) and sink their ships. We will obey.

"Aircraft flying off the *Henan*, and missiles fired by our destroyers, will catch the Americans by surprise and lay waste to their fleet.

"Meanwhile our submarines will circle around the north end of Luzon, and launch missiles. Then they will close with the enemy, and make good use of their torpedoes."

Jing noticed that no mention had been made of the *Sea Dragon*. Because Wen thought of the semi-submersible cruiser as a barge? Yes, Jing thought so. He wasn't surprised when Captain Ko spoke. "I have a suggestion, sir. Since our submarines are to circle around Luzon, the *Sea Dragon* could accompany them, and flank the Americans to the north."

The suggestion was met with a long moment of silence. What was Wen thinking? The admiral had to deploy the *Sea Dragon*, Jing reasoned, because the semi-submersible concept was popular with the "new wave" admirals, as well as certain members of the Central Military Commission. Even junior lieutenants knew that.

Wen cleared his throat. "That makes sense, Captain Ko ... Although I suspect that the American carrier will be sinking by the time your ship gets into position.

"You have your orders. Execute them."

***

Aboard the aircraft carrier *USS Concord*, east of Luzon

Admiral Hoyer was still on the bridge. Captain Danby was in the Combat Direction Center (CDC) where he could best monitor the *Concord's* tactical and operational defense systems. The lighting was dim, amber colored data scrolled down screens, and the subdued buzz of conversation could be heard.

The air defense weapons coordinator (ADWC) was responsible for defending the ship. LT. Commander Nancy Allard had the duty, and was feeding information to Danby. "Both Phalanx close-in weapons systems are on line sir. The second transport is en route to Palau. The Chinese are launching fighters. Chinese missiles are enroute from the west. Our RIM-Six-Sixes are in the air."

The U.S. frigate and both destroyers were armed with RIM-66 medium range surface-to-air missiles. It was Danby's hope that the weapons would intercept most, if not all, of the incoming threats.

"We have five, no six, F-16s in the air on a course to intercept," Allard continued. "The incoming fighters appear to be Shenyang J-15s, which have twin engines, and are likely to be armed with Kh-41 ramjet powered anti-ship cruise missiles."

Danby felt an emptiness in his stomach and strove to ignore it. Odds were that the Six-Sixes would intercept the incoming weapons. Failing that, the Phalanx CIWS "sea-wiz" close-in weapon system could handle the job. Meanwhile Danby knew that the *Concord* was launching fighters at the rate of three every thirty-seven seconds. And it wouldn't be long until every flyable plane was in the air.

The air battle was going to be fought over the island of Luzon which, if memory served, was something like 460 miles long, and 140 miles wide. And, since Luzon was the largest and most populous island in the Philippines, collateral damage was a lead pipe certainty.

Danby could imagine President Costas in front of the cameras, complaining about the Americans, and demanding reparations without any mention of the Chinese. But that wasn't his job. No, *his* job was to defend the strike force, and take the battle to the Chinese if he could.

"The *Johnson* took a hit," Allard announced. "No, *two* hits."

Danby swore. The dying had begun.

***

Aboard the Chinese semi-submersible cruiser Sea Dragon off the north end of Luzon

Junior Lieutenant Jev Jing listened as the submarine captains delivered their reports in quick succession. Each boat was armed with sixteen JL-2 ship-to-ship missiles, all of which had been fired. And that, according to the chatter from the CIC, was one of the reasons why the Americans were losing. The combined throw weight of the Chinese destroyers, along with the submarine launched weapons, was more than the enemy's anti-air missiles could handle.

And that was to say nothing of the air launched Kh-31 air-to-surface supersonic missiles which were capable of reaching Mach 3.5. Two 31s had been able to target an enemy destroyer which was, according to multiple reports, sinking.

Hits had been scored on the American frigate as well. All of which was good, but not good enough, since the carrier was the grand prize.

"I'm watching you," a voice said. And, when Jing turned, there was Lieutenant Commander Ang standing with hands on hips.

"Sir, yes sir," Jing replied. His face was empty of all expression. But secretly, deep within, Jing was filled with hatred. *I will find a way to screw you*, Jing thought, *and you won't see it coming.*

***

Aboard the aircraft carrier USS *Concord*, east of Luzon

LT. Commander Jayson Greer, aka "Gun Daddy," felt the usual butterflies in the pit of his stomach as he taxied up to the catapult.

It was the same sensation he'd felt stepping out onto the football field as a high school kid, only worse, because this was the real banana. A combat mission.

Planes were going off every minute or so, and Greer's would be among the last to get airborne as Chinese missiles and planes swept in from the west. Greer took a moment to scan his controls and instruments, found all of them to his liking, and tossed a salute.

After looking to make sure everyone was clear, the catapult officer, or "shooter," put one knee on the deck. His arm snapped forward. That was the signal for the deck edge operator to press the launch button. Greer felt as if an elephant were sitting on his lap as the plane hurled forward. Then everything became a blur as the end of the deck rushed at him.

Within seconds the screeching, whirring, and hissing noises associated with a takeoff were replaced by a steady hum. Greer was airborne, but not just airborne, he was a fucking target.

Most of the action was taking place at around 20,000 feet over Luzon. That's where the Chinese Shenyang J-15s were trying to fire ship killers at the American strike force while American F-18s sought to shoot them down.

But Greer, along with Lieutenant Katie "Soccer Mom" Bowers, had orders to go after the enemy carrier. And to accomplish that it didn't make sense to go high.

Greer kept his F/A-18E Super Hornet 200 feet above the waves and therefore well below Chinese radar. A quick glance confirmed that Bowers was off his left wing and hanging back.

Luzon was a dark line up ahead at first. Then the island took on more definition, turned green, and flashed below. Greer knew where the Chinese carrier was because his plane knew. Had they been spotted yet? *Hell no*, Greer decided. *And I know that because I'm alive.*

It seemed logical to suppose that most of the Chinese J-15s were to the east, attacking the group, and equally logical to assume that two or three were flying CAP (combat air patrol) over the enemy flattop. They would be at twenty thou or so. That would allow them to dive on the Americans.

But before the Chinese pilots could intervene, the American pilots would try to hit the carrier with AG-88 HARMs (High-speed Anti-Radiation Missiles). The HARMs were designed to home in on the ship's main surface-to-air radars, as well as those that controlled the carrier's close-in weapons systems.

And Greer knew that if the effort failed the F-18s would be met by a devastating curtain of 30mm cannon fire. "Gun Daddy to Soccer Mom," Greer said over the radio. "All HARMs on three. Over."

"Roger that," Bowers replied. "On three. Over."

Each F-18 was carrying four of the anti-radiation missiles for a total of eight. The hope being that at least half of the HARMs would get through.

Greer cleared his throat. "One, two, *three*. Over."

"Birds away," Bowers replied. "Over."

Once fired, Greer knew the HARMs would take care of themselves. He could see the carrier by then. It was little more than a speck but getting larger with every passing second. "Standby to fire the AGMs. Over."

The F-18s each carried four AGM-158C Long Range Anti-Ship Cruise Missiles. Unlike previous systems the AGMs could independently target enemy vessels without support from Global Positioning Satellites or data links. And assuming that the HARMs were able to blind the carrier's anti-air capability, the AGMs were going to pound it.

"All AGMs," Greer said. "On three. One, two, *three*. Over."

"Birds away," Bowers responded. "Go Navy. Over."

Flashes were visible ahead as the HARMs struck the carrier. A scant minute passed before the first AGM arrived. Greer would never know how many of the cruise missiles got through before he was forced to pull up and climb. But he saw at least three explosions, and knew that major damage had been done.

There was no time to celebrate. Two Shenyang J-15s were coming down to play, and since his Radar Warning Receiver was buzzing, Greer knew a missile was tracking him.

The F-18's ECM (electronic counter measures) jammer was on. But, since the Chinese plane was less than twenty miles away, it could burn through Greer's ECM.

That left Greer with chaff and flares. He fired one of each, went into a hard-right turn, and prepared to fight.

***

Aboard the Chinese aircraft carrier *Henan*, west of Luzon

The *Henan* shook like a thing possessed as the anti-radiation missiles struck. Some of them hit the towering structure called "The Island," which was home to radar installations, flight deck operations, and the bridge where Admiral Wen was standing.

The impacts threw him to the deck. And that's where Wen was, when a cruise missile slammed into the flight deck, and blew a large hole in it. Alarms sounded as *more* weapons arrived—each striking a different part of the carrier.

A sailor helped Wen to his feet. Damage reports were flooding in. Senior Captain Kwan was in command of the ship, and it was his job to supervise damage control efforts, and assess the Henan's readiness to fight.

All Wen could do was stand with hands clasped behind his back, and a scowl on his face, as planes were recalled and ordered to fly CAP above the carrier. And when Kwan delivered his assessment Wen wasn't surprised.

"The *Henan* is seaworthy, sir," Kwan reported. "And the ship can return to port without assistance. But the flight deck was holed in two places. That means we can't launch or retrieve planes. I recommend that the fighters that have enough fuel return to Yulin. And I suggest the others land on Luzon, consistent with the emergency assistance pact we have with the Philippine government."

All of that was to be expected. Wen nodded. "I concur. But the battle isn't over yet. Request additional air cover from the mainland, and disperse the ship's planes as you see fit. But the *Henan* is to remain here until the battle is over. We cannot, and we will not, run."

***

In the air over the South China Sea

Greer shouted "God damnit!" as Bower's F-18 disappeared in a flash of light. More Shenyang J-15s had arrived on scene, and even though Soccer Mom had scored a kill, the Americans were badly outnumbered.

All Greer could do was run, or try to, with a pair of J-15s on his tail. He was over Luzon by then, and firing flares, when a missile exploded. It was a miss. But his starboard engine shut down as pieces of shrapnel tore into it.

And, as Greer lost half his power, a Chinese fighter opened fire with a GSh-30-1 cannon. Alarms sounded, indicators turned red, and he had to punch out.

Greer pulled the handle, the ejection seat fired, and the F-18's canopy blew off. He felt the full force of eighteen Gs as a rocket motor fired him up and out of the plane. Restraining straps tightened as the drogue chute stored behind the seat opened. All in less than two seconds.

The main chute deployed shortly thereafter. Greer felt a jerk as he parted company with the seat and swayed from side-to-side as the ground rushed up to meet him.

That was when Greer had a chance to look around. Trees, all he could see was trees, and they were rising fast. *Knees and feet together*, Greer thought. *This is going to hurt.*

***

Aboard the semi-submersible Chinese cruiser *Sea Dragon*, northeast of Luzon.

Senior Captain Ko was secretly pleased. He knew that the emotion was inappropriate, and felt guilty about it. But, to Ko's way of thinking, Wen was getting his much-deserved comeuppance. Carriers were important because of their capacity to expand China's strategic reach, and project its power to every nook and cranny of Southeast Asia.

But flattops were difficult to defend. And, had Wen been willing to send the *Sea Dragon* in first, it was quite possible that the *Henan* would have come through undamaged.

But such thoughts were not only unpatriotic, they were a waste of time, and therefore counterproductive. Thanks to the footage supplied by a drone, Ko could assess the situation with his own eyes. And it was clear that, even though the Americans had been able to inflict damage to the *Henan*, they were in a vulnerable position and could be defeated.

One of the *Sea Dragon's* submarine escorts had been able to torpedo and sink an American frigate. Since then, contact had been lost with *both* Chinese subs, suggesting that they were radio silent for defensive purposes—or had been destroyed.

Shi feared the later, and Ko was inclined to agree, because the Americans made no secret of the fact that at least two attack submarines were normally assigned to each carrier strike group to defend their ships from enemy subs.

Ko's primary target was a carrier named the *USS Concord,* assuming the Intel people were correct, and a ship worthy of the *Sea Dragon's* railgun. The first for any navy.

Unlike conventional guns that use gunpowder to force a projectile out of a barrel, the *Dragon's* railgun relied on electricity to create strong electromagnetic fields between two rails. Then, once in the grip of a conductive device called an armature, a projectile would be propelled down the pathway between the rails and fired downrange.

By launching smaller projectiles at extremely high velocities from the *Sea Dragon's* railgun, it was possible to deliver kinetic energy impacts equal to, or superior to, the destructive energy of a 5"/54 caliber naval gun. And to do so at a greater range. Up to 124 miles during sea trials.

There were ancillary benefits too, including the elimination of the hazards associated with carrying propellants and explosives aboard ships, not to mention a significant reduction in the size and weight of projectiles. Couple the railgun's virtues with the semi-submersible's stealthy characteristics and a new class of warships was being born.

Ko was in Operations One, standing behind the rating who would actually fire the gun, and well aware of what was at stake. The outcome of an important battle? Yes. But, more than that, the fate of a new technology. And one that could make an important difference in the way that World War III turned out. That was why Ko felt a sudden emptiness in the pit of his stomach.

When not in use the *Sea Dragon's* railgun was below deck, protected from the weather, and easier to maintain. Now it was elevated and ready to fire. The coordinates of the enemy ship had been loaded and were being updated every five seconds.

All Ko had to do in order to fire the weapons was give a few simple commands. "Prepare to fire the railgun."

"All lights are green," the gunnery tech replied. "The railgun is ready to fire."

Ko drew a deep breath. *"Fire!"*

***

Lieutenant Jing's superiors were on duty in the duplicate CIC. So he, as a junior officer, was stationed in the aft conning tower. The overlapping white contrails looked like childish scribbles. Smoke boiled up to the south and the distant thump of an explosion was heard.

Large though the *Sea Dragon* was, Jing could feel the cruiser lurch as the crack of what sounded like lightning was heard, and a "smart" shell soared upwards.

Thanks to an automated loading system the railgun could fire a shell every sixty seconds. And Jing watched in awe as four additional shells flew downrange. Would they strike the target? And, if they did, how much damage would the projectiles cause?

***

Aboard the aircraft carrier *USS Concord*, east of Luzon

After reaching apogee the first smart shell fell at a steep angle. It was travelling at 5,000 mph. As a result, the *Concord's* computers were just starting to process the event when the projectile hit the flight deck, forward of the carrier's superstructure.

The shell wasn't armed with an explosive charge. Nor did it need to be. Kinetic energy was enough to drill a hole through the flight deck, the crew quarters below, *and* the hangar deck, before the projectile shattered and sent shrapnel flying in every direction.

Admiral Hoyer and Captain Danby were in the CDC, celebrating the hits on the *Henan*, when the railgun shell arrived. "What the fuck was that?" Hoyer demanded as the carrier shook and alarms sounded.

"Some sort of missile," Danby guessed, as flames appeared through the hole in the flight deck. And then the second shell slammed into the ship, quickly followed by three more. The last of which scored a direct hit on the island, destroying the carrier's CDC, and killing everyone in it.

***

Aboard the semi-submersible Chinese cruiser *Sea Dragon*, northeast of Luzon.

Thanks to the *Henan's* drone, and satellite imagery, Ko could see the *Concord*. And Ko knew that every shot the *Sea Dragon* fired had been on target.

But crippled though the carrier was, it remained afloat, and that was unacceptable. In order to win the battle, *and* the acceptance that Ko hungered for, he had to send the American ship to the bottom. And he had the means to do so.

Five shots had been enough to cook the railgun's barrel. A new one was being installed. But the *Sea Dragon* was armed with 200 surface-to-air and surface-to-surface missiles. That's why some officials referred to the cruiser as "an arsenal ship."

The Sea Dragon's vertical missile launchers were loaded and ready. Ko gave the orders: "Fire missiles 1 through 10 in standard sequence." The sea-skimming YJ-91 anti-ship missiles were good, but with a range of only 30 to 75 miles, they weren't comparable to the American Harpoons, some of which could strike targets more than 150 miles away. But improvements were on the way ... Or so the authorities claimed.

Ko watched from above as seven explosions blossomed along the length of the *Concord's* hull. The remaining destroyer rushed to rescue those she could, while tiny boats and rafts could be seen bobbing around the carrier.

Slowly, almost majestically, the *Concord* sank until what remained of its island disappeared from view. "We have a fix on the destroyer," Shi said. "And we're ready to fire."

Perhaps it was the sight of fellow sailors struggling to survive. But for whatever reason Ko couldn't kill any more. Admiral Wen might criticize his decision. But the goddess Tianfei would not. "Secure all missiles," Ko ordered. "The battle is over."

CHAPTER TWO

Istanbul, Turkey

After stepping onto the narrow passageway alongside the hydrofoil's superstructure, U.S. Navy Commander Max Ryson paused to look across the moonlit Bosporus to Istanbul.

Most of the Turkish city was blacked out. But jewel-colored traffic lights twinkled, a police car flashed blue, and rectangles of buttery light marked windows where a shade was up.

Closer in, about a hundred yards away, boats of every possible description slid through the moonlit channel, their engines thrumming, as they journeyed east and west. The Bosporus strait was an important link between the Sea of Marmara and the Black Sea further east. That's why human beings had been fighting to control it for thousands of years. And were about to do so again.

The air felt warm as Ryson made his way around the boat's superstructure to the gangplank, and from there to the dock, where a sailor named Farley saluted. "Good evening, sir."

Ryson returned the salute and paused. "Guard duty again? What was it this time?"

Farley grinned. "A bottle of booze in my locker, sir. The chief took offense."

Ryson laughed. "Keep a sharp eye out Farley ... Istanbul is full of spies and saboteurs."

"I will, sir. Enjoy the party."

Ryson nodded agreeably, but knew he wouldn't. Ryson didn't like parties, but British Admiral Jerome Canby did. And since Canby was in command of Special Sea Command 2, the group Ryson's squadron was attached to, he had to attend.

People were filing off other boats as Ryson made his way along the pier. American boats, British boats, and Israeli boats. Ryson could hear the thump, thump, thump of bass and caught a glimpse of light as the door to the warehouse opened and closed.

A cyclone fence and gate barred the way. So the procession slowed as the party goers were forced to stop and show ID. A Royal marine checked Ryson's card against a list. "Sorry about the delay, sir … But we have orders to keep the Russians out."

It was supposed to be a joke but the jest contained a kernel of truth. English speaking members of Russia's foreign Intelligence Service would love to attend Canby's party.

Of course, the Russians didn't need secret agents to inform them that an Allied attack was imminent. The concentration of naval resources in Istanbul was very visible to the naked eye and from space. Still, there was no reason to provide the Ivans with operational details regarding the coming attack. "Your card sir," the marine said, as he returned it. "Have a good time."

Ryson followed a French officer to a door where a woman was waiting to give him two drink chits. "There's a two-drink limit tonight," she said. "And that includes beer. Please stick to it."

Had it been up to Ryson there wouldn't have been a party or drinks. But Canby thought the gathering would boost morale. "Play hard and fight hard," the mercurial officer said. But Ryson wasn't so sure.

A blast of music escaped the warehouse as the group in front of Ryson opened the door and went in. He followed. Not surprisingly, the interior of the building looked like the inside of a warehouse, complete with harsh lighting, concrete columns, and yellow lines on the floor.

Ryson guessed that something like two hundred people were present, most of whom were Allied navy personnel, all wearing the cammies peculiar to their particular service.

Ryson couldn't help but notice how egalitarian the crowd was. Both officers and senior enlisted people had been invited and were mingling in a manner typical of special operations units. And that made sense. If these men and women were going to die together, why not party together? Ryson's respect for Canby went up a notch.

A temporary bar had been established against one wall. Thanks to the presence of six bartenders, the lines were short. Ryson began to work his way through the crowd. A Brit called his name. Ryson waved but kept going.

To Ryson's ear the Europop music was loud and frantic. Not the sort of thing he wanted to hear on the eve of battle. But others felt differently and were dancing. Something he was completely unqualified to do.

After surrendering a chit, and collecting a gin and tonic, Ryson scanned the crowd. Where was Canby? His plan was to find the admiral, stage a short conversation, and exfil.

"Commander Ryson," a voice said from behind him. "I'm glad you were able to join us."

Ryson turned to find that Admiral Canby was standing behind him, glass in hand. The admiral was built like a fire plug, and was good looking in a Rugby-player sort-of-way.

Canby's face was flushed. Because he'd been drinking? Or as a function of his mercurial personality? There was no way to know.

Ryson started to come to attention but Canby waved the formality off. "No need for that sort of thing, old fruit. Save it for the

Queen Elizabeth's flight deck. How's Squadron 3? Ready to go I should imagine."

"It is," Ryson assured him.

"You're a lucky man," Canby said. "Forty feet up off the waves, wind rushing through your hair, pumping 76mm shells downrange! Who could ask for more! You're a lucky dog. I wish I could trade places with you."

Judging from the look on Canby's face the admiral meant every word of it. "I'm sorry, sir ... But I refuse to trade. The paperwork would drive me crazy."

"I don't blame you," Canby said, as his face darkened. "The paper shuffling bastards at the admiralty are relentless. But, should we take control of the Black Sea, all the bureaucratic bullshit will be worth it. As it stands the Black Sea is like a cyst filled with Russian pus. And the longer we wait, the more pus there is. We need to act before the cyst bursts."

Ryson got the feeling that the analogy had been used before. Canby's eyes had a messianic quality to them. "'The clock is ticking,' old boy. We need to act now."

Ryson frowned. "Are the Russians about to break out? And enter the Med?"

"No," Canby said. "Not so far as I know. The problem is Turkey."

Turkey was the most controversial member of NATO (North Atlantic Treaty Organization). And Turkish troops deserved a huge amount credit for defending Bulgaria and Georgia from the Russians.

But the Turks were obsessed with the Kurd separatists to the south. And stood accused of using the war effort as cover for a thinly disguised strategy to seize control of Kurdish territory.

Canby took a quick look around as if to ensure that no one else could hear. "Keep this under your hat, Commander ... But there's a significant group of people within the Turkish government who want to renounce NATO membership and move against the Kurds.

"If that occurs, they sure as hell won't let us travel through the Bosporus. But, if we have control of the Black Sea, they'll be forced to tolerate our presence. And that, Commander Ryson, is what makes this outing so urgent."

Ryson finished his drink. "We'll do our best sir. What about our supply line—should the Bosporus be closed to us?"

"Then we'll take supplies in through Bulgaria," Canby replied. "That would be extremely tiresome. But it's feasible."

Suddenly the sunny personality was back. "You're out of gin, Commander," Canby said. "I suggest that you take on fuel. The bar will close in forty-five minutes." Then the admiral vanished into the crowd.

Ryson had no desire for a second drink. His goal was to exit the warehouse and return to the *Mammatus*. He was halfway to the door when Rav-Seren (Lt. Commander) Yaakov Segal stepped out of the crowd to block his way. "Max! Surely you aren't leaving yet … We must toast the old days."

Five years earlier, when Ryson had been a lieutenant commander, and Segal was a seren (lieutenant), they'd been assigned to a joint task force operating out of Israel's Haifa naval base. Both were ambitious and competitive. And the competition continued when they were off duty.

The girl's name was Noa Shapira. In addition to a quick mind, and a wicked sense of humor, she was beautiful. So much so that both men were willing to do just about anything to win her affections.

Looking back Ryson realized that Noa had been playing them off against each other. But that wasn't the way it seemed at the time. The situation came to a head in a bar when Segal bragged about having sex with Noa. A claim that may, or may not, have been true. Ryson hit him in the face and a brawl ensued.

Ryson won the fight, but lost the girl. So, the last thing Ryson wanted to do was toast old times. "Hello, Yaakov. I didn't know you were part of Command 2."

"I wasn't," the Israeli said, "until yesterday. One of our squadron commanders has appendicitis. I jumped at the opportunity to replace him. I have six kills now. I plan to double that number by the end of the day tomorrow."

Ryson knew that Squadron 5 consisted of four Israeli Super Dvora Mark III-class patrol boats. They could make 50 knots, and were armed with everything from automatic grenade launchers to Hellfire missiles, all packed on ninety-foot hulls that looked the way a fast patrol boat should look. Better than Ryson's hydrofoils, truth be told, although his Pegs were faster and more maneuverable.

"It doesn't matter how many kills you make," Ryson said. "The purpose of the mission is to seize control of the Black Sea."

"So, you still have a stick up your ass," Segal replied. "Some things never change."

"No," Ryson replied. "They don't. Goodnight Yaakov." And with that Ryson made his way toward the door.

"My squadron will score more kills than yours!" Segal shouted.

Ryson felt dozens of eyes on him as he stepped out into the night. Special Sea Command 2 was a relatively small unit. And some people, the stupid ones, would think that the challenge was important. *Well*, Ryson thought. *Fuck them.*

***

Aboard the Russian cruiser *Omsk,* on the Black Sea

The Allies were about to invade the Black Sea, and Vice Admiral Viktor Belkin was in a good mood, because his men were ready. But first it was necessary for Belkin to complete his morning workout. Phase one involved pumping iron in his cabin to keep his six-foot two-inch frame in good shape. No, *excellent* shape, especially for a man in his fifties.

Then it was time for phase two, which required him to don a Speedo, and make his way out onto to the deck where a section of railing had been removed for his convenience. The sun was just starting to rise and an easterly breeze chilled his skin.

The swim was a tradition by that time, and one that roughly twenty crew members were waiting to witness. They cheered for their admiral as Belkin stepped up to the edge of the deck, brought his hands together, and dived head-first into the Black Sea.

He went deep. The water was relatively warm at that time of year. So, there was none of the icy shock Belkin felt upon entering the North Pacific. As he'd done in the past.

Belkin surfaced, waved to his audience, and swam back to the ship where a rope ladder equipped with wooden rungs was waiting. He scrambled up to the main deck where he paused to take a bow. That was part of the act, part of the mystique, and one of the reasons why Belkin's sailors loved him. Who else could, or would, do such a thing? Certainly not the mostly rotund admirals in charge of the other fleets.

Belkin accepted a towel, wrapped it around his midriff, and addressed the crowd. "Go have breakfast. Tell your shipmates. The enemy will come today and we will defeat him!"

And that was almost certainly true. In order to enter the Black Sea, the Allies would have to send mine sweepers to neutralize the five hundred so called "influence mines" that would block their way.

Influence mines were equipped with fuses that could detect pressure, not to mention magnetic, electronic, and acoustic activity. That made them equally deadly against submarines and surface ships alike. And once the Allied minesweepers went to work, Russian fighter jets would harvest them like wheat. A cheery thought indeed.

Would the Allies manage to break through? That seemed doubtful. But, if by some miracle they did, five 100-foot-tall defense towers were waiting to greet them. Each armed with remotely operated radars, guns and missiles. And that was to say nothing of the fast patrol boats waiting to pounce.

Finally, there was the *Omsk* herself. Though not as agile as the patrol boats, the cruiser was more than 600 feet long, and was armed with 16 Vulkan anti-ship missiles. That was on top of surface-to-air missiles, guns, and antisubmarine mortars.

After a shower, followed by a shave, Belkin got dressed. A hearty breakfast was waiting when he entered the day room located next to his cabin.

Members of Belkin's senior staff arrived moments later. They included Captain 1st Rank Shubin, who was the Omsk's CO, and second in command of the Black Sea Fleet. Also present were Captain 3rd Rank Garin, who was in charge of the fleet's air arm, and Lieutenant Volkov, Belkin's Intel Officer.

"So," Belkin said from behind his desk. "Have the *inostrannyye svin'i* (foreign pigs) entered the slaughterhouse yet?"

Both of the more senior officers turned their eyes to Volkov. She had short hair, a plain face, and thin lips. "Yes," she said. "And no."

Belkin washed a mouthful of *kasha* (porridge) down with hot tea. "What the fuck does that mean? Are they in the minefield or not?"

"Our mines are detonating," Volkov said. "But we don't know why. In the meantime, the Allied boats are in the Bosporus waiting to enter."

Belkin put his spoon down. "What about submarines? Maybe submarines triggered the mines."

"That's possible," Volkov agreed. "But it's unlikely. Rather than localized explosions, which we would see if a sub set the mines off, they're exploding in waves. That suggests some sort of electronic or electromechanical clearing process."

That was unexpected. And Belkin didn't like unexpected things. But, mines or no mines, the outcome would be the same. The Black Sea was his, and it was going to remain that way.

***

The entrance to the Bosporus Strait

The "*Mother Ship*," as the USV operators generally called the 262-foot-long steel barge, was heavily armored and propelled by two diesel engines. It was remotely operated by a civilian located in Maryland.

The space forward of the engine room was filled with racks of so-called "Otters." That was the name bestowed on the semi-autonomous mine killers being fired through underwater launching slots into the Black Sea.

By that time the first two waves of machines had destroyed more than one hundred Russian mines by spoofing the signals "influence" mines were waiting for. In most cases, but not all, the Otters were destroyed by the explosions they triggered. Those that survived continued on their way.

Now the *Mother Ship* was coming under attack by Russian planes, as the third wave of Otters slipped into the Black Sea. But, as the Russian planes swooped in to attack, Allied fighter jets were waiting to pounce on them from 30,000 feet.

Thousands of eyes watched as contrails twisted and turned to create what looked like scribbling in the sky. Meanwhile the Allied ships and boats stood ready to fire on the enemy aircraft with SAMs, and shoulder launched missiles, when Russians came into range.

Ryson felt impatient despite his attempts to look calm, cool, and collected. The vessels under his command were Pegasus II Class PHMs (Patrol, Hydrofoil, Missile boats). Often referred to as "Peg Twos."

The Pegasus Class I boats had seen service from 1977 to 1993. And, when the program came to an end, it seemed as though hydrofoils were gone for good. But that was before Admiral Hartwell came along.

Hartwell, and some equally visionary Congress people, succeeded in securing seed money for a Class II prototype in 2018. And when that proved to be successful, they managed to fund a full-on PHM program.

The program's formal objective was: "To operate offensively against hostile surface combatants and other surface craft—and conduct surveillance, screening and special operations." And the Peg Twos were everything a "small navy" sailor could possibly want. They were fast, steady when foilborne, and armed to the teeth.

The PHMs were, as one reporter put it, "The 21st century equivalent of PT boats." And the only boats equipped with hydrofoil technology. But when hull borne, they had a slightly retro gunboat look to them.

Thirty states belonged to NATO and squabbles were common. Israel wanted its Super Dvora Mk III patrol boats, rather than the Pegasus IIs, to lead the way. And after some high-level negotiations they received permission to do so. Ryson's nemesis Segal would be pleased.

Ryson's squadron was next, followed by some up-gunned British Scimitar patrol vessels, and a hodgepodge of vessels representing Greece, Italy and France.

An equally diverse selection of destroyers and frigates were to follow, along with two transports, both packed with troops. Admiral Canby knew he couldn't occupy the entire sweep of the Black Sea's coastline, but he sure as hell planned to seize the Russian naval base in Sevastopol, and return it to Crimea.

Ryson's train of though was interrupted as Lieutenant Commander Stacy Sterling stepped out of the wheelhouse. She was the USS *Mammatus's* CO, and Squadron 3's XO. She had green eyes, a spray of freckles that crossed her nose, and navy-short hair. "The Israelis are going in, sir … And it sounds like the Russian boats are waiting for them."

"All right," Ryson said. "Let's keep the formation tight. And, Stacy …"

"Sir?"

"Keep at least half of your Harpoons in reserve. Just in case."

Sterling knew what Ryson was thinking. Everyone was aware that the *Omsk* was out there somewhere. And, if the *Mammatus* had to engage the cruiser, the boat's Harpoon anti-ship missiles were the PHM's only hope of putting a dent into the Russian behemoth. Sterling grinned. "Yes, sir. You can count on it."

Ryson followed Sterling into the wheelhouse. There were three high-backed seats. One for Sterling, one for her coxswain, and one for a guest. Ryson in this case.

Communications were being monitored by a tech in the Electronic Equipment Room, located midship, but the chatter could be heard on the bridge as well.

A lot of the radio traffic was focused on the Italian boat that had run aground, the effort to rescue a seaman who had fallen off the stern of a Scimitar, and a civilian freighter which was trying to enter the Black Sea ahead of the navy vessels. Never mind the fact that it would be sunk.

One-by-one the problems were solved. The *Mammatus* was ready to follow as Segal's boats roared into the Black Sea. Like other PHMs, the "M" could operate in the hull borne mode for low-speed travel, or "fly" with the foil extended.

And at the moment, the *Mammatus* was hull-down, and gradually increasing speed from 8 knots, to about 29 knots, when the boat would become foilborne. The Peg Twos had a great deal in common with the original boats, but there were significant differences too. Not the least of which were superconducting propulsion systems that consisted of two engines, sometimes referred to as "prime movers," along with generators, and the electric motor controllers that were connected to the ship's propeller shafts.

In order to deliver greater reliability, two drive motors were connected to each foilborne propeller. So even if one drive motor failed, the boat could still operate at foilborne speeds of up to 36 knots per hour.

Sterling made the announcement that the *Mammatus* was foilborne, followed by her boat's motto, which was: "*Omnes interficere.*" (Kill them all.)

A cheer went up over the intercom and Ryson grinned. Morale was high, and that was good. The *Mammatus* was blasting along at 52 knots by that time, and the main deck was high above the sea. Rather than what a novice might expect, the ride was rock steady. Just one of the reasons why hydrofoils were good gun platforms.

But steering required considerable skill. The boats were designed to "fly by wire." And the analogy was apt, since the foils had aileron-like flaps, similar to aircraft wings.

The flaps were coupled to the helm via redundant systems of computers, gyros and accelerometers. Once a course was dialed into the ACS (Automatic Control System) the *Mammatus* could steer herself. But always under the watchful eyes of the coxswain and a deck officer.

Under combat conditions however, it was impossible to follow a set course. And that meant Petty Officer Po, Sterling's coxswain, would have the ticklish job of steering the boat as the ACS tried to second guess him.

Squadron 3 was spread out by then with all four boats foilborne and traveling abreast of each other. The Peg Twos carried scaled down versions of the AN/SPY-6 integrated air and missile defense radars used on destroyers.

Electronics Technician Deen was hunkered down in the PHM's tiny CIC, his eyes flicking from screen-to-screen. He described the action. "We have six, repeat *six*, bogeys inbound from the northwest," Deen said. "Based on the feed from the fleet drone they are Russian Raptor patrol boats. Range ten miles and closing."

Sterling went off intercom in order to query the ship's AI, which the crew referred to as "Aunt Ida," because of its soothing female persona. "Give me a readout on Russian Raptor patrol boats."

Ryson could hear the response. "Russian Raptors are 55 feet long, powered by 2000 hp engines, and equipped with a full suite of cutting edge nav and com systems. Raptors are armed with a remotely operated 14.5mm machine gun located aft of the wheelhouse and high enough to fire over it. Two 7.62mm machine guns are mounted in the stern. Say 'Details,' for additional information."

"No missiles," Ryson observed. "Good."

Ryson selected Squadron 3's frequency and spoke into his mike. "This is Scepter Six. We will engage the incoming targets with guns. After they pass through our formation, pull a one-eighty and reengage. Be careful who you shoot at. Over."

There was a flurry of confirmations followed by radio silence. But there was no end to the traffic on the fleet freq, where Admiral Canby had some major problems to deal with, including a troop ship that sat dead in the water.

But that was Canby's problem. Ryson was fighting a battle with himself.

He had to let Sterling command her vessel without offering unsolicited advice, signaling his opinions via body language, or otherwise being a pain in the ass.

But once a boat skipper, always a boat skipper. And keeping his mouth shut would be difficult.

The Raptors were clearly visible by then, white water spraying away from their bows as their large caliber machine guns opened fire. "Target dead ahead," Sterling said. "Stand by to engage with the 76. Fire."

The remotely operated 76mm autocannon was housed in a forward mounted turret and capable of firing 85 rounds per minute. GM (gunner's mate) Ronny Silva, better known as "Guns," was controlling the weapon via a joystick in the CIC, where he was back-to-back with Deen. "Roger that," Silva replied. "Outgoing."

Puffs of gray smoke blew away from the 76 as it opened fire. As he had many times before Ryson marveled at how steady the Peg was when foilborne. Not only that, but the hydrofoil was higher than the oncoming patrol boats and could fire down on them.

By contrast with the PHM, the Russian boats were bouncing in a slight chop which forced their remote operators to constantly re-aim the top-mounted machine guns.

The enemy shells threw up fountains of sea water along the Peg's port side as the Raptor approached. Guns was hitting the Raptor and hitting it hard. Ryson could see the flashes as thirty mike-mike HE (high explosive) rounds struck the enemy boat. But only for a few seconds.

The *Mammatus* had a .50 caliber machine gun on each side, just aft of the wheelhouse. And Ryson heard a rhythmic thud, thud, thud as the port gunner raked a passing boat from end-to-end.

The battle was far from one-sided however. The Raptor had two stern-mounted machine guns, both of which fired at the PHM as the vessels parted company.

"The bastards killed the RIB boat!" a sailor exclaimed. "How will we go ashore for beer?"

"Belay that bullshit," Master Chief Atkins growled from his position adjacent to the CIC. "You and I will chat later."

All the Pegs had passed through the enemy line by then. "This is Six," Ryson said. "All boats will turn and chase the Ivans down."

The hydrofoils had numerous virtues, one of which was the capacity to execute incredibly tight turns. Ryson had an instinctive desire to shift his weight from one foot to the other as Po put the wheel over, but there was no need to do so, as the ACS put the vessel into a coordinated turn. The Russian gunboats appeared ahead.

They were just starting to come around. As they did so the Ivans exposed the entire length of their hulls to the streams of 76mm HE shells fired by the American vessels.

"Yes!" Sterling exclaimed, as geysers of spray led to the nearest Raptor and bright flashes marked hits. At least three hit the wheelhouse. Armored glass broke, a shell detonated, and the patrol boat slewed around prior coming to a stop.

The top mounted machine gun was still firing as the *Mammatus* circled its prey and Sterling was having none of that. "Kill that weapon!"

Silva responded with a terse, "Aye, aye, ma'am," and brought the 76 to bear. Six shells struck the enemy gun in quick succession and the firing stopped.

"Well done," Sterling said. "I owe you a beer."

A faint cheer was heard, and Ryson forced himself to refocus. The problem with riding on a boat, *any* boat, was a loss of situational awareness. Sterling was responsible for one PHM. Ryson had *four* vessels to worry about. As he scanned the area, Ryson was pleased to see the amount of damage Squadron 3 had done.

Silva's target was dead in the water and burning. Another Raptor was down at the stern and about to sink. Two vessels were fleeing northeast toward Sevastopol. Another was turning listless circles, as if under power, but with no one at the helm. But where was boat six?

Ryson opened his mike. "This is Six. I see 5 Russian boats? Where is number six?"

"This is Four-Six," a male voice replied. "The vessel you're referring to went boom. Over."

Ryson had a vague memory of an explosion. "Nice work, Four-Six. Six-Two will set a course for Objective 2. Form a line astern. Over."

As Po brought the *Mammatus* around Ryson took a moment to assess the larger battle. It wasn't easy. Ryson could access individual pieces of data—only Canby and his staff understood the full sweep of events.

But according to the tidbits Ryson could glean from the fleet drone feeds, and the choppy radio traffic, it was clear that the drifting troop ship had been attacked by Russian planes and was sinking.

That meant critical resources were focused on rescuing hundreds of men and women from the dying ship and the surrounding water. That effort included two destroyers.

From what Ryson could tell the air war wasn't being won or lost. Both sides had thrown everything they could into the sky and the result was a bloody draw.

As for the other small boat squadrons, Segal's Super Dvora Mk III patrol boats were engaged with a hulking Project 22160 patrol ship, which was more like a destroyer than a missile boat, and heavily armed. If Segal's sailors managed to defeat the 160 no one, Ryson included, would hear the end of it.

But with the *Mammatus* speeding north, it was time for Ryson to turn his attention to Objective 2, which was part of the so-called "Belkin Line" of defense towers, named after Russian Vice Admiral Viktor Belkin—the man credited with having created it.

And, according to the fleet Intel briefing Ryson had attended two days earlier, the entire Black Sea fleet was under Belkin's command. Where was the bastard anyway? The spooks weren't sure, but figured the vice admiral was aboard his flagship, the cruiser *Omsk*.

But the *Omsk* wasn't the focus at the moment. The Belkin Line consisted of five towers, located approximately fifty miles apart, in a line that stretched from Constanta in Romania, to the city of Sevastopol in Ukraine.

According to Allied Intelligence each tower was one hundred feet tall and equipped with independent radars and tracking capabilities to support remotely operated surface-to-surface and surface-to-air missiles. That meant the towers had overlapping fields of fire, and were positioned to prevent vessels from reaching occupied Ukraine, and the Sea of Azov.

Ryson's orders were to punch a large hole in the line, thereby preparing the way for the troop transports that would follow. "We have two, repeat *two*, targets inbound from the northwest," Deen said. "They're low, sea skimming missiles, range fifteen miles and closing."

Sterling gave orders and the combination of evasive maneuvers and mortar launched decoys worked. Explosions marked the spots where the Russian weapons detonated.

In the meantime, the other vessels were being targeted as well. Ryson thumbed his mike. "This is Six. All boats will take evasive action, fire decoys and attack their preassigned targets. Over."

The other three boats peeled away as they fired flares and chaff while Po put the *Mammatus* through an unpredictable series of high-speed course alterations, all of which took the PHM in a generally northwesterly direction. "Requesting permission to engage the target with missiles," Sterling said formally.

"The *Flammagen* took a hit," Deen said. "She's gone."

Ryson winced. Twenty-five lives snuffed out. Just like that. "Permission granted," he said, and felt the *Mammatus* flinch as two Harpoons took to the air. Were the towers equipped with close-in missile defense systems?

The spooks didn't think so. But they were believed to have decoy launchers. Ryson could see the tower by then. Which meant he could also see the explosions as the Harpoons chased decoys and blew up. "Shit, shit, shit," Sterling said.

"Close with it," Ryson ordered. "Tell the RPG crews to get ready. We'll fire up at the weapons platform. Who knows? Maybe we'll get lucky."

Sterling gave him a look. Did she think he was crazy? Or brilliant? Ryson couldn't tell. And it didn't matter. All that mattered was for the *Mammatus* to survive long enough to get in under the tower's weapons platform. Because there was little, if any, chance that the tower had a sea level defense system.

More missiles came streaking in and either missed or blew themselves up. Then the hydrofoil entered the shadow under the Russian platform where the Russian weapons couldn't reach it. Ryson said, "Standby for an emergency stop. *Now!*"

That was the pilot's signal to push the foil depth lever down. And, because the turbine was at full power, that had the effect of driving the vessel down into the sea.

At that point the helmsman hurried to throttle the turbine back. Buckets of water fell as the boat bobbed up out of the sea and stopped within her own length.

The RPG teams were now free to stand out in the open, aim their weapons at the structure above, and fire round after round. The explosions were all over the place. Ryson turned to Sterling. "Contact the other boats. Tell them what we're doing. Now, back her off to the point where we can see the radar array."

Then Ryson went down to stand between the RPG teams. "Target the radar enclosure!"

The sailors understood. The tower-based system wouldn't work without targeting information. And the radar enclosure was fully exposed. It took five rounds to crack the boxy structure open and three rounds to destroy the array inside. "Well done," Ryson told them. "Keep those weapons handy."

Ryson returned to the bridge where Sterling was ready with a report. "Two additional towers have been neutralized, sir."

"Good," Ryson replied. "Send a report to the fleet."

***

Aboard the Russian cruiser *Omsk,* on the Black Sea

Vice Admiral Viktor Belkin was eating lunch. It consisted of a thick ham and cheese sandwich, some Ukrainian grapes, and a bottle of Baltika Number 8 beer. Alcohol was prohibited on Russian ships. But rank hath privilege. And who was going to report him?

Belkin heard a knock and looked up to see Lieutenant Volkov standing just inside the door. It was impossible to read the woman since she frowned all the time. "Come in. So, are we victorious yet? Should I give President Toplin the good news?"

It was a joke but the intelligence officer's expression remained unchanged. "That would be premature, sir. Three of our defense towers have been neutralized."

Belkin swallowed and took a sip of beer. "And the other two?"

"They are located at the extreme ends of the line, sir. And too far away from each other to provide mutual support."

"So at least one Allied officer has a brain," Belkin remarked. "What type of ship or ships brought the towers down? A couple of destroyers?"

"No, sir. Four high-speed hydrofoil missile boats. Three now. One was destroyed. There is some other good news as well. At least 25 percent of the Allied fleet is tied up reacting to the loss of a troop ship."

Belkin belched, wiped his lips with a napkin, and placed it on his desk. "We will take advantage. Tell the captain to increase speed. Who knows? Maybe we can break out of the Black Sea and enter the Med. I like Greek food."

***

Aboard the *USS Mammatus*, in the Back Sea

Ryson hadn't had time to review the strategic situation since the attack on the towers began. And he was surprised by what he saw. Rather than the orderly process Admiral Canby and his aides described during their briefing two days earlier, it appeared that the battleplan had been severely disrupted by the loss of the troopship.

The plotting screen was filled with arcane symbols. Allied surface ships appeared as a dot within a circle. Hostile vessels were represented by dots in diamonds. And a dot at the center of a box signified an unidentified surface contact.

What jumped out at Ryson was the number of ships scattered about, the diamonds that were still in play, and two unidentified surface contacts.

But most concerning of all was the group of six diamonds, all in formation, all steaming southbound from Ukraine—headed straight for the heart of the shit show. Ryson put his right index finger on the group. "Do we have aerials for this group? What are they?"

The fleet drones were still online. And, as video appeared on-screen, Ryson found himself looking down at a large ship with five smaller escorts. "That looks like a cruiser," Sterling observed, as she zoomed in. "Yup, here we go … That sucker is an 87.2 percent match with the cruiser *Omsk*."

"And the *Omsk* is Admiral Belkin's flagship," Ryson mused. "He can see how fucked up we are, and he's coming down to play."

"So it would seem," Sterling agreed.

"Show me the Black Sea chart," Ryson said.

The video morphed into a chart. Ryson was well aware of the fact that his squadron was blasting north at 52 knots, while the Russian battle group was traveling south at something like 26 knots, which meant he had very little time in which to make a decision. The squadron would fight. That was a given. But *how*?

Ryson scanned the chart looking for something, *anything*, that might offer a way to slow the oncoming behemoth down. If Squadron 3 could accomplish that, perhaps Canby could send some tin cans to lend a hand.

But a head on collision with a cruiser and five escorts would be nothing less than suicidal. Especially after losing 25 percent of his command. A sick feeling seeped into the pit of Ryson's stomach as Sterling stared at him. He could imagine what she was thinking. *Make a decision god damnit. That's what they pay you for.*

According to the chart the Black Sea was empty. No islands. Unless you were willing to count the nameless rock off the coast of Romania as an island. It was marked with a capital "K," the letter that stood for rocks, wrecks and obstructions. But, so what?

Then a thought occurred to him. A stupid thought most likely, but a thought nevertheless. And something was better than nothing. Ryson thumbed his mike. "This is Six. I know you can see the battle group that's coming our way. Boats 1 and 4 are going to try and slow it down. Meanwhile boat 3 will proceed to the only rock on your chart. Get in as close as you can, drop the hook, and prepare to fire missiles on my command. Over."

The acknowledgements came in quick succession as the *Altostratus* turned east and cut speed. "The Russians will assume the three boat is having mechanical problems, and will focus on us," Sterling said. "Plus, the *Alto's* radar image will merge with the blip from the rock. So maybe the Ivans will forget about her."

"That's the plan," Ryson admitted. "Send a message to the fleet. Tell them that the enemy is north of us, and Squadron 3 will engage. Request air support."

Ryson saw the subtle change in Sterling's expression. She knew they were going to die. "Aye, aye, sir."

The sun was peeking through scattered clouds, and the wind was starting to pick up, as the distance between the American boats and the Russians continued to dwindle. The enemy ships were well within range of the PHMs' Harpoon missiles, and the reverse was true as well. Yet neither party had chosen to launch.

Ryson knew why he hadn't chosen to fire, and assumed that Admiral Belkin was thinking the same thing. By closing with the enemy, the travel time for each missile would be shortened. And that meant less time for the enemy to respond with anti-air measures. The difference would be a matter of seconds, but that's what modern warfare was about.

According to Aunt Ida the *Mammatus* had six Harpoon missiles remaining, and the *Pileus* had all eight, for a total of fourteen. Each of which could be individually targeted.

So, which was best? Should Ryson spread the love around? And put a couple of missiles on each Russian vessel? Or go all in, and try to stop the *Omsk*?

Ryson decided to pursue the second strategy on the theory that the cruiser was the most significant threat to the fleet, and that if seriously damaged, the *Omsk's* escorts would be forced to stay and defend her.

The horizon was about twelve miles away, so Ryson couldn't see the enemy with his eyes, but they were on the plot. And after choosing a strategy Ryson wanted to draw first blood. He turned to Sterling. "Contact the *Pileus*. Tell Hanson to put all of his missiles on the *Omsk*. And we'll do the same. Sixty from now."

"What about the *Alto*?"

Ryson glanced at the plot. The three boat was nowhere to be seen. "Tell them to hold their fire but to be ready."

The ensuing sixty seconds seemed to last forever. What if he had waited too long? What if Russian missiles blew his boats out of the water before they could launch?

Finally, the moment came. The *Mammatus* continued to speed along as the missiles raced away. The full ECM (Electronic Counter Measure) package was on by then, decoys were in the air, and the deck began to tilt as Po put the boat into a hard turn.

"Incoming from the north," Deen said phlegmatically. "One, 2, 3, 4, 5, 6 missiles."

Ryson closed his eyes, but opened them again, as a series of explosions were heard. The last was like a clap of thunder.

"The *Pileus* is no longer on-screen," Deen said.

Ryson felt slightly nauseous. Fifty percent of his command had been destroyed. A male voice interrupted his train of thought. "Shag and Digger in from the west with missiles and guns. There are six Ivans north of your location. Smoke is pouring off the big boy ... But he's still underway. Your wish is our command. Over."

Ryson felt a sense of elation. Some of the Harpoons had struck home! He thumbed his mike. "Welcome to the party, Shag. See if you can stop the big boy. Then, if you have something left over, put it on the escorts.

"Be advised that we have a boat to the west with a full load of eight Harpoons. Once you've completed your run give me an assessment. Then we'll put those missiles where they can do the most good. Over."

"Roger that," Shag replied cheerfully. Over."

Meanwhile the *Mammatus* continued to hurtle toward the Russian battle group at 52 knots. "I see smoke," Sterling said. "The bastards are just over the horizon." Then, to all hands,

"Prepare for a surface action. I want the RPGs and the SLMs on deck and ready to fire."

It was crazy really. A single hydrofoil attacking six enemy ships. But Ryson hoped that Shag and Digger would make a difference. As would the missiles fired by the *Alto*. Time seemed to slow.

***

Aboard the Russian cruiser *Omsk,* on the Black Sea

Vice Admiral Viktor Belkin was standing on the cruiser's bridge trying to reconcile his expectations with reality. His line of defense towers had been penetrated. And, even though the mighty *Omsk* had been able to destroy most of the incoming missiles, two had been able to penetrate the ship's anti-air defenses. One hit the stern, punched a hole in the plating, and started a fire below. The other sea-skimming missile slammed into the port missile launchers, where it triggered a secondary explosion. None of which was supposed to happen.

"Two enemy planes in from the west," a voice said. "They're a match for Pindo F-16s."

"One, 2, 3, 4 missiles in from the west," a second voice said. "Where's our air cover?"

Elsewhere, Belkin thought morosely. *Or dead.* He saw a blur and was trying to process it when his world exploded.

***

Aboard the *USS Mammatus*, in the Black Sea

"Four Harpoons, and four hits," Shag reported. "The big boy is dead in the water, and burning. Over."

Ryson felt no sense of joy. Not after the loss of two boats. Just a feeling of relief. He opened his mike. "Roger that, and thank you. I hereby retract all the things I've said about the 'chair force' in the past. Destroy as many escorts as you can. Hit the largest ones first. And be sure to stand off. There will be incoming from the west. Over."

"Your apology is accepted," Shag replied. "Going in. Over."

Ryson thumbed his mike. "Six to the *Alto*. You are to engage the cruiser's escorts. At least one Harpoon each. And be careful. The *Mammatus* is to the south. Over."

There was a squawk of static followed by a female voice. "This is Three actual. One each. The *Mammatus* to the south. Over."

Ryson could see the enemy by then. Smoke trickled out of the cruiser's badly mangled superstructure as waves washed across the *Omsk's* main deck. Boats and rafts were in the water. A corvette was in close and pulling sailors aboard. Ryson turned to Sterling. "Don't attack the corvette unless it opens fire."

No sooner had he spoken than the missiles from the *Alto* arrived. Some were blown out of the air, two followed decoys into oblivion, and four found targets.

A missile boat disappeared in a flash of light, a destroyer took a hit, and so sadly enough, did the corvette. And, after additional hits from the F-18s, it began to sink.

That left a tug and a patrol boat. Sterling went after them with a vengeance.

The patrol boat tried to fight, but quickly fell victim to Guns and his cannon. The tug had a heavy machine gun mounted in the bow. But the HE rounds from the starboard .50 caliber machine gun, as well as a solid hit from an RPG, destroyed the gun as the *Mammatus* roared past. A sailor pulled the Russian flag down while another waved his white tee shirt.

"The *Omsk* sank," Sterling said.

Ryson turned to look. There wasn't much to see. Just an oil slick, flotsam, and a flotilla of dead bodies. "Call fleet. Tell them that we sank the *Omsk* with assistance from two zoomies. And tell them that we neutralized a missile boat, a corvette, and a destroyer. Three enemy vessels remain afloat, but are no longer offering resistance."

Sterling eyed him quizzically. "That's all?"

"Yes," Ryson replied. "And that's enough."

CHAPTER THREE

Luzon Island, the Philippines

LT. Commander Jayson Greer, aka "Gun Daddy," was falling out of the sky. And the lush, green jungle was waiting to receive him. *This is gonna hurt,* Greer told himself. *Gotta protect the boys. Knees and feet together.*

He was falling at a theoretical rate of 17 mph. But it seemed to be much faster than that. And suddenly he was there. His boots penetrated the upper canopy of the triple canopy forest. Branches broke, vines snapped, and a bird took flight. Then Greer felt a stab of pain and came to a sudden stop.

When Greer looked up, he could see the torn chute, the hole in the foliage, and a patch of blue sky above. How long had it been since he punched out? Five minutes? Ten? And where was his F-18? On the ground somewhere was the obvious answer. *I hope it didn't hurt someone,* Greer thought. *Please God, make it so.*

Greer looked down at the point past his bloody pant leg, past his boots, to the ground waiting below. What was it? A twenty-foot drop? Yeah, something like that. *That's going to hurt too,* Greer decided. *But it's like Daddy said. "Do want your whupping now? Or do you want it later on? It's gonna hurt either way."*

Greer drew his survival knife, thumbed it open, and went to work. He felt a jerk as the risers on the left came free. Then it was time to hack his way through the straps on the right. The ground came up hard. His boots hit, he fell forward, and struggled to breathe. "*Radio. SAR.*" (Search and rescue.) Then he fainted.

***

The city of Sanya, Hainan Island, Southeast China

Sanya was a modern city with a population of nearly 700,000 residents, tall buildings, and a constant flow of tourists eager to enjoy the city's warm weather.

The local economy had taken a hit when the war started, and travel restrictions were imposed. But, thanks to the adjacent navy base, the influx of additional navy personnel had been sufficient to compensate for the loss in tourism. And Mayor Chee was well aware of how important the military was to Sanya's wellbeing.

So, when the victory over the Americans was announced, followed by the news that President Enlai and Premier Lau were going to be present for a military parade, Chee pulled out all the stops.

For Lieutenant Junior Grade Jev Jing, and all the personnel from the *Sea Dragon*, it was a proud moment as they followed the *Henan's* 3,896-person crew down Sanya's main street and past the reviewing stand where the president and the premier were seated.

Like most sailors Jing didn't spend much time marching. As a result, the goose step, or *zheng bu* (straight march), was beginning to hurt by the time they passed the Yifang Shopping Mall. And from that point forward Jing was forced to grit his teeth during the rest of the two-mile-journey.

Finally, after being marched into a parking lot, the sailors were ordered to form up, threatened with all manner of punishments if they misbehaved, and released into the city.

Most made straight for the bars, restaurants, and shopping malls. Jing was the exception. His desire to get back at political officer Bohai Ang was undiminished. However, since Ang outranked him, the process would have to be circumspect. But *how?*

Jing wasn't absolutely sure. But as one of the *Sea Dragon's* communications officers, he knew that Ang sent an encrypted message off every three days. A *uniquely* encrypted message which only Ang could access.

That sort of thing was to be expected where political officers were concerned. They were spies after all, whose job it was to ferret out sailors who questioned communist doctrine, or had an affinity for western culture. That meant Ang's reports were probably within the purview of his job.

As far as Jing had been able to ascertain from his brother officers however, the use of specially encrypted messages was specifically prohibited, lest an Allied spy use such an app to communicate with his handler. But the other Com officers were too scared to report the issue. So, what was Ang hiding?

Such were Jing's thoughts as he rode a bus back to the Yulin naval base, cleared security, and entered the maze of passageways that led to the cavernous sub pens. And that was where the semi-submersible cruiser *Sea Dragon* was moored. *This*, Jing reasoned, *is probably the only day of the year when there will be no more than ten people aboard.*

Would Ang be one of them? Possibly. But Jing didn't think so. Ang was a suck up. And as such wouldn't be able to resist all the opportunities to mingle and kiss ass in Sanya.

Once aboard Jing made his way to the CIC, told the duty tech to take a thirty-minute break, and promised to monitor incoming radio traffic himself. The moment the tech was gone Jing checked to see which cameras covered the approaches to Ang's cabin and turned them off.

Confident now that he could enter Ang's tiny cabin without being seen, Jing went there, opened the door and slid inside. There was barely enough room for a bunk, some storage, and a fold down desk. A laptop was sitting on top of it.

Less than five seconds were required to install the Wi-Fi compatible keylogger which, thanks to a remote access feature, would allow Jing to track every keystroke the political officer made. The interesting stuff would be encrypted. But Jing hoped to solve that problem later.

Would Ang discover the tiny unit? And understand what it was? Maybe. But even if he did, the logger couldn't be traced to Jing.

The moment Jing was back in the CIC he turned the surveillance cameras back on and glanced at his watch. The whole exercise had taken less than ten minutes. Jing smiled.

***

Luzon Island, the Philippines

Greer felt a tickling sensation as if something was walking across his face. His leg hurt. And, when the pilot tried to open his eyes, he couldn't. It felt as if they were glued shut.

Greer pawed at them and tried again. Then something warm was pressed against his eyes. And when he opened them, a blurry face appeared. "There," a voice said. "That better. No worry. Doctor coming."

As the face came into focus Greer saw that his nurse was an old man. He had brown skin, a wrinkled countenance, and was chewing something. He turned to spit into a rusty can.

Greer struggled to form words. "Where am I?"

"You in my house," the man answered.

Greer discovered that he could turn his head. "The house" was a hut with a thatched roof. And, when a bug fell on his face, he slapped it. "My leg, what's wrong with it?"

"Deep wound," the man said laconically. "Pus."

Pus. That wasn't good. "You said a doctor is coming."

"Doctor Diwa come soon. Here, you drink."

The man cupped the back of Greer's head with one hand, while holding an ancient Pepsi bottle to his cracked lips with the other. The water was sweet and cool. "Thank you," Greer said, as he allowed his head to fall onto a foam pillow. "My radio...I need my radio."

"No radio," the old man said sternly. "It bring troops. Kill you, kill me, kill everyone."

Greer tried to get up, felt dizzy, and fell back. Something like sleep pulled him down. When he awoke it was to find that night had fallen and a different face was staring down at him. A female face with wideset eyes, a delicate nose, and full lips. "You're black," the woman observed.

"And good looking," Greer said. "Is being black a problem?"

"Yes," the woman replied. "There are relatively few black people in the Philippines, and that will make it easier for the government to find you."

Greer remembered what the old man had said. "Kill you, kill me, kill everyone." And that's when he remembered the briefing. Though theoretically neutral, the Philippine government was very friendly with the Chinese. "So, they're looking for me?"

"Yes. And there's a bounty on your head. Five-thousand American."

"Shit, I'm worth more than that."

The woman smiled for the first time. "You were lucky. Datu hates the government. And the people in his village hate the government too."

"And *you*?"

"I'm here, aren't I? My name is Marikit. I'm a doctor. How does your leg feel?"

Suddenly Greer realized that the pain had disappeared. "I feel good. The pain is gone. What did you do?"

"I drained half a gallon of pus out of your wound, put in half a dozen sutures, and shot you full of ampicillin. Which is all I have. Take it easy for a few days, and voila, you'll be ready to go."

"Go where? I would call for a ride, but Datu told me not to."

"And Datu is right," Marikit replied. "The government is quite good at locating downed pilots. They claim to have captured three in the last few days.

"So, the best thing you can do is let Datu put you in touch with the underground. They can send you south to Indonesia. That will take a while however."

Greer nodded. "Tell me about those pilots. Where are they?"

Marikit shook her head. "Don't even think about it."

Her expression softened. "Jayson, there's something you need to know."

"What?"

"You were on the aircraft carrier *Concord*. Is that correct?"

Greer felt something akin to cold lead trickle into his stomach. "Yeah … Why do you ask?"

"It sank," Marikit replied. "The Chinese are very proud. Their TV networks play footage of that moment twenty-four hours a day."

Greer closed his eyes. How many of his fellow sailors had died? Hundreds? Or thousands? He felt sick. "And the other ships? What about them?"

"The Chinese claim that all but two were destroyed."

Greer opened his eyes. "Seriously?"

"Yes."

Tears began to flow. He wiped them away. "Sorry."

"Don't be," Marikit replied. "I understand."

The visit ended shortly after that. And contrary to Marikit's advice, Greer's thoughts turned to the captured pilots. He couldn't save the *Concord*. Maybe he could save them.

***

The city of Sanya, Hainan Island, Southeast China

The celebratory dinner was held at the Mandarin Oriental Hotel in Sanya which, in the interest of security and privacy, was entirely reserved for President Enlai, Premier Lau, and their respective retinues. The Mandarin was located on Coral Bay, where visitors could snorkel, or lie on the beach.

But, except for the old men who were paid to rake the sand each day, the beach was mostly populated by members of two different security organizations. The MSS (Ministry of State Security) personnel were there to protect Enlai, and uniformed officers of PAP (People's Armed Police Force) were equally determined to guard Lau. And while outwardly civil toward each other, a feeling of barely contained hostility hung in the air.

The problem was baked into the system. Technically Lau, as Premier, outranked President Enlai. But since 1993 China's top leader had been allowed to simultaneously serve as president, the leader of the party (as General Secretary), and the commander-in-chief of the military (as the chairman of the Central Military Commission).

That enabled Enlai to carry out different duties under separate titles. For example, as president, Enlai was the one who met with foreign dignitaries. As Chairman of the Central Military Commission, Enlai issued orders to the military, and as the General Secretary of the Communist Party, Enlai controlled it as well. All of which made Lau angry.

As one hundred and thirty-seven people sat down to dinner in the hotel's main meeting room the air was thick with suspicion, envy, and hostility.

Because of his position as Premier, Lau was seated at the head of the main table facing east. Enlai was on his right. Lesser officials sat to either side of the table in order of precedence, with the lowest of the low being located at the west end of the beautifully set table—by the service doors. Hot tea was served, immediately followed by appetizers, and soup.

Conversation was stilted and for good reason. Enlai suspected that Lau was plotting a coup. And Lau had every reason to fear that Enlai would have him killed before he could launch a coup.

While good for China, Admiral Wen's victory over the Americans had strengthened Enlai's position. He could distract the population from the appalling number of casualties in India, by launching a propaganda blitz on the victory in the Philippine Sea.

"So," Enlai said, as the main courses began to arrive. "How's your family? Did your son get into Tsinghua University?"

Tsinghua was the top ranked university in China. And the answer to the question was "Yes." Something that Enlai was almost certainly aware of. That meant the question was a threat rather than a question: "Consider what will happen to the members of your family if you try to replace me and fail."

Lau forced a smile. "I'm pleased to announce that he did. And how is the home in Shanghai coming along? Is work going well?"

Threat, and counter threat. As China's Premier, Lau had the means to not only withdraw the permissions required to construct Enlai's third home, but to review his taxes, and those of family members too. Maybe the Enlai family had nothing to hide. And maybe sows would learn to climb trees. Enlai paused with chopsticks halfway to his mouth. Their eyes met. "Be careful," Enlai said. "Be very, very careful."

"I will be," Lau replied. "Please pass the *Hong shao rou*." (Red-fried pork.)

***

Luzon Island, the Philippines

Two days had passed since Marikit's departure. Greer was feeling better, so much so that he could walk, albeit at a slow pace. And Datu wanted him to leave.

Greer understood. He was a threat to the village. And the last thing he wanted to do was bring the government soldiers down on members of the underground.

With help from Datu's adult daughter Lita, Greer got dressed. The outfit consisted of a long-sleeved barong tagalog, worn over trousers, with dress shoes. "We have to hide as much of your skin as possible," Lita said. "And tell a story."

"What story?" Greer wanted to know.

"*This* story," Lita replied, as she gave him a hard-sided briefcase. "You are a businessman from South Africa."

"It feels heavy," Greer commented. "What's in it?"

"Take a look," Lita suggested.

Greer did as she asked. And found himself looking at a Bullpup submachine gun, a screw-on suppressor, and two extra magazines. "Wow! A Chinese QCW-05."

Lita looked surprised. "You know it?"

"I know a lot about weapons," Greer replied matter of factly. "That's why my squadron gave me the callsign, 'Gun Daddy.' Where did you get it?"

"The Chinese ship weapons to the government. President Costas uses them to kill Filipino citizens. Then we kill his soldiers, take their weapons, and put them to good use. Here's the pistol you were carrying when my father found you."

Greer accepted the nine-mil. It was tucked into a hand-tooled belt holster. Just right for wearing under the baggy shirt. "You don't think I'm going to make it, do you?"

"No," Lita replied. "I don't."

***

Aboard the Chinese semi-submersible cruiser, Sea Dragon, Yulin Harbor

Lieutenant Junior Grade Jev Jing was sitting on his bunk, with the privacy curtain pulled, studying for the lieutenant's exam. That's what he was prepared to tell anyone who asked. But the truth was quite different.

After successfully installing the keylogger on political officer Lieutenant Commander Ang's laptop, he'd been able to record every keystroke the other officer entered into his computer, and retrieve the information via Wi-Fi. That was the good news. The bad news was that the data had been encrypted using an unauthorized program.

But Jing had majored in computer technology at the Dalian Naval Academy. And as one of the ship's communications officers he had the permissions necessary to access various outside networks, including the one set up for students at the academy.

The first step was to submit a snippet from one of Ang's messages. The second step was to request an ID. The answer came back right away. The encryption program was called "Strong Sword," after the popular Chinese video game, with the appendage NIK7854 after the name.

Jing felt a sense of satisfaction. Now that he knew what the program was, he could go looking for the necessary decryption software. And that, Jing knew, would be available somewhere on the deep web. Not the dark web, but the considerably larger *deep* web.

After half an hour of surfing, Jing located a non-indexed site where Strong Sword NIK7854 encryption and de-encryption software was for sale. And that's where Jing stalled out. The price for a de-encryption key was $1,000 USD.

That was way more than Jing had in his savings account. Not that he could take it from there, because such a transaction would be easy to identify should there be an investigation.

After signing out Jing was careful to delete his browsing history before turning the laptop off. Where was he going to get $1,000? The answer was obvious. He would steal it.

***

The aircraft carrier Henan, Yulin harbor, China

In spite of the work already done to repair the *Henan's* flight deck, the carrier wasn't operational yet. That didn't stop Admiral Wen from using the flattop as his flagship however. And the command conference scheduled for 0900 that morning was just the latest of the meetings Ko had been summoned to over the past couple of days.

The purpose of the conference was, according to the agenda distributed the day before, "… to formulate an interim plan by which Carrier Battle Group 3 can continue to operate while the *Henan* is being repaired." It was a subject that Senior Captain Peng Ko had strong opinions about.

And, since Ko was aware of Wen's love for military pomp and ceremony, he was careful to wear a spotless uniform, complete with the recently authorized Hero of the State medal awarded to those who reported to the admiral.

A launch took Po from the submarine pens across the bay to the pier where the *Henan* was moored. A floating platform was waiting to receive Po and his fellow captains, all of whom arrived within seconds of each other.

As the only senior captain present it was Ko's responsibility to lead the others up two flights of metal stairs to the hangar deck. There a coterie of lesser officers was waiting to escort the visitors to the elevator that carried them up to the Flag Bridge.

Besides Wen's quarters, the Flag Bridge was home to a large war room, typically used for staff meetings. There was theater style seating for attendees and a buffet along the port bulkhead. After getting a cup of tea, Ko made his way over to the front row where a seat had been reserved for him. Five minutes passed while the officers checked their cell phones, traded bits of gossip, and in one case dozed off.

All of them stood when the Henan's executive officer shouted, "Attention on deck!" and Wen entered the room. He had a huge personality for a such a small man and Ko could feel it fill the compartment. Wen said, "As you were," and the other officers took their seats.

Wen was extremely proud of his victory over the Americans and about to celebrate it again. Something which, though understandable, struck Ko as unseemly. "Here," Wen said pompously, "are the heroes of the glorious battle for the Philippine Sea! A victory so great it will be celebrated a hundred years from now."

Ko had doubts about that, but was careful to keep his face professionally blank.

"But incredible though our achievement was," Wen continued, "there's more to do. Much more. You'll be happy to hear that we have new orders. As you know, the *Xiao Riben* (Japanese Devils) have a blue-water navy which they keep under lock and key in Tokyo bay, rather than risk combat. Our job will be to lure the *hundan* (bastards) out of their hidey hole, and into the Pacific, where we will send them to the bottom of the ocean."

The line had been written for the occasion. But that didn't stop the assembled officers, Ko included, from jumping to their feet and shouting "*Shengli*!" (Victory!)

Wen grinned. "Yes, victory. Please be seated. Commander Sun is here to tell us how we are going to win."

***

Village of Bogo, northeast Luzon Island, the Philippines

The village of Bogo was located on the lower slopes of a mountain, with jungle all around, and serviced by a dirt road rife with potholes. The delivery van carrying Greer and his "shepherd" downhill rocked, rolled, and bounced as the driver veered from side-to-side in a vain attempt to avoid the deepest craters.

Greer was in disguise and carrying a doctored South African passport. The forgery consisted of a tiny photo of Greer glued over the picture of a man named Noel Zondi. Greer could feel the bump as he ran his thumb over the document.

When asked who Mr. Zondi was, and how the underground came to have his passport, Lita shrugged. "Who knows?"

Greer's guide, or "shepherd," was a teenager named Wally. That wasn't his real name of course but, as Lita put it, "You can't tell the interrogators what you don't know."

Another indication that seemed to suggest that Lita was far from optimistic about Greer's chances. Wally was styling an Under Armour tee, patched jeans, and a pristine pair of Nike Air Force shoes. A pair of reflective sunglasses completed the look. He seemed like a good kid, but Greer wasn't going to take that for granted.

It took the better part of a painful hour to reach a paved road that would, according to Wally, take them to the town of Kasa.

"Kasa is located on the highway that connects west Luzon with east Luzon," Wally explained. "We'll spend the night there."

"Then what?" Greer wanted to know. "Are we going to go west, or east?"

"West," Wally replied. "The east side of Luzon is more developed. And the president's security people have checkpoints on the highways. We'll run into roadblocks to the west as well, but not as many."

Greer was impressed by both the extent of the boy's knowledge, and his ability to communicate. "You speak very well."

Greer couldn't see Wally's eyes. They were hidden by the sunglasses. But Greer got the feeling that he had inadvertently touched a nerve. "My father lived in America for three years," Wally replied. "And he was an English teacher."

Greer took note of the past tense. "Did your father pass away?"

Wally's voice was cold. "My father was murdered by the police."

Greer was curious but didn't want to pry. So, he took the statement at face value. "I'm sorry, Wally. I'm sure he'd be proud of you."

The moment cell service became available Wally focused on whatever it was that Filipino kids were interested in. And that was scary. Would Wally post something dangerous? That seemed unlikely, given his father's murder. Assuming the story was true.

You're getting paranoid, Greer told himself. *Keep it up! Paranoia is a survival trait.*

After pursuing a winding path through the foothills, the van entered the town of Kasa, which existed to provide cross-island travelers with food, gas, and lodging. "Get ready," Wally said. "We'll get out in a minute. Then we'll grab a taxi."

"Why?"

"So the driver won't know where we went," the teenager replied.

Greer looked forward. If the driver was offended, he gave no sign of it. And, sure enough, the van pulled over to the curb a few seconds later. Greer was carrying a back pack that contained an extra set of underwear, some cheap toiletries, and a box of nine-mil for the pistol. The briefcase was ready in his right hand.

Wally waited for the van to disappear before crossing the street midblock and turning to hail a cab. It, like all cabs in the Philippines, was white. The interior stank of stale cigarette smoke, there was litter on the floor, and the radio was tuned to a talk show in one of the nation's 120-plus languages. The best guess was Filipino, a standardized version of Tagalog which, along with English, was one of two official languages.

Wally gave instructions to the driver and they lurched into traffic. After a number of turns the car entered what was a mostly industrial area complete with machine shops, a junkyard, and a scattering of houses with tin roofs.

Wally ordered the car to the curb, paid the cabbie with pesos, and got out. Greer followed. "We're going to stay in a safe house," Wally said. "It's about three blocks away. How's the leg?"

"It's okay so far," Greer replied. "But don't walk too fast."

It was hot and Greer started to sweat after a block or so. Eventually Wally turned off the sidewalk and led Greer through the narrow passageway between two buildings and into the shade cast by a tall Bagoadlau tree.

The safe house was a simple affair with a metal roof, a covered porch, and gray siding. A dog came out to meet them and collect a pet from Wally. An elderly woman was sitting on the porch prepping vegetables and chewing betel nuts. She barely looked up as Wally walked past her and into the house.

"The bedroom belongs to Lola (Grandma). But we can use the cots," Wally said. "Lola doesn't talk much, but she's an excellent cook. Wait until you taste her Adobo. The bathroom is out back."

Greer was in need of a shower. With his shaving kit in hand the American went out through the back door to discover an open-air shower and a screened commode. The remains of a tumbledown factory backed up to the yard, which made for plenty of privacy.

The lukewarm shower felt wonderful. A shave followed. Dinner was waiting by the time Greer reentered the house. True to Wally's prediction, the Adobo was a treat. The dish consisted of chicken cooked in vinegar, salt, garlic and pepper with a mound of white rice on the side. It was both delicious and filling. "Thank you, Lola," Greer said, as he cleaned his plate. "That was a wonderful meal."

"You're welcome," Lola replied. "All three of my husbands liked it."

Greer laughed. "They were lucky men."

"Yes," Lola agreed. "They were."

The couch that Greer wound up on was lumpy, and even though Lola was sleeping in her own room, he could hear the snoring. Where were the other pilots Greer wondered? And how were they doing? When Greer fell asleep it was with the nine-mil clutched in his right hand.

He awoke to find that Lola was not only up, but baking pandesal (bread rolls) which she served with slices of cheese, and mugs of Filipino coffee. "Remember this," Wally said, when breakfast was over. "We won't be so lucky during the next few days."

Greer paused to say goodbye before leaving the house. "Thank you, Lola."

Lola turned a wrinkled cheek toward him and tapped it with a finger. "Pay me."

Greer kissed Lola's cheek. And, for the first time since Greer had met her, she smiled. Her teeth were reddish-black after years of chewing parcels of areca nuts and tobacco wrapped in betel leaves. "Let me know if you need a wife. I can find one for you."

Greer nodded. "Thank you, Lola, I will."

A box truck was waiting outside. A sun-faded watermelon was displayed on the side along with the words, "Jonny's Produce."

Once in the back Greer discovered that the cargo area was mostly full of tubs, filled with mangoes, bananas, and pineapples. Thanks to the external refrigeration unit the cargo area was cool. *Too* cool.

Fortunately, the driver had anticipated the problem, and two neatly folded blankets were waiting behind a false wall consisting of stacked crates. An old mattress was there to soften the ride. "There's a checkpoint twenty-five miles west of here," Wally said. "And when the soldiers open the back, they will see nothing but containers of fruit. Then they will pull the door down, and give the driver permission to proceed."

Greer eyed the boy. "And if they enter? And find us?"

"Then we will die fighting," Wally said. And, judging from the determination in the teenager's eyes, he meant it.

There were no windows. Nor was there a way to interact with the driver. So, Greer took the submachine gun apart, and put it back together while Wally surfed the internet. That gave Greer an idea. "Do me a favor Wally ... See what you can find out about the other pilots. The ones who were captured."

Like most kids his age Wally was very internet savvy. And over the next half hour he shared about a dozen articles with Greer. Most were worthless propaganda stories filled with hyperbole about how evil the fliers were.

But one story actually had some content, including photos and names. And Greer knew them. He'd flown with them, gotten wasted with them, and gone to one pilot's wedding.

The pilots had, according to the article, been taken to the Bataan Prison and Penal Farm.

"Because the Penal Farm is already operational, and well-guarded, it's the perfect place to house the American psychopaths," the story read. "Once the necessary arrangements are complete, the prisoners will be sent to China, where they will go on trial."

The last sentence sent a chill down Greer's spine. Because he had little doubt that once his fellow aviators went to trial, they would be found guilty, and executed. He gave the phone back. "Thanks, Wally. I think I'll take a nap."

Greer closed his eyes, but was thinking rather than napping. And it wasn't long before the truck slowed and came to a stop. "There will be a line," Wally predicted. "There always is."

The teenager was correct. The truck advanced in a series of fits and starts that lasted for the better part of thirty minutes. That was when Greer heard muffled voices, the latch was freed, and daylight flooded the cargo area.

Wally put a finger to his lips but there was no need. Greer's heart was pounding like a trip hammer, and the submachine gun was ready in his hands. "Fruit, huh?" a voice said. "How do I know if it's any good?"

"Would you like to try one of our watermelons?" a second voice said. "Just to make sure? They were picked early this morning."

"That sounds like a good idea," the first voice said. Scuffling noises were heard as the driver climbed up into the truck, chose a watermelon, and returned to the doorway. "Here, please accept this with my compliments."

"Thank you," the policeman said. "We will test it during lunch."

The door rattled closed, Greer heard the engine start, and felt the truck get underway. "We'll spend the night in Dingras," Wally announced. "We'll be there in a couple of hours."

Wally's prediction proved to be true. And, when the driver pushed the big door up and out of the way, his passengers were eager to get out. The truck was parked in a warehouse. Rays of light streamed in through gaps in the siding, spraying streaks of gold across the floor. "This is it," Wally announced. "Home sweet home. We're on our own for dinner. Fortunately, a good restaurant is located nearby."

Greer didn't want to go out. But knew it wasn't realistic to expect home cooked dinners at each stop. The driver was a short, stocky man named Angel. He was in a hurry to head home. He locked the side door behind them and gave Wally the key. "Don't let anyone in," Angel said. "And be ready at eight in the morning." With that he left.

It was hot and humid. The sidewalk was cracked where tree roots pushed up from below. Shanties lurked in the shadows between commercial buildings. The sinister thump, thump, thump of bass emanated from a Toyota Vios as it passed by. Greer felt as if he was being watched. Because he was the only black guy in sight? Probably. But he was used to that. A black man could attract hairy eyeballs in the good old U. S. of A. too.

Wally led Greer around a corner and onto a narrow street. Greer saw signs advertising a laundry, an internet café, a convenience store, and much to his surprise—a Mexican restaurant. It was called "The Blue Cactus." "I hope you like Mexican food," Wally said, "because that's where we're going."

"I love it," Greer replied. "Are Mexican restaurants common in the Philippines?"

"Of course," Wally answered. As if Greer had asked a silly question.

The Blue Cactus was very busy which forced Greer and Wally to eat at a standup table. "Order two San Miguel Pale Pilsens," Wally said. "What's a taco without a beer?"

That was when Greer realized that Wally wasn't old enough to drink. Should he play dad? Hell, no. He ordered the beers.

The beer was cold, and the chicken tacos were hot, which was the perfect combo in Greer's opinion. And all three went down in a hurry. That was partly due to the fact that Greer was hungry. But he figured the faster they ate, and the faster they left, the better.

Greer couldn't shake the feeling that he was being watched. The sensation followed Greer out onto the street where he paused to check his six. But it was clean, or so it seemed anyway, and that would have to do.

It was nearly dark by the time they reentered the warehouse, turned the lights on, and locked the door. "I'll get the blankets out of the truck," Wally volunteered. "We can sleep on the floor against the wall."

Greer eyed the inside of the warehouse while Wally was gone. And was ready with a question when the teen returned. "What is that stuff?"

Wally followed a pointing finger over to a fifteen-foot-high pile of baled fiber. "That's copra," Wally answered. "It comes from coconuts."

"Let's sleep on top of the pile," Greer suggested. "The copra will be softer than the floor, and we'll be up and out of sight."

Wally shrugged. "Sure, if you want to."

After making use of a filthy washroom, they climbed up to the top of the pile, where they spread their blankets. It was too hot to crawl under the blankets and the copra was scratchy.

Greer thought he would have trouble falling asleep but didn't. The dream was achingly familiar. Greer was back at Annapolis, and sitting in a class, when he realized that he hadn't done his homework. That was when a large truck smashed through the door.

Greer heard the roar of an engine, followed by a shout. "Police! Come out with your hands up!"

Greer was trying to decide how to handle the situation when Wally stood and opened fire with what sounded like a .22 semi. *Pop! Pop! Pop!*

Greer swore, fumbled with the latches on the briefcase, and opened the lid. The police were firing back by then, and it sounded as if they were armed with all manner of pistols, assault weapons, and shotguns. The slugs couldn't penetrate the copra however.

Wally took a very sensible dive as Greer took hold of the submachine gun and wormed his way over to the edge of the pile. The cops were firing at the place where Wally had been.

That gave Greer a moment to assess the situation. There were four of them, all dressed in black uniforms and tac gear. Did that include body armor? Most likely. Greer aimed low.

There hadn't been time to screw the suppressor on, nor a reason to, since the police were making one hell of a racket. The Bullpup chattered as Greer swept the weapon from left to right. The bullets hit ankle high and dumped three of the cops on their asses.

Greer missed the fourth but gave himself a do-over and shot the policeman in the head. That was when the submachine gun clicked empty.

Greer dumped the magazine and was in the process of seating another when Wally went over the side. Greer shouted, "No!" but the command came too late. The wounded cops were swearing as they rolled around on the cement floor trying to stop the bleeding. But any one of them could take a timeout to shoot Wally. Greer stood in hopes of distracting them.

There was no need. Wally had reloaded by then, and was firing. One to the head, one to the chest, one to the head, and one to the chest. The policemen died within seconds of each other. Greer slid down the stack to the floor. "God damnit, Wally… We killed four policemen. The entire force will be after us."

"No," Wally said coldly, "they won't. These assholes are criminals. Chances are they spotted you out on the street, and planned to hold you for ransom."

"Not police? How can you be sure?"

"Look at their shoes. Cops wear boots, not running shoes."

Greer looked. And sure enough, the blood-soaked shoes the men wore were sneakers. "I'll call for a pickup," Wally said. "We need to get out of here."

Greer took the opportunity to scrounge some 5.8x21mm and nine-mil ammo for his weapons, and to cram everything into his knapsack, while Wally talked on the phone. "Okay," the teenager said, as he broke the connection. "We're going to depart on foot, and meet our ride four blocks from here. Let's haul ass."

CHAPTER FOUR

The Pentagon, Washington D.C.

In spite of gas rationing, traffic in Washington D.C. was bad. And no wonder, since tens of thousands of civilian workers and members of the military had been added to the city's population, all vying for cabs, apartments, and reservations at local restaurants.

Ryson's orders had arrived two days after the battle in which the Russian cruiser *Omsk* had been sunk, along with most of her escorts. And the Black Sea was a Russian pond no more.

Commander Maxwell Ryson had, for reasons unknown to him, been afforded the full VIP treatment, including a seat on a small jet all the way from Turkey, followed by a ride to his hotel in a black SUV, and eight hours of sleep. Now he was in a cab on the way to the Pentagon. The suspense was killing him. *They have something in mind,* Ryson reasoned as the cab came to a stop. *I hope it isn't a staff job.*

A perky ensign was waiting to greet him. She was, Ryson assumed, a ninety-day wonder and right out of officer candidate school. She was holding a sign with his name on it. "Good morning, sir. I'm Ensign Bradley. This is your temporary ID. Please wear it at all times. The SecNav is running half an hour late. But Admiral Simmons and Captain Dorsey are available to meet with you. Would you like to freshen up on the way?"

"I don't need to pee," Ryson replied. "But thanks for checking."

Bradley grinned. "Please follow me."

It took the better part of fifteen minutes to pass through a pre-screening, and a final screening, before being admitted to the building. Ryson had done a tour there, and knew the ropes. But there was a new sense of urgency in the air.

As Bradley led him through the maze Ryson saw American uniforms, British Uniforms and more. Some of which were completely foreign to him.

"This is the room where the SecDef meets with the Joint Chiefs," Bradley said brightly. A marine corporal snapped to attention. "Commander Ryson and Ensign Bradley to see Admiral Simmons and Captain Dorsey," Bradley said. "They're expecting us."

The marine opened the door, said something to a person inside, and turned back. "The admiral and the captain will see you now."

Bradley stood to one side so Ryson could enter first. He'd never been in the room before. An oil painting of Lincoln meeting with his generals was hanging on a light gray wall. A well-lit table flanked by nine high-backed leather chairs claimed the center of the room. Two senior officers were waiting to receive Ryson, along with a navy steward and a civilian.

Bradley withdrew as the officers came forward to meet Ryson. Admiral Simmons was mostly bald, wore wire rimmed glasses, and had a firm handshake. "I don't believe we've met, Commander. But you have an excellent rep."

"That's right," Dorsey put in. "It's good to see you Max. What's it been? A couple of years? All spent on those little piss pots."

"Those piss pots did the job," Simmons said stolidly. "Would you like some coffee? Some java for the commander please. The SecNav is running late. But that means we can pre-brief you. Please grab a chair."

A mug of coffee appeared at Ryson's elbow along with cream and sugar. "Let's start with the basics," Dorsey said. "We have a problem, a BIG problem, and we think you could be an important part of the solution."

"That's right," Simmons said, as he aimed a remote at a screen. "I know you've been busy, but I suspect you're aware of what happened to the *Concord*, and her battle group."

"I am," Ryson agreed. "Chinese propaganda footage was all over Turkish television. According to what I heard a Chinese battle group, centered around the carrier *Henan*, sank the *Concord*."

"That's true up to a point," Dorsey put in. "But there's a pretty good chance that the *Concord* would have survived had it not been for one of the *Henan's* escorts. It delivered the final blows and, interestingly enough, hasn't received any mention by the ChiCom bullshit machine. And here it is."

A series of grainy black and white satellite images appeared, and none of them were worth much. All Ryson could make out was a long gray oval with vertical structures at both ends. He turned his gaze to Dorsey. "It looks like a whale with two heads."

Dorsey laughed. "In some ways it is. First because it's *big*, well over six hundred and fifty-feet long, second because it's semisubmersible, and third because it does have two heads. Or, in this case, conning towers. One forward and one aft. The Chinese call it the *Sea Dragon*. And it was the *Sea Dragon* that killed thousands of our sailors."

Ryson frowned. *"How?"*

"That's the right question," Simmons said, as a diagram appeared. "Here's the way the battle unfolded. The *Concord*, and her battle group, were *here*, east of Luzon. The *Henan,* and her battle group, were *here*, west of Luzon.

"The Chinese started the fight, and the *Concord* responded. But in the meantime, the *Sea Dragon*, along with what we think were two attack subs, circled north. Due to the ship's low radar profile, and the fog of war, no one noticed the half-submerged cruiser as it rounded the north end of Luzon. That's where the *Sea Dragon* fired five shots from a railgun, along with what we estimate to have been a dozen surface-to-surface missiles. Game over."

"Seriously?" Ryson demanded. "A railgun?"

"Yes," Dorsey replied. "We have one under development, but it isn't ready for prime time. The bastards beat us to it."

A knock was heard, the door opened, and Ensign Bradley appeared. "Secretary Moran is here."

Moran entered, paused to look at the people who were present, and smiled. It was a famous smile, thanks to three years as a successful talk show host. The only talk show host who had graduated from Annapolis, served twenty years in the navy, and been elected to congress prior to becoming secretary. She had a shock of gray hair and even features. "Good morning, gentlemen. I'm sorry to be late. I see our victim is present."

Ryson stood as Moran made her way over, hand extended. "Congratulations, Commander. What you accomplished in the Black Sea was nothing less than amazing. Thank you for coming on such short notice."

Moran's eyes were sky blue and her grip was professionally firm. The part about coming on short notice was bullshit of course, since Ryson had no choice, but it was a nice thing to say. "It's a pleasure to meet you Madam Secretary. As for the Black Sea, I had a lot of help."

A cloud seemed to fall over the secretary's face. "You took 50 percent causalities."

The fact that Moran knew that, and cared, meant a lot. Ryson nodded. "Yes, ma'am. I miss my shipmates."

Moran forced a smile. "It sounds trite, I know that, but we have to keep on. And that's why you're here." She turned to Simmons. "How much does the Commander know?"

"We brought him up to speed on the *Sea Dragon* and her role in the loss of the *Concord*," the admiral replied. "But we haven't addressed Operation Red Tide."

"I'm just in time then," Moran said, as she took her seat. "Let's jump in."

Dorsey nodded. "The objective of Operation Red Tide is to find the *Sea Dragon* and sink her. The National Reconnaissance Office (NRO) is looking for the ship, but it's difficult. You saw the satellite imagery. At least half the cruiser is underwater at any given time, and there are thousands of square miles to search.

"The sky spooks believe the *Dragon* is in port right now. But there's no way to be sure. So they have to scan the South China Sea and the Philippine Sea just in case. And that takes a lot of person power and machine time."

"How about our subs?" Ryson inquired. "I assume they're looking as well."

Moran was an ex-submarine skipper. She nodded her head. "We're short of everything. Submarines included. But yes ... We put additional resources into the area."

"And one of them might nail the *Sea Dragon*," Simmons said. "Let's hope they do. But here's the problem. In addition to being difficult to see, the *Dragon* is hard to hear, thanks to a nuclear-powered waterjet propulsion system. That's what the Intel people believe, and for good reason. The *Sea Dragon's* Chief Engineer is a Captain named Bohai Hong. He's a longtime proponent of waterjet technology for surface ships."

Ryson was quite familiar with waterjet technology since Class I and Class II PHMs were equipped with it. Hong's face appeared on the screen. He was a handsome man with a high forehead, a long nose, and a well-shaped mouth. But most interesting of all was the look of calm determination in his eyes. "That photo was taken about a year ago," Dorsey said. "At a meeting of the National People's Congress."

"And that's where things become even more interesting," Moran added. "Hong was there as a guest of his brother-in-law Premier Li Lau. And, according to some high quality humint (human intelligence), no love is lost between Lau and President Enlai. How that might impact the situation is unknown."

So, the *Sea Dragon* was hard to see from space, and hard to hear underwater. That sucked. But for the life of him Ryson couldn't understand why he was in the room. He looked from face-to-face. "No offense, but why am I here?"

Moran laughed. "Spoken like a true surface warfare officer. I like that. Here's the deal Commander ... Operation Red Tide has three components. They include satellite surveillance, subsurface surveillance, and surface surveillance.

"We believe that a multi-national squadron of high-speed patrol boats might happen across the *Sea Dragon*. Or develop Intel sources that will lead us to her."

"But that isn't all," Dorsey added. "The squadron that Secretary Moran mentioned will have other duties too including, but not limited to, special ops insertions, anti-smuggling operations and counter terrorism missions."

"And you," Simmons said, "will be in command of Squadron 7. I don't know whether to congratulate you or commiserate with you."

Ryson felt a wild mix of emotions. Excitement, fear, and uncertainty all battled each other for dominance. "Thank you, I think."

The others laughed. "Time is of the essence," Moran said. "We need to find and destroy the *Sea Dragon* as quickly as possible. So, there won't be time for leave. I'm sorry about that. But *this* might put a smile on your face."

Moran pushed a velvet covered box across the table. "Go ahead, open it."

Ryson flipped the lid back and found himself looking at a Navy Cross. The United States Navy and the United States Marine Corps' second-highest decoration—awarded for valor in combat. "You earned it," Simmons said. "Congratulations."

"Under normal conditions there would be a ceremony, the admiral would give a speech, and I would pin it on your chest," Moran said. "But these aren't normal times. May you have fair winds, and following seas."

***

Luke's Steak House, Washington D.C.

Ryson didn't have time to go home to his grandfather's house in Westport, Connecticut. But shortly after arriving in Turkey, Ryson had spoken with his grandfather by phone, and suggested a meal in D.C. And now, as he sipped a gin and tonic, the navy officer was watching the door. George Ryson was pushing 80. But, as he entered the room, the marine architect didn't look a day over 60. He was tall, lanky, and burned sea-sun brown.

Ryson stood and waved. George smiled and made his way over to the table. "Maxwell! It's good to see you Son … I missed you Boy."

"Maxwell," and "Son," and "Boy." Those were names George always used to address his only grandchild who, after losing his parents to an auto accident, had come to live with his grandfather at the house named "Sea Salt."

"I missed you too Pops. You look good."

"I'm glad to hear it," George said, as he sat down. "But I have a lot of aches and pains. Old age sucks."

Ryson smiled. "I think everyone agrees on that. How's the boat?"

George and his grandson had constructed the twenty-six-foot sloop *Serene* with their own hands. A boat which George insisted on sailing almost everywhere while making minimal use of the *Serene's* small inboard engine. "She's a sailboat," George liked to say. "Not a stinkpot."

"She's fine," George replied. "I just had the bottom painted. I wish you could come up."

"I wish I could too," Ryson said. "But I'm leaving in the morning."

"I don't suppose you can tell me where you're headed."

"No, I can't."

"I saw a news story about the battle in the Black Sea. They aren't allowed to mention names, but I knew the Pegs were in your squadron. How bad was it?"

"Bad."

George nodded. "I'm sorry."

The waiter arrived, took their orders, and departed. "I ran into Marisa a few days ago," George said. "She asked after you."

"That was nice of her," Ryson responded.

"She's single you know," George said pointedly. "And pretty."

"And she's self-centered, too focused on money, and a social climber," Ryson replied. "All the qualities my grandfather warned me about."

George laughed. "Touché."

The next hour was spent eating, drinking, and telling stories. Finally, when the time came to part company, they hugged. "Take care of yourself, Pops. I'll send emails when I can."

"You do that Son. Give them a broadside for me." And with that they parted.

***

Yulin Harbor, Hainan Island, China

It was late in the day. Thousands of citizens, all bused in for the occasion, stood on docks and waved victory pennants as the ships steamed out to sea. Because the *Henan* was still in port undergoing repairs, Admiral Wen had been forced to shift his flag to a new Type 055 destroyer. The *Baotou,* in company with another destroyer and a frigate, were headed north toward Japan.

Normally such deployments were concealed to the extent that such a thing was possible. But Wen wanted the Allies to see the relatively small armada in hopes that the Japanese would send their nascent fleet out to do battle.

Two Chinese submarines were waiting to join the group beyond the seawall and, under the cover of darkness, the *Sea Dragon* would sail as well. The cruiser's assignment was to hang back about fifty miles or so, where she would be ready to support the other vessels with her railgun and missiles. Wen felt sure that another great victory was in the offing, so long as the Japanese took the bait.

***

Aboard the semi-submersible cruiser *Sea Dragon*

Captain Peng Ko was frustrated. He understood Admiral Wen's plan, but believed the Japanese were too smart to engage the battle group without having an American carrier on hand, and were likely to remain in port.

But had the *Sea Dragon* and the submarines been allowed to venture forth on their own, it might have been possible to catch the Japanese by surprise during one of the fleet exercises they were so fond of. And Ko had said as much.

It was clear however, that even after the role the cruiser played in sinking the *Concord*, Admiral Wen viewed the semi-submersible as little more than a toy, rather than a key element of his battle group.

So as Ko knelt before the statue of Tianfei in his cabin, he called upon her to help Wen understand the *Sea Dragon's* true value, and grant his ship its rightful place in the battle group. He finished with the words, "I am a sailor. I ask your blessing on my ship and my crew."

The Princess of Heaven remained mute—one hand extended as if to bless him. Ko hoped that she would.

***

Lieutenant Junior Grade Jev Jing was terrified by the extent of his own success. After harvesting Ang's key strokes Jing had been able to access the political officer's banking information and remove $1,000 from an account that had a very large balance. Jing spent the money on an encryption and de-encryption tool called Strong Sword NIK7854.

Now it was time to use Strong Sword, and do so quickly, before Ang discovered the illicit transaction. And before he could call on others for help. Because although Jing lacked proof, he felt sure Ang was more than a communist zealot. If so, it would behoove Jing to get whatever he could, make use of it and refor-mat the hard drive on his laptop.

But, just as Jing was about to start work, Commander Shi's voice came over the loudspeaker system. "Attention on deck.

We're about to cast off. Report to your duty stations immediately. We're going to sea."

***

Sam Ratulangi International Airport, near the city of Manado, Indonesia

Ryson was exhausted. The trip from Washington D.C. to Manado, Indonesia had taken a day and a half, and involved three connections, some of which required long waits.

Sam Ratulangi had been a mostly civilian airport prior to the war. That was no longer the case. Because Manado was on the very north end of the Indonesian Archipelago, and just south of the Philippines, it was home to an important airbase. Most of the base was dedicated to military cargo planes, and Airborne Early Warning and Control (AWACS) aircraft, which were used to track Chinese air, land and sea movements.

But since Manado was within range of the Chinese airfield on Hainan island, the Allies kept a multi-national air wing there too, which was ready to respond if the enemy sent their long-range bombers south.

And such a thing was possible since the H-6Ns could make the round trip without refueling if necessary, and were equipped to carry air-launched cruise missiles.

To keep the airport safe the area was protected by surface-to-air missile batteries and C-RAM (Counter Rocket, Artillery, and Mortar) installations. One of which was a thousand yards away as Ryson clattered down the roll-up stairs. It was early in the day, but the temperature was already uncomfortably warm, and the air was muggy.

A female Master Chief was there to greet Ryson at the foot of the stairs. The salute was followed by a handshake. "My name is Jo Jensen, sir. Welcome to Indonesia and Squadron 7. Royal Australian Navy Lieutenant Commander Linda Vos is your XO. She's out on patrol, but sends her regards, and is looking forward to meeting you. Do you have any checked luggage?"

Jensen appeared to be forty-something, had navy-short hair, and a lanky build. Ryson liked her professional no-nonsense manner. As the squadron's senior enlisted person Jensen would play an important role as an advisor and go-between. "It's a pleasure to meet you Master Chief. I checked a duffle bag. Let's see if it survived the transfers."

Jensen led Ryson inside where she spoke to an air force sergeant, and presto, the duffle bag appeared. An unarmed Land Rover was waiting in the parking garage. It soon became clear that Jensen knew her way around as they left the airport and merged with traffic. "Manado is about eight miles away, sir. So, the trip won't take long."

"Tell me about the harbor," Ryson said. "It isn't much from what I could see online."

"No, it isn't," Jensen agreed. "The main problem is size. It's too small. There are two freighters in port at the moment, plus three warships, and some interisland steamers. Never mind the fishing fleet and the liner that serves as Admiral Nathan's headquarters. So, it's very crowded."

"Admiral Nathan is Australian? Do I have that right?"

"You do," Jensen replied.

"What do you think of him?"

Jensen gave Ryson a sideways glance. "Permission to speak freely, sir?"

"Granted."

"The good news is that Nathan believes in fast patrol boats. He took part in the annual Key West Offshore Races before the war. And he was the runner-up."

Ryson knew that, when the water was smooth off of Key West, specially designed super boats could achieve speeds in excess of 121 knots per hour. That seemed to suggest that Nathan was knowledgeable about basic seamanship and the technical issues associated with fast boats. "And the bad news?"

"He's egotistical," Jensen replied. "And might have an eye on a postwar political career."

The extent of Jensen's forthrightness raised her up in Ryson's estimation. There was good reason to be cautious however. An American Master Chief was unlikely to have much exposure to an Australian admiral. Therefore, it seemed safe to assume that Jensen's opinions were based on hearsay. Ryson decided to wait and form his own opinion of Nathan.

As they entered Manado, Ryson was struck by the absence of high-rise buildings. Homes and businesses stood shoulder-to-shoulder on narrow streets. A cloud-capped mountain could be seen in the distance. It was shaped like a volcano.

When a bay appeared at the foot of the street they were on, Ryson saw a vessel with the unmistakable silhouette of a cruise ship anchored there. "That's the *Agger*," Jensen said. "She's on loan from Denmark. You'll have to take a launch to reach her. The Harbor Master was forced to reserve the dockside moorage for container ships."

Someone had given the *Agger* a haze-gray paint job so she could fit in with convoys. And Ryson knew she could keep up. Most cruise ships could make 20 knots or so. "So where is the squadron moored?" Ryson inquired.

"A couple of miles that way," Jensen said, pointing north. "Our boats are moored to floating docks underneath a steel-reinforced concrete warehouse. There isn't much clearance at high tide, and it's pretty gloomy down there, but the bad guys can't watch us from orbit. And we're safe from old-school bombing raids."

"Have there been air raids?"

"A few," Jensen replied. "But they weren't very successful. The Chinese have to fly more than a thousand miles to reach Manado. So by the time they arrive, our planes are waiting for them. But that could change if President Costas allows the bastards to fly out of the Philippines."

Ryson could imagine it. If the Chinese had a base on the island of Mindanao, they would be only minutes away by air. Jensen stopped the SUV a hundred feet away from a sign that read, "Passenger Terminal. Military Personnel Only. No weapons allowed."

"Thank you, Master Chief," Ryson said. "Assuming things go the way I hope they will, I'll see you tomorrow."

Ryson lugged his knapsack and duffle bag to a metal grate where soldiers from the 2nd Battalion, Royal Australian Regiment, were providing security. A sergeant came to attention and popped a British style palm-forward salute. Ryson returned it. "Good morning, sir. Are you headed for the *Agger*?"

"I am," Ryson replied.

"All right then," the noncom responded. "I'll need to see your ID, plus a copy of your orders."

It took the better part of twenty minutes for Ryson to pass through the checkpoint, follow a stairway down to the dock, and make his way out onto one of the *Agger's* waiting launches. After taking a party of civilian crew people aboard, the boat left the dock, and made straight for the cruise ship. The sun was setting and the ship's lights were on.

The landing stage was bobbing up and down, forcing Ryson to time his jump. A miss would not only be humiliating, but dangerous, should he be caught between the launch and the float. He made it. An aluminum gangplank led to an open hatch and the reception area where thousands of tourists had been required to show their ID prior to the war.

And it was no different with the military in charge. A female warrant officer was waiting to greet him. "Welcome aboard, Commander Ryson. My name is Riley. Admiral Nathan is ashore at the moment, but would like you to join him for breakfast in his cabin at 0800. Would that be acceptable?"

Ryson grinned. And Riley did as well. Both knew that there was only one possible answer. "Yes," Ryson said. "Thank you."

Riley led Ryson to a cabin on Deck 6, which was still referred to as "The Verandah Deck." Once inside Ryson discovered that a stack of paperwork was waiting for him on a counter. But he was too tired to do anything more than take a brief shower, slip into bed, and close his eyes. Sleep was waiting. It pulled him down.

***

Aboard the semi-submersible cruiser *Sea Dragon,* south of Japan

Captain Peng Ko was standing in the forward conning tower, binoculars to his eyes, thinking about his personal hero Zheng He, a 14th century mariner, explorer, diplomat and fleet admiral during the Ming dynasty. Zheng He was also a eunuch—which was one of the reasons why Ko had chosen to remain celibate—to focus all his energy on his profession.

But that left Ko with nothing else to live for. And it was painful, so very painful, to watch Admiral Wen squander China's precious resources on a plan that was doomed to fail.

As the American General George Washington had said, "Never underestimate your enemy." Especially the same navy that successfully attacked Pearl Harbor, forced the British out of Southeast Asia, and occupied China.

The plan to tease the Japanese out of their safe harbor to do battle with Wen's battle group was a nonstarter. And it would be only a matter of hours before Wen would have to admit that and return to port. *And then*, Ko decided, *is when I will strike. The high command will listen to me after Wen's failure. And, like the Bismarck in WWII, the Sea Dragon will prowl the seas alone.*

***

After being relieved, Lieutenant Junior Grade Jev Jing made his way to officer country, and his shared cabin. The door opened easily and there was Political Officer Bohai Ang. "Aha!" Ang said. "Where have you been hiding?"

That was when Jing saw that his locker was hanging open and his belongings were scattered on the deck. The sight filled him with dread. Ang had sent and received half a dozen encrypted messages earlier in the watch. Had he discovered the keylogger? And the bank transfer? That seemed likely. "I was on duty, sir. I just got off."

"I will check on that," Ang growled. "Give me the password for your computer. That's an order."

"Yes, sir," Jing said, secure in the knowledge that there was nothing incriminating on his laptop. That stuff was on a password protected thumb drive, hidden behind the ventilator grill, in Stall 2 of the junior officers' head.

Jing wrote his password on a scrap of paper and handed it over. Ang snatched it out of the junior officer's hand, tucked the laptop under his right arm, and left.

Unfortunately, Jing hadn't had time to page through Ang's secret messages. *But now*, Jing told himself, *you'd better make time.*

***

Aboard the Allied transport *Agger*, in Manado Harbor, Indonesia

Ryson was somewhere, running from something, when the phone next to his bed began to ring. He reached for the sound and found the receiver. "Yes?"

"This is Warrant Riley. The Admiral's steward would like to know if there's anything you do or don't want for breakfast."

Ryson looked at the clock. *Shit!* It was 0713 and he was due to meet with Nathan at 0800. "Coffee please," Ryson croaked. "And crispy bacon if you have it. Thank you for asking."

"You're welcome, sir," Riley replied.

Ryson swore as he put the phone down. What an idiot. He'd gone to bed without setting the alarm. What followed was a rush to shower, shave, and prep a summer uniform. Perhaps Admiral Nathan was a camo kind of guy. But maybe he wasn't. And, as his grandfather had taught him, "It's always better to be overdressed, rather than underdressed."

In keeping with his rank Nathan was quartered in what had been called the "Penthouse Verandah Suite" prior to the war. It sat atop all the rest, with sweeping views of the harbor. An Australian Navy petty officer was there to receive Ryson and show him into a beautifully appointed cabin complete with sitting area and separate bedroom. "Breakfast will be served on the verandah," a civilian steward said. "Please follow me."

Ryson followed the steward out onto a sun splashed verandah where a white clad officer and a woman with shoulder-length auburn hair were sitting. "Good morning," Nathan said, as he stood. "I'm Admiral Nathan and this is Special Envoy Kelsey Parker. She's an expert on interisland shipping and works for our State Department."

Nathan had a ruggedly handsome face, a slightly sunburned complexion, and a steely grip. Parker's handshake was firm and cool. Her eyes were green and filled with what? Intelligence? Curiosity? Yes. And something else that Ryson couldn't quite put a finger on. Calculation? Perhaps.

"Please," Nathan said. "Have a seat. Your coffee is waiting. A whole pot of it! I'm a tea man myself. How was the trip? No, no need to answer … It was horrible. How could it be otherwise? Let's dig in. We'll talk business once our stomachs are full."

As it turned out that was typical of Nathan. He had a tendency to ask questions and answer them himself. That would have been disconcerting but Ryson preferred it to the squinty-eyed interrogation he'd been expecting. And it seemed that Parker shared his opinion. She even went so far as to wink at him when Nathan asked her a question about Indonesian shipping and proceeded to tell her the answer.

"And so," Nathan said as he put his fork aside, and allowed the steward to pour him another cup of tea. "Enough chatter. Let's discuss the so-what of the situation.

"The Chinese have a new weapon. A semi-submersible cruiser armed with a railgun and hundreds of missiles. And, according to our intelligence blokes it was this cruiser, the *Sea Dragon*, that sank the *Concord*, not the carrier *Henan*. Even though the enemy's propaganda machine claims otherwise.

"It isn't clear whether the Chinese elites are trying to downplay the *Sea Dragon's* capabilities, or are so focused on the mechanics of traditional sea power, that they don't grasp how truly revolutionary the cruiser is.

"Not that it matters," Nathan added, as he took a sip of tea. "What is, is. So, all of us are looking for the *Sea Dragon*, and with no luck thus far. She's a stealthy bitch, with a lot of ocean to hide in. Perhaps they'll spot her from space. Or a spy will deliver the goods. Or maybe Squadron 7 will hunt her down! And that, Commander Ryson, will be your primary task.

"But there are pirates to deal with, smugglers, and all sorts of other riff raff. Not to mention merchant ships to protect. Many belonging to Kelsey's father. Isn't that right, Honey?"

Suddenly Ryson understood. Nathan was a friend of Parker's father who, as a shipping magnate, might be a political force. That matched what Master Chief Jensen had told him.

So, was something corrupt afoot? Or was it more a matter of common interests? The navy was supposed to protect Allied shipping. And if people knew each other, so what?

Parker's eyes narrowed. Ryson had the feeling that she didn't like Nathan's use of the endearment "Honey." "The admiral is correct," Parker said. "My father's company, *our* company, specializes in interisland shipping. Most of our vessels are only 200 to 300 feet long. Just right for small ports like this one. And they make tempting targets as well.

"But that isn't why I'm here," Parker added. "We have extensive contacts throughout Indonesia, Cambodia, and Vietnam. And it's quite possible that one or more of those contacts will either spot the *Sea Dragon*, or receive information about her location. If that occurs a speedy response will be required to take advantage of the information."

"That's right," Nathan added. "By the time we summon a carrier, and all the rest of it, there's a high likelihood that the *Sea Dragon* will have slipped away.

"I trust that the two of you will work together to create the intelligence network that Kelsey mentioned, and to ensure a quick response in case of a sighting."

The meeting came to an end ten minutes later. And, as Ryson returned to his cabin, a number of unanswered questions went with him. What if the plan succeeded? What if one or more of his boats managed to close with the *Sea Dragon?* What then? He didn't have a clue.

CHAPTER FIVE

The town of Currimao, The Philippines

Currimao was a small town in the province of Llocos Norte. And, according to Wally, most of the 12,000 or so residents made their livings either directly or indirectly from the sea. That wasn't unusual since roughly 800,000 Filipinos were fishermen.

The plan called for Greer to board one of the larger boats, which would carry him down Luzon's west coast to the south end of the island where the plan became somewhat fuzzy.

"They'll let you know," Wally said vaguely. "Good luck Gun Daddy…You are a good man." And with that the teenager delivered a good imitation of a salute, did an about face, and marched out the door. Bright sunlight flooded the shack for a moment and vanished when the door closed. That left Greer sitting in a hot, humid fishing shack that stank of rotting fish. "Don't worry, someone will come," Wally had promised. But *who*? And *when*?

The cross-island trip to Currimao had been tedious but uneventful. After a taxi ride to a safe house, and a two hour wait, a beat-up travel agency van had arrived. There was very little tourism because of the war. But there was a trickle, including a few business people from Africa. Which was consistent with Greer's cover story and altered passport.

Sadly, the van's AC wasn't working, and it was hot. So much of the day was spent sitting on a hot vinyl seat, with air rumbling past the open windows, listening to an evangelical preacher on the radio. They had to stop at two checkpoints along the way.

Fortunately, the soldiers who manned them were more interested in the van's driver than Greer. And no wonder since she was pretty.

Greer's thoughts were interrupted by a knock and the squeak of a hinge. A man entered the shack. He was dressed in a ball cap, a dirty tee, and baggy boardshorts. A pair of ancient flip flops completed the outfit. "Put this on," the man said without preamble. "Then grab the net that's piled in the corner and wrap it around your briefcase."

Greer did as he was told. The outfit was new but otherwise nearly identical to what the fisherman hand on. And while not entirely convincing, the disguise was better than walking around the docks dressed as an African businessman.

Once Greer was ready the man led him out of the shack and onto a rickety pier. High-bowed Banca boats were tied up along both sides of the jetty. There was some variety, especially where masts were concerned, but most of the fishing boats were yellow.

Greer noticed that unlike the small craft pulled up on the beach, these boats weren't fitted with outriggers, and could probably venture further out to sea. A motor rumbled, pop music floated on the air, and a power drill whined nearby.

A sway-backed gang plank led from the pier to the *Saint Andrew's* cluttered deck. Greer followed the fishman over the narrow gap and down some steep stairs, into the cramped living quarters below. The overhead was so low that Greer had to duck his head. The air was thick with the combined odors of fish, diesel, and spicy food. Greer put the bundle down.

A man was standing under a light. He was relatively young, and dressed in a blue polo with immaculate white pants. A sure indication that he was something other than a fisherman. He was talking on a cellphone. "Yes, yes, I know that. But we can't let them get away with it. Make the bastards pay. Yeah, later brother. Stay safe."

"Sorry," the man said, as he slipped the phone into a pants pocket. "Please allow me to introduce myself. My name is Roberto Dalisay. And you're the American flier called 'Gun Daddy.' You and I have something in common."

"And what's that?" Greer inquired, as they shook hands.

"We both have a price on our head," Dalisay replied. "Although mine is much higher than yours."

"I'm not in the least bit jealous," Greer responded.

Dalisay laughed. "Please have a seat. The boat will depart soon, and I need to speak with you first."

The table was little more than a polished two-foot-wide wooden plank, resting on pipes that were screwed to the deck. Stools lined both sides so that the men faced each other.

"I hope you like fish," Dalisay said, "because you're going to eat a lot of it. Luzon is 460 miles long. And it will take four to five days for the *Saint Andrew* to reach the town of Bagao, where you'll transfer to a different boat, and make your way to Indonesia."

"Thank you," Greer said. "I'm grateful."

"You fought for us," Dalisay said. "That's how we see it. So, we're duty bound to help you if we can. But I must admit that I have an ulterior motive as well."

"Which is?"

"I hope that after seeing the conditions here, and receiving assistance from the underground, you'll become a spokesperson for our cause. We need weapons, ammo, and medical supplies. And, since Costas provides support to the Chinese, our fight is your fight."

Greer nodded. "I'd be happy to tell my superiors what I've seen, and suggest that the United States send more supplies to your organization. But I think there's an even more effective way to accomplish what you have in mind."

Dalisay cocked his head. "I'm listening."

"Good," Greer replied. "Let's gather intelligence on the prison where the American pilots are being held. Then, with help from your organization, we'll steal a private plane.

"I'll fly it to Indonesia where we'll propose a special ops mission to rescue the pilots. And you will take the opportunity to make the case for additional support. Believe me, at that point you'll have their undivided attention."

Dalisay stared across the two-foot space separating them. Greer thought he could see the wheels turning. At least thirty seconds passed by.

"He who speaks first loses." That was a negotiating tactic the pilot's father swore by, and Greer was determined to win.

Dalisay spoke first. "If your superiors agree to the plan, and if the raid is successful, would the Allied press report on it?"

"They'll shout it from the rooftops," Greer assured him. "The story will be everywhere."

"I will make the necessary arrangements," Dalisay said. "And I'll meet you in Bagao."

***

Manado, Indonesia, aboard the Allied transport *Agger*

Prior to the war the Mermaid Room had been used to stage lectures about the major attractions available in the next port of call, as well as musical performances after dinner.

Now, as Ryson took his place behind the podium, the tastefully decorated room was half filled with Squadron 7's commanding officers and their senior enlisted people. He cleared his throat. "Good morning, and welcome. My name is Maxwell Ryson, and it's an honor to join Squadron 7. I didn't have the pleasure of speaking with your last CO, but I understand he's out of hospital, and the prognosis is good."

Ryson's eyes scanned the room. He had some basic information about each man and woman, but he couldn't put faces with names yet. That would come soon.

"It would have been nice to have your executive officers present for this meeting," Ryson said. "But duty requires that our fast patrol boats be *fast*. And among other things, that means the ability to clear the harbor within fifteen minutes, day or night, except when vessels are in for maintenance. With that in mind either the CO or the XO will need to be aboard their boats at all times."

There wasn't any applause, nor did Ryson expect any, since he was imposing a higher level of response time than they were used to. "And that isn't all," Ryson added. "To maintain that state of readiness, 75 percent of your crews will need to be on board or nearby. Please adjust your liberty rotations accordingly."

"Now, a word or two about what Squadron 7 is, and is not," Ryson added. "Squadron 7 is a multinational naval combat unit, rather than two units operating under a single name.

"Take a look around. You chose to seat yourself in groups according to nationality. That's understandable. But it needs to change. Part of fighting as a unit is to *be* a unit. Please rearrange your seating so that Squadron 7 is fully integrated."

Ryson saw some frowns as officers changed seats. And he could practically read their minds. *"What a load of crap,"* at least half of them were thinking. *"This guy is a full-on asshole."*

"Good," Ryson said, as the exercise was completed. "Now, if *that* pissed you off, then you'll love this. It is my intention to cross train all of the COs and XOs so they are qualified to command any boat in the squadron.

"No, you won't have to become experts. But it's important for American officers to know what the Armindales are capable of, and for Aussies to be sufficiently familiar with PHMs, so they could take one into battle if that becomes necessary.

"And understand this…Each mission is unique. When a boat is on patrol the crew will have to deal with whatever comes their way.

"But when we plan a mission, we will assign to it the type of boat most likely to succeed. And if that isn't known, we'll use secondary criteria such as maintenance, crew condition, and arm wrestling to settle the matter." That got a few chuckles, but not many.

"As you know, Lieutenant Commander Linda Vos is not only the *Perth's* commanding officer, but the squadron's XO, and will no doubt set me straight on all sorts of things."

That line got a laugh because Vos had a rep for not only speaking her mind, but lacing her comments with profanity. She was thirty something, with bright blue eyes, and a shaggy hair cut.

"And," Ryson said, "you are already acquainted with Master Chief Jensen. She is, and will continue to be, our senior enlisted person…Ah, I see that breakfast is being wheeled in. Please enjoy it. I will see many of you this afternoon when I tour the boats that are in port. I hope to ride with each of you on patrol. Thank you."

Breakfast was a chance to chat with Vos, Lieutenant Commander George Trygg of the *Stratus,* Lieutenant Commander Marie Moreno of the *Nimbus*, and the others. With the exception of Vos, the rest were polite, but reserved. And Ryson understood that. Seeing was believing. And they hadn't seen anything yet.

"Don't worry," Vos said as they parted company. "They'll come around."

The next few hours were spent reviewing personnel files, a maintenance summary for each boat, and the squadron's budget. Expenditures were right on target. That was a surprise. But consistent with the relatively small number of patrols authorized by his predecessor.

Why was that? Had Commander Pierson been more concerned with hitting a number than strategic success? Or were there mitigating factors he didn't know about? Perhaps weather, a lack of Intel, or command interference were factors.

But for his part Ryson was determined to find the *Sea Dragon*, cost be damned. The decision to delay that discussion had been intentional. It would take place in a location that was a lot more secure than the Mermaid Room.

Master Chief Jensen had a navy launch waiting for Ryson when he arrived on the float. Ryson stood for most of the trip so he could see the full sweep of the harbor. *It's tight*, he concluded. *Very tight. And busy too.*

One of the major destinations in the port was the Manado Marine Terminal, where interisland steamers docked to deliver cargos and load huge bins of locally grown produce.

In contrast to many of Manado's buildings, the terminal was well constructed. And the pilings that supported the warehouse were so tall that even a tsunami would be unlikely to touch the underside of the building.

So it was there, in the shadows below the warehouse, that all ten of Squadron 7's patrol boats could be moored. Although it was unlikely that the entire force would be in port at the same time.

The squadron consisted of six hydrofoils and four Armindale patrol boats. And, as the launch left the sunlight for the relative darkness beneath the warehouse, Ryson saw that two PHMs and an Armindale were missing and presumably on patrol.

The Australian boats were of particular interest to Ryson because he'd never seen one first hand. The Armindales had a sleek, almost yachtlike appearance. Whereas the PHMs had a rather retro profile when hullborne.

Ryson knew that each Armindale was 186 feet long, which meant the boats were more than fifty feet longer than their American counterparts. Plus, they drew less water, which could be an advantage when fighting inshore.

On the other hand, ton-for-ton, the hydrofoils were better armed. Each PHM carried four missile launchers, plus a bow-mounted auto cannon, and two .50 caliber machine guns. Whereas the Aussie vessels were armed with a single 25mm Bushmaster autocannon.

The other major difference was speed. The Class II Pegs could do 52 knots per hour in a pinch, compared with about half that for the Armindales. Yes, the PHMs could cut speed in order to accompany the Armindales, but doing so would reduce their effectiveness.

Yet, to truly integrate the Americans with the Australians, it would be necessary to have them fight side-by-side occasionally.

Ryson's train of thought was interrupted as the coxswain brought the launch alongside a floating dock, and applied just the right amount of reverse.

Ryson turned to thank him before making the jump to the dock. Vos was there to greet him. "Good morning, sir … And welcome to Squadron 7. If it's all the same to you, I thought we would begin with a tour of the *Perth*."

"I'm looking forward to it," Ryson said. And he was.

***

Aboard the semisubmersible cruiser *Sea Dragon*, at the Yulin Navy Base, China

Jev Jing was terrified. After obtaining the program called Strong Sword NIK7854, and using it to de-encrypt the back-and-forth correspondence between Ang and an MSS official named Diu Zang, Jing knew he was in way over his head.

Now it was clear that political officer Ang was a lot more than a pain in the ass. He was an MSS agent who'd been sent to keep an eye on the *Sea Dragon's* Chief Engineer, Captain Bohai Hong. A man who, if Ang's correspondence was to be believed, was a member of a shadowy group called *Shi Quan* (The Circle of Ten). A secret society pledged to remove President Enlai from office and replace him with Hong's brother-in-law Lau.

So, how to extricate himself? There were two choices, or so it seemed to Jing. He could do nothing and hope for the best. Or, he could anonymously pass the information to Hong, in hopes that the Chief Engineer would find a way to rid himself of Ang. And that was the option Jing chose.

But *how?* After considering all sorts of farfetched possibilities Jing decided that the direct approach would be best. After downloading all the messages to a thumb drive, Jing placed the device in an envelope and addressed it to "*Shi Quan.*" A name which was sure to grab Hong's attention. Then Jing went to the tiny postal cubby located next to the officer's mess, and slid the envelope into Hong's mailbox.

After returning to his bunk, Jing he wiped his browsing history, and took the time required to reformat the thumb stick he'd been working from. Jing tried to fall sleep. He couldn't.

***

Aboard the *HMAS Eucia* in the Celebes Sea, north of Manado, Indonesia

The *Eucia's* bow rose, and spray flew port and starboard, as the patrol boat cut through a six-foot wave on her way north toward the Philippine island of Mindanao. The Armindale's bridge was considerably more spacious than a hydrofoil's.

Ryson was seated next to Lieutenant James Atworthy. Due to the exigencies of war the Australians, like the Americans, had been forced to give young officers commands that would normally go to someone more senior.

But according to Vos, Lieutenant Atworthy was quite competent, and Ryson had to agree. Part of that competency stemmed from the fact that Atworthy knew the local waters, which showed in the confident way that he pushed his boat north.

Thanks to radar, GPS, and the Armindale's computer, the Australian knew exactly where he was. The *Eucia* was westbound between the Philippine island of Palawan, and the northern extreme of Malaysia.

"The Spratly Islands are right over there," Atworthy said, as he pointed west. "Which puts them more than a thousand miles from China. That's a long supply chain.

"So, thanks to the sweetheart deal they have with President Costas, the Chinese airlift supplies to Palawan Island, and pay Filipino fishermen to run them out to the bases on the Spratlys. Our job is to disrupt that supply chain, put pressure on those locations, and force the Chinese to evacuate."

Ryson knew that the Spratlys were part of a long running dispute between China, Taiwan, Malaysia, the Philippines and others concerning the ownership of the islands, which had strategic importance. And might be adjacent to oil deposits as well.

That's why the Chinese had spent years turning reefs into islands, complete with military outposts. "What you say makes sense," Ryson said. "But what if you succeed? And the Chinese send supplies in via submarines?"

"Then we force them to tie up subs that they would rather use elsewhere," Atworthy replied easily. "Plus, it would set them up for our attack subs."

"I like it," Ryson said admiringly.

"It was Admiral Nathan's idea," Atworthy replied.

Nathan suddenly went up a notch in Ryson's estimation. Never mind the political aspirations the man might, or might not have, Nathan was a real honest-to-God admiral. And that was a good thing.

Ryson's train of thought was interrupted by a voice on the intercom. "We have four targets to the northwest," an electronics technician announced. "They were traveling west single file. One of them is turning our way and increasing speed."

"That's typical," Atworthy said. "Three heavily laden fishing boats and a Chinese escort. Sound general quarters. It looks like they want a fight."

A klaxon sounded. But that was little more than a formality, since most crew members were at their stations already. Atworthy turned to the helmsman. "Steer to intercept."

"From what I can see," the ET said, "and the speed with which we're closing with them, the enemy vessel is a Chinese C 14 missile boat."

Having done his homework Ryson knew that C 14 missile boats had catamaran style hulls, which were originally designed for use in the Middle East. And, as any sailor knows, catamarans are faster than monohulls, in this case *much* faster. According to what Ryson had read a C 14 could do about 52 knots per hour, while Atworthy's Armindale would max out at 26. And that disparity might have something to do with the Chinese skipper's eagerness to engage.

There was another difference too … C 14s were typically armed with short-range guided missiles, or a pair of torpedo tubes, the latter being something of an anachronism. Which were they about to face? The *Eucia* was armed with a remotely operated 25mm Bushmaster autocannon and crew-served-weapons that could be brought up from below.

That was a concern. Not just where the impending battle was concerned, but regarding the Armindales generally, and their usefulness. Should Ryson try to up-gun them? Or, limit how the boats were employed? It was an important choice.

The distance between the boats had closed by then and Ryson waited to see what Atworthy would do. Surely the Australian knew what a C 14 was capable of and had a plan in mind. What looked like sparks appeared as missiles took to the air. What would happen next? Ryson waited to learn his fate.

***

Aboard the semisubmersible cruiser *Sea Dragon*, at the Yulin Navy Base, China

Chief Engineer Bohai Hong was scared. And for good reason. After opening the envelope with "*Shi Quan*" written on it, and opening the thumb drive, Hong's worst fears were realized. Not only was he under surveillance by an MSS agent, President Enlai was preparing to move against his brother-in-law Premier Li Lau, and there was an urgent need to warn him.

As for the person who had intercepted and decrypted the email chain, there were only so many people on the ship who had the necessary skills, and Hong knew who they were. It hardly mattered which officer it was though, since he was clearly an ally rather than a threat.

Thanks to Hong's rank, and the fact that the ship was in port, he could come and go as he pleased, so long as his number two was on board, and ready to run the engineering department in an emergency. So, Hong left *Sea Dragon,* and took public transportation into Sanya, where he spent the better part of an hour pretending to shop—while checking for any sign that he was being monitored in an unusual way.

That was made more difficult by the fact that *all* of Sanya's citizens were monitored. Thousands of computer-linked cameras were watching the city's residents go about their daily lives and facial recognition software was being used to surveil certain individuals.

But the need for private communications between Hong and his brother-in-law had been anticipated. And the best way to commit the crime was to do it in plain sight.

Hong chose a table in an open-air restaurant, ordered tea, and eyed his cell phone. At least half the people seated around him were doing the same thing. The first step was to select a fictious name from his contact list and send a one-word instant message: "*Jinji.*" (Urgent.)

Lau was a busy man so Hong knew there would be a wait. He spent his time drinking tea and reading the nonsense on CGTN's (China Global Television Network's) website. The victory over the American Battle Group had faded from the news by then. But still, according to the functionaries who wrote for CGTN, the Axis was winning every battle it fought.

Hong's phone chirped. As he thumbed it on Hong knew the conversation would be scrambled both ways. "Hello, Admiral," Premier Lau said. "What's up?"

Hong wasn't an admiral. But Lau had referred to him as such when he was still a lieutenant.

"Nothing good," Hong replied. "Here's the situation." That was followed by a concise description of the envelope he'd received, and the nature of its contents, including the message that ordered Ang to "neutralize" Hong on the eve of "the consolidation."

"I see," the Premier said. "It sounds like they are preparing to take action against me. You're sure this information is genuine? What if it's a trick? An attempt to provoke us?"

"No," Hong said. "I'm not sure of anything. So, I'm going to send you an attachment that includes both the encrypted and decrypted messages. Surely you have technicians who can determine whether the material is authentic."

"I do," Lau said. "Send the attachment."

"What if your technicians decide that the messages are genuine. What then?"

"Then," Lau said, "some changes will have to be made."

***

Aboard the *HMAS Eucia* in the Celebes Sea, north of Manado, Indonesia

"There are two bogeys, probably missiles, in from the north," the radioman announced.

Lieutenant James Atworthy was unmoved. The orders he gave were identical to the ones Ryson would have given. "Activate ECM, fire flares, blow chaff and take evasive action."

Ryson was standing rather than sitting. He felt the deck tilt under his feet as the wheel went over, and the helmsman began a series of random course changes, which might or might not be effective against the Chinese guidance systems.

There was no way to assess which defensive measures, or combination of measures, prevented the missiles from striking the Armindale. But one missile missed and the other exploded.

Meanwhile both of the *Eucia's* diesels were producing maximum power as Atworthy hurried to close the distance with the enemy patrol boat. And Ryson knew why. Once the Armindale was within two or three miles of the C 14 its missiles would be ineffective.

And more than that, it was highly likely that the Chinese boat's secondary armament consisted of little more than a machine gun. If so, the *Eucia's* 25mm cannon would win the day.

But what if the C 14 was armed with torpedoes? They would be even more effective at close range. Atworthy was placing a very important bet. And one which he won since the catamaran *wasn't* armed with torpedoes.

As the combatants came within range of each other's guns it became clear that the Chinese skipper was no push over. He was, it seemed, keenly aware of the fact that his catamaran could literally run circles around the Armindale and proceeded to do so.

Muzzle flashes were visible as the heavy machine gun on the C 14's bow began to chug. And only seconds passed before the slugs were striking the *Eucia's* port side and stern. Ryson battled the desire to duck as shells hammered the port side of the Armindale's superstructure but failed to penetrate the boat's armor.

In the meantime, the Armindale's 25mm cannon had nothing to shoot at, since it couldn't be brought to bear. *Maybe we could mount fifty caliber machine guns just aft of the superstructure*, Ryson mused. *Where they could defend our flanks and the stern.*

Though less than perfect Atworthy had a solution for the problem. And that was to order the helmsman to put the wheel all the way over, and put one engine into reverse, causing the *Eucia* to rotate. That brought the bow cannon on target. And with some judicious help from the boat's helmsman, the 25mm proceeded to pump shells into the C 14 at a rate of 100 rounds per minute.

There was a bright flash as the Chinese boat exploded, followed by a blast wave that caused the *Eucia* to shudder, and cheers from the CIC. "Well done," Ryson said over the intercom. "The first round of beers will be on me."

The announcement triggered even more cheers. But Ryson's thoughts were elsewhere. The Armindale's crew was first rate. But their boat was badly outgunned. And God help any Armindale that made contact with a frigate or a destroyer—never mind the *Sea Dragon*. Something would have to be done.

***

The Chaoyang Park neighborhood, Beijing, China

The 18th century Spring Palace was located in what was considered to be the wealthiest section of the capital, on the periphery of the sprawling green area for which it was known. Chaoyang Park residents were typically rich. And President Enlai was no exception. He was a billionaire who, in spite of the war, had assets hidden within some of the countries China was at war with.

The Chinese government seized the Spring Palace immediately after the American owner left the country at the beginning of the war. Enlai purchased it shortly thereafter for the token price of 100,000.00 USD. And, as the morning sun inched higher in the sky, the president was standing at the exact center of the beautifully appointed central courtyard preparing for his morning workout.

After bowing to each direction of the compass, Enlai began the highly ritualized series of moves taught to him by a *Jian* (Sword) master during his youth. Some said that practicing with such an outdated weapon was silly. But they missed the point. Sword fighting was about focus, harmony, and strength. Glints of sunlight reflected off the narrow double-edged sword as it rose, fell, and cut the air.

In fact, Enlai was so engrossed with his workout that he was oblivious to the real-world battle occurring all around him. Premier Lau and his loyalists had spent years infiltrating the ranks of Enlai's household retainers and security detail with members of the PAP (The People's Armed Police). And that effort was paying off.

Even though Lau's agents represented only a small fraction of the president's staff, they had the advantage of surprise. Enlai's wife and children were the first to die, immediately followed by the members of his security detail who happened to be on duty.

It wasn't until Enlai completed his highly stylized series of moves, and returned the sword to the resting position, that he sensed something was wrong. But *what?*

Enlai turned a slow 360. His bodyguards, all four of them, had been replaced by men wearing black hoods. They were armed with suppressed weapons and stood like statues.

Enlai felt a terrible sickness enter his stomach as Li Lau appeared from the shadows. The Premier made a show of looking around. "No matter how splendid this is, it represents only a tiny fraction of your wealth, much of which is hidden abroad.

"The Chinese people will be treated to a video tour later today, along with photos of your other homes, and documents listing your foreign investments. Some of which are making large sums of money manufacturing weapons used to kill our soldiers."

In seconds everything Enlai had worked so hard for, and hoped for, had come crashing down. "And my family?"

"All dead. Slaughtered by you before you committed suicide."

"But I didn't…"

Enlai dropped the sword as a bullet hit his head. His body fell on top of it.

CHAPTER SIX

The village of Bagao, in the Province of Bataan, the Philippines

The fishing village of Bagao was located down the coast from the town of Morong. And after a week at sea Greer was thrilled to see it. During his voyage the pilot had been able to overcome bouts of seasickness, learn some Tagalog, and make peace with the name "Hey-you!" As in "Hey-you, pull on that rope!" "Hey-you, empty the garbage can!" And, "Hey-you, throw up over the side."

Now he was, in the words of the skipper, "As useful as a three-legged dog." And that, according to a fisherman named Pedro, was a compliment.

There was no dock. Just rows of brightly painted Banca boats which had been beached. "It's Sunday," Pedro said. "They aren't fishing today."

The *Saint Andrew* was too large to beach, so a rusty anchor went over the side, as a sun-bleached RIB boat was lowered from the stern davits. Greer asked if he could go ashore and the skipper said, "Hell no. Not until Roberto says so." Then he left.

It was hot. But a much-patched sail had been rigged to throw some shade onto the deck. And, when a bright blue rowboat came alongside, Pedro bought 2 six packs of ice-cold beer. Greer savored a bottle of San Miguel, and wondered if he could get it in the states.

Time passed. The hammock Greer was lying in swayed with the boat. His parents came to mind. Did mom and dad think he was dead? Of course, they did. But, if the plan worked, he'd call them from Indonesia. Or he'd email them … Or …

Greer heard a thump as another boat came alongside. That was followed by the sound of the skipper's voice. "Hey you! Roberto's here."

Greer felt a rising sense of excitement as he stood and went to shake hands with the underground leader. "Damn, it's good to see you Roberto."

"And you," Dalisay replied. "Are you ready to go ashore?"

"More than ready. Is the plan intact?"

"Yes," Dalisay answered. "A local woman knows a prison guard. She can't ask direct questions without revealing too much. But the man is quite loquacious. Especially when drunk. Which is most of the time. So, we know roughly how many guards there are, and which building the Americans are housed in."

"What kind of condition are they in? That will make a big difference if a special ops team goes in to rescue them."

"We don't know," Dalisay confessed. "That's why we made arrangements for you to go in and talk to them."

"You did *what*?"

"You heard me," Dalisay said. "A South African journalist named Noel Zondi is scheduled to interview the American prisoners at 4:00 pm this afternoon. South Africa is neutral. And China wants to win hearts and minds there. That's why my government is willing to let you visit the Bataan Provincial Detention Center, and write what they assume will be an anti-American story. I can't accompany you. Photos of me are posted everywhere. But an agent named Mary will act as your guide and interpreter."

"Is that her *real* name?"

Dalisay grinned. "No, of course not. Do you have any luggage? If so, get it. We're leaving."

All Greer had were the clothes on his back and the hard-sided briefcase full of guns. With that in hand he followed Dalisay to the gangplank and from there to the dock. Greer waved to Pedro and got a one fingered salute in return. So much for fond farewells.

The dock led to a well-trod path, which took them into a tin roofed fish market and the street beyond. A white taxi was waiting. Dalisay slid in beside the driver which left Greer to sit in back. A well-dressed woman was waiting there. She wrinkled her nose. "You stink."

Greer's sense of smell had been numbed by weeks of life on a fishing boat. "Sorry about that," Greer said. "I'm looking forward to a shower and some clean clothes."

"They're waiting for you," Dalisay assured him. "You must look like a journalist, and smell like one as well."

The cab followed a turning-twisting path through the streets of Bagao to the far side of town and a little hotel with a big name. The "El Grande" was two stories tall and, judging from the number of windows out front, home to no more than a dozen rooms.

Dalisay didn't pay prior to getting out which suggested that the driver was a member of the underground. A mangy dog was asleep on the front porch. Greer had to step over the animal in order to follow Mary inside. The lobby was delightfully cool. AC! Greer had damned near forgotten what it felt like.

The man behind the front desk kept his eyes focused on his cellphone as the threesome trooped past him, climbed the stairs to the second floor, and made their way to Room 003. *Why bother with the zeros?* Greer wondered, as Mary led them inside. "The bathroom is over there," she said pointedly. "I hope the underwear fits. You're a big man."

Dalisay grinned. "I have to go. Mary will take over from here."

"What about later on?" Greer wanted to know. "What about the plane?"

"It will be waiting," Dalisay assured him. "As will I."

Greer took the briefcase filled with guns into the bathroom and put the pistol within reach. The shower stall was small, and the water was tepid, but the pressure was good. Greer spent the better part of fifteen minutes lathering, rinsing, and toweling off.

The underwear Mary had promised was there still in its original packaging. Greer ripped the plastic open. The boxers were labeled XL but a bit too tight. Ditto the V-necked tee shirt. But they were clean, and Greer was happy to have them.

The pilot didn't have a robe, which left him with no choice but to leave the bathroom in his underwear, gun in hand. Mary was sitting in the room's only chair, hands clasped in front of her. Her eyes widened slightly as Greer appeared.

A shirt, tie, and suit were laid out on the bed. A highly polished pair of black shoes were on the floor next to the dresser. Mary glanced at her watch. "Get dressed. The prison is an hour away and, once we arrive, we'll have to go through security."

"Tell me how this is going to go down," Greer said, as he examined the shirt.

"We will arrive at the front gate, identify ourselves, and present our IDs," Mary answered. "Then we will be taken into the prison where we'll be searched. According to our informant that could consist of a pat down, or if the guards are suspicious, a more intrusive search.

"Once that process is over, we will be escorted to the cell where the Americans are being held. You will have thirty minutes to interview them. Once the session is over, we will exit through the main gate. A private car will be waiting. Here's a brand-new cell phone," Mary added, as she tossed the device onto the bed. "You can use it to record the interviews, and take pictures, to the extent that the guards allow you to do so."

Greer was looking in the mirror mounted over the dresser as he tied his tie. He could see Mary behind him. "Are you wanted by the police?"

She frowned. "No. That's one of the reasons why I was chosen for this mission."

"But what about later on?" Greer wanted to know, as he turned to look at her. "There will be cameras in the prison. Even if everything goes perfectly, and we leave without incident, the shit will hit the fan. Have you considered that?"

Something changed in her eyes. "Yes. Of course."

"And?"

"And I will hide."

"Maybe you should come with us. The flight will be risky. But, if the authorities connect the stolen plane with our visit to the prison, staying on Luzon will be even riskier."

Mary's eyes searched his face. "Why do you care?"

"I care because you're risking your life for me," Greer answered simply. "And for a common cause. So how 'bout it? Will you come?"

"Maybe," Mary said. "I'll think about it."

"You do that," Greer said, as he pulled the pants on. "Is there any chance we can grab something to eat on the way?"

"Yes," Mary answered. "We'll stop at a McDo."

"A McDo?"

"A McDonalds. That's what we call them here."

Once Greer was dressed, they left the hotel. Another one of the ubiquitous white taxies was waiting. Greer's nine was tucked into his waistband and the briefcase was at his side. When they stopped at McDonalds it was Mary who went in to get the food.

Even though he was inside a car Greer felt very exposed as the minutes ticked by. The driver was surfing the internet as a police car pulled in next to them. Greer pulled the pistol and waited to see what the cops would do. The driver got out, paused to hitch his gun belt up, then made his way to the front door. Mary passed him going the other way.

Once Mary was in the taxi, she gave each man his food. "Let's hit the road," Greer said, as he accepted a bag. "*Now.*"

Mary passed the order to the driver, who was already eating his McRice burger, as he backed out. Greer's bag contained a double cheeseburger and a large coke. The food was delicious after weeks on the fishing boat.

After passing through the outskirts of town the taxi followed a winding road through a succession of villages, between carefully tended fields of green, and over rushing rivers.

Greer saw very little of it however because he was watching their six, trying to anticipate what would go down at the prison, and wondering if he was batshit crazy. The obvious answer was, "Hell yes."

The sun was beginning to sink in the west as the taxi turned off the highway and onto the road that led to the prison. What Greer saw surprised him. There were walls, yes. Plus, an inner fence topped with concertina wire and two guard towers.

But a building that sat perched on the rise beyond looked like a Hilton Hotel. The roof was red, the walls were white, and palm trees lined the drive. "Appearances can be deceiving," Mary said. "What you see is what President Costas *wants* you to see. The truth is hidden within.

"About 20 percent of the prisoners in Filipino prisons die each year. Many of the deaths result from pulmonary tuberculosis. The others can be attributed to gang fights and summary executions."

As Greer took the information in, he realized that his mission was even more urgent than he'd thought. Unless the Allies launched a rescue mission right away, the POWs might die before they could be sent to China.

The taxi came to a halt in front of a drop-down barrier which was sandwiched between two stone guard houses. Both structures had slit-style windows through which weapons could be fired.

Mary got out of the taxi with some paperwork clutched in her hand. A noncom spoke to her and consulted a clipboard. More words were exchanged. Mary came over to speak through the open window. "So far so good. Leave everything other than your passport, wallet and cellphone behind. The taxi will turn around and go back the way we came."

With my weapons, Greer thought. *That sucks.*

But it was too late to back out. He slipped the nine into the briefcase which he placed on the floor. Then, with a big smile on his face, he got out of the car. The noncom looked him up and down. "Good afternoon. Your passport please."

Greer gave it over, and the police officer made a show out of comparing the recently taken photo, to the American's face. Then he gave the passport back. "Thank you. We are required to search you. I'm sure you understand."

Greer stood with legs spread and arms extended as a second guard scanned him with a wand and a third administered a pat-down. Meanwhile, a female cop was running her hands up and down Mary's slim frame.

Greer could imagine doing the same thing. And admonished himself for thinking about sex instead of the task in front of him. *What the hell is wrong with you?* he wondered. *Belay that shit.*

After clearing the security check the visitors were invited to board a nine-seat van which, judging from the mesh covered windows and the U-bolts attached to the floor, was used to transport prisoners. Greer felt his stomach muscles tighten as the vehicle passed between neatly mowed swaths of grass, past a statue honoring a guy on a horse, and up to the prison.

Once they were closer, the building no longer resembled a hotel. Hotels don't have sharpshooters positioned on their roofs, windows protected by bars, and surveillance cameras.

A man in a business suit was waiting to greet them. "Hello!" he said brightly. "My name is Carlos Ruiz. I'm an attaché with the Department of Foreign Affairs. It will be my pleasure to facilitate your visit with the American criminals."

The remarks were directed to Greer as if Mary didn't exist. "You are Mr. Noel Zondi. I read the opinion piece you wrote about the war, China's philanthropy on the African continent, and the need for your country to align itself with the Axis. We couldn't agree more."

That was the first Greer had heard of the opinion piece that someone else had written. He smiled as they shook hands. "Thank you. May I call you Carlos?"

"Yes, of course," Ruiz replied. "And I shall call you Noel. Come … Please don't be disturbed by the conditions inside. I assure you that the crowding is only temporary, and will be resolved the moment new beds become available."

Greer had to give Ruiz credit. The bastard was an accomplished liar. They followed their guide through a door into a lobby. Two heavily armed guards were waiting for them. After showing their IDs the visitors were led through the reception area to a steel door. Metal rattled as the barrier slid from left to right.

The first thing Greer noticed was the overwhelming miasma that filled the air. And no wonder, hundreds of prisoners were packed into cells intended for fifty.

Some stood. But many lay like corpses on the filthy floor too tired, too sick, or too dispirited to rise. The combined stench of their unwashed bodies and the overflowing toilets made Greer gag. He took pictures anyway, hoping that they would help convince the chain of command to stage a rescue operation.

Then the yelling started. It was directed at Mary in English, Tagalog, and other languages that Greer didn't recognize. All the shouted commentary had to do with Mary's appearance and the things the men wanted to do to her. To her credit Mary remained expressionless, her head up, and her eyes forward.

That was when Ruiz yelled something to a guard. The man stopped, drew his pistol, and shot a prisoner in the face. Blood and gore splattered those around the dead man. The press of bodies held him vertical for a moment. Then, as the living hurried to distance themselves from the dead, the body slumped to the floor. The shouting stopped.

Total silence reigned, and hundreds of eyes stared at the visitors, as they followed the passageway to the far end of the cavernous room. "Sorry about that," Ruiz said breezily. "The boys get a little out of hand sometimes. The American war criminals are in the last cell."

Greer snapped a series of photos as they arrived in front of a large cell with only three men in it. Greer recognized the emaciated faces right away. Ames was the tallest, Symons was the thinnest, and Wix had a look of astonishment on his face. "Holy shit, guys … That's …"

Wix wasn't able to get the rest of the words out because Ames put a size 12 on the smaller pilot's foot and interrupted him. "Who the fuck are you people?"

"My name is Carlos Ruiz," the diplomat said, "and this is Noel Zondi. He writes for the South African Express newspaper."

"The Chinese province of South Africa, huh?" Symons replied. "Remember this Mr. Zondi. "What goes around comes around. That's all I have to say."

Greer held the phone out to record the conversation. "Do you have a message for the families of the people you killed? An apology perhaps?"

"Yeah," Ames said. "I have a message for China … Fuck you."

Greer was busy snapping photos. "That's it? That's all you have to say for yourselves?"

"Eat shit and die," Wix said. "How's that?"

Greer turned to Ruiz. "I've got enough. Once I file my story the people of South Africa will get a firsthand look at the baby killers."

Symons rattled the bars. "Step in here asshole! So I can kick your lying ass!"

Ames pulled Symons back, and Ruiz turned to Greer. "Please send me a copy of your story."

"I will," Greer lied. "And the people of South Africa thank you." Was he laying it on too thick?

Apparently not. Ruiz smiled blandly and turned to the guards. "We're ready to leave."

None of the prisoners made a sound as the visitors left. Greer noticed that the dead body was still sprawled on the floor. The van was idling outside. Greer wanted to relax but couldn't. Not until he was safe in Indonesia.

It took what seemed like an hour, but was only a matter of minutes, to reach the main gate. A car was waiting for them. Not a taxi, but a black Mercedes. Dalisay was inside. And when Greer began to describe the visit, the underground leader shook his head. "You're here," Dalisay said. "That's all I need to know."

It seemed that Dalisay didn't want Greer to talk in front of the driver and that made sense. What the man didn't know he couldn't reveal. And he knew enough already.

Cars passed. Lights could be seen. The Mercedes passed through a small town, slowed, and took a righthand turn. Greer felt a rising sense of excitement as the limo approached a small airport. The dimly lit terminal was the size of a two car garage and, except for a two-engine passenger plane, the rest of the aircraft were small prop jobs.

Greer made eye contact with Mary. She was seated across from him with her back to the driver. "So, what's it going to be? Yes? Or no?"

Dalisay had no idea what Greer was talking about, but Mary knew. She sat as he'd seen her before, with hands clasped, her eyes locked with his. "The answer is yes."

Greer smiled. "I'm glad to hear it."

Then, in an aside to Dalisay, Greer said, "Mary's coming with us."

If Dalisay had any doubts about the arrangement he left them unspoken.

The car jerked to a stop. Dalisay thanked the driver and got out. The others did likewise. The Mercedes pulled away. "That's the one," Dalisay said, as he pointed to a plane. "I hope you know how to fly it."

The plane was half lit by the spill from a pole-mounted light. Greer recognized it right away. The Cessna 172 Skyhawk was very similar to the one he'd flown as a kid. Tens of thousands of the single-engine, fixed-wing aircraft had been manufactured since the first one had taken flight in 1955. In fact, based on the plane's longevity, it was easily the most successful aircraft in history.

But was the 172 in good shape? Were the tanks full? Did it have a functioning radio? Those questions and more crowded into Greer's mind.

"The plane is, or was, the property of a local drug dealer called Johnny Wong," Dalisay said. "His nickname was Kilo Wong. So, if you use the radio, be sure to use that name."

"*Was* the property?'" Greer inquired.

"Mr. Wong had an unfortunate accident earlier today," Dalisay replied. "But the authorities don't know that yet."

"So, they'll think Wong is fleeing the country," Greer concluded.

"Exactly," Dalisay agreed. "Thereby protecting your fake identity."

"Alright," Greer said. "Wong it is. Let's see what we have."

Greer circled the 172 looking for problems, didn't spot any, and entered the cockpit. The key, thank God, was in the ignition.

Greer checked to make sure that the Avionics Master switches were off. And that was important because, when the engine began to crank, the system's voltage would be low. But when the engine started, and the alternator kicked in, there would be a momentary power surge. A surge that could fry the 172's electronics.

The next item on his mental check list was the fuel selector valve located at the center of the cockpit on the floor. It was set to "both," which was ideal, since Greer had no need to monitor the wing tanks separately.

Then it was time to pull the throttle out a quarter of an inch, set the mixture to "Idle Cutoff," and turn the Master Switch on.

Greer checked to ensure that all the avionics were off and pushed the mixture to "Full Rich." At that point he opened the door long enough to instruct his passengers to enter.

Finally, it was a simple matter to set the carb to "cold," pump the primer a few times, and toe the brakes. The ignition key turned easily, and the engine started with a satisfying roar.

That was when Greer eyeballed the fuel gauge and saw that the plane had about 90 percent of its forty-gallon total capacity onboard. That equated to something like 550 miles worth of range. Not nearly enough to get the job done. Greer had done his homework on the fishing boat. And, according to the captain's charts, the closest airport in Indonesia was Miangas on the island of Karakelong. That was 900 plus miles away.

It couldn't be helped however. All Greer could do was try. "I hope both of you know how to swim," Greer said, as he released the brakes. "Here goes nothing."

Greer hadn't flown a prop plane in years. But the old habits were waiting. *It's like riding a bike*, Greer thought. *You never forget.*

Once he had sufficient ground speed Greer pulled the yoke back and felt the 172 lift off. It wasn't like being shot off a carrier … But it felt good nevertheless.

Greer's plan was to fly south over Marinduque island in the Sibuyan Sea. From there they would overfly the islands of Mindoro, Panay, Negros and Mindanao, before arriving over the Celebes Sea, where they would have to ditch.

First however Greer had to stay low, well under Philippine radars, to avoid detection. Meanwhile, by using a lean fuel mixture, and 75 percent power, Greer hoped to maximize the distance he could cover with the existing fuel supply. At 125 knots, or 143 mph, it would be three plus hours before the fuel gave out.

Ideally Greer would maintain radio silence until the last minute. But, if he did that, Allied forces wouldn't be able to respond quickly enough to help. So, what to do?

It was dark by then, and lights glittered like gemstones strewn on black velvet, as the Cessna droned its way south.

The decision, Greer decided, was no decision at all. He had to contact Allied forces while there was time for them to react. And time for him to consider a forced landing on Mindanao Island if he didn't get a response.

The first step was to put out calls on three frequencies typically used for search and rescue operations. Those included the Aeronautical Auxiliary Frequency at 123.1 MHz, the U.S. military voice SAR frequency at 138.78 MHz, and the Joint/combat on-the-scene voice and DF frequency used throughout NATO at 282.8 MHz.

Greer turned the radio on, put the pilot's headset on, and selected the first frequency. "My name is Johnny Wong. Some people call me Kilo Wong. I am enroute to Karakelong Island. But I don't have enough fuel to make it, so I'll be forced to ditch north of there.

"I want to apply for asylum in Indonesia. And, as a gesture of goodwill, I will provide the Indonesian government with a list of Chinese sleeper agents in the Philippines. So please send someone to pick me up. Oh, and your SARs boat will need air cover. Over."

Greer heard a response thirty seconds later. But it was in broken English, and staticky to boot. So, he took a run at the U.S. SARs frequency. The response was immediate. "This is Reacher-Three. What's your call sign and approximate position. Over."

"It wouldn't be wise to share either one," Greer replied. "Not yet anyway. Will you send a boat? Over."

"I'll get back to you on that," Reacher-Three replied. "Please continue to monitor this frequency. Out."

"So," Dalisay said. "What's going to happen now?"

"The Filipino air force will send planes to shoot us down."

"Will they? Shoot us down?"

"Don't be silly," Greer replied. "We have plenty of sky to hide in."

That made sense and Dalisay nodded.

As for Greer, he knew better than to believe that bullshit, and was waiting to die.

***

The Celebes Sea, north of Manado, Indonesia

U.S. Navy Commander Max Ryson was stretched out on a bunk with his clothes on, and oblivious to the fact that the *PHM Cumulus* was hullborne, and pushing her way through three-foot seas. The dream was nothing new. He was ten or twelve and trying to find his way through a corn maze. Pops was somewhere nearby and yelling instructions like, "Take the next right!"

But each turn led to a dead end and Ryson was frightened. Then a second voice was heard. "Sorry to bother you, sir … But the skipper wants you on the bridge."

Ryson awoke, swung his feet over onto the floor, and remembered where he was: perched on Katie Barkley's bunk while she conned the ship. "Tell her I'll be there in a minute. I need to bleed my tank."

The com tech's name was Evers. She grinned. "Sir, yes sir."

Ryson felt the bow rise on a wave before sinking again as he entered the head. A moderate sea was his guess and nothing to worry about.

That assumption was proven correct after Ryson made his way forward and up the ladder to the bridge. It was dark outside but Ryson knew that the *PHM Fractus* was half a mile to port and on the same course.

Barkley was present, along with Quartermaster Chris Sanchez, and Combat Systems officer Marsha Lee. She started to say, "Attention on deck," but Ryson waved the courtesy off. "What's up? And it better be good. I was dreaming of an ice-cold chocolate milkshake."

Barkley grinned. "Good luck with that, sir. A mug of coffee is the best we can do. According to the SAR folks some guy named Wong is flying a plane our way. He claims to be low on fuel, and will be forced to ditch north of Karakelong Island.

"But here's the weird part … Wong claims to have a list of Chinese sleeper agents in the Philippines, which he's willing to turn over in return for asylum."

Ryson accepted a mug of coffee from Lee. "Do we have a recording?"

Barkley said, "Yes sir." She was wearing a headset and clicked it on. "Hey, Evers … Play the SAR message to the bridge."

"Okay," Ryson said, once the recording stopped. "That *is* strange. Is it my imagination, or does Wong have a southern accent? And would a civilian request air cover?"

Barkley had bangs and narrow set eyes. She nodded. "Exactly. There isn't much to go on. But we think he might be one of ours. A downed pilot perhaps."

Ryson sipped his coffee. "Right. But why pretend to be a guy named Kilo Wong?"

"Because he *is* one of ours," Lee offered.

Ryson nodded. "What do you think? Could we make it in time?"

"That depends on what he's flying," Barkley replied. "Assuming it's a prop job, I'd say yes."

"What does the Indonesian navy have on Karakelong?" Ryson inquired. "Maybe they can respond."

"I'll find out," Barkley answered, and summoned Evers up to the bridge.

Ryson took a moment to reflect. If Wong was Wong, and in possession of the kind of list he described, then a rescue was consistent with the squadron's orders. And if Wong *wasn't* Wong, but an American pilot, it was his duty to make the pickup.

It took fifteen minutes to find out that, while the Indonesians had a couple of launches stationed at Karakelong, they were lightly armed, and no match for what the Filipinos and/or the Chinese would probably send south. "Okay," Ryson said. "Send the following message to fleet headquarters. 'Aircraft carrying an American pilot, or what could be an intelligence asset, is going to ditch north of Karakelong. Planning to intercept. Request air cover.' And sign my name."

"Yes, sir," Evers replied.

Ryson turned to Barkley. "Plot a course to an arbitrary point north of Karakelong. Get the *Fractus* on the horn, brief Conte, and tell him we're going foilborne in five."

Barkley nodded. "Aye, aye sir."

"Oh, and one more thing," Ryson said.

"Sir?"

"Send the crew to battle stations."

***

Two-thousand feet above Panay Island, the Philippines

Greer needed to pee. And no wonder. His last leak had been prior to the prison visit. And Greer wasn't wearing an AMXD (Aircrew Mission Extender Device) which could detect pee and pump it into a collection bag. So, all he could do was pee his pants, or manage to hold it.

The sound of a voice broke his reverie. "This is Seadog-Three. We're inbound to your projected ditch area. Let us know when you go feet wet. Over."

Greer said, "Roger that, over," and thought better of it. A guy like Wong wouldn't understand carrier slang like "feet wet," to describe the moment when a plane is no longer over land. Was someone testing him? Trying to suss out whether he was military? If so, that was fine. The navy was a lot more likely to rescue an American pilot rather than some dude called "Kilo Wong."

Greer turned so Dalisay and Mary could hear him. "Good news! The U.S. Navy is going to help us. Or try anyway. Root around and see what you can find. We could use some life jackets and a flare gun."

"I'll look back here," Mary volunteered.

Greer turned to Dalisay. "You said Wong had an accident. What kind of accident?"

"A fatal accident," Dalisay answered. "He's six feet under."

Greer was about to reply when a jet fighter roared past so close that the turbulence threw the Cessna sideways. "Shit, shit, shit," Greer said as he battled for control. "The bastards found us! Tighten your seat belts. This is going to get hairy."

All sorts of thoughts flickered through Greer's brain as he pushed the yoke forward. What was the other plane anyway? An aging South Korean made KAI T-50 was his best guess, since that's what he and his fellow pilots had been told to expect if the Filipino air force came out to play.

What was the pilot trying to accomplish? *They want to force us down*, Greer thought. *And pump us dry. That ain't a-gonna happen.*

So, what to do? The T-50 had every possible advantage except one. And that was too much speed. The problem was nothing new. Jet fighters had an average takeoff speed of something like 150 mph, while single engine prop jobs could lift off at about 70 mph.

So anytime a fighter tried to intercept something like a Cessna it was impossible for the jet to pull up next to the smaller plane and hang there. A differential that Greer planned to take full advantage of.

"Roll through all the frequencies," Greer ordered, as he passed the headset to Dalisay. "Find the jet jockey. Chances are he's trying to talk to us. Tell him you're Wong, and stall for time."

Greer pulled out of the dive about 500 feet off the ground and began to zig zag as a stream of tracers shot past him. Thanks to its speed the T-50 had been able to circle back around and come up from behind!

Greer heard Dalisay speak. "This is Johnny Wong. Stop shooting!"

The key was to ignore the back and forth and look for an opportunity of some sort. Greer's eyes were drawn to a pair of strobing lights in the distance. Cell towers? It didn't matter. What mattered was that they were close together. *Very* close together. Could the asshole on his tail fly? Greer was going to find out.

Dalisay continued to babble all sorts of nonsense into the mike as the Cessna closed on the towers. Where was the T-50 anyway? Circling? Or on his six? Greer hoped for the latter. Some right stick put the 172 on target. But Greer was having second thoughts as the flashing beacons rushed at him.

Then, before he could chicken out, the red beacons flashed past both wings. Greer pulled back on the yoke and was starting to climb—when a flash of light lit the inside of the cabin—and a blast wave hit the Cessna. "Something blew up!" Mary exclaimed, as she looked out through the back window.

Greer banked to the right, saw a pile of burning wreckage, and realized that the T-50 was down. Would the government send another T-50? Of course, they would.

The fiery wreck would serve as an excellent marker. Start there and head south. That's all the next plane or planes had to do.

But the 172 would cover some important miles while the Philippine air force was getting its shit together. Greer glanced at the fuel gauge, didn't like what he saw, and decided to ignore it.

***

Aboard the PHM *Cumulus*, west of Karakelong Island, in the Celebes Sea

The incoming call was heard on the bridge. "This is Longjohn and Smoker inbound from the south with missiles and guns. Whatcha got? Over."

Barkley spoke into her headset. "This is Seadog-Three. We're expecting a light plane. It will ditch north of Karakelong Island. Philippine and/or Chinese fighters may be chasing it. Keep them off us but don't overfly any Filipino territory. That would constitute an act of war on a neutral country. Do you read me? Over."

"Loud and clear," came the reply. "Over."

Ryson turned to Lee. "Put a call into the sky spooks," Ryson said. "Ask them for any imagery they may have regarding shipping south of Mindanao Island, and north of Karakelong. I want to know what kind of assets the Filipino government sends to intercept us."

"Yes, sir," Lee said, and left the bridge.

"We're rounding Karakelong," Barkley said. "And turning onto our new course. ETA at the projected crash site is just under an hour."

"Confirm with the *Fractus*," Ryson replied. "And tell Conte that, in the case of a ditching, I want him to pull the pilot out of the drink. The *Cumulus* will take up a position to the north and shield him from surface craft that may enter the area."

"Aye, aye," Barkley replied. "Permission to rotate the crew through the galley."

"That's a good idea," Ryson said. "Assuming Wong makes it to the rendezvous we're going to be busy."

***

One-thousand feet above Mindanao Island, the Philippines

The headset was unplugged so the voice boomed through the plane's ceiling mounted speaker. "This is Filipino air force plane Cat-2. You will immediately execute a one-eighty and follow my directions. Otherwise, I'll shoot you down."

Greer executed a tight 180 degree change in heading, and pulled the yoke back into a near vertical climb. That caused the airspeed to drop. Then, before the 172 could stall, he applied a hard rudder, putting the plane into a vertical flat-turn, with his port wing pointing straight up.

The maneuver was called a wingover. And something Cessna 172s weren't designed to do. But Greer knew he was near Mindanao's southern coast, and hoped to shake his purser just long enough to go feet wet, and reach the ditch site.

As the Cessna's speed fell off Greer made a 180 degree flat-turn over the top of the climb, dived to his original altitude, and was back on course. He thumbed the mike. "This is Kilo Wong. I have a T-50 on my ass, and I'm about to cross the coast at 1,000 feet. I'm turning my navigation lights on. Be advised that I have *two*, repeat *two* passengers, both wearing PFDs."

The response came as a surprise. "Roger that, Kilo. This is Longjohn and Smoker. Two 18s in from the west with missiles and guns… We've got you buddy… Lead the sucker out over the water. Over."

Greer felt his spirits soar. He didn't know either one of the pilots, but that didn't matter. He was close, so damned close, if only… A stream of tracer shot past, the plane shook as the starboard wing took a hit, and Greer saw nav lights blur past.

***

At the projected ditching site 30 miles south of Mindanao Island

"We have surface targets inbound from the north," Combat Systems Officer Marsha Lee announced from the tiny CIC. "The larger blip could be the Kagitingan class patrol boat which was docked in the port of General Santos late yesterday. The smaller blips are likely to be patrol boats."

Ryson was on the bridge with coffee mug in hand. "What kind of armament are we up against?"

"Assuming it is a Kagitingan class, we're looking at an Emertec 30mm, or a Bofors 40mm, depending on which vessel it is. They also carry 4 fifties, and a couple of 7.62mm machine guns."

Ryson turned to Barkley. "Try and raise them. Tell them who we are. And warn them. They will change course or be fired on."

"Here comes the plane!" a lookout shouted. "It's on fire!"

***

Three hundred feet above the Celebes Sea, south of Mindanao Island

The starboard wing was on fire. That was the bad news. The good news was that there was very little fuel remaining in the plane's tanks. And the flames would make the 172 that much more visible to the SAR people.

Meanwhile Greer was trying to pull up the rules about ditching from his mental files. A process which, thank God, he'd never been required to use before. "Touch down on the top of a swell." He remembered that much. But it was impossible to see that kind of detail.

"And ditch at low speed." No problem there … His airspeed was falling.

"But what about ditching into the wind?" Greer had no idea which way the wind was blowing. He thumbed the mike. "Gun Daddy to Seadog. Wind direction please. Over."

"South to north," came the reply. "We can see you. Veer to Starboard by five degrees. Then you'll be straight in. Over."

Greer did as he was told. He was skimming the surface of the sea by then. And thanks to his nose light he could see the foam topped swells. "Brace yourselves!" Greer warned. "We're about to …"

Greer never got to finish the warning. The Cessna hit the crest of a wave, skipped like a stone, and bellyflopped into the trough between two swells. "Out, out, out!" Greer shouted.

The water wasn't up to the doors yet which meant they could still be opened. "Roberto … Help Mary."

"Mary took a hit!" Roberto shouted. "I'll pull her out."

Greer turned to look and saw that Mary was slumped sideways in her belt. A dark stain marked the center of her PFD. Her hands were clasped in front of her. As if sitting in church.

"Get out!" Dalisay shouted, as the nose dipped.

Greer released his belt, pushed the door open, and threw himself out. A wave of cold seawater washed him back past the tail and the beacon perched on top of it. The red glare lit the ocean swells as the light flashed on and off.

Geysers of water leapt into the air as cannon shells struck all around Greer and a jet roared overhead. Some of the shells struck the Cessna. It shuddered and sank. The beacon vanished with the plane. A bright flash lit the surface of the sea. The sound of an explosion followed. Longjohn? Or Smoker? One of them had scored. And payback was a bitch.

The rumble of engines announced the boat's arrival. As seen from below, it looked huge. A searchlight snapped on, swept back and forth, and nailed Greer in its glare. The pilot felt a stab of fear. What if the boat was Filipino? But the voice on the loudhailer put that concern to rest. "This is the *PHM Fractus*. Grab the PFD!"

Someone knew what they were doing. The life preserver slapped the water not two feet away. It was attached to a line. Two strokes were enough for Greer to grab on. Strong arms pulled him in.

CHAPTER SEVEN

Aboard the PHM *Cumulus*, the Celebes Sea

Barkley appeared from below. "I just got off the horn with the patrol boat's skipper, sir. He has orders to capture our boats, and bring them into port."

Ryson was surprised. "Does he understand that our boats are armed with Harpoon anti-ship missiles?"

"He understands sir, but I got the impression that he's more scared of President Costas, than he is of us."

"Okay," Ryson replied. "I think discretion is the better part of valor here. We can out run them so there's no need to blow the Filipino boat out of the water. *Fractus* has the survivors on board. That's what we came for. Set a course for Manado. Copy the *Fractus*."

"Permission to speak freely, sir?"

"Of course."

"The Filipinos will claim they chased us away."

"True," Ryson said soberly. "Plus, they won't mention that they lost two jets or the fact that three people escaped the country in a stolen plane. But it wouldn't be right to kill two dozen Filipino sailors for the sake of a headline."

"Will Admiral Nathan agree with you?"

Ryson smiled. "I don't know. It could go either way."

Barkley nodded. "I will notify the *Fractus*."

***

Aboard the Chinese cruiser Sea Dragon in the South China Sea

Ex-Premier Li Lau had taken over in the wake of President Enlai's "suicide." A well-organized purge followed. Enlai's financial crimes were revealed to the public, including his ongoing investments in Alliance countries, some of which were clearly treasonous.

A timeline was released detailing the year-long inquiry that preceded Enlai's death, along with "confessions" from members of his personal staff, detailing how they learned of the investigation from an informer, and warned Enlai. Then according to the government approved narrative, Enlai chose to murder his family and commit suicide rather than face the punishment he so richly deserved.

But, as newly named President Li Lau made clear, "The moral rot does not end with Enlai. No, it reaches much deeper into our government, and that includes the military. Painful though it will be, we must find each tendril of corruption and cauterize it, just as the ancient text, the *Su wen*, recommends."

Few if any Chinese citizens were fooled. They knew Enlai had been assassinated. But they also knew that he was a profligate spender. That made the evidence against him all the more compelling. Plus, who in their right mind would go up against Li Lau? He was president now... And all powerful.

So more than a thousand public officials and military officers were fired, imprisoned, or "disappeared." Among them was a Ministry of State Security official named Diu Zang, an MSS agent named Bo Ang, and Senior Captain Peng Ko's commanding officer, Admiral Jinhai Wen. All of whom had been sent to work in the cavernous gypsum mine in Pingyi County, Shandong Province.

A development that left Ko, and his Chief Engineer Bohai Hong, free to employ the *Sea Dragon* as a semi-autonomous raider. And that's what they were doing.

It was just past 0500 and the cruiser's YJ-91 surface-to-surface missiles were almost within range of Singapore, which was located 252 miles to the southwest. Its port had been ranked as the world's top maritime hub prior to 2005, when it was surpassed by the Port of Shanghai in China. Singapore's container facilities alone boasted 50,000 feet of docks, 52 berths, and 190 quay cranes. Which was to say nothing of the terminals, warehouses, and other structures related to shipping.

Any other ship of the *Sea Dragon's* size would have been identified by that time and attacked by Singapore's modern navy. But the *Sea Dragon* wasn't just any ship. Traveling at barely ten-miles-per-hour, the cruiser managed to creep into Singapore's primary defensive zone with only her twin conning towers showing above the water. A stratagem that made the cruiser look like two fishing-boat-sized blips on Singapore's radars. Blips like hundreds of others.

As for sonar, Singapore had both the money and the expertise to deploy a system similar to the U.S. Sound Surveillance System (SOSUS), which made use of fixed arrays on the sea floor to track submarines as they approached Singapore.

But thanks to the *Sea Dragon's* nuclear-powered waterjet propulsion system, she was as quiet as the submarines assigned to protect her, all three of which managed to penetrate Singapore's outer defenses.

Captain Ko was eager to unleash the full weight of his arsenal on the enemy. The *Sea Dragon's* primary target was the port's container docks and cranes. But there were secondary objectives as well, including the Changi Naval Base, the Tuas Naval Base, and carefully selected government structures.

To whatever extent possible, civilians were to be spared. And for good reason. Nearly 75 percent of Singapore's 5.6 million population were ethnic Chinese. A group that President Lau hoped to subsume after the war. A war which Lau was certain the Axis would win.

Present among Singapore's Chinese population were hundreds of spies. And thanks to their efforts, cameras had been placed throughout the city, which meant Ko would be able to monitor the effects of his bombardment in real time via encrypted video feeds. The time had come. "Prepare to fire the railgun."

"All indicator lights are green," the gunnery tech replied ritualistically. "The railgun is ready to fire."

Ko took a quick look at the faces around him. They were largely expressionless, the single exception being that of his executive officer Commander Shi. He was smiling. *"Fire!"*

The deck lurched as the popup railgun fired and sent a smart shell arching high into the air. No sooner had the first shell departed than another was loaded and sent toward a preprogrammed target. Death was falling from the sky.

***

Newly promoted Lieutenant (OF-2) Jev Jing was stationed in the CIC as the shells landed. As a result, he could see the screens and witness the devastation first hand when the first shell struck the container cargo terminal. The resulting explosion tossed pieces of wreckage high into the air, threw cranes to the ground, and destroyed a freighter.

The other shots were no less impressive as a shell scored a direct hit on a navy frigate, another plunged down through the roof of a submarine pen, and a third laid waste to the building where Singapore's naval operations staff were headquartered.

And so it went. Nine shots were fired before the railgun's barrel burned out. But the attack wasn't over. Ko still had 150 individually targeted surface-to surface missiles to call upon, along with 50 anti-aircraft weapons, which the *Sea Dragon* could use to protect herself from planes.

The YJ-91s had a maximum range of about 75 miles, could be launched from ships and planes, and used against shore targets if necessary. Once in flight the supersonic weapons would travel at a speed of Mach 2.5 before slamming into their targets.

"Prepare to fire missiles 1 through 150 in sequence," Ko ordered. "*Fire!*"

Jing could feel the deck shudder as missile after missile shot out of their vertical launchers and rocketed upwards before reorienting themselves for horizontal flight. Each weapon was traveling at roughly 1,900 miles-per-hour. That meant Singapore's armed forces would have very little time in which to detect the incoming YJ-91 and intercept them.

Fortunately, Singapore was a wealthy state. Wealthy enough to buy and install Raytheon's S-3 Interceptor system, which was designed to destroy short to intermediate range missiles. Rather than an explosive warhead the interceptor missiles were designed to "hit-to-kill." A process which had been likened to intercepting a bullet with another bullet. And they worked.

But the magnitude of the incoming onslaught was beyond anything Singapore's military planners had anticipated. And even though half of the *Sea Dragon's* YJ-91s were intercepted, the rest struck their targets. As Jing watched the monitors, he witnessed dozens of hits on everything from warships, to power plants, and two of Singapore's three desalinization plants. That allowed Ko to attack the populace without actually blowing them up.

The combined effect of the explosions was to send more than fifty columns of smoke up into the sky, where they came together to block the light from the rising sun, and throw a gray pall over the "Lion City."

In spite of the hits it took, the shared Singapore and United States Air Force base located in the central-eastern part of the city, still managed to launch fighters. And the Allies knew where their tormentor was by then.

Captain Ko expected to be attacked from the air and gave the necessary orders. "Fire anti-air missiles as the enemy planes come into range. Reverse course, give me flank speed, and make for Hainan Island. Contact the 323rd Home Defense Squadron on Mischief Reef and order them to take off.'

Jing knew that Mischief Reef was an atoll that surrounded a large lagoon in the east Spratly Islands. And he knew that the Chinese government had spent years transforming the reef into an island, complete with buildings, defenses, and a military air strip.

The fact that Mischief Reef was located along the *Sea Dragon's* line of retreat was no accident. Thanks to Ko's foresight and influence, twelve Chengdu J-20 fighters were prepositioned at the reef, ready to provide air cover while the arsenal ship made its way home.

The jets, along with the fifty HQ-9A anti-air missiles in the *Sea Dragon's* launchers, should ensure a safe escape. Jing certainly hoped so, because he didn't want to die.

***

Aboard the ship *Agger*, in Manado Harbor, Indonesia

After arriving in Manado, and turning both Lieutenant Commander Greer and Roberto Dalisay over to navy intelligence, Ryson returned to his cabin aboard the *Agger*. A message was waiting: "Admiral Nathan requests your presence at breakfast at 0800 tomorrow morning." Ryson looked at his watch. It was 0230. But there was no helping it. He made a point of setting his alarm for 0700 this time, laid out a white uniform, and took a nap.

Ryson awoke a 0658, looked at the clock, and turned the alarm off. By then Ryson knew he could phone the galley and order a half pot of coffee *before* the breakfast meeting.

With that out of the way he took a shower, shaved, and emerged to find the coffee waiting. It was good. Damned good. Which shouldn't have been a surprise since Indonesia was one of the leading coffee producers in the world.

After getting dressed, and consuming two additional cups, Ryson left the cabin. A slim binder was tucked under his right arm as he made his way to the Penthouse Verandah Suite. A steward was waiting. "Good morning, sir. Admiral Nathan was called away. He'll be back soon. In the meantime, he suggested that you start breakfast without him. You want a pot of coffee and an order of crispy bacon. Is that correct?"

"You have an amazing memory," Ryson replied. "Thank you. And I'd like to have an English muffin too, if one is available."

"It is," the steward assured him. "Please have a seat."

A pair of binoculars, a tablet computer, and a half empty cup of tea marked Nathan's chair. So Ryson took the one next to it. An awning had been rigged to throw some shade on the table. His coffee arrived. Ryson settled in to watch a pair of tugs guide a container ship into port. "There you are," Nathan said, as if Ryson had been MIA. "Pretty, isn't it? Of course, it is. Glad to see you have your coffee."

"Sorry to be late," Nathan added, as he sat down. Even though Ryson knew he wasn't. "I had to take a secure call," Nathan added importantly. "The *Sea Dragon* attacked Singapore shortly after

0500 this morning. The bastards went after the container terminal first, followed by the navy bases, and individual targets. They
sank three frigates. Then, after firing their damnable railgun and
more than a hundred missiles, they ran for the Spratlys.

"Our fighters gave chase. But twelve Chinese fighters were
waiting for them, along with dozens of surface-to-air missiles
fired by the *Sea Dragon*. All of which is to say that they kicked
our asses and returned to Yulin Harbor without sustaining so
much as a scratch. General Haskell is furious."

Ryson knew that Haskell was in command of the United
States Indo-Pacific Command, under which non-NATO countries like Australia had agreed to fight. The news that Singapore
had been attacked, and severely damaged by a single ship, would
come as a terrible shock.

Their breakfasts arrived at that point. And, in spite of the
terrible news, Ryson discovered that he was hungry. "Haskell
is of the opinion that none of his people are doing enough to
find the *Sea Dragon*," Nathan said. "And that includes you and
me. Normally your effort to snatch an escaped flier out from
under Costa's nose would have produced an 'attaboy.' Not this
time.

"In fact, when I raised the matter, Haskell's response was,
'Well, that's just lovely. What's the sonofabitch doing to find the
Sea Dragon?'"

Ryson took a sip of coffee. "I understand the general's pain.
And, as it happens, I have something in mind. A plan which will
increase my squadron's chances of finding the *Sea Dragon*. It's
all in here."

Nathan accepted the binder. "Strike while the iron is hot, eh
what? Pour yourself another cup of coffee while I take a look."

Ryson was both pleased and fearful. Pleased that Nathan was
going to read the proposal, and fearful of how he might react.

There were two kinds of senior officers in Ryson's experience. Skimmers and divers. When skimmers read a document, they're looking for the big so-what.

And when divers read a document, they're were looking for the so-what plus the who, what, why, when and how. Which group did Nathan belong to?

As minutes passed, and Nathan turned pages, it soon became obvious that the admiral was a diver. That meant Ryson could expect a detailed grilling. And that was fine with him.

Finally, after fifteen minutes of uninterrupted reading, Nathan looked up. There was a frown on his face. "My God man, you want the sun, the moon, and the stars."

"Yes sir," Ryson replied. "But that, in my judgement, is what it's going to take."

"All right," Nathan replied. "You want your own island. Justify that."

Ryson was ready. "Yes, sir. As things stand now, we're too far away from the enemy. Half of each patrol is spent traveling north into enemy waters and returning to base.

"You mentioned the Chinese base on Mischief Reef in the Spratlys. I want to establish an FOB (forward operating base) on one of the islands south and west of there.

"So, if we learn that the *Sea Dragon* is steaming south from Hainan island for example, we would be able to quickly intercept her. Slow her down if you will, and call for help."

"That makes sense," Nathan said grudgingly. "And, if you get approval for the island, you'll need all the rest of it. A supply ship, a C-RAM system on a barge, and a land-based air defense system. To protect your supply ship and patrol boats. Did I miss anything?"

Actually, he had. The squadron would need an oiler too. But Ryson sensed it would be best to ignore that requirement for the moment. "No, sir. I think that pretty well covers it."

"All right then," Nathan said. "I will take your proposal to General Haskell along with a wild estimate of how much it would cost. In the meantime, keep on keeping on. I'll get back to you when I have an answer."

Ryson knew a dismissal when he heard one. He stood. "Sir, yes sir." The meeting was over.

The rest of the day was spent on the minutiae of command: requests for supplies, fitness reports, three disciplinary actions, a pissing match between two skippers, the need to motivate a recalcitrant dockyard crew, an emergency leave for an engineman on the *Arcus*, and the need to take part in a promotion celebration. It was being held at a waterfront tavern, and that's where the Australians found him. The Australians being an army captain and a lieutenant. "Sorry, to crash the party sir," the captain said. "My name is Dancy. And this is Lieutenant Kapoor."

Dancy was wearing a green beret, and looked like the rugby player that he probably was. Kapoor was a Sikh. And the camo pattern on his turban matched his uniform. His parachute wings were sewn on.

Ryson glanced from Dancy to Kapoor and back again. "Don't tell me, let me guess: Special ops."

"Yes, sir," Dancy replied. "The 2nd Commando Regiment to be exact. We'd like to have a chat if that's possible."

"Of course," Ryson said. "We can step outside if you like."

"Sorry, sir, but that won't work. With your permission we'll take you to the other side of the harbor where our chaps are prepping for an ocean cruise."

Ryson sighed. It was already 1930 and he was functioning on a couple hours of sleep. "Alright, if that's how it has to be. Give me a moment."

Ryson went over to congratulate the newly made E-6, before handing command off to his XO, Lieutenant Commander Linda

Vos. "You're in charge Linda. Your people want me to attend some sort of meeting."

Vos eyed the army officers. "Yes, sir. Be careful what you agree to. Those blokes are batshit crazy."

Ryson laughed. "Will do. I have my radio. Call me if the *Sea Dragon* enters the harbor."

"Count on it," Vos replied, and turned away.

The army officers led Ryson outside. A dark green Land Rover was waiting at the curb. Ryson sat in the back next to Dancy. The ten-minute drive took them along the waterfront to a dilapidated warehouse. The driver honked and a much-abused steel door rolled out of the way. The SUV then entered the building. Ceiling mounted lights threw pools of light down onto oil-stained concrete. Ryson could see men moving about, vehicles parked to one side, and piles of equipment.

The Aussies got out and Ryson did likewise. Together they made their way over to a door marked "Manager." It opened into a large office. And there, seated at a long wooden table, were Admiral Nathan, Kelsey Parker and two strangers. "They found you," Nathan said. "Well, done. Sorry I couldn't brief you this morning, but we were still putting the pieces together, and waiting for a green light. You know Kelsey. The man sitting opposite me is Lieutenant Commander Greer—the pilot your people pulled out of the drink—and a very resourceful man."

Greer stood and came around to shake hands. "It's a pleasure to meet you, sir ... And thanks for saving my ass. This is Roberto Dalisay. He leads the Filipino resistance movement. Without the resistance I'd be sitting in a prison cell waiting for a trip to China."

Ryson shook hands with Dalisay as Nathan nodded approvingly. "That's right. And thanks to the underground we have an opportunity to rescue three American pilots. Believe it or not

Commander Greer was able to enter the prison where the POWs are being held and take photos!

"But time is of the essence," Nathan added. "The Chinese want to put the pilots on trial in Beijing. And President Costas agreed to give them up. That's where Dancy and Kapoor come in. They're going to lead the rescue.

"We considered using helicopters," Nathan said. "But they would have to refuel in both directions. And there's no secure place to do that. So, we decided on a ship. But *what* ship? Now, thanks to Kelsey here, that piece of the puzzle has fallen into place."

"And the ship is?"

"A roll on/roll off ferry named the *Setiawati*," Nathan replied.

"It means loyal and faithful," Parker explained. "She looks like hundreds of other interisland ferries, her engines are in good shape, and she can transport both the commandos and their vehicles."

Nathan gestured toward some empty seats. "Please join us."

The commandos chose chairs and Ryson wound up next to Parker. Her perfume was distracting. "So, how does Squadron 7 fit in?"

"Seven will provide escorts coming back."

"And going in?"

"You'll sail separately," Nathan said. "From all appearances the *Setiawati* will be doing what ferries do. Meanwhile you, and your boats, will be on patrol.

"Then shortly after dark, the day after tomorrow, the task force will come together at Bataan in the Philippines. Captain Dancy?"

The commando cleared his throat. "Our lot will roll off the ferry in the vehicles you saw outside, and drive to the prison. Mr. Dalisay and Commander Greer will guide us.

"Once we have the POWs in protective custody, we'll turn all the rest of the prisoners loose. They'll run every which way, making it difficult for the authorities to know what's going on. Then, using the same vehicles, we'll return to the ship."

"And that's where your boats come in," Parker added. "I think it's safe to say that both the Filipinos and the Chinese will give chase. And *Setiawati* will be easy to catch."

Ryson could imagine it. Planes, boats and even ships would be sent to intercept the ferry. "Tell me something," Ryson said. "Are both the vehicles and the ferry expendable? If so, we can load the soldiers, the POWs, and the ferry crew onto my boats."

Nathan looked at Parker. "What about that?"

Kelsey shrugged. "It would cost the government something like a million U.S. to buy the *Setiawati*. You'd have to speak with my father."

"Realizing that you'll most likely lose the ferry either way," Ryson put in. "It will represent a rather large, not to mention slow, target."

"There's that," Nathan agreed. "I'll look into it. In the meantime, I suspect you'll want to discuss tactical concerns with Captain Dancy, Commander Greer, and Mr. Dalisay."

"That makes sense," Ryson agreed. "Is the ferry captain around? We should bring him into the loop."

"I will serve as captain," Parker put in. "I have an unlimited master's license."

A mariner with an unlimited master's license could command any ship regardless of type, tonnage, power or location. And the fact that Parker had such a ticket was impressive. And an important asset where the family business was concerned. Parker was sitting only inches away and Ryson could see the curiosity in her eyes. She was waiting to see how he would react to a female captain. "Perfect," Ryson said. "Let's get to work."

***

Borgo Catholic Cemetery, Manado Indonesia

The rising sun threw three black shadows across the yawning grave, as the wooden coffin was lowered into the ground, and a Catholic Priest named Father Wijaya led the mourners in the Lord's Prayer. Then he added some words of his own.

"Her true name was Maria Avilar. But when it came time to choose another name, one which would offer hope, Maria chose 'Mary.' The name of Mary, mother of Jesus, blessed be her name. Now, with the mother Mary in mind we recite *her* prayer, knowing that Maria would be pleased.

'Hail Mary,
Full of Grace,
The Lord is with thee.
Blessed art thou among women,
and blessed is the fruit
of thy womb, Jesus.
Holy Mary,
Mother of God,
pray for us sinners now,
and at the hour of our death. Amen.'"

Greer wasn't Catholic. Or anything else for that matter. But the words moved him. And as he went forward to kneel by the grave, tears trickled down his cheeks. Mary, because that was how he continued to think of her, had been struck by a shard of metal that entered her body from behind, and came out through her chest.

Greer had been battling to keep the plane in the air and fly them to safety. So, rather than distract him—Mary died quietly—with her hands clasped in front of her.

Then, after the plane hit the water Dalisay, in what could only be described as an act of heroism, managed to cut through Mary's seatbelt and drag her free of the sinking plane. She was wearing a PFD. And that, plus Dalisay's efforts, kept her afloat until sailors on the *Fractus* were able to hoist her body out of the water.

Now, as Father Wijaya, Dalisay and four gravediggers looked on, Greer spoke to her. "I am so very, very sorry. I urged you to come. I said you would be safe here. And I thought you would be. But there was something more on my mind as well. A desire to learn all about you, to spend time with you, and to look into your eyes. I'd like to believe that you felt something similar.

"I hope you're out there somewhere, in a place where you're happy, and I will be able to find you."

Greer stood, nodded to the grave diggers, and turned to Father Wijaya. "I'd like to make a donation Father. Please make sure that someone tends to Mary's grave, and those of the people buried around her. If you'll give me an address, I'll send money from time-to-time."

Wijaya produced a business card. And Greer gave the priest most of the emergency pay the navy had given him. The money was sorely needed. Although Catholicism was one of the six approved religions in Indonesia, less than three percent of the country's population were Catholics, and budgets were tight. A fact which accounted for the toppled monuments and the rampant weeds that threatened to overwhelm the graveyard.

"It shall be as you say," Wijaya said, as he accepted the money. "Once Maria's headstone is finished, I will make sure that the workers install it properly."

Greer thanked the Father, and with Dalisay at his side, made his way back to the waiting taxi. The ferry was going to depart at 1500. And both men would be on it.

***

Aboard the ferry *Setiawati,* Manado harbor, Indonesia

The ferryboat's main cabin was packed with naval personnel, both American and Australian. The purpose of the gathering was to announce assignments, coordinate missions, and resolve problems. The first problem was the fact that the American hydrofoil captains were pissed off, because they'd been left out of Operation Free Eagle, and the Aussies were going to get all the glory. And Ryson was aware of that thanks to a download from Master Chief Jo Jensen.

So as Ryson made his way to the front of the half-hostile crowd, he knew he had his job cut out for him. "Good morning … By now you know we're prepping for a very important mission. Please allow me to remind you that it is top secret, and do not share any of what you are about to hear with anyone other than your XOs.

"At 1500 hours this afternoon a ferry loaded with Australian commandos and their vehicles will depart Manado bay, and proceed north to carry out a highly classified raid.

"All four of the Australian boats will depart as well, traveling separately and in pairs, to convey the impression that they are on patrol. Later in the day the Armindales will meet the commandos after their raid has taken place, take them off a beach, and bring them here.

"Meanwhile the PHMs will continue to carry out their regular duties. Lieutenant Commander Vos will be in command. When this meeting is over, I will meet with the Armindale captains to discuss tactics. Do you have any questions?"

Arms shot up. One of them belonged to the *Nimbus's* skipper, Lieutenant Commander Marlo Moreno, who described herself as "loud and proud." Ryson pointed to her. "Yes, Marlo."

"Why are you taking all of the Armindales, and none of the Pegs?"

The truth was that Ryson had a secret bias in favor the PHMs, due to their speed and the fact that they were armed with Harpoon missiles. But, after studying the matter, he 'd been forced to conclude that the Australian boats were better suited for the mission at hand.

"Without diving into the classified details," Ryson said, "I can tell you this. The Pegs have a range of 1,380 miles. And the Armindales have a range of 3,452 miles.

"Plus, each Armindale can accommodate twenty passengers, each carries two RIB boats, and each has stern mounted ladders. That will make it easier to board the commandos—especially if some are wounded. Does that answer your question?"

Moreno could read between the lines. It didn't take a genius to figure out that the objective was a long way off. And the Aussie boats were bigger. *Bigger and slower*, Moreno thought to herself. But she knew better than to say that. "Sir, yes sir. Thank you."

After the PHM officers left, Ryson sat down and invited the Australians to do likewise. They included Vos's XO, Andy Tyson, who would command the *HMAS Perth*.

Then there was the *HMS Kalbarri's* skipper LT. Carl (Foxy) Fox who, according to the rumors Ryson had heard, was very popular with the ladies.

Ryson had already been to sea with the *HMAS Eucia's* boy-ish Captain, LT. James (Jim) Atworthy, as well as the *HMAS Rockhampton's* commanding officer Mike Christian, an officer known for his pranks.

During the next hour the group reviewed all sorts of things, including the need to triage wounded commandos on the beach, and put the most serious cases on *Eucia*, which would have a doctor on board.

Then there was the matter of rations. There would be extra mouths to feed on the journey home. Towing rigs would need to be ready just in case. Extra loads for the RPGs and missile launchers would be required too. Along with additional ammo for the Armindales' M242 Bushmaster autocannons. It went on and on.

Finally, at about 1000 Ryson returned to the *Agger* where he took a three hour nap. Then it was time to get up, shave, shower, and get dressed. His personals and a change of underwear went into a black AWOL bag. There was just enough time to hustle down to the cafeteria style restaurant on *Agger's* Promenade deck and gulp three cups of coffee while eating a French dip sandwich.

From there it was a short trip down to the landing stage where Master Chief Jensen and a RIB boat were waiting. She saluted. "Good afternoon, sir. Which boat do you want to travel on?"

"The *Rockhampton*, please."

Jensen gave the information to the coxswain and spoke into a handheld radio. Ryson eyed the sky as the boat bounced through a light chop. The sun was hidden behind a layer of clouds. And that was a good thing. The less the enemy could see the better.

The *Rockhampton* was moored under the Manado Marine Terminal with the rest of Squadron 7's boats. Thanks to an advance warning from Jensen, Lieutenant Commander Christian was waiting to greet Ryson as he came aboard. The Aussie had brown eyes, dark skin, and a ready smile. The open palm slaute was rendered British style. Ryson delivered an American salute in return and the men shook hands. "I'm glad you chose the *Rockhampton*, sir. You'll be happy to know she's faster than the other Armindales."

Ryson frowned. "Really? How much faster?"

"Three-miles-per-hour, sir."

Ryson laughed. "The enemy has no idea what they're up against."

The conversation was interrupted as a sailor appeared. "Excuse me, sir. The ferry is getting underway."

Christian nodded. "Thank you, Smitty."

Ryson thought about the ferry and the woman in command of it. After negotiations between Admiral Nathan and George Parker, a contract had been agreed to. The *Setiawati* would be sacrificed. And the Austrailian government would pay Parker Marine $900,000 American.

But while the ferry could be replaced, Kelsey Parker couldn't, and Ryson hoped to keep her safe.

***

Aboard the ferry *Setiawati*

As the ferry departed Manado's harbor, and made her way out to sea, Greer was leaning on a wooden rail watching the city dwindle in the distance. The rescue mission was underway. And that was good. But there were plenty of unknowns. Were the pilots still in the same prison? Dalisay's sources said, "Yes." But what if they were wrong?

And how would the raid go? The prison was an hour's drive from the commandos' landing point. Of course they would be traveling in British-made Simba personnel carriers, identical to those used by the Phillipine army. And the troop trucks bore Phillipine army insignia as well. So that would be helpful.

But what about the return trip? The Filipinos would know about the attack by then, and send every available unit after the raiders. *We'll have air cover though*, Greer thought. *And that could make the critcal difference.*

Suddenly Greer felt tired. The ferry had six first class cabins, and he was sharing one with Dalisay. He made his way down a ladder, and back along the side of the main cabin, to the point where Cabin 2 was located. He knocked, paused for a moment, and opened the door. Dalisay wasn't there.

It felt good to stretch out on the clean coverlet, pull a pillow over his left ear, and fall asleep. Mary was waiting for him.

***

Aboard the Interisland Steamer *Alcona*, passing through the Northwest Danger Shoals, into the South China Sea

The *Alcona* was classified as a "self discharging cargo vessel." That meant she was equipped with a deck-mounted, hydraulically-operated crane which could load and unload cargo without assistance from the shore. And that would be absolutely necessary on the island of Samir. The ship had been built in 1978 in Germany, and had seen service all over the world since then.

But in spite of the dents in her hull, the creeping rust, and the peeling paint, the old girl still had virtures. The crane was one of them. Her capacity to haul deck cargo was another, and a draft of only thirteen feet was the third.

Such were Lieutenant Commander Linda Vos's thoughts as she made her way forward along the port side. Past the well tarped deck cargo, past the windlass, and into the *Alcona's* V-shaped bow. Vos was wearing a pair of aviators and civilian clothes. Her short hair blew in the breeze as she inhaled a deep draught of the sea air.

Vos was as happy as she could be anywhere other than on the bridge of her own ship. Because, even though her current assignment was sideways from the Squadron's long list of secondary objectives—it was laser focused on the unit's *primary* purpose—and that was to find the *Sea Dragon.*

Plus, Vos liked to organize things. And there would be a whole lot of organizing to do, assuming that Captain Albert Finster remained sober enough to con the *Alcona* through the Danger Shoals, and into the South China Sea.

The ship's destination was an Indonesian possession called Samir Island. It was no more than a speck on the nautical chart taped to a cabin wall. But size didn't matter. Not in this case. What mattered was Samir's location west of the island of Palawan, and south of Mischief Reef, which was controlled by the Chinese.

As conceived by Commander Ryson, a base on Samir would allow the boats of Squadron 7 to extend their patrol areas, and increase the odds of spotting the *Sea Dragon.* And that explained why General Haskell had been willing to approve the considerable expense involved.

That was the good news. The bad news was that, once the Chinese took notice of what the Allies were doing, they would send planes to attack Samir. And possibly ships as well.

But Ryson had anticipated that. Also in transit to Samir was a barge loaded with camouflaged weapons, including an American C-RAM (Counter Rocket Artillery and Mortar System), and a tracked missile system called the Tor SA-15 Gauntlet.

Ironically enough the Tor system was Russian made, and one of six units found aboard a Russian ship bound for Karrachi, just days after hostilities began.

The problem would be the need to secure an adequate supply of 9M330 missiles. Squadron 7 would have thirty-two of the little bastards. After that? Well, good luck.

A male voice broke into Vos's thoughts. "Excuse me, ma'am … Lunch is served."

Vos turned to find Lieutenant Chin standing behind her. Chin was an American Combat Systems officer who, along with his techs, would be in charge of both the C-RAM and Gaunlet systems. Vos smiled. "In other words the sandwich buffet is open."

Chin grinned. "Yes, ma'am."

"Should I visit the bridge? And check on the captain?"

"No need," Chin replied. "First officer Loe has the con. The captain is in his cabin."

"Drunk?"

"I assume so," Chin answered. "Fortunately Loe seems to be quite competent."

"I agree," Vos said. "Let's grab some tucker. I'm hungry."

Hours passed and the Danger Shoals were behind them. The two foot waves were just enough to cause the ship to curtsy as they rolled under the bow, and the high overcast made it less likely that the *Alcona* was being tracked from orbit.

Vos was on the bridge, as was Captain Finster, when the island appeared in the distance. The atoll was a low-lying smudge at first. But eventually a grove of palm trees appeared, along with a tight grouping of metal clad buildings. The complex had been constructed by an Indonesian fishing company ten years earlier and abandoned after the start of the war.

The South China Sea accounted for at least 12 percent of the global fish catch each year, and more than half of the world's fishing vessels were operating there. So the fishing company's goal had been to shorten the time fishing boats spent offloading their catch to reefer ships, and maximize the time they spent competing for fish. Not that different from Commander Ryson's plan, come to think of it. In any case, the presence of some buildings and the 30,000 gallon water bladders would be helpful, and Vos planned to take full advantage of what she found.

Finster belched and the smell of alcohol misted the air. "I'll anchor offshore," Finster said. "Then you can go in and take a look around."

"No," Vos replied, "you won't. The channel is 20 feet deep. And so's the lagoon. Don't waste time. Take her in."

Finster's face was flushed. He wiped it with a rag. "This is *my* ship."

"For the moment." Vos said. "But that could change. Do what I say."

Finster left the bridge and First Officer Loe appeared. He was a good looking young man, who, had it not been for the loss of a leg in a motorcycle accident when he was younger, would have been in the military. But Loe had a good prosthetic and was fully capable of executing his duties. He smiled and took command.

The channel leading into the U-shaped lagoon had been dredged by the fishing company, and was, theoretically, the same depth as it had been before. But just to be safe Loe ordered his boatswain to lower a boat and lead the *Alcona* in. "Tell him to keep his eyes peeled for mines," Vos suggested. "Who knows what the Chinese have been up to."

The international orange lifeboat had an inboard engine which produced a trail of gray smoke as it motored into the channel, paused to take soundings, then proceeded into the lagoon. The azure water was crystal clear, almost completely calm, and bordered by a thin band of white sand. A tattered flag flew from an aluminum pole that marked the complex of buildings.

The first thing Vos noticed as the *Alcona* crept forward was the rusty wreck lying half submerged on the north side of the lagoon.

The second thing that caught her eye were the orange mooring buoys which dotted the lagoon, all carefully spaced so that fishing boats could swing freely, regardless of what direction the wind blew from. That was an unexpected bonus because the buoys would allow the Pegs and Armindales to tie up rather than anchor.

Last, but certainly not least, was the concrete quay where company's reefer ships had docked. Could the *Alcona* do the same? Yes, of course she could. "Put her alongside the wharf," Vos ordered, and watched approvingly as Loe took the single screw ship in. A tricky task in such cramped quarters.

The yellow sun was hanging low in the sky by then, and barely visible through the overcast. Vos faced a decision. Should they unload the ship immediately, before assessing the buildings, or push the task off to morning? *The Alcona is a sitting duck*, Vos reasoned, *and a sure sign that something's going on. If we can turn her loose tonight we should.*

Finster didn't like the navy officer's decision, since it would require him to negotiate the channel at night, but Vos didn't give a shit. She gave the necessary orders and it wasn't long before the ship's yellow crane was plucking blocks of cargo off the deck and depositing them on the quay.

The first item to go across was a Yale gas-powered forklift, which immediately went to work moving pallets of supplies up a concrete path, and into the steel frame building. Chin's job was to organize the generators, tools, cordage, ammo, food and other items.

That left Vos free to inspect the rusty train tracks that led away from the water to a free-standing tin roof, where a fishing boat sat on a trolley awaiting repairs. A path led to the barracks beyond which, while in desperate need of a good cleaning, would offer those who were off duty a place to crash rather than sleep on their boats.

The small building ajacent to the flag pole was clearly the office, and would serve Squadron 7 as such. Her radio crackled and Chief Becker spoke. "We have company, ma'am. Enemy drone at eleven o'clock."

There was still a bit of light to see by. And, as Vos looked up, there it was: a sizeable quadcopter, circling the island as it took pictures, feeding them to who knew where.

Vos had no idea what model of UAV she was looking at. The Chinese had more than a hundred different makes and models. Nor did it matter. What mattered was that the Tor and C-RAM systems hadn't arrived yet, which left Vos and her tiny command virtually defenseless. Yes, she could call for air support if attacked, but would it arrive in time?

Vos held her right hand up with middle finger raised, and shouted: "Fuck you!"

Some of her people were close enough to hear. They laughed and offered defiant gestures of their own. "*Fuck you!*" they yelled in unison, as the UAV banked away. The Allies had arrived.

CHAPTER EIGHT

Off the coast of Luzon, the Philippines

D arkness had fallen, and lights twinkled in the distance, as a gentle swell caused the *HMAS Rockhampton* to heave. Off to port the *HMAS Kalbarri* was waiting as well. And further out to sea, the *HMAS Eucia*, and the *Perth,* were lurking in the gloom.

Ryson knew that military operations rarely went off as planned, and that's why there was some pad in the schedule. But the fact that the ferry had broken down, and been adrift for thirty minutes, had been cause for worry. Now the ferry was running again, and would arrive shortly.

But what if something else happened? And the team lost even *more* time? That could force the patrol boats to run for Manado in full daylight. A prospect Ryson didn't care for at all. But if he cancelled the raid, and the POWs were taken to China, Ryson would never forgive himself. So, the rescue was on. In the meantime, every minute carried the risk that a Philippine patrol boat would happen along, or a Chinese satellite would spot the intruders from space.

Ten long minutes passed before the ET spoke over the intercom. "The *Setiawati* is five out and headed for the beach."

Ryson knew the tech was referring to the beach that fronted the village of Bagao. No pier or wharf was available. So the plan was to run the *Setiawati* up onto the beach, drop the bow ramp, and drive the vehicles off. If they arrived dry, good. If they didn't, no problem. All of the vics (vehicles) had four-wheel drive, or in the case of the trucks, six-wheel drive.

Once the commandos were ashore, another long wait would begin. *I hope it will be boring*, Ryson thought. *Boring is a good thing.*

***

Aboard the ferry Setiawati just off the village of Bagao, the Philippines

A Simba armored personnel carrier was going to lead the way, followed by the trucks, and a second Simba. Greer was riding in the second six-by-six, along with ten Australian commandos, all of whom were gunned up.

In accordance with the Geneva Convention, Greer was wearing U.S. Navy camos and was armed with American weapons. Not that he would allow himself be captured. No fucking way.

The ferry was going full tilt as it hit the beach and ran up onto the sand. The boat came to an abrupt stop, hydraulics whirred as the bow ramp went down, and the first Simba roared away.

There was a short wait followed by a violent jerk as the driver of the second six-by-six let the clutch out too quickly and killed the engine. A torrent of friendly abuse was directed at the unfortunate driver: "Hey, Dickhead, learn to drive!" "What a fucking Drongo," and "How am I supposed to sleep?"

Greer grinned as the driver produced an equally profane torrent of words, and a sergeant told the commandos to zip it. Silence reigned.

The back of the truck was covered which meant Greer couldn't see out. But he could feel the truck bounce through potholes, slow for intersections, and make a sharp left-hand turn.

The ride began to smooth out as the vic left town and made its way onto a highway. That's when the driver ran through the gears and put his boot down. The forty-five-minute wait began. People handled the situation in different ways.

Corporal Boyle went to sleep. A medic made changes to his kit. And a dull-eyed private sharpened his knife. It might have been Gallipoli in 1915, Korea in 1950, or Vietnam in 1965. Young men, their thoughts astray, waiting for the worst.

Greer's thoughts turned to the men they were hoping to rescue, the pilots who'd been killed, and a burning need for revenge. *I want a carrier*, Greer thought. *And a plane.*

Greer closed his eyes but found he couldn't sleep. Not behind enemy lines on a noisy truck. After forty minutes on the highway, Greer heard Captain Dancy's voice via the plug in his ear. "All right men, we're almost there. Check your weapons and remember your assignments. Oh, and don't stop to pee. That means you Cooper."

The comment produced gales of laughter just as it was supposed to. Greer hadn't been briefed on the backstory, but grinned, and felt sorry for Cooper. No wonder they called him "the pisser."

Greer's job was to lock onto Corporal Boyle, follow the noncom, and defend himself if necessary. Other than that Greer's mission was to be present when the prisoners were freed, so they'd have a familiar face to look at. At that point he was supposed to lead the POWs out of the building to a waiting truck.

Greer's radio was tuned to the command frequency. So, he was a firsthand witness to what occurred next. "Cat-Four to Alpha-Six," a female voice said. "It looks like a trap. Something like a hundred tangos are gathered around the main gate. Over."

Greer knew that Cat-Four was a UAV pilot located back in the states. She was flying an MQ-9 Reaper drone which, due to its range, wasn't likely to make the return trip to Indonesia. Other drones had more range but were unarmed.

There had been a leak somewhere. But from whom? Greer hoped to live long enough to find out. Even though the news came as a surprise, the possibility had been discussed, and Dancy had a plan. "Roger that, Cat-Four. Take them out. We'll make our own gate. Over."

Cat-Four's voice was devoid of emotion. "A Hellfire and a couple of 500-pound bombs should do the trick Alpha-Six. Warn your people and plug your ears. Over."

Dancy gave a warning as the truck veered to the left and bounced wildly. Then, just short of the razor wire topped fence, the driver braked. "Out! Out! Out!"

Boyle bawled. "Make a hole in that fence Cooper … And be smart about it."

Greer heard a series of loud explosions as Cat-Four put some of her ordinance on the locals. Greer followed Boyle into the night. A search light snapped on and a shaft of light began to probe the prison grounds. That was accompanied by the rattle of gunfire as the remaining defenders fired in every direction.

It took Cooper three minutes to place the charges and detonate them. The result was a ragged hole through which the commandos could pass so long as they were careful. "High step and mind your balls," Boyle advised, as he led the way.

Greer took the advice to heart, saw muzzle flashes off to the right, and realized that the surviving defenders were going to stay and fight. Prison guards were coming out to serve as reinforcements. Like generations of noncoms before him, Boyle shouted, "Follow me!" and ran straight at the enemy.

Greer was lumbering along behind the Aussie, his M4 carbine at the ready, as defenders fired from the prison's roof. It was Greer's first experience with ground combat and he didn't like it.

The search light found Boyle and pinned him in its glare. Bullets threw divots of dirt up all around the corporal and knocked him down.

Greer ran to help. The medic arrived seconds later, felt for a pulse, and shook his head. "He's gone."

Greer took a quick look around, realized that Boyle's team had gone to ground, and waved them forward. "Follow me!" And with that the pilot began to zigzag forward. The Australians followed.

A second commando counter sniper team was at work by then, and the fire from the roof stopped, as the Aussie marksmen found their targets. Lieutenant Kapoor was shouting orders. "Bring the vehicles in! Establish a perimeter! Treat the wounded!"

Greer heard the words, but his mind was focused on reaching the door to the prison, and the sand-bagged machine gun position in front of it. Muzzle flashes lit the area around the belt-fed weapon as it began to swivel their way. "RPG!" Greer shouted. "On the machine gun!"

It was the correct order, but a projectile was already on the way by the time the pilot gave it. There was a flash, followed by a boom, and a series of secondary explosions as grenades went off. "Cooper!" Greer yelled. "Blow the door!"

Cooper had to step over badly mangled bodies to access the door. The charge had been prepared prior to departure, and was ready for placement.

Cooper backed away. "Fire in the hole!"

The explosion was more modest than what Greer expected. And that made sense, since the purpose of the charge was to destroy the lock, not the door. Smoke swirled as Cooper hurried forward, gave the barrier a kick, and saw it swing open.

A private named Pinder hurried to toss a smoke grenade through the opening. "Now!" Greer shouted as he entered the space beyond. Bodies were strewn all over the reception area's floor. A casualty said something, raised a pistol, and paid the price.

A metal door blocked their way at that point. But, thanks to Greer's description of the barrier, Cooper was ready for the challenge. "Fire in the hole!"

The explosion was larger this time, and not only destroyed the lock, but blew a hole through the door. There was no response from inside. And that made sense. The guards had been sent out to fight.

With help from Pinder, Cooper managed to push the door aside, revealing the hellhole beyond. Nothing had changed since Greer's previous visit. Cages were crammed with prisoners. The stench was sickening. Hundreds of eyes stared. Greer spoke over the command frequency. "This is Gun Daddy. We're inside. Give me a sitrep. Can we turn the prisoners loose? Over."

Greer *wanted* to release the prisoners, knowing they would run every which way, causing Filipino soldiers to chase them. But turning them loose into the middle of a firefight would be a monstrous thing to do. So, Dancy had to make the call. "This is Alpha-Six. Let 'em go. We're in control out here. And you can bet your arse that reinforcements are on the way."

"Roger that," Greer replied. "There are a lot of loose weapons lying around, so watch the people coming out. We're going in after the pilots. Over."

Greer heard two clicks by way of a response. He turned to a corporal. "Cut the locks. Start at this end."

Two commandos, each armed with a pair of bolt cutters, went to work on both sides of the corridor. A cheer went up and the prisoners battled for positions in front of cell doors.

Greer, M4 at the ready, led the rest of the squad down the central walkway to the cell where the pilots had been previously.

His heart sank. Some terrified Filipinos were being held in the cage where the pilots had been confined.

Had the aviators been taken to China? If so, Corporal Boyle had died for nothing. "Who speaks English?" Greer demanded. "Where are the American prisoners?"

There was a stir as a man with a bloody bandage wrapped around his head pushed his way to the front of the crowd. "The guards took them."

"When?"

The man shrugged. "They took my watch. Three, maybe four hours ago."

"Did the guards say where they were taking the prisoners?"

The man shook his head. "No. But there are interrogation rooms in the basement. I would look there if I were you. Open the door and I'll take you there."

A soldier carrying a bolt cutter arrived. Greer pointed to the padlock. "Cut it."

The lock rattled as it hit the floor and a cheer went up as prisoners pushed the door aside. There was a rush to get out. Greer half expected the man with the bandage to flee. But he didn't. "Follow me," the man said, and turned toward a door Greer had paid scant attention to during his prior visit. It was made of steel. A head-high, wire mesh window made it possible for jailers to see who was about to enter. Not surprisingly the door was locked. But Cooper was there to set a charge and trigger it. "Fire in the hole!"

Greer spoke into his headset. "Gun Daddy to Alpha-Six. The prisoners were moved. We're going to search the basement. Over." Dancy offered two clicks by way of an acknowledgement.

Hinges squealed as Greer pushed the door open. There were no defenders to block the way. Metal stairs led down. Greer followed them, turned into a switchback, and immediately took fire.

A burly private shoved Greer aside, fired a shotgun, and nodded. "Sorry sir, but there's a reason why we don't put pilots on point."

Greer grinned. "Sorry, my bad."

Three commandos slipped past Greer. A dead guard lay sprawled on the floor, a pistol not far from his right hand. The man with the bandage paused to scoop the weapon up and Greer allowed him to keep it.

Overhead lights led the way through a long corridor with rooms on both sides. Commandos checked them one by one. Then they paused. "This one is locked!" a private shouted.

Greer was about to send for Cooper when the commando with the shotgun stepped forward. He shouted "Stand back in there!" and fired. The door gave. A second commando kicked it open. Greer entered. The aviators were standing with their backs to a wall. All three of them.

Ames was on the left, Symons was in the middle, and Wix stood to the right. He was the first to speak. "Holy shit, it's Gun Daddy!"

Greer nodded. "That's right Dickhead … Where's the fifty-bucks you owe me?"

Ames laughed and Symons began to sob. Wix gave him a hug. "Come on Drew, we're going home."

***

Off the coast of Luzon, the Philippines

Ryson was sitting on the *Rockhampton's* bridge when the report came over the intercom, and all hell broke loose. "Two-three targets inbound! Repeat, two-three targets inbound. ETA three minutes!"

Mike Christian, the *Rockhampton's* skipper, was about to issue an order when a call came in over the radio. Ryson recognized Atworthy's voice. "Seadog-Seven to all units…We have contact, repeat contact, with …"

"Fire!" a lookout shouted, "at ten o'clock!"

Ryson turned and saw that the lookout was correct. A low-lying fire was burning west of the *Rockhampton's* position. *The Eucia?* Yes, it had to be. But *what?* How?

The answers came quickly. "This is Six," the *Kalbarri's* skipper said. "We're in contact with approximately six Jet skis. They're carrying two men each—a driver plus an armed passenger. Engaging. Over."

By that time Ryson could hear the rhythmic thud, thud, thud, of the *Kalbarri's* fifty caliber machines interspersed with automatic fire from the jet ski riders. After getting word of the attack on the prison someone in the Filipino chain of command had the good sense to wonder if the invaders had arrived by sea and dispatched a unit to investigate.

Maybe the jet ski armada already existed. Or maybe some enterprising officer threw it together on the fly. But it was dangerous either way. He turned to Christian. "Try to contact the *Eucia*," Ryson ordered. "And offer assistance if you raise her."

Then he snatched the bridge mike off its hook. "This is Seadog-Six. Be careful with the fifties. What we don't need is casualties from friendly fire. All units will rally around the *Rockhampton*. Execute. Over."

That was when a half dozen jet skis arrived. One came so close that the port fifty couldn't depress far enough to hit it. A Molotov cocktail sailed through the air, landed on the flat surface forward of the bridge, and shattered. The resulting fire spread quickly, but was extinguished by two sailors with fire extinguishers.

Ryson opened his mouth to give orders, and forced himself to close it. He was responsible for the squadron. But Christian was in command of the *Rockhampton*, and should be left to fight the enemy as he saw fit.

"The missile teams will prepare to engage the enemy," Christian said formally. "Do not, I repeat, do *not* fire in the direction of a friendly, because you will probably hit it. Choose targets with care. Fire at will."

Ryson knew that each boat had two Stinger missile teams, and that the Stingers were fire-and-forget weapons equipped with passive infrared seekers. That meant the weapons should be able to target the heat produced by a jet ski engine.

It also meant the Stingers could identify the heat produced by a patrol boat as well. And, if an Armindale was in line with a jet ski, a Stinger was likely to choose the hottest target. That meant Christian was placing a great deal of faith in his missile teams.

The gamble paid off. A sailor waited for a Jet ski to pass on the starboard side and fired. The Stinger took off, achieved lock on, and hit the watercraft dead-on. The resulting flash of light was accompanied by a clap of thunder. The Jet ski disappeared.

Three of the other patrol boats had closed in around the *Rockhampton* by then, forcing the attackers to change their tactics. Now, rather than pass between the Armindales, strafing them as they passed, the Jet skis were circling all three boats in a clockwise direction.

Flares fired by the Armindale crews reflected off the oily black waves as they lit up what looked like a scene from hell. Jet skis threw water sideways as they wove in and out, and continued to spray the gunboats with small arms fire.

But that was a mistake, because it allowed the Australian sailors to fire their weapons without fear of hitting a friendly boat. Ryson watched as a series of watercraft ran into fifty-caliber fire and were torn to shreds.

Then, as quickly as the battle had begun, it was over. *Is that it?* Ryson wondered, as the surviving Jet skis roared away. *Or is the worst yet to come?* He feared the latter.

But the battle was far from one-sided. Because by that time the *Eucia* had sunk.

After lobbing a Molotov cocktail aboard the unsuspecting boat, the attackers managed to attach an IED to her hull, and detonate it from afar. That meant Lieutenant James Atworthy was dead, along with all of his crew.

How many people has Dancy lost by now? Ryson wondered. *To free three prisoners? Does the whole thing make sense?*

No, he decided. *Not logically. But, in some other way, it makes perfect sense. For morale? Yes. But for some ineffable reason as well. Something which can be felt, if not fully rationalized.*

"Get a message off," Ryson ordered. "*Eucia* lost to enemy fire. Enemy repelled. Holding station. Over." It wasn't much of an epitaph. But it would have to do.

***

Creech Air Force Base, Nevada, USA

The first Simba had been destroyed in the fighting, killing two commandos, and wounding another. Now the surviving Simba was leading the 6x6 trucks west toward the town of Bagao where RIB boats would be waiting to take both the soldiers and the POWs off the beach.

Cat-Four knew that much. What she didn't, *couldn't*, know was what it felt like to be sitting in a truck with a bunch of Australian commandos racing for the west coast of Luzon. Because weird though it might be, she was sitting in a high-backed leather chair, in a secured building on Creech Air Force base in Nevada.

Cat's job was to fly the drone. Her sensor operator, call sign "Samsonite," was in charge of monitoring the Reaper's infrared and night vision sensor systems.

They were seated side-by-side with ten monitors arrayed in front of them and a console in between. Cat's controls consisted of a keyboard, joystick, and throttle plus switches that controlled everything from transponder codes to flap deployment. It was difficult to master all the technology at first. But after a year of training, plus three months experience, flying the Reaper was second nature.

Later, after completing her shift, Cat would head home to a rented condo where she would attempt to decompress. That involved watching children's cartoons while downing two gin and tonics. Never less, and never more, because men and women all over the world were counting on her.

Cat's drone couldn't match the convoy's relatively slow ground speed without falling out of the sky. So, she was flying circles overhead watching for threats. The most likely of which would be an attempt catch up with the convoy and/or cut it off from the coast.

But, when trouble arrived, it was different from what Cat expected. "We have two tangos at ten thousand," Samsonite said. "They're helos rather than planes, and Mr. Computer says that they're a 96 percent match with MD 500 Defenders."

MD 500s were observation choppers armed with TOW anti-tank missiles, 7.62 mm miniguns, or Stinger air-to-air missiles.

The Reaper was at fifteen thousand. And judging from what Cat could see on the monitors, the helo jockeys were blissfully unaware of the drone's presence as they began to close on the convoy. If they were armed with TOWs the Australians would be toast.

"They made us," Samsonite said. "Or, some radar operator did. Here they come."

The helicopters were climbing. What to do? Reapers weren't designed for dog fights. But newer units were armed with AIM-92 Stinger missiles, and Cat was "riding" one of them. That was the good news. The bad news was that Cat had zero experience with the missiles.

Oh, she'd been through the virtual training course all right, but nothing more. Still, what else could she do? Try to drop a 500-pound bomb on a moving target?

"I'm arming a Sidewinder," Cat said, as she pushed the drone's nose down.

"Sidewinder armed."

A grid appeared over the target. "Firing."

"Missile away, tracking, tracking, shit!"

It appeared that the MD 500 pilot was firing flares as a precaution and it paid off. Cat's Sidewinder swerved, homed on a flare, and blew up.

Cat saw flashes of light as the helicopter's machine gun fired. However the Reaper was in a tight turn by then, and the stream of tracer missed.

The Reaper could climb and run. But if Cat did that, the convoy would be easy meat for the helos. At that point she had one air-to-air missile left, with two targets on the loose. *I need to get closer before I fire*, Cat decided. *So the Sidewinder will choose the chopper instead of a flare.*

The second helo was closer by then. Cat banked, advanced the throttle, and watched the distance close. Tracer rounds stuttered her way, bent, and seemed to veer away when she applied some left stick.

The second MD 500 was firing flares just like the first one had. But Cat was closer by then. *Much* closer. And the moment she pickled the missile off, the UAV operator knew it was on the money.

Cat was turning as an explosion strobed the night and Samsonite made the call. "Tango down. One A-hole left. Whatcha going to do?"

That was a good question. With no air-to-air missiles left to fight with, Cat was out of options. Or was she? The thought put a grin on her face. "We're gonna ram the bastard, Sammy. So, stand by for that."

Samsonite stared at her. "A Reaper costs 64 million buckaroos!"

"That's true," the pilot admitted. "But we don't have enough fuel to make it back, do we? And if we bag another helo, the brass will celebrate."

"You're smarter than you look," Samsonite said admiringly.

"And you're a pain in the ass," Cat said, as she aimed the Reaper's nose at the helo.

The MD 500 pilot didn't know how many Stingers the American drone was carrying. And, after having seen his wingman vanish in a ball of flame, he decided to run for it.

That was a serious mistake. The helo could travel at 160 mph full out. The Reaper had a max speed of 300 mph.

It appeared that the helo pilot knew the drone was closing on his six. He began to fire flares, and jink from side-to-side. And that made sense. Or would have if Cat was going to fire a Stinger. But she wasn't.

The collision alarm sounded as the Reaper slammed into the helicopter at 293 mph. Their screens registered a flash of light before cutting to black.

"Okay, then," Sam said. "That's one way to get off work early."

After checking out with Seadog-Six and Seadog-Three, Cat wrote her after-action report, hit "send," and left. She arrived home forty minutes later.

Then it was time to make a gin and tonic, and watch a Scooby Doo episode titled: "*The Glowing Bug Man*." The tears were waiting. But Cat refused to let them flow.

***

Off the coast of Luzon, the Philippines

The surviving Armindales wallowed offshore as long, lazy rollers swept in from the west, passed under the boats, and made for the beach. Ryson's nerves were on edge. *All* the RIB boats had been sent ashore to retrieve the shore party and the POWs. That left his force vulnerable to a Filipino or Chinese surface attack. One or more patrol boats would be bad. A destroyer or a frigate would sink his flotilla in seconds.

Meanwhile the air cover that Ryson had been counting on, which was to say the Reaper drone, had been destroyed. F-18s had a range of 1,253 miles. They couldn't make it from the carrier group that was cruising east of Luzon, or from Indonesia, and make the return trip as well.

Normally a KC-46 Pegasus aerial refueler, or a venerable 396 KC-135 Stratotanker, would have been the app for that. But 46s had been grounded for another round of retro-fixes, and the so-called "Stratobladders" were like gold. Everyone wanted to get more of them and keep what they had. The situation would improve once the Armindales entered Indonesian waters, but that moment was in the future.

As an angry looking sun began to rise in the east as Ryson eyed the shoreline through a pair of binoculars. Everything was riding on how quickly the Aussie sailors could collect Dancy's people and get off the beach. Fortunately, they were doing a good job of it.

The RIBs had landed and been loaded. Now came the tricky task of pushing the boats stern first into the surf, where the coxswains could start their engines, and back out through the low-lying surf. Then, once it was safe to do so, they would turn and head full-speed out to the Armindales.

That was when the metal stairs on the stern of each patrol boat would prove their worth. Once the commandos and POWs were aboard it would be time to recover the RIBs, strap them down, and haul ass. Ryson spoke into his headset. "Radar … What have you got?"

***

The radar tech was a sailor named Sykes. He turned to the tech next to him and rolled his eyes. The American commander was like a teenager on his first date. If Sykes saw something worth reporting he'd sure as hell say so. "We have a target that looks like a northbound container ship off to the west, sir … And plenty of fishing boats. None of which are headed this way."

***

Ryson frowned. The report was too good to be true. After losing scores of troops at the prison, not to mention a couple of helicopters since then, the Filipinos were sitting on their hands? He didn't believe it.

Ryson raised the binoculars. The RIBs were underway. Spray flew away from their blunt bows as they muscled their way through the waves and began to close with the patrol boats. That was when the first artillery shell fell. The explosion threw a fountain of water up into the air, and a RIB roared through the briny spray, on its way to an Armindale.

"They're wasting ammo," Christian observed calmly. "Artillery isn't designed to track and hit fast moving targets."

"True," Ryson replied. "But the *Rockhampton* isn't small, nor is it moving. It's the Armindales I'm worried about."

Ryson opened his mike. "This is Seadog-Six. All RIB boats are to head west until further notice. The Armindales will get under way and follow. Over."

A shell exploded off the *Rockhampton's* port bow and water droplets hit the windshield like a hard rain. The *Rockhampton* shuddered and began to increase speed. "How far can they lob those shells?" Ryson asked of no one in particular.

A good thirty seconds passed while Christian's XO consulted her laptop. Her name was Tracy Devin. "They have a range of approximately seven miles, based on the assumption that the shore batteries consist of U.S. made M101, or M102, 105mm towed howitzers."

"Thanks, Sub," Ryson replied, and spoke into his mike. "All units will rendezvous eight miles offshore, load passengers, and secure the RIBs. Over."

A flurry of acknowledgements was followed by the steadily dwindling thud of artillery as the RIBs and the Armindales drew further away from land. It took the better part of twenty minutes to transfer the passengers and retrieve the RIBs. And it was during that time that Greer, along with three gaunt looking strangers appeared on the bridge. "I thought you'd like to meet the POWs," Master Chief Jensen said.

Greer made the introductions and Ryson shook hands with Ames, Symons and Wix. Their expressions were somber. "Thank you, sir," Ames said. "We're sorry about all of the casualties."

"And we're very glad that their bravery paid off," Ryson replied. "Thank you for your service to our country."

Jensen led them away. Greer paused. "That was nicely said, sir. They've been through hell. Symons is going to need a lot of help."

Ryson nodded. "What you accomplished was truly remarkable, Commander ... I have it on good authority that Admiral Nathan plans to hang some sort of Australian gong on you ... And I'm sure our people will do likewise."

Greer started to reply, but Ryson interrupted. "I know you're a modest man, Commander. But the brass will have their way with you. Look at it this way—the rescue will make news all over the free world—and inspire millions of people. And that's a good thing."

Greer came to attention and saluted. Ryson returned the gesture and the pilot left the bridge. *Stage 1 is over*, Ryson thought. *But Stage 2 is just beginning. And Indonesia is 1,000 miles away.*

***

On the island of Samir, in the South China Sea

The sky was blue, a light breeze was blowing, and three flags snapped from their poles. One each for Austrailia, Indonesia, and the United States.

Progress had been made. But FOB Samir was vulnerable. Lieutenant Commander Linda Vos was standing on top of the newly designated headquarters building looking north toward Mischief Reef. It was a race. Who would arrive at the island of Samir first? The Chinese? With planes and ships? Or the tugboat *Hercules* which was *towing* a barge loaded with weapons? *Please God*, Vos thought. *Make it the Hercules.*

God wasn't listening. That's how it seemed as two Chengdu J-7 fighters swept in from the north and opened fire.

Vos hurried to vacate the roof and Squadron 7 personnel scattered in every direction as they searched for places to take cover. Gravity bombs fell. And, judging from the size of the explosions, they were large. Something like a thousand pounds each. One scored a direct hit on the barracks building and blew it to smithereens. Sections of aluminum siding took flight, reached apogee, and slip-slid to the ground.

Rockets arrived next. The wharf took hits as they came sleeting in, as did the building that housed a fishing boat. There were near misses too … Lots of them. Including one that exploded only yards away from the warehouse where the detachment's supplies were stored.

Gun runs followed. Vos didn't know what kind of cannons the planes had. Only that the strafing attacks didn't seem to be well targeted. A fact for which she was extremely grateful.

After clearing their racks, and expending all the ammo from their cannons, the jets banked away. The attack was over. Lieutenant Chin was the first to arrive at Vos's location. "So much for the welcome wagon," he said. "This is a tough neighborhood."

"No kidding," Vos replied. "Did we take any casualties?"

"No," Chin replied. "Not so much as a scratch. And I have some good news for you."

"Which is?"

"The *Herc* and the barge are about two hours out."

"That's wonderful," Vos replied. "Let's get everyone fed. We'll have a lot of work to do once the barge arrives."

Time passed quickly and it seemed like only a matter of minutes before a sturdy looking tug pushed the heavily loaded barge into the lagoon. That was exciting.

But of equal interest to Vos were the hydrofoils that had been sent as escorts. They included the *Nimbus,* under Lieutenant Commander Marie Moreno, and the *Fractus,* with Lieutenant Mark Conte in command. Between them the PHMs could launch sixteen Harpoon missiles at any Chinese vessel that might venture near. A fact that made Vos feel better.

There were challenges however. Getting the barge alongside the quay took some doing. Then there was the matter of unloading weapons systems that had to propel themselves off the barge and onto the wharf. That meant constructing a ramp, using extremely heavy steel plates brought along for the purpose.

The Russian built Tor missile system was the size of a heavy tank and mounted on treads. Considerable maneuvering was required to turn the beast onto the narrow ramp and nurse it up slope onto the concrete quay. But after an hour of fits and starts the behemoth was finally ashore.

Vos had chosen a place for the Tor system well away from everything else where, if it was destroyed, nothing else would be harmed.

According to Chin, set-up and testing would take the remaining daylight hours. But by midnight, Vos hoped to have the all-weather system up and running. Then the Tor system could defend the island from airplanes, helicopters, cruise missiles, drones, and precision guided munitions. And she'd be able to sleep.

The C-RAM system was on multiple trailers and a small tractor had been sent to tow them off the barge. Vos had chosen to locate the C-RAM system at the opposite end of the curving land mass and well away from the Tor setup.

Ryson's plan called for keeping at least one PHM at or near the island at all times, ready to fire on long-range surface targets if necessary. But, should the Chinese engage the hydrofoil, and send fast boats into the lagoon, the Counter rocket, artillery and mortar system would defend itself *and* the anti-air Tor installation. It was, Vos thought, a clever strategy.

But cleverness would only get Squadron 7 so far. If it decided to exert itself, and bring the necessary amount of force to bear, China could swat Samir like a fly. And the results wouldn't be pretty.

***

Aboard the HMAS *Rockhampton* off the east coast of Palawan, in the South China Sea

There weren't any good choices. Just bad choices. If Ryson took his flotilla down the west side of Palawan island they'd be vulnerable to the Chinese forces stationed on Mischief Reef. And if he ventured further to the west, in an attempt to give the Spratly Islands a wide berth, he might encounter a Chinese task force— because the ChiCom bastards pretty much "owned" the South China Sea.

So, Ryson had chosen to cruise down the east coast of Palawan. At the moment the boats were entering the Cuyo West Passage, with the Cuyo islands off to port.

Once through the narrow passageway they would enter the Sulu Sea where Filipino naval units could be waiting. Then assuming it survived, the flotilla would make the transition into the neighboring Celebes Sea, and proceed to Manado. Or not. Time would tell.

Things went well at first. The sea state qualified as "slight," with seas that were roughly two feet high, and running to the northeast. The sky was mostly clear, with broken clouds, some of which threw asymmetrical patterns onto the cerulean water.

Contrails clawed the sky, and served to remind Ryson of the war above. Were the planes Chinese? Or Allied? There was no way to know.

As for surface ships, there were hundreds of radar blips. And that was normal in an area frequented by fishing boats representing half a dozen nations.

That situation continued for the better part of an hour. And Ryson was napping in his chair when ET Sykes spoke over the intercom. "There's some unusual activity taking place south of us, Captain. I thought you'd want to know."

Ryson opened his eyes and sat up. Christian frowned. "What sort of activity?"

"Some of the fishing boats are bunching up, while others are spreading port and starboard," Sykes replied. 'It's weird."

"I'm coming down," Christian said, and left the bridge. Ryson followed. Sykes was in the CIC, sitting next to a radio operator. And sure enough, most of the blips on his screen were swarming, while a few were motoring away. "It's a scrum," Christian said.

Ryson frowned. "A *what?*"

"A scrum. As in Rugby. It means an orderly formation of players used to restart play. We've seen it before. At least one in ten Chinese fishing boats are equipped to gather intelligence, and fight if necessary, which they are preparing to do. We call them 'X-boats.'"

"You're sure?"

"I'm positive," the Australian answered. "Look... See how the boats are forming a funnel? The whole idea is to guide us into the middle of the scrum where the X boats are waiting. If we change course, they'll reform to block us."

"But we can fight our way through," Ryson suggested.

"Yes, probably," Christian agreed. "But some X boats have hydraulically operated gun turrets that pop up from below."

"On fishing boats."

"Yes. Most of those fishing boats are roughly the same size as the *Rockhampton*."

"Shit."

"Yes, sir."

"All right. Notify the other boats. Tell them to form a line ahead."

The same order had been given during the Battle of Trafalgar in 1805, when ships on both sides of the conflict formed columns prior to what became a melee.

The purpose of the maneuver was to ensure that the second and third boats could make use of their heavy machine guns to the port and starboard, while the *Rockhampton's* bow-mounted M242 Bushmaster autocannon blew a hole through the enemy line.

Then, if it became necessary, Ryson would order boats two and three to move sideways in opposite directions to free their bow guns. Meanwhile sailors, with help from the commandos, would hose the "fishing" boats down with small arms fire including RPGs.

As for air support, they were still too far away from Manado, and would have to handle the situation by themselves. Would Chinese planes take part in the ambush? That was a scary thought.

Ryson could see the fishing boats through his binoculars by that time. The Chinese trawlers were nearly identical. Each had a white superstructure, a blue hull, and a high flared bow. The boats were deployed in the way Christian said they would be. Except for one thing— two trawlers were traveling toward each other from opposite sides of the U-shaped formation. After a careful examination Ryson realized that the boats were dragging nets! *Why?*

There was only one possible answer: the Chinese had anticipated Ryson's plan, and hoped to ensnare one or more Allied
boats by fouling their propellors. A plan that would bring the
Armindales to a stop and, if things went well, allow the enemy to
board and take *more* POWs! Thereby transforming what would
have been a propaganda disaster into a propaganda victory.

Ryson turned to Christian. "Pass the word ... The flotilla will
form a line abreast. All Stinger teams will target the trawler to
port ... Which is to say the one moving east to west with a net in
tow. Fire when ready."

Christian looked surprised, brought his binoculars up to
confirm the net, and passed the order to the other boats. The
Rockhampton's crew was already at battle stations so it was a
simple matter to send the Stinger teams forward.

The distance between the Armindales and the trawler was
closing fast. Missiles lashed out, six in all, and most were on target. Ryson saw a flash on the superstructure, just aft of the bridge,
another on the hull and two near the waterline.

The second flight of Stingers was even more effective. All
of the missiles hit. Including two that slammed into the bridge.
Ryson could imagine the slaughter inside. The blood-splattered
bulkheads, the bodies sprawled on the deck, and no one at the
wheel.

But there was no further time to consider the trawler's fate as
the rest of the Chinese fishing boats swarmed the Armindales.
The net strategy had failed. But the enemy had sheer numbers on
their side. And, by pressing in and around the Allied vessels, the
Chinese could immobilize them as effectively as a fouled prop
would.

Jets of black smoke issued from exhausts as boats vied with
each other to reach the Armindales. Just as Christian predicted,
some of them were armed with pop-up machine guns which

immediately opened fire on the Australian vessels. "RPGs! Stingers!" Ryson shouted over the din. "Kill those guns!"

Meanwhile, the auto cannons mounted in the bows of the Armindales, plus their recently installed .50 machine guns, were hard at work. Fishermen, some armed, but most not, were cut down by the dozen. Grenades exploded, fires appeared, and boats were holed.

But even that wasn't enough. Fishermen in aluminum skiffs and rubber rafts jostled each other in a crazed competition to board the enemy patrol boats first. "This might come in handy, sir," Master Chief Jenson said, as she gave him a twelve-gauge pump gun and a bandolier of ammunition. And she was correct.

Ryson heard a sailor yell, "They're about to come over the port side! We need help over here."

Ryson stepped out of the wheelhouse, saw a face appear over the bulwark, and fired. The blast of double ought buck blew half of the boarder's skull away and threw his body back onto a much-abused tender.

More boats were coming alongside. Ryson fired seven rounds into the nearest skiff and saw three men fall. Then it was time to step back, get reoriented, and reload. A sailor lay dead on the deck. Christian had taken the helm himself, and was shouting encouragement to his crew. "Kill the bastards! Kill them all!"

A quick check confirmed that the other patrol boats were still side-by-side next to the *Rockhampton,* using their fifties to good advantage, and leaving a trail of broken boats and dead bodies bobbing in their wakes. "The stern!" someone yelled over the intercom. "They're coming over the stern!"

"I'll go," Ryson said, leaving Christian to con the boat. Ryson arrived in the stern to find that Sub-Lieutenant Devin was already there, pistol in hand, firing at a fisherman armed with a wicked looking knife. A .9mm bullet hit the man between the eyes and he toppled over backwards.

But more men were swarming up to replace him. *The stairs,* Ryson thought. *They were critical to getting the POWs aboard quickly, and now they're working against us.*

Ryson fired the shotgun again and again. Boarders fell but were soon replaced as more fishermen appeared. That was when a basso voice said, "Make way for the second commando."

A huge soldier appeared. He was armed with what would normally be a crew served machine gun, but looked like a toy in his arms. And when he fired a hail of bullets wiped the stern clean of intruders.

"That's how it's done, son," the commando said to a teenage sailor. "Now lend a hand. Let's take a peek over the stern railing."

Ryson couldn't see what the two of them saw. But after firing some long bursts, the commando gave a thumbs up. "They won't be bothering you again, sir … This lot is finished."

The commando's words were prophetic. The boats broke free of the trap at roughly the same time and continued south. None suffered major damage. But there had been casualties, and Ryson wasn't looking forward to the butcher's bill. *Still,* he thought, as he looked back at the burning fishing trawlers: *We won. And that's what we're supposed to do.*

CHAPTER NINE

Yulin Naval Base, Hainan Island, China

Senior Captain Peng Ko eyed himself in the mirror. His uniform was perfect. A horizontal row of ribbons represented each of his major achievements. That was one of the many things Ko liked about the military. A single glance was enough to assess what another officer had accomplished and his position in the naval food chain.

In Ko's case he was wearing a ribbon that signified the Order of August the First. The highest military award a Chinese sailor or soldier could receive. A rare honor indeed.

But that wasn't all. Ko was also wearing a ribbon representing the Medal of Heroic Exemplar. The *second* highest decoration awarded by the Chinese government.

Would Admiral Yong Chao be suitably impressed? *He should be*, Ko mused. *Since he has neither one.*

The thought produced a wave of guilt. "The superior man has a dignified ease without pride." That was what Confucius said. And it was true.

You must humble yourself, Ko thought. *And remember your many failings lest you repeat them.*

Thus chastened, Ko made his way out into the *Sea Dragon's* main passageway. It was two sailors wide and ran almost the full length of the semi-submersible's 667-foot-long hull.

Sailors saluted as they passed Ko and the air was filled with the familiar odor of amine. A compound used to remove carbon dioxide from the air. A ladder led up to Conning Tower 2 which was unmanned while the cruiser was in port. A sentry was on duty at the foot of the metal gangway.

The cavernous sub pen was dark and gloomy in spite of the sunshine outside. Pools of light led to a bank of elevators, one of which whisked the officer to the surface.

A black Hongqi (Red Flag) H7 sedan was waiting for him along with a uniformed driver. The sailor snapped to attention, delivered a salute, and opened a door. The interior was on a par with anything that Mercedes or Audi offered, and the air was delightfully cool. The engine purred as the car followed the highway into the resort city of Sanya.

And it was there, in a high rise, with a sweeping view of the sea, that Admiral Chao and his staff were quartered. A bright-eyed ensign was waiting to receive Ko and escort him through a maze of corridors to a spacious office with a wall of windows. Unlike some senior officers, who liked to make subordinates wait, Chao was ready to receive his guest.

The officers had met on two previous occasions, both of which had been ceremonial. That meant they had no personal relationship to speak of.

But, as Chao came forward to shake Ko's hand, the navy officer was impressed by the other man's relative youth and vitality. "Captain Ko!" Chao said enthusiastically. "I've been looking forward to this meeting. I read your proposal, and I like it."

Ko felt his spirits rise. *So far so good*, he thought. *It sounds like he's willing to approve the plan.*

Chao led Ko into a conference room with a sweeping view of the South China Sea. A tea pot was waiting for them, along with cups, and a bowl of peanuts. Chao had a reputation as a *Zhengzhi jia* (politician) as well as a skilled administrator. Both talents were on display as the admiral poured tea and made small talk.

But once the social niceties were out of the way, Chao wasted no time getting down to business. "As I said, I like your proposal which—like the attack on Singapore—is very imaginative. Not to mention daring! Only thirty-six miles from Okinawa … That's the part that worries me however. How will you reach the island of Tonaki without being detected? Forgive me Captain, but your proposal was a bit vague in that regard."

It was the right question, and Ko's respect for Chao went up a notch. "You have a keen eye, Admiral … That question lies at the very heart of the concept. And it was my hope that I would have a chance to provide an answer during a meeting like this one. Partly because the idea is somewhat unorthodox."

"As is the *Sea Dragon* herself!" Chao said enthusiastically. "I'm ready to listen."

"Well, as you know sir, the *Sea Dragon* is 667 feet long. And, as you also know, there are container ships longer than that. The idea is to find a neutral cargo vessel of the correct length, with a legitimate reason to stop in Japan, and convince the owner to let the *Sea Dragon* travel alongside for a while."

Ko stopped at that point so Chao could extrapolate. And, when a big smile appeared on the other officer's face, Ko knew he had scored. "The Americans will see *one* radar signature," Chao said. "Then, at the right moment, the *Dragon* will slip away. And because of her low profile she's likely to escape unnoticed."

"Exactly," Ko said. "But I need the cargo ship in order to make the plan work."

"And you shall have it," Chao said. "A great many countries owe China a great many favors. We will call on one of them.

"Now that I understand the magic involved, I would like to share an idea of my own, an embellishment if you will. Something that will set the Allies back on their heels."

Ko felt the first stirrings of despair. Where Admiral Wen refused to accept the *Sea Dragon* as a useful weapon, Admiral Chao had embraced it, but was about to make an already difficult mission more so. Or was he wrong? *Give Chao a chance*, Ko thought. *Don't jump to conclusions.* He forced a smile. "How interesting! Please tell me more."

"Imagine this," Chao said. "Once the *Sea Dragon* is in position, we will launch one hundred Dongfeng 26 missiles at Okinawa! The *Gweilo* (pejorative term for white people) will see them coming. And they'll throw lots of defensive weapons into the sky, including missiles and decoys. As a result, most of our weapons won't reach their targets.

"Meanwhile you will fire your railgun and missiles at carefully chosen command and control targets on Okinawa, causing tremendous damage. The Americans will use their satellites to backtrack your missiles to Tonaki Island.

"Their first reaction will be to assume some sort of technical glitch, or computer hack, because the launch site is only thirty-six miles away! But as you continue to fire, they will conclude that yes, Tonaki Island *is* where the missiles and shells are coming from.

"Then, they'll target your location to the extent they can, remembering that our DF-26 missiles, combined with your missiles, will have destroyed key radars and offensive systems. But, before they can fire on you, the Americans will have to get permission from the Japanese. And that will take time since there are over 400 Japanese citizens living on Tonaki.

"Meanwhile," Chao added, "it seems likely that Japanese warships will be sent to the scene. And that, Captain Ko, is when you and your submarine escorts will sink as many of those vessels as you can before running home."

Chao had been leaning forward with elbows on the table. Now he leaned back. "So, Captain, what do you think?"

Ko was impressed in spite of himself. Chao's plan was daring to say the least and, assuming everything worked the way the admiral imagined it would, the admiral would receive the Order of August the First within days of the attack. But the devil would be in the details. And, as with any complex plan, there were lots of details.

But Admiral Chao was an admiral. And there was only one thing Ko could say. "I like it, sir ... Let's get to work."

***

Da Nang, Vietnam

Three days had passed since the meeting in Sanya. There had been more meetings. Lots of meetings. Because Operation Hammerfall had a lot of moving parts. And there were some, especially within the army, who questioned the wisdom of firing one hundred expensive missiles as a diversion.

But Admiral Chao was not only fully invested in the plan, he was a skilled bureaucrat, and more than a match for grumpy generals. And, some subtle messaging from the *Sea Dragon's* Chief Engineer to his brother-in-law President Lau, didn't hurt either.

So, the plan was approved. And Ko and his chief engineer were on a trip to Da Nang, where they were going to inspect the container ship *Java Dawn*, and interview her captain.

The ship was registered in Liberia, like thousands of other ships, but owned by a shadowy company called Neptune Rising. Not that Ko cared, so long as the ship's captain did his bidding. His name was Frank Bristol. And he was, according to Chinese intelligence, an American. More than that, a mercenary who, like all mercenaries, was for sale.

The *Java Dawn* was docked at a pier just inside the entrance to Da Nang Bay where the water was deepest. The naval officers were dressed in business suits as they paid the taxi driver, left the car, and paused to inspect the vessel docked in front of them.

The forward section of the ship was loaded with multi-colored shipping containers which were stacked three high. The four-level superstructure was painted white, and topped by a single stack. "What's she carrying?" Hong wanted to know.

"She's loaded with machine parts, electronics and textiles," Ko replied. "All from India, and bound for South Korea."

"So, she's traveling from an Allied country, she's in a neutral port, and she's headed for an Allied country," Hong observed. "That's good. The Americans and the Japanese have no reason to pay special attention to her."

"Exactly," Ko said. "From here the *Java* will sail due east, pass the north end of Luzon off to the starboard, and turn north. Then she'll pass Taiwan on her port side, and head toward Okinawa."

"And the island of Tonaki."

"Yes," Ko agreed. "That makes her perfect for what we have in mind, so long as her captain is competent, and her engines are in good repair. I will evaluate the captain while you take a tour of the engine room."

A man in a blue jumpsuit was stationed at the gangplank that ran from the pier into the ship's gloomy interior. He didn't speak Chinese or English. The officers were forced to wait while a crewman was dispatched to fetch a petty officer.

The petty officer was dressed in khakis, rather than the blue overalls the deckhands wore, and carrying a radio which he used to contact the bridge. After a brief exchange the naval officers were led across what seemed like a half-acre of oily steel to a hatch marked "Stairs" in three languages.

The metal stairs switch-backed up three levels to the bridge. There a large sweep of windows framed the view of the harbor. A curving console and a dozen screens fronted that. Two raised seats were positioned next to duplicate sets of controls. The sort of setup Ko would expect to see on a navy vessel.

But what he *wouldn't* expect to find was the mat behind the chairs and a set of free weights. The American stood at least six-two; he was stripped to his waist. Muscles bulged and tattoos squirmed as he performed alternating curls with fifty-pound weights.

"Welcome aboard gentlemen," the man said in English. "I'm Captain Bristol. The home office instructed me to cooperate with you. And for a ten-grand bonus, I agreed to do so. What's the plan?"

"Our requirement is really quite simple," Ko replied. "You will depart for South Korea as scheduled. At a predetermined time and place our vessel will join yours and cruise alongside."

Bristol placed the weights on a rack. "Define 'alongside.'"

"About one hundred feet off your starboard side."

Bristol's eyes flicked from Ko to Hong and back again. "For how long?"

"Approximately four hours at your cruising speed of 24 knots."

Bristol went over to get a towel. "So, we're going to hold hands for a hundred miles. And this will take place during the hours of darkness?"

"Yes."

"With or without running lights?"

"Our vessel will be blacked out."

"And in case of bad weather?"

"Then dress appropriately," Ko replied.

Bristol laughed. "I like your style. Okay…The *Java Dawn* will depart Da Nang at 1800 the day after tomorrow. Do you have the coordinates for the rendezvous? And a time?"

"Yes," Ko answered as he gave Bristol a piece of paper.

The merchant captain eyed it. "Ah, you included a radio frequency as well. Good. Although I suggest that we use it as little as possible."

"Agreed."

Bristol made a show out of folding the paper, and tucking it into a pocket. "Is there anything else?"

"Yes," Ko said. "We want a tour of the engine room."

Bristol smiled. "Of course, you do. I'll send for Chief Abidi. He will show you around."

***

Aboard the semi-submersible cruiser *Sea-Dragon* in the South China Sea

It was dark and the *Sea Dragon* was steaming north with the island of Taiwan to the west. Most of the cruiser's hull was submerged leaving nothing more than her twin conning towers exposed. In keeping with his new rank Lieutenant Jev Jing was standing watch in Tower 1, along with the cruiser's third officer, and two ratings.

The ship was traveling at a steady 22 knots and pushing swells away from its rounded bow. The lights of Taipei twinkled off the port bow, where they served to symbolize Taiwan's precarious neutrality.

China had, as was the case with Vietnam, chosen to leave the heavily armed country alone for the moment, rather than spend the resources required to conquer it. But later, during what the president referred to as the *Weida de tongzhi* (The Great

Dominion) there would be plenty of time in which to "train the dogs."

Lieutenant Commander Yu's thoughts were on Taiwan as well. "Look at those lights, Jev," Yu said. "Some of them are bars. And do you know what's in those bars? Booze. But more importantly, women. Some of whom are bound to pretty, and willing to make a sailor happy for the right price. I wish we could go there."

"Yes, sir," Jing said obediently. "That would be nice."

"Attention on deck," a rating said as Captain Ko appeared.

"As you were," Ko said, before anyone could snap to attention. "We should be coming up on the *Java Dawn* at any moment … Keep your eyes peeled."

Jing stared into the darkness, hoping to be the first to spot the container ship, but a sharp-eyed rating beat him to it. "There she is, Captain … Off our port bow."

Jing saw the white glow of a stern light, followed by a green running light, and the checkerboard glow of lights associated with the ship's superstructure. The *Sea Dragon* by contrast was blacked out.

Ko was wearing a wireless headset, and giving orders to those on duty in the CIC. "Warn the freighter that we're coming alongside. Match her speed. Tell the *Dawn* to engage their autopilot if they are steering manually. And ask them to provide advance warning if they disengage it.

"Bring the *Dragon* to a point one hundred feet off the *Java Dawn's* starboard side and engage our autopilot. Monitor our position constantly to ensure that we remain in position."

Everyone, Jing included, knew what the captain was up to, and had complete faith in his ability to pull it off. And why wouldn't they? After the victory over the *USS Concord*, and the successful attack on Singapore, Ko could no wrong. So, if he thought the *Sea Dragon* could sneak up on Okinawa, and attack it with impunity, they were happy to be part of what promised to be a third thrilling victory.

Jing went off duty a half hour later. He was thankful for the tiny cabin that he shared with another lieutenant, because two platoons of marines were crammed into the cruiser's various nooks and crannies. That meant the air was even more fetid than usual, the already cramped conditions felt more oppressive, and Jing had to stand in line to use a urinal.

But Jing knew the marines were going to play an important part in completing the mission. Their job was to go ashore on Tonaki Island and prevent the locals from using phones or radios to warn authorities about the impending attack.

And, much to his satisfaction, Jing had been selected to go with them to supervise communications. The prospect was not only exciting, but the sort of outing that could produce a favorable mention, or even some sort of award.

It was important to be rested, or so it seemed to Jing, who was determined to take a two-hour nap prior to joining the shore party. He found it impossible to sleep however, and kept looking at his watch, until it was time to roll off the bunk and get dressed.

The *Java Dawn* and the *Sea Dragon* had been traveling in company for four hours by then. And as far as Jing knew, they had done so without difficulty. It felt strange to wear marine camos and the holstered Type 67 suppressed pistol. Jing hadn't fired a handgun or a rifle since officer training school, but had no reason to worry, since the marines would handle that sort of thing.

A lieutenant named Ma was in charge of the marine detachment and Jing didn't like him. There were a number of reasons for that, starting with Ma's tendency to shout everything, the officer's overbearing manner, and his coarse sense of humor.

Fortunately, Jing wouldn't have to deal with Ma for very long, and took comfort from that.

***

Captain Ko felt a tremendous sense of relief as the *Java Dawn* and the *Sea Dragon* parted company. The subterfuge had been successful. He knew that because he was still alive. Had the Allies been able to spot the cruiser, long range missiles would have fallen on it in a matter of minutes.

But *Sea Dragon* wasn't safe yet. Not by a long shot. The next step was to close with the island of Tonaki, enter its harbor, and discharge Lieutenant Ma's marines. The rest would depend on stealth. The plan was to send teams to disable cell service, regular phone service, and the radio transmitter the islanders used for emergencies. Lieutenant Jing would see to that.

Once that was accomplished the locals were to be rounded up and held in a warehouse until the attack was over. Perhaps they would survive. Or, if the Japanese government decided to sacrifice them, the residents of Tonaki would be killed by the Americans. Such were the vagaries of war.

Of immediate concern was the need to put the marines ashore. A tricky business because it required him to blow enough water out of the *Sea Dragon's* ballast tanks to raise the main deck above sea level. But not too far above sea level lest Ko make it difficult for the crew to launch the inflatable rafts the marines were going to use.

Would that make the ship more visible to radar? Yes, it would. But Ko planned to keep the process short by loading the rafts on the deck, taking water into the tanks, and floating them off. A process for which Jing was also responsible. *He's a bright lad*, Ko thought. *If it weren't for him Enlai would be president. This will be the making of him.*

***

Jing was acutely aware of the responsibilities that had been heaped upon him. Load the rafts. Make sure the marines landed in the right place. Establish and maintain communications with the *Sea Dragon*. And, destroy the island's communications infrastructure. Not personally of course, but through Lieutenant Ma.

Nothing had been said. But it was obvious that Captain Hong, and therefore Captain Ko, were aware of his role in uncovering then President Enlai's agent on the ship. And they were giving him an opportunity to distinguish himself.

Jing made sure that he was the first man to exit the hull via Conning Tower 2, and the first to arrive on the main deck, where a team of sailors was inflating the rafts. Air hissed from portable tanks, and the rafts began to take shape, as Ma barked orders.

It took less than a minute for the marines to board their assigned rafts and connect the inflatables together with pre-cut lines. That was Jing's idea. And it stemmed from a deep-seated fear that, if left to their own devices, at least some of the marines would stray and land in different places.

Jing had assigned himself to the first raft, and assigned Ma to the last raft, to minimize the amount of harm the marine might do.

In spite of the late hour lights twinkled on Tonaki. And the lights, combined with the red beacon on the island's radio tower, would keep Jing on course. The raft wobbled as the *Sea Dragon* sank into her semi-submerged state and seawater sloshed over the deck. Then the rafts were afloat and free to depart.

Every member of the landing party was wearing a wireless headset and night vision gear. Jing spoke softly. "Paddle in unison. Hold noise to a minimum. And maintain situational awareness. Over."

Jing was amazed by how clear the green-hued imagery was. Water splashed as someone missed a stroke and a noncom told him to "*Sushen*." (Shape up.)

Jing's eyes were focused on the village of Tonaki. It took on more detail as rafts drew closer. Jing was looking for any signs of alarm. There were none. "Get ready," Jing said. "My raft will land sideways. Do the same with yours. That will enable everyone to exit quickly. Assume a defensive posture and await orders. Over."

Jing knew Ma was jealous, but didn't care. More than that, and much to Jing's surprise, he was enjoying himself. Would he feel the same way if American soldiers were waiting on the beach? No. But the sense of anticipation persisted.

Jing felt the raft make contact with the steeply shelving beach and heard the rattle of loose gravel. "Now! Swing sideways! Don't forget to drop your anchors. We'll need the rafts later." Jing knew that the marines in the last raft would need extra time to reach the beach. That was factored into the plan.

Jing stepped out into cold seawater that immediately flooded his boots. He barely noticed. The tower was designated as "target one" because of all the cell phone antennas, splitters, couplers and attenuators that were attached to it. The mast was used for emergency radio communications as well.

Meanwhile Ma, with roughly 75 percent of the marines at his disposal, had orders to roust the locals out of their beds, confiscate their cell phones, and cut their land lines if any.

The moment those tasks were accomplished Ma was to herd the civilians to the school gymnasium and place them under guard. "Team 1 will follow me," Jing said, as he drew his pistol.

"Team 2 will split into fire teams and take control of the village. Don't forget to neutralize public phones if you see any. Execute. Over."

Ma barked only slightly subdued orders, noncoms led fire-teams away, and it was time to report in. "This is Alpha-One. We are ashore and proceeding to our preset objectives. Over."

"Understood. Over," came the reply.

Navigation was easy. All Jing and his team of seven marines had to do was head for the red beacon. They jogged through twisting-turning streets to the point where the tower loomed above them. A small equipment building and the tower were protected by a locked gate and an eight-foot, wire mesh fence.

Bolt cutters were used to slice through the padlock. Hinges squealed as Jing pulled it open. A demolitions expert hurried forward to plant a prepared charge on the equipment shed's door. There was a warning, followed by a flash, and a loud bang.

Would someone hear it? That didn't matter because Ma and his marines were going door-to-door rounding up residents.

Now the demolitions tech was inside placing thermite charges on equipment racks, the emergency power supply, and a metal casing of unknown purpose. Then the tech left the shed.

Meanwhile a second engineer was up on the tower placing a charge next to the radio mast. As soon as that was accomplished, he hurried down. "It's ready, sir."

"Take cover and blow the charges," Jing ordered.

A warning was given, the team took cover behind a wall, and the charges were detonated. There weren't any explosions as each charge produced a fountain of sparks, followed by a tremendous amount of heat and a flow of white-hot molten metal.

That was when Jing heard gunfire. He yelled, "Follow me!" and ran toward the sound. Had the Americans or the Japanese arrived? Was a firefight underway? If so, the *Sea Dragon* was about to be destroyed, the plan was in the toilet, and he was going to end up dead.

Yelling could be heard, some in Chinese, and some in Japanese. The first thing Jing saw was a headless marine lying sprawled out in a pool of light from a street lamp. A severed head, a samurai sword, and an old man lay nearby. A corporal rushed over to speak with him. "He came out of nowhere, sir! Private Guo never had a chance."

Jing heard a burst of automatic fire. Flashes could be seen through the thin curtains of a neighboring house. "What's going on?"

"Lieutenant Ma is executing the old man's family, sir."

That was understandable in a way. But stupid, since the gunfire was sure to wake the entire village, and could trigger more resistance.

Jing hurried over to the house where the gunfire had taken place and hurried inside. That's where he became part of a horrible tableau. A woman lay dead on the floor. A child was clinging to her body and sobbing. And there, standing erect in her night clothes, was an old lady. The dead man's wife perhaps?

Ma was aiming an assault weapon at the woman and screaming insults. Two marines stood motionless. The woman knew she was going to die. But her head was up, and her eyes focused on Ma's face.

Perhaps it was that, as much as the need to prevent more noise, that caused Jing to raise his pistol and fire. Not at the woman, but at Ma. Two shots missed. One didn't. It struck the officer's temple and pulped his brain. Ma went down like a fifty-pound sack of rice.

Jing was as surprised as the marines and the old woman were. Surprised and scared. How would Captain Ko react to his decision? Not well, Jing assumed. But one thing was for sure: it was necessary to take control before the marines turned against him.

"Take the woman and child outside," Jing ordered. "Do not harm them. Your mission is to search houses for communications devices and herd the population into the high school gymnasium. Do it."

Perhaps other soldiers, in another army, might have questioned Jing's authority. Especially after they had watched him shoot their platoon leader. But the marines were quite familiar with the "Three Rules of Discipline and Eight Points for Attention" issued in 1928 by Mao Zedong and his comrades, when they were battling the Chinese nationalists. And the first rule was, "Prompt obedience to orders."

They said, "*Shì de xiānshēng*" (Yes sir), in unison. One went over to take the old lady by the arm, while the other took the child and led the way out of the house.

Jing paused to collect one of Ma's dog tags which he slipped into a pocket. Then he went out onto the street. Fortunately, fireteams led by noncoms had been hard at work. Jing was a witness to what might have been seventy prisoners being marched down the street. A third-class master sergeant hurried over to greet Jing. "We're making good progress, sir. Where is Lieutenant Ma?"

"He was killed," Jing said, without offering any details. "As was private Guo. But everything is under control now. You will take the lieutenant's place."

The noncom saluted. "Sir!" And turned away.

Jing allowed himself to exhale. And was surprised to learn that he'd been holding his breath. He saw a flash on the horizon, followed by a moment of silence, and what might have been thunder. Except it wasn't thunder. Missiles were falling on Okinawa. And people were dying.

***

Aboard the semi-submersible *Sea Dragon*, in Tonaki bay, 36 miles from Okinawa, Japan

Captain Ko was standing in the Sea Dragon's CIC peering over a tech's shoulder. The atmosphere was tense as targeting data arrived from a variety of sources, including Yaogan-30 satellites. The one hundred Dongfeng 26 missiles promised by Admiral Chao had begun to fall. On command-and-control targets? Yes. But on selected houses and apartment buildings too. All identified by Chinese spies who lived on Okinawa.

Would the hits entail collateral damage? Or course they would. But that was necessary. Command and Control was more than radars, operations centers, and computers. They were tools. The *real* threat was resident in the minds of the men and women who commanded them.

Dead officers could and would be replaced. But it would take time for their replacements to arrive, learn, and start to function. Valuable time which China would use to good effect.

Of course, most of the incoming D-26 missiles were being intercepted—just as Chao predicted they would be—thereby sparing some of the targets.

But computers were tracking "misses," and sending that data to the *Sea Dragon*, where one hundred of the ship's two hundred missiles were waiting to receive it. The rest were reserved for surface targets the ship might encounter on the way home. Ko's eyes were on the countdown clock. "Missiles one through one hundred. Report."

"Ninety-eight are programmed, or have been reprogrammed, and are ready for launch," the CICWO (Combat Information

Center Watch Officer) reported. "Missiles 52 and 79 reported technical issues and were taken offline."

"Understood," Ko replied. "Stand by to fire missiles, fire!"

The *Sea Dragon* lurched as the surface-to-surface missiles left their launchers and sped downrange.

"The railgun," Ko ordered. "Report."

"Targets loaded. All lights are green. The railgun is ready to fire," the CICWO replied.

Ko was ready. "Fire!"

There was no need to give orders after that. The railgun would fire until it overheated. Progress had been made since the attack on the *Concord*. Now, the railgun could fire nine shots before it was necessary to replace the barrel.

That meant the *Sea Dragon* could put to sea. There was no way to know if the Japanese would let the Americans attack Tonaki island, but they might. And Ko planned to be elsewhere if that occurred. "Shore party. Report."

"Two dead," the officer of the deck reported. "No wounded. The last of them are boarding now."

Two dead? That was a surprise. "Cut the rafts loose. Get the marines below. And raise the anchor. We're about to get underway."

The last shot was fired. The railgun was lowered into the hull, and a crew immediately began the process of replacing the old barrel with a new one.

Once clear of the harbor Ko gave the order to submerge most of the ship and sent a message to Admiral Chao: "Mission accomplished. Departing."

The reply came quickly: "This moment will live for a thousand years. Congratulations."

Try as he might Ko was unable to resist the feeling of pride that the admiral's words produced. Ko sought to push it away.

The original plan, *his* part of it anyway, had been to use the *Sea Dragon* and her submarine escorts to ambush one or more Allied ships as they left Japan's Yokosuka navy base. But now he wasn't so sure. "There will be times you need to disengage from a fight so you can be in a position to fight another day."

The great Chinese general, strategist, writer and philosopher Sun Tzu had written that in the 5th century BC. And Ko felt it in his bones. Rather than seek the enemy, he would let the enemy seek him. And if a fight ensued, then so be it.

Ko's thoughts were interrupted by his executive officer Commander Shi. "Excuse me, sir. We have a situation. May we speak privately?"

Ko frowned. "What kind of situation?"

"One we should discuss privately."

"All right, let's duck into the chartroom."

After asking the navigator to leave, Ko turned to Shi. "Okay, what's up?"

Shi's face was expressionless. "A villager killed one of the marines with a Samurai sword. Lieutenant Ma began to execute people. Lieutenant Jing shot him in the head. Then Jing took command and completed the mission."

Ko stared. "You're joking."

"No, sir."

"How do we know this?"

"Jing told the head of Communications who told me."

"So, it's all over the ship."

"Yes, sir. But, strangely enough, there's been no complaint from Lieutenant Ma's marines."

"Hmm," Ko said. "That would suggest that he wasn't popular. And that his noncoms agree with what Jing did."

"I think so, yes," Shi replied.

"Let's convene a disciplinary panel, go through the motions, and find Jing innocent of murder before we reach Yulin. You might want to speak with a couple of noncoms ahead of time."

Shi knew what that meant and nodded. The hearing would go smoothly.

CHAPTER TEN

Manado, Indonesia, aboard the Allied transport *Agger*

It was not just raining, it was pouring. Water pounded the ship's decks as if determined to penetrate steel. Rain droplets ran down the window in Ryson's cabin as he looked out across the bay. But his thoughts were elsewhere.

While Ryson and his boats had been up north rescuing pilots, the Chinese cruiser *Sea Dragon* had been on another rampage. Okinawa was the target this time. With support from launchers on the Chinese mainland the cruiser had been able to destroy dozens of command and control targets, and assassinate the Commander of U.S. Forces Japan.

It was depressing. Very depressing. And the only thing the media was focused on at the moment. As a result, the rescue mission had received scant attention. And a story which might have lifted spirits around the world was subsumed by grief.

Once clear of the fishing boats, the Armindales had been able to make good time. And it wasn't long before Allied fighter planes appeared to protect them.

Now Ryson was seated at the cabin's built-in desk, drinking coffee while he sought to plow through the pile of work that had accumulated during his absence. Supply requisitions, a disciplinary action, and a missing assault rifle. It went on and on.

The phone rang and Ryson picked it up. "This is Commander Ryson."

"Of course it is," Admiral Nathan said irritably. "Pack a bag, and be sure to bring a dress uniform. I'll meet you at the gangway in half an hour. We're flying to Port Moresby."

"May I ask why?"

"Because General Haskell is pissed," Nathan replied. "And no wonder ... The attack on Okinawa could cost him his job. So, he's going to hold a command conference and light a fire under senior management."

Ryson took note of the way the situation had been framed. Haskell, and perhaps Nathan as well, saw the attack on Okinawa as a resume killer. "Yes, sir. I'll see you in half an hour."

Ryson put the receiver down. Rain pattered against the window. Kelsey's family lived in Port Moresby. Would she be there? He hoped so.

***

Lieutenant Command "Gun Daddy" Greer was going home. That's what his orders said. First to Washington D.C. for a recognition ceremony that the POWs would participate in. Then to the TOPGUN school where he would serve as XO. All over his objections. Because while Greer was eager to grab some leave, he wanted to fly planes. Not a desk.

But, in the words of the local interservice tasking officer, "I asked, and the people at the Pentagon said, 'No fucking way.' What if you were on a mission, got shot down, and were captured? Can you imagine what the Chinese would do to you? And the propaganda they would pump out?"

Greer *could* imagine. And knew the brass were correct. But, before leaving Manado, Greer wanted to say goodbye to Mary. So, he dashed from the hotel to the store across the street, where he bought a hat and a cheap plastic raincoat.

But when Greer stepped out into the rain, he realized that something was missing. And that was the 9mm pistol he'd been issued and "forgotten" to return. Not a must for visiting a graveyard. But nice to have without Dalisay as a guide.

After retrieving the weapon from his room Greer returned to the street. Rain rattled on plastic as Greer got his bearings. Three taxis were waiting, and he stuck his head into the first. "Do you speak English?"

"Speak English number one," the driver replied.

Greer figured that was good enough, opened the rear door, and slipped inside. The smell of stale cigarette smoke permeated the air. A half empty baby bottle was rolling around on the floor, Indonesian pop music was blaring from the radio, and a statue of Jesus was perched on the dashboard. "Take me to the Catholic cemetery," Greer ordered. "And turn the radio off." The driver glared at Greer in the rearview mirror as he turned the music off.

Greer didn't know Manado well enough to be sure that the driver was headed for the right location. But when the car came to a stop, he recognized the sagging wall, the overgrown shrubbery, and the ornamental gate. "Stay here," Greer ordered. "Don't worry. I'll pay extra if you wait."

Water splashed away from Greer's combat boots, and seeped down the back of his neck, as he passed through the gate and entered the cemetery beyond. The relentless downpour made the graveyard even more depressing than it had been the first time he'd been there.

But death wouldn't wait. Four grave diggers, all wearing ponchos, were hard at work under a structure consisting of bamboo poles and a ragged tarp. Were they the same men Greer had seen last time? Probably.

Greer walked past them to the section of the cemetery where Mary had been laid to rest. Everything was the same. The weeds were just as tall. Headstones still lay where they had fallen. And the grave that Greer knew to be Mary's was marked by nothing more than a wooden cross. That in spite of the money Greer had given to Father Wijaya.

The pain was waiting deep inside of him. And as Greer knelt in the mud, he could feel his emotions churn as sorrow morphed into rage. "I'm sorry Mary," Greer said, tears trickling down his cheeks. "I will punish the bastard. And, when the war is over, I will return. A monument will be constructed on this spot. I love you."

And with that Greer stood, turned his back on the grave, and made his way out to the street. The taxi was gone. Revenge? For the radio? Or boredom? Greer would never know.

But it caused Greer to change course. He had Wijaya's card. And, after digging it out of his wallet, Greer saw that the priest lived on the same street as the cemetery.

There was a parsonage then, and close by, which made sense. Greer performed a slow three-sixty, spotted a steeple in the distance, and knew his theory was correct.

With the steeple to guide him Greer followed the street west. A shabby church appeared. That was when Greer saw that the steeple wasn't a steeple, but a steel tripod, with a bell and a crucifix mounted up top.

Memories stuttered through Greer's mind. The convoy, the ambush, and Boyle dying. All because the Filipinos knew the rescue party was coming. And *how* did they know that? Because a spy told them, that's how. A spy who, despite a vow of poverty, was eager to make some money. Or, was that a reach? Greer was determined to find out.

Thunder muttered as Greer approached the entrance to the church. One of the double doors was open. The interior was lit by wall sconces and the candles in front of the altar. The flames wavered uncertainly as a gust of wind entered the nave.

All of the parishioners were women. And looked up from their prayers as Greer made his way along the right side of the cavernous room to a door. A sign said, "Private" in English, and what Greer thought was Bahasa. The door was equipped with a hasp. An open padlock dangled from it. Did that mean the priest was within?

Greer drew his pistol and turned the knob. The door opened easily. Music was playing, classical music. And the lighting was dim. Sculptures lurked in the gloom—celebrations of male beauty copied from well-known Greek and Roman artifacts.

A spotlight threw a circle of light onto the planked floor. And there, lit from above, was Wijaya. The priest was naked. And though no fan of ballet, Greer recognized the Arabesque for what it was. Wijaya was standing on one foot, his arms extended.

Greer shot the priest in the knee. Blood flew and Wijaya screamed as he fell. Greer waited to see if the parishioners would come running. None of them did.

Wijaya was lying on his back holding onto his bloody knee while rolling back and forth. "Fuck! Fuck! Fuck! *Why?* Why did you shoot me?"

Greer knelt just beyond the puddle of blood. "I gave you money. You made promises. None were kept."

Wijaya seemed to recognize Greer for the first time. "The headstone? This is about the fucking headstone?"

"Yes," Greer answered. "And it's about the information you passed to the Philippine government. Information that led to dozens of deaths."

Greer had no proof of that. But the priest assumed that he did. "No! That's impossible. I sent them a picture of her face. I told them about you, and the man who was with you, that's all."

The photo came as a shock. Mary had been dead when Wijaya snapped it. But that, plus a written description of Dalisay, would be enough to trigger an investigation.

And, after the authorities compared Mary's photo to the images of her taken at the prison, they'd been able to put the rest of it together.

Greer stood. Wijaya stared into the barrel of the pistol. "*No!* I'm a priest. God will punish you!"

"He already has," Greer said. And he pulled the trigger.

Greer hadn't touched anything up to that point, and was careful to avoid doing so, as he left through a rear entrance. America was waiting. And that at least, was a good thing.

***

Port Moresby, Papua New Guinea

The flight from Manado, Indonesia to Port Moresby, in Papua New Guinea, had taken more than four hours. So, by the time the eight passenger C-21 began its approach into Jacksons International Airport, it was midafternoon. The Air Force pilot put the jet down with a gentle bump.

But rather than the main terminal, the pilot taxied to a remote hangar located next to Joint American/Australian command headquarters. Fighters were parked there. All protected by revetments.

Once on the ground the navy officers were greeted by an Aussie lieutenant. He rendered a salute which Nathan returned. "Welcome to Pom City. Lieutenant Swallow at your service. The meeting with General Haskell is slated for 0900 tomorrow morning. But, according to what I've been told, he'll be present at tonight's party."

Nathan frowned. "Party? What party?"

A party? Ryson wondered. *In the wake of the attack on Okinawa?* That was strange. But maybe the Parkers were trying to boost morale. A stiff upper lip and all that.

"The party will be held at the Parker mansion," Swallow replied. "Which, as it happens, is where you've been invited to stay."

"I see," Nathan replied. "That was very nice of the Parkers. What have we got by way of ground transportation?"

"The vehicles are over there," Swallow said, as he gestured to a column of armored cars. "Nothing fancy, sir … That wouldn't be safe here. Pom City was dangerous before the war, and it's worse now. There's a great deal of government corruption. And, because of that, the Raskol (Rascal) gangs are even more assertive. Car jackings are common. As are kidnappings."

Ryson saw that a Bushmaster PMV was waiting to lead the parade, followed by two Land Rovers, and a second Bushmaster. All heavily armed.

"I see," Nathan replied. "Thank you for the efforts on our behalf. This is Lieutenant Commander Ryson by the way … He's American, but don't hold that against him."

Swallow smiled. "We'll do our best, sir. Please follow me."

The fact that both visitors were issued body armor, and told to put it on, served to emphasize the dangers resident in Port Moresby.

So why live there, Ryson wondered? Especially since the Parkers could live anywhere. The answer was obvious. For better or worse, the family business was headquartered in Pom City. And they had to defend it.

"Parker House is located on Touaguba Hill, overlooking Port Moresby," Lieutenant Swallow informed them, as the Land Rover bumped through a series of pot holes, and sped past a row of shacks with rusty roofs. "The house provides them with a terrific view of the harbor. Not to mention their ships as they come and go.

"The Chinese try to bomb the Parker freight terminal on a regular basis but, thanks to our fighters, they haven't been able to score."

That caused Ryson to wonder. Was Kelsey acting as a patriot, out to protect Australia? Or the daughter of a shipping magnate, with an ax to grind? And did it matter? So long as her motivations were consistent with each other?

Swallow was an amateur historian, and proceeded to describe the air battles that took place over Port Moresby between February of 1942 and August 1943. "It was a bloody affair," Swallow said, as the convoy passed through a seedy business district.

"On March 31st our chaps were joined by the American 8th Bombardment Squadron which flew A-24 bombers. And for two weeks in May, six P-39 Airacobras of the American 36th Pursuit Squadron joined the fray.

"But, in spite of American assistance, the daily battles reduced the No. 75 Squadron RAAF to just three airworthy machines.

"Eventually elements of the American 35th, and the full 36th Pursuit Squadron, arrived to lend a hand. The No. 75 Squadron lost twenty-one aircraft and twelve pilots. It was a close thing."

While Swallow continued talking, the lead Bushmaster led the convoy through narrow streets, and onto the road that climbed the side of Touaguba Hill. "There's the bay," Swallow said. "As you can see two Indonesian destroyers are in port."

Ryson knew that Western New Guinea was governed by Indonesia, which was clearly doing a piss poor job of it. But there was no reason to say that and he didn't.

The convoy slowed, then came to a stop in front of a military style checkpoint, complete with concertina wire and machine gun positions. Smart looking soldiers, most of whom were black, came forward to check IDs and search the vehicles for IEDs.

"They're mercenaries," Swallow explained. "All veterans of the South African Special Forces Brigade. That's something Mr. Parker insists on. 'You can't trust the locals.' That's what he says. And I agree."

Once cleared, the convoy was allowed to pass through a gate, and follow a paved road up through a series of switchbacks to the sprawling mansion above. It was painted an eye-searing white and much given to right angles, gleaming windows, and verandahs. All boasting views of the city and bay.

The convoy took a hard turn to the left, climbed the last stretch of driveway, and came to a stop under a flat-roofed portico. "Duty calls," Swallow said, as the navy officers got out. "I'll see you tomorrow."

Two white clad servants appeared to greet the guests. One was a young woman in a sari. "My name is Nia," the girl said, as she brought the palms of her hands together and bowed. "Welcome to Parker House. Please allow me to take your bag, and show you to your room."

"Thank you," Ryson replied. "I'll carry the bag."

"As you wish," Nia said, with another bow. "Please follow me."

Glass doors slid out of the way as Nia approached them. The reception area was large and beautifully furnished. An enormous portrait confronted each guest as they entered. The woman was Asian. Chinese? Ryson thought so.

She was dressed for a formal occasion. A large diamond dangled from her neck. Matching diamonds glittered on her ears. The skintight evening dress fit like a glove. The woman's eyes were focused on a point somewhere in the distance. "And who," Ryson inquired, "is *she?*"

"That's Li jing," Nia answered. "Her name means beautiful spirit. She was Mr. Parker's first wife."

"Was?"

"Yes. She died of cancer over twenty-five years ago."

"And Mr. Parker's second wife?"

"They're divorced. She lives in Sydney."

So, Kelsey's mother was alive, and living in Australia. Ryson filed the fact away.

Servants bowed, as Nia led Ryson to a bank of elevators, and stood to one side as he entered.

"Your suite is on the second floor," Nia informed him, as the elevator carried the officer upwards. The doors swished open onto a small lobby. Nia led Ryson down a hall to a door. The name plate read, "*The Celine II.*"

"Each guest suite is named after one of the family's ships," Nia explained, as she opened the door.

Ryson entered to discover that the room was beautifully furnished with a dazzling view of the bay. A white envelope with his name on it was waiting on the king-sized bed. "If you need anything dial zero and ask for me," Nia told him.

"Thank you," Ryson said. "I will."

Nia withdrew and Ryson opened the envelope. The calligraphy was beautiful. "Lieutenant Commander Ryson ... Please join George and Kelsey Parker at six for cocktails, followed by dinner, and entertainments. Formal dress is required."

Ryson eyed his watch. It was nearly 5:00 PM. So there wasn't enough time for a nap. He laid out his whites, took a long shower, and continued to towel off as he entered the bedroom. The window beckoned and there, waiting on the windowsill, was a pair of powerful binoculars. Just the thing for enjoying the view.

But Ryson had very little interest in the city. His gaze went straight to the Indonesian warships anchored in the bay. The flotilla consisted of the destroyers he'd seen earlier, plus two patrol boats, which Ryson recognized as Mandau-class missile boats circa 1977 or 78.

The boats were badly outmoded, but Ryson understood why they remained in service. With WWIII raging Indonesia needed every hull it had. And since the vessels were well armed, and could do nearly 43 knots, the boats could give a good account of themselves in a shootout with any adversary of their size.

But what Ryson found to be most interesting were the torpedo launchers mounted next to the Mandau superstructures. The tubes were in addition to a pair of missile launchers. *Why?*

So, they can duke it out with destroyers and frigates if necessary, Ryson decided. *And do so at ranges where missiles don't make sense. What about the Armindales? Could they be fitted with torpedo tubes? That would give us an option we don't have now.*

Ryson put the binoculars down and began the process of getting dressed. He hated parties. Especially parties thrown by VIPs for VIPs. Only the fact that Kelsey might attend prevented Ryson from descending into a bad mood.

Two Asian men, both wearing tuxedos, were in the elevator that delivered Ryson to the first floor. Servants were everywhere and one of them bowed. "Cocktails are being served in the Bay Room, sir … The door is over there."

Ryson thanked him and followed a well-dressed couple through double doors and into a beautifully appointed lounge. The bar was an eye-catching combination of polished brass and Southeast Asian rosewood. A material so precious that poachers were stripping Thailand's national parks of it. Did the Parkers know that? It seemed safe to assume that they did.

Ryson made his way over to the bar where he ordered a gin and tonic. "Empress 1908 if you have it please."

"We do," one of six bartenders answered. "With lime?"

"No. Thank you."

The bartender smiled. "I agree."

"I was looking for you," a female voice said.

Ryson turned to discover Kelsey Parker standing there. Her hair was up. A large amethyst rested in the hollow of her throat. The skintight red gown fit perfectly. "You are very beautiful," Ryson said.

"And you are very handsome," Kelsey replied.

"We didn't get to see each other following the rescue mission," Ryson said. "I want to thank you. No one runs a ship aground the way you do."

Kelsey laughed, and Ryson liked the sound of it. A voice came from behind him. "Your drink is ready, sir."

Ryson turned to collect his drink and thank the bartender. "Follow me," Kelsey said, as she took control of his free arm. "This is a meet and greet. So, let's get to work."

What followed was a seemingly endless round of introductions to people Ryson didn't want to know, the inevitable questions about how the war was going, and complaints of wartime shortages. None of which were in evidence as waiters made the rounds carrying trays of hors d'oeuvres and glasses of champagne.

Ryson was still nursing the gin and tonic when George Parker emerged from the crowd. "There you are my dear … And who is this chap?"

"Commander Ryson, this is my father George," Kelsey said. The men shook hands.

In spite of his perfectly tailored tux there was something elemental about George Parker. The bushy brows, the prow-like nose, and the thin lips were reminiscent of sea captains from a bygone era. And the shipping magnate's voice was loud enough to hail the masthead lookout during a roaring typhoon. "Ryson is it?" George demanded.

"Admiral Nathan thinks very highly of you. I however, am of a different opinion, since you saw fit to send my daughter into harm's way."

Ryson looked at Kelsey and back to her father. "Is that what she told you, sir?"

George laughed. "I should have known! My daughter has a mind of her own. She comes by it honestly I'm afraid."

The conversation was interrupted by the clang of a ship's bell. "Dinner is being served," Kelsey said. "And you're sitting next to me."

Ryson allowed himself to be led into a vast dining room where he wound up being seated between Kelsey and Admiral Nathan near the head of the table. "Mind the weather," Nathan cautioned sotto voice. "You could be blown ashore."

"I'll keep that in mind," Ryson promised. "Who is the officer seated to Mr. Parker's right?"

"That's General Haskell," Nathan replied darkly. "The man who recently referred to you as 'a sonofabitch.'"

Ryson was about to respond when George Parker stood, and began what turned out to be a long list of toasts. The first of which honored the Allied soldiers, sailors, marines and airmen killed or wounded during the attack on Okinawa, as well as the Japanese citizens who'd lost their lives as well.

That was followed by toasts to the Alliance, individual countries and VIPs, including Haskell. And it was during the latter that Kelsey placed her right hand on Ryson's left thigh. And, as her father spoke, the hand slowly but surely slid up towards his crotch.

Ryson was hard long before the hand arrived at its destination, and made him even harder. Then it became necessary to remove it or run the risk of an embarrassing accident. Kelsey smiled knowingly as she raised her glass to General Haskell.

Dinner was a long grueling affair in which dish after exotic dish arrived at the table, finally culminating with the presentation of three suckling pigs, all of which had spent the day baking in a stone lined pit.

Once the chicken wire that held the meat in place was removed servers moved in to heap roast pork on each plate. It was delicious. And Ryson would have eaten more if he hadn't been so full already.

By the time an elaborate dessert arrived, all Ryson could do was pick at it. Fortunately, Kelsey was schmoozing the businessman at her left, while Admiral Nathan flirted with the forty-something newswoman to his right. An arrangement which left Ryson free to sip coffee and wonder when the torture would end.

The answer was fifteen minutes later when George Parker stood and announced that a fire dance was about to take place on the verandah. That struck Ryson as the perfect moment to slip away. He was about to do so when the family's major domo arrived. "Excuse me gentlemen. Coffee will be served in the library, and General Haskell asks that you join him."

Ryson had a bad feeling about that. But like Admiral Nathan, he couldn't say "no." He turned to say goodbye to Kelsey, only to discover that she was no longer there. Because she knew about the meeting with Haskell? Or because she was expected to be present on the verandah? Either way it would have been nice to say goodbye.

The major domo led the officers back to the reception area, through a decorative door, and into a library that didn't contain any books. Or shelves to put them on. Just a long table and four computer stations which, Ryson assumed, could access a private network and the digital books stored there.

A U-shaped seating area lay beyond. And there, standing with his back to a gas fireplace, was General Haskell. He was holding a cup of coffee which he put down in order to greet the new arrivals. "It's good to see you Alexander," Haskell said, as they shook hands.

"This is Commander Max Ryson," Nathan said. "The man largely responsible for rescuing three American pilots a couple of days ago."

"That was quite a feat," Haskell said. "And one which would have been all over every news network in the free world, if it hadn't been for the attack on Okinawa. I'm sure some sort of recognition will come your way eventually."

Ryson wanted to say that he didn't care about recognition. But Haskell clearly did. So he left the thought unsaid. "Thank you, sir. But the men and women who carried out the ..."

"Yes, yes," Haskell said impatiently. "Credit where credit is due, and all that. I'll leave the awards to you. I'll sign whatever you send me.

"We're not here to talk about attaboys gentlemen," Haskell continued. "We're here to discuss the *Sea Dragon* and how to stop her.

"I asked you to join me so we could have a private conversation prior to the meeting tomorrow. The simple truth is that Squadron 7 is performing well in every category—other than the one that the President of the United States and Australia's Prime Minister are most interested in. And that's the destruction of the *Sea Dragon*.

"No, you aren't in this alone. Surveillance satellites, spy planes, drones and submarines are all searching for the bitch day and night.

"But like an archer with a quiver full of arrows, I don't know which one has the correct profile—just the right heft—to strike the target. And Squadron 7 is one of those arrows. I'm aware of the forward operating base. It's damned expensive. How's that effort going?"

"My XO is there now," Ryson replied. "She tells me that all of our defenses are up and running. Regular patrols will begin soon."

"Good," Haskell said. "So long as 'soon' means tomorrow. But patrols rely on luck. Maybe you run into something. Maybe you don't. What we need is more *humint*."

"I agree," Ryson replied. "And with some help from the Parkers, I think we could assemble a pop-up intelligence network in a very short period of time."

That was news to Admiral Nathan. But Ryson couldn't help it. It was a nascent idea. And far from fully formed. But if he could sell the concept to Haskell the rest would follow.

"I'm listening," Haskell said. "What do you have in mind?"

"Tens of thousands of fishing boats ply the South China Sea," Ryson said. "Not to mention hundreds of interisland steamers and ferries. And between them that's a lot of eyeballs. Thanks to their shipping interests the Parkers know everyone there is to know. And, if they put their network to use, we could harvest the kind of Intel that you need.

"Perhaps some sort of reward should be offered for images of the *Sea Dragon* and the coordinates for where the photos were taken."

"That sort of system would be likely to produce a lot of false positives," Haskell observed. "But a photo taken at the right place and time could make all the difference. What do you think Alexander? I assume you're onboard?"

Nathan cleared his throat. "Yes, or course. But as Commander Ryson indicated, we would need help from the Parkers to pull it off."

Haskell nodded. 'I'll talk to George. Thank you, gentlemen. Please keep the concept under your hats."

"We will," Nathan promised.

"Good. Let's join the rest of them on the verandah."

Haskell left right away which gave the other men an opportunity to talk. Admiral Nathan was pissed. "Why didn't you tell me about the intelligence network *before* the meeting?"

"Because I hadn't thought of it yet," Ryson replied honestly.

Nathan was at least partially mollified. "Well, let's do better next time. It's important for us to be on the same page. Are you going to join the rest of them on the verandah?"

"No," Ryson replied. "I'm going to crash."

Nathan nodded. "I'll see you in the morning."

Ryson took the elevator to the second floor, slipped the key card into the lock, and saw the indicator light turn green.

The lights were dim within. So much so that it took Ryson a moment to see the clothes puddled on the floor, and realize that Kelsey was waiting in his bed. She smiled. "Hello, sailor. It took you long enough to get here. Now strip and come to bed."

***

Ryson awoke on time. And was halfway out of bed when Kelsey pulled him back. "Oh, no you don't!"

What happened next took the better part of twenty minutes. And by the time Ryson had showered, shaved, and put his uniform on, he was fifteen minutes late for Haskell's Command and Control conference. Fortunately, the meeting room was packed with officers and senior enlisted people representing half a dozen Allied countries. And outside of Nathan, who shot him a dirty look, Ryson managed to enter the room largely unnoticed.

Breakfast consisted of a danish and coffee from the back table. The only chairs available were in the back row. It soon became apparent that all of the presentations had one thing in common, and that was the need to find the *Sea Dragon,* and sink her.

And the overall strategy was quite simple. Locate the bitch, try to pin her down, and call for help. The problem was that, depending on the circumstances, it might take hours for help to arrive. Unless the brass hats had something special up their sleeves, that is. Like the satellite-based laser weapon which had been used to destroy the Russian cruiser *Admiral Konev* many months earlier.

But insofar as Ryson knew, Derringer hadn't been used since. He wondered why. And so, as it turned out, did a navy captain from New Zealand. She not only wondered about it but was brave enough to inquire about the weapon's status.

Haskell's face darkened. "Suffice it to say that Derringer was destroyed by a kinetic attack from another space vehicle. I have been assured that more weapons of that sort are coming. But they aren't likely to arrive quickly enough to solve our problem.

"That's top secret of course. But you need to know that, if you get a crack at the *Sea Dragon,* there won't be any bolt of lightning coming down from the sky."

That was depressing, since Ryson had been secretly hoping that the laser weapon *was* in the mix, and might save the day.

The conference ended at noon, a flood of people left the room, and Nathan appeared. "You were late. Overslept I suppose. I expect better."

"As you should," Ryson said contritely. "I apologize."

Nathan might have said more if General Haskell hadn't joined them. "A quick word before you go," Haskell said. "I spoke with George, and he agreed to help us with the matter we discussed last night. His daughter Kelsey will work with you to put the pieces together. I will brief the spooks so they're in the loop. Keep me informed." Then he was gone.

Ryson felt a mild sense of alarm. His relationship with Kelsey was growing ever more complex. It was never a good idea to mix business with pleasure. Yet that was exactly what he was doing. He forced a smile. "Congratulations, sir ... Game on. You must be pleased."

Was that too thick? Would Nathan demur? Nope. The plan had his stink on it now, and he was proud of it. "Yes, of course. It can't hurt, eh what? Well, we need to pack up and get to the airport."

"Yes, sir," Ryson agreed. "But I wondered if you would accompany me on a side jaunt first. Some naval research if you like, that might pay off for us. I took the liberty of making a back-channel appointment."

Nathan's eyebrows rose. "An appointment? With whom? And where?"

"With the captain of the Indonesian patrol boat *Nyai Roro Kidul*, which means *Goddess of the Sea*. She's anchored in the bay."

Nathan eyed him. "You never stop, do you?"

Ryson tried to look innocent. "Stop what, sir?"

"Stop coming up with all sorts of harebrained schemes."

"No, sir. I like to keep my hand in."

"All right," Nathan replied. "But our plane departs at three, and I intend to be on it."

"You will be sir," Ryson assured him. "Let's take our bags so we won't have to return for them."

Thanks to an advance warning from Ryson, Lieutenant Swallow had another four-vehicle convoy waiting when they left the mansion. And after receiving instructions from Ryson, the first Bushmaster's driver led the rest through the downtown business district, into an area dominated by warehouses, and out to the military pier.

The fact that an Australian admiral was about to inspect a lowly patrol boat created quite a stir. Salutes flew as an Indonesian *Letan Satu* (first lieutenant) led the visitors to a smart looking launch. It was too large to belong to the patrol boat and was most likely on loan from a destroyer.

Engines burbled as the forty-footer pulled away from the dock, and began to pick up speed. It was a nice day. And for one brief moment Ryson was enjoying himself as birds wheeled overhead, sunlight glittered on the surface of the bay, and a fisherman waved.

But the moment came to an end as the launch drew alongside the *Nyai Roro Kidul* where the ship's captain was waiting to greet them. "Welcome aboard Admiral ... We don't get very many visitors. Especially those seeking advice regarding torpedoes."

Nathan looked surprised. "Torpedoes?"

"Yes, sir," Ryson said smoothly. "Torpedoes."

"But *why?*" Nathan demanded.

"Because," Ryson replied, "our Armindales are armed with nothing more than an auto cannon and a brace of fifties. Most boats of their size would carry missiles. But it's a bit late for that. By mounting torpedo tubes port and starboard we could give the Armindales some additional punch. The sort of thing that might come in handy if they were to confront a large warship."

"I take your point," Nathan replied. "But torpedo tubes would be so—so ugly! No offense Captain."

The Indonesian smiled. "And none taken."

"I get that," Ryson said. "But please give the idea a chance. Is your gunner's mate available Captain? I'd like to inspect the launchers, and ask some questions."

"Yes. *Sersan Mayor* (Master Chief) Darwis is present. Please allow me to introduce you."

Once the introductions were complete, the captain excused himself, and allowed Darwis take over. As it turned out the ship was equipped with four launchers, with two vertically stacked tubes on each side of the ship, all equipped to fire NATO compatible torpedoes.

The ensuing Q & A session lasted for half an hour. It ended with a question from Nathan. "So, tell me the truth Master Chief... In the final analysis are the torpedoes an asset? Or a pain in the ass?"

Darwis smiled. "That depends, sir. If the target is a long way off then missiles are ideal. But in close? Against a large vessel? Torpedoes are the answer. Especially since our bow-mounted autocannon isn't likely to win that kind of contest on its own."

The officers went ashore shortly thereafter. Ryson wanted to push for an answer where the torpedo launchers were concerned, but managed to restrain himself. Nathan liked to make his own decisions. Or at least have the room to pretend.

The convoy took them to the airport and Ryson slept through most of the flight home. And it wasn't until they were aboard the *Agger* that Nathan broached the subject that was still on Ryson's mind. "Against my better judgement I am going to take the torpedo idea up the chain of command. But it will, I suspect, run aground immediately."

Ryson nodded. "Thank you for trying, sir. May I ask why you believe the concept will face resistance?"

Nathan made a face. "You won't like this. But there are those in senior posts who are, shall we say, a bit out of step with the realities of this war. They may object to the way the Armindales would look were we to hang tubes on them. Please don't take offense, but one admiral said that your hydrofoils, 'Resemble tug boats on skis.'"

Ryson frowned. "You're serious."

"Yes, I am."

Ryson sighed. "I appreciate your honesty, sir. Please let me know how it goes. I'll be leaving for Samir in the morning."

"Good hunting," Nathan said. "Find the bitch, Commander. And put her down."

CHAPTER ELEVEN

Port Moresby, Papua New Guinea

After a lengthy discussion with her father, and a good night's sleep, Kelsey Parker was ready to leave. The first leg of her trip would take Kelsey to the city of Balikpapan, in Borneo, which was about 2,160 miles away. That necessitated a stop for fuel at Kokenau, New Guinea, since the family plane had a factory-built range of just over 1,000 miles plus an auxiliary tank that would provide the aircraft with a sufficient safety margin.

The floating hangar was located in among the Parker family docks, warehouses, and administrative buildings that stood shoulder-to-shoulder along the south shore of the bay. Kelsey's luggage consisted of a beat-up TUMI backpack and an equally disreputable leather briefcase. The bag was home to her laptop, three phones, and a .9mm Glock 26. Because, as her lead bodyguard liked to say, "Shit can happen."

The lead's name was Ronda Chaney. And, as Kelsey entered the hangar, Chaney and her crew were hard at work loading the flying boat with luggage and gear.

The Dornier Seastar was a parasol wing plane, powered by two Pratt & Whitney Canada PT6A-112 engines, both mounted over the wings in a push-pull configuration. Two engines being a must for the sort of long, over-water trips the Parkers made.

Other things that made the plane unique included a fuselage fabricated from composite materials, a low center of gravity, and enough room to carry twelve passengers. Although the Parkers' plane was equipped with only eight seats aft of the cockpit. A configuration that allowed for more legroom, a cramped lavatory, and the cargo compartment located in the tail.

"Good morning, boss," Chaney said. "Let me take that pack."

Chaney was a thirty something ex-marital arts fighter, ex-surfer girl, and ex-wife. And though pretty, Chaney had a tendency to frown all the time, as if there was no reason to expect anything other than the worst.

Her "associates" included six-foot six-inch Larry Howe, aka "The Hulk," and Michael "Pretty Boy" Donnelly.

The flight crew consisted of an ex-airline pilot Candice Wride, who was starting to show some gray, and the only member of the team with a smoking habit.

Her co-pilot was an American named Jeremy Brody, better known as "Spock," due to the vague resemblance. He paused in the middle of his pre-flight walk-around. "I hear Borneo has some great diving."

"It does," Kelsey agreed. "Sipadan Island being the most famous. But you won't be going there. Sorry."

"Bummer," Brody said. "Maybe next time."

"Yeah," Kelsey said unsympathetically. "A guy can always hope."

The third member of the crew was aircraft mechanic Justin Smith, aka "Toolz." A man who could carry out repairs in remote locations, and lend a hand if things got hairy, which they sometimes did.

Once everyone was aboard, and Wride had a clearance, the plane taxied into the bay. There was some chop but nothing the Seastar couldn't handle. The plane took off to the north. Their immediate destination was a bay in the coastal town of Kokenau, New Guinea where they would stop to refuel.

One of the things that Kelsey liked about long trips in the plane was the opportunity to get a lot of work done. There were financial statements to review, insurance policies to renew, and the construction of a new ship to keep an eye on. Never mind wartime shortages and regulations associated with them.

Time flew. And it seemed that only minutes had passed when they landed on the bay fronting Kokenau, and taxied in. Wride, Brody and Toolz took care of the refueling process while Kelsey was left to stretch her legs. There wasn't much to see, and no threats other than swarms of flies, but Chaney was never more than a few steps away.

After a drink in the town's only bar the women returned to the dock. "Here," Kelsey said, as she gave two 6-packs of beer to the Hulk. "Pass 'em around. Who knows where this stuff was brewed. I hope you survive." Those who were close enough to hear laughed.

The plane took off and headed west. Sack lunches were traditionally Brody's responsibility, and a thankless one at that, since no matter what he provided to the crew it was never considered good enough.

As for Kelsey she enjoyed the steak sandwich which was loaded with onions, parsley, tomatoes and a touch of salad dressing. Then she put a sleeping mask on, stuck earbuds in, and closed her eyes. Her thoughts turned to Max Ryson. He was good in bed and scary smart. What more could a girl want? Sleep came quickly.

When Kelsey awoke it was to the sound of Chaney's voice. "We're descending, boss. Time to buckle up."

Kelsey sat up straight and turned to look out the window. Balikpapan was a seaport city located on Borneo's east coast. It was a financial center with busy air and seaports. The city had been established as a fishing village in the 19th century, and fishing still ranked as an important part of the economy, even though the oil industry had eclipsed everything else in terms of overall revenue.

The sun was starting to set. Wride took advantage of what light there was to put the flying boat down, thread her way between the ships anchored in the bay, and taxi to the Balikpapan Seaplane Base. It was a modern facility, with six slips, half of which were occupied.

Brody was the first person to deplane. His duties included securing the mooring lines, or in this case supervising the local dock jockeys, while they secured the mooring lines, and making arrangements to refuel the plane. A task he was expected to complete ASAP in case Kelsey wanted to leave early.

Meanwhile, aft of where Kelsey sat, the bodyguards were drawing straws. Standard operating procedure required one of them to sleep on the plane during the night. A security precaution that had paid off in the past. Howe drew the short straw, and was about to complain, when Chaney put a finger to her lips.

The rest of the party went ashore with duffle bags in hand. All of them were armed. That was illegal of course. But the Parkers had high-priced lawyers everywhere. And a night in jail was preferable to an eternity spent in a coffin. Because like every other big city in the world Balikpapan had its share of criminals.

In keeping with the Parker family's unwritten code Kelsey and her team had been booked into a mid-priced, yet nice hotel, near the company's Balikpapan office.

Once her retinue had checked in Kelsey took them out to dinner at a Japanese restaurant. The same unwritten code that specified staying in mid-priced hotels prevented anyone, Kelsey included, from having more than two alcoholic drinks with the meal.

The entire party was back in the hotel by eight PM. "We'll meet in the lobby at 7:00," Kelsey told them. "I have an appointment at 8:30."

Donnelly and Chaney had rooms adjacent to Kelsey's. And both would be on-call throughout the night. But there was no need.

The night passed peacefully, the group had breakfast in the restaurant off the lobby, and checked out. Two SUVs were waiting outside along with a rep from the rental agency. After searching each vehicle for IEDs and surveillance devices, bodyguards took their places behind the wheel.

One SUV would have been sufficient to move five people. The second was a spare. And, in the case of a car chase, would be used to block pursuers. In keeping with standard operating procedures, a pilot was assigned to each car.

Both SUVs were equipped with nav systems which made it easy to find the Dyak Fishing Company. "Dyak," or "Dayuh" were loose terms for more than 200 riverine and hill-dwelling indigenous subgroups who inhabited the central southern areas of Borneo.

According to company lore, the company's founder Aito Eguchi named his company "Dyak Fishing" as a way to honor the indigenous peoples.

But, according to George Parker, Eguchi knew that a Japanese surname wouldn't fly in the wake of WWII, and chose "Dyak" for marketing purposes. Not that it mattered anymore. The old man was gone now. And his grandson, Milo Eguchi, was in charge.

As the lead SUV arrived in front of the Dyak Company's sleek, modernistic headquarters building, Kelsey was reminded of how successful the enterprise was, in spite of cutthroat competition.

Or had been prior to the war. But now? Kelsey could only imagine that the current situation was a good deal more difficult.

Donnelly got out to open the door for her. "Ronda will go in with me," Kelsey said. "You know the drill."

"The drill" for what was considered to be a low-risk meeting was for Kelsey to take one bodyguard with her, and leave the rest of them with the vehicles.

Kelsey had a small radio in her jacket pocket. And, after a quick radio check, she put it back. Kelsey was wearing an all-white outfit consisting of a waist length jacket, a tee shirt, and peg pants. A pair of red high heels completed the look.

Chaney's black business suit was one size too large for her in order to provide room for a bullet proof vest, two handguns, and backup mags. She was wearing black high-tops which, though covered with glitter, would allow the bodyguard to fight effectively should something bad come their way. She followed Kelsey to the front door which swished out of the way as they approached.

The lobby was cold in contrast to the muggy atmosphere outside. A young man came forward to present his business card. "I am Mr. Eguchi's Executive Assistant, Shiguru Okada. It's a pleasure to meet you."

"And I am Kelsey Parker, Executive Vice President of Parker Shipping."

Okada bowed. "Mr. Eguchi is expecting you. Please inform your bodyguard that her weapons are to remain holstered."

"She knows," Kelsey said. "Thank you."

So, the front door was more than a door. A scanner was built into the frame. And it was Okada's duty to inform Kelsey that the company's security people were watching. Mr. Eguchi could have refused to see her of course ... But nearly every executive Eguchi met with had at least one bodyguard. And no wonder given all of the potential threats.

An elevator whisked the party up to the fifth floor. Okada led his guests to a conference room, showed them inside, and gestured to a side table. It was loaded with western and eastern breakfast items. "Mr. Eguchi will be with you shortly. Please help yourselves."

Kelsey poured a cup of coffee and took it over to a huge picture window. The Dyak docks were immediately below with the busy harbor beyond. The company's boats were white over green. Good luck colors.

But very few of them were in port. Most of Dyak's fleet was out fishing. And Chinese competition was fierce. Estimates put China's pre-war fleet at more than twelve-thousand vessels, fishing in waters all around the world, even as far away as Argentina. And doing so with government subsidies that averaged three hundred and fifty-thousand dollars a year.

That put companies like Dyak at a tremendous disadvantage. And Kelsey couldn't imagine how the war was making things any better. "Hello," a male voice said. "Sorry I'm late."

Kelsey turned to see a middle-aged Japanese businessman in a dark blue suit. They already knew each other, so there was no need to exchange cards.

"I was on the phone with my manager in the UAE," Eguchi said, as he came forward to shake her hand. "Diesel fuel is in short supply as I'm sure you know."

"We do," Kelsey said. "That's why we accept government cargoes at below market prices. The fuel allotments make up for the losses."

"That's clever," Eguchi said. "Very clever. I wish we could do the same. Please, have a seat. I see you have coffee. Can I get you something else?"

"No, thank you," Kelsey replied.

"Then we'll get down to business," Eguchi said. "What brings you to Balikpapan? It's been a while."

"I, which is to say the Alliance, need your help."

"Japan is part of the Alliance, that's true," Eguchi said. "But this is my home. And Borneo is neutral."

"No one is neutral," Kelsey replied. "Every country has a preference, even if they pretend otherwise. And Borneo is no exception."

Eguchi smiled. "It's been twenty-five years since I went to school in Australia. As a result, I tend to forget how direct Aussies can be. There is something to what you say. So, what does the Alliance want from Dyak Fishing? More fish?"

Kelsey smiled. "No. What the Alliance wants is information. Specific information regarding the Chinese cruiser *Sea Dragon*."

Eguchi's expression darkened. "The ship that attacked Okinawa."

"Yes."

"What sort of information?"

"Information about her movements."

"So, you can attack her."

"Exactly. You have boats in the South China Sea. Hundreds of them. Each carrying three or four men. That's a lot of eyeballs."

Eguchi frowned. "Spying for the Alliance would be extremely dangerous. But I will say this … One of my relatives was killed during the attack on Okinawa. And I regard Japan as my second country. How would the reporting system work?"

"Let's say a crew spots what might be the *Sea Dragon*," Kelsey said. "They upload an encrypted photo if they can. And they send their position. Then, if the information results in a successful attack on the *Sea Dragon*, ten million U.S. will mysteriously appear in your bank account. Plus one million for the crew to split."

Eguchi's eyebrows rose. "I like that part. But it would be naïve to think that all of my crews are sympathetic to the Alliance. Plus, more likely than not, some of employees are parttime spies. Reporting everything they see to China."

Kelsey nodded. "I hear you ... Perhaps your security people can do some sorting."

Eguchi nodded. "I think we can come to an arrangement. And—and here's something to seal the deal. Some of my captains tell me that there are days when most of the Chinese fishing fleet remains in port. And those who are in the South China Sea suddenly return home. My people love that, needless to say. But the question is *why?*"

The answer was obvious. When the *Sea Dragon* was going to pass through a particular area the Chinese fishing boats were ordered to remain in port, or return home, lest someone photograph the ghost ship and post pictures online. That would happen eventually, of course. But it appeared that the Chinese government wanted to shroud the cruiser in mystery for as long as possible.

The so-what was that—if the Allies saw China's fishing boats sitting in port, or all returning home at the same time—it might presage an impending cruise by the world's most dangerous ship. And that could be helpful.

"Wow," Kelsey said. "That's interesting. Thank you. I'll pass it along. Someone will contact you to work on logistics. He or she will identify themselves with the code name Kratos."

"Meaning 'strength?'"

"Yes. Because that's what it will take to win."

The meeting came to an end shortly thereafter and the team returned to the Seaplane Base where Howe was waiting for them.

The plane was in the air forty-five minutes later, and westbound to Kelang, Malaysia where they stopped to refuel.

The final leg of the journey took them to Yangon, formerly the city of Rangoon, in Myanmar. It was dark by the time they arrived and checked in. Parker Shipping had an office there, but Kelsey didn't want to advertise her presence, and was happy to order dinner from room service.

Work began shortly after Kelsey got up. Her goal was to find and make contact with a criminal named Mickey Fanon. He was, according to her sources, neither a drug kingpin nor a street dealer. He was a middleman. And that was said to be a profitable slot in the drug dealer ecosystem. Especially in that part of the world.

Myanmar was the world's second largest producer of illicit opium, and had been a major player since WWII. Largely thanks to China, which had forced opium production south into the Golden Triangle, rather than let it flourish inside the country's borders.

Fanon's role was to buy opium from the producers, process it into morphine, and turn the morphine into heroin—large quantities of which were sold to dealers. But like most men and women in his profession Fanon had to move from place-to-place on a frequent basis.

So, Kelsey took her sat phone out onto the balcony. She placed dozens of calls to contacts, and contacts of contacts, before hearing what purported to be Fanon's voice. "This is Mickey. Leave your message at the tone. Beep."

Kelsey was ready. "I represent a group of clients who are willing to pay a large sum of money for certain types of information. Please call me." After providing the long string of numbers required to reach her sat phone, Kelsey broke the connection.

The wait began. Kelsey continued to follow leads as the hours ticked by, but without any luck. Eventually she took a nap, and was sound asleep, when her phone chimed. She rushed onto the balcony. "Yes?"

A male voice read off an address in Mingalor Zay, which he said was in the Mingalor Taung Nyunt Township. That was followed by the words, "Eight tonight." Then a click.

Kelsey eyed her watch. It was a few minutes past five. That wouldn't allow enough time to inspect the meeting place ahead of time. Chaney wouldn't like that.

But Kelsey was determined to make contact with Fanon. By all accounts the middleman ran small boats in and out of ports throughout southeast Asia. And, if she managed to recruit Fanon, his drug runners might be able to provide information about the *Sea Dragon's* whereabouts.

Kelsey called the bodyguards to her room for a briefing. Chaney was adamantly opposed and said so. Kelsey nodded. "Everything you say is true, but we'll have to take the chance."

"Okay," Chaney said reluctantly. "But I want Justin on the team. He can drive and protect our vehicle."

"Agreed," Kelsey said. "Let's gear up and get going."

The decision had been made to use one of the team's two vehicles. The van had seats in the back, but no windows, which was just as well.

Kelsey couldn't see much. But she could catch glimpses through the windshield. Most of the buildings were western in appearance and five or six stories tall. Traffic was heavy. Motorcycles roared as they wove in and out of traffic. A chaotic maze of power, telephone, and TV cables crisscrossed each other thirty feet above the street.

A sickly sun was hanging low in the sky by the time the van passed through the prosperous part of the Taung Nyunt Township, and entered a seedy area dominated by bars, thinly disguised brothels, and dilapidated hotels. Kelsey leaned forward. "Find a place to park, Justin. You know the drill."

Justin Smith was even featured, had dark skin, and was sporting a two-day growth of stubble. He knew that "the drill" meant a spot where it would difficult to block the van in, there was good visibility, and he could pull straight out. "Roger that, boss. Your destination is coming up on the right."

Kelsey was watching as they passed a garish bar called "The Lucky Seven." A couple of what might have been lookouts were lounging out front. They turned to watch as a young woman in a short skirt entered.

A delivery truck pulled out into traffic and Smith wasted no time sliding into the empty parking slot. It was at the end of the block which meant he could pull straight out.

Kelsey had made her way forward by then and was sitting next to Smith. Most of the pedestrians were locals. But she saw Europeans too. Men mostly, looking for sex or drugs. But a scattering of couples were visible too. And that was a good thing if the team was going to fit in. "Okay, Ronda ... We need to split up. What would you suggest?"

"I'll pair with the Hulk," Chaney replied. "And that puts you with Pretty Boy. You'll make a great couple."

Kelsey made a face. "I don't date guys who smell better than I do."

She looked at her watch. "It's 7:45. Let's de-ass the van and enter separately. Mickey is an Australian aborigine. He's about 5'8', and he's got a thing for tropical shirts. According to what I was told he'll have bodyguards with him. Questions? No? All right. Donnelly and I will enter first. The dynamic duo will follow two minutes later. Keep your eyes peeled Toolz ... If you see anything iffy holler."

Each team member was packing a radio, a tiny wireless microphone, and a pair of ear buds. Smith grinned. "No prob, boss lady. I've got this."

Kelsey and Donnelly left the van through the curbside sliding door. Both wore jackets, jeans and sneakers. Kelsey's were red. The first thing Kelsey noticed was the smothering heat. Even though the sun had set, the temperature was still in the mid-eighties.

The second thing Kelsey noticed was the throat clogging smell. Not a single scent, but many odors mixed together, creating a fuggy mix of drifting cigarette smoke, rotting vegetables, human urine, roasted peanuts, and the betel nut juice that both adults and children squirted into the street.

And that was to say nothing of the cacophonous street noise which consisted of motorcycle engines, pop music that drifted out of bars, and the wail of a distant siren. None of that was surprising and the input served to sharpen Kelsey's senses. She was entirely in the moment, with every sense activated, and her mind racing.

Men stared. Why? Because she was a Euro? Because they wanted to fuck her? Or both?

Donnelly pulled the door open. Cool air waited to greet her. The lighting was dim. Tables occupied the area in front of her. A bar ran down the righthand wall. People turned to look. Some stared. Others lost interest. *Fanon.* Where was Fanon? Was it some sort of trap?

Donnelly placed a hand on Kelsey's back, as if to guide her, and she shook it off. Only a few of the empty tables had been bussed. Kelsey chose to sit with her back to the wall with a glowing "7" mounted on it. A position that would enable her to watch the front door.

So Donnelly sat with his back to the front door which gave him a view of the "7" and the exit located next to it. Between them they had both points of entry-egress covered.

Kelsey watched Chaney and Howe enter, look around, and take a table near the entrance. She eyed her watch. It was 8:03. Fanon was nowhere to be seen.

Kelsey scanned the room for security cameras but didn't see any. Maybe that was one of the reasons why Fanon liked the place. There might be hidden cams of course. That was a chance she'd have to take.

A teenage waitress arrived. She was wearing too much makeup and not enough clothes. Her English was rough but serviceable. "What you want?"

Donnelly was the team's beer snob. "Two beers. Myanmar Black Shield please."

Like most females the girl had eyes only for Donnelly. "You bet. Any else?"

"Nope," Pretty Boy said. "That will do it. But make them cold please. *Real* cold."

"So, you've had Black Shield before?" Kelsey inquired.

"Never. But I did my research," Donnelly said. "And according ..."

"There he is," Kelsey interrupted. "Coming in the front door. He has one, two, three, four, five people with him. Four men and a woman. I think she's arm candy rather than a shooter. But hey, you never know."

There was a stir as waiters hurried to bus a large table and Fanon sat down. A pair of reflective sunglasses were parked above the drug dealer's forehead. His eyes scanned the room; they found Kelsey and stopped. Did Fanon know who she was? Or was he guessing?

Kelsey stood and made her way over. "Mr. Fanon? I'm the woman who left the message. Can we talk?"

Fanon looked her up and down as if inspecting a side of beef. He had an Australian accent. "Sure, sweet stuff. We can talk, and you can take a ride on my stiffy. Have a seat."

Fanon's girlfriend had to move in order for Kelsey to sit down, and was far from pleased. Kelsey had just settled into the empty chair, and was getting ready to make her pitch, when Smith spoke into her ear. "Six, repeat, six armed men just arrived. And they're headed for the front door."

"Get down!" Chaney ordered. "We'll form on Donnelly and exit through the back."

"Two men entering through the back," Donnelly warned. "I see a gun!"

Then the shooting began. Fanon was the target. Kelsey scrabbled across the floor, as the gunmen entered from the street, and opened fire. Two of Fanon's bodyguards and his girlfriend jerked spastically as bullets struck them.

Fanon was on his knees, returning fire with a pistol, as his surviving bodyguards did the same. Then Chaney joined the battle, along with Howe. And their fire sent the attackers diving for cover.

Kelsey had the baby Glock in her right hand, and was aiming at the men at the back of the room. They were firing at Chaney and Howe by then. But not for long as both Kelsey and Donnelly opened fire. The gunmen were caught by surprise.

Kelsey saw blood spray as her bullets tore through a man's throat. He stumbled backwards, fell, and hit the floor hard. Thanks to Donnelly his buddy was down too. The body jerked as Pretty Boy shot him again.

The other battle was still underway. And as Kelsey turned in that direction, she saw bodies sprawled all about. Fanon was wounded, but on his feet and firing when a bullet struck his head. Gore flew and his body toppled.

Two of the invading gunmen were still vertical and one was armed with a machine pistol. The auto fire forced Chaney and Howe to duck as bullets tore splinters out of their table. That was when Smith entered the bar with the 12-gauge leveled in front of him. He fired one barrel, followed by the other, killing both men instantly.

Then, like a duck hunter in the field, Toolz broke the weapon open. Shook two empties onto the floor, and replaced them. "Anybody need a ride?"

***

The island of Samir, in the South China Sea

The PHM *Arcus* was roughly a hundred miles north of Samir Island, on foil, and making a good 47 knots. Ryson was on the bridge along with the boat's skipper Charlie Moy, and the duty helmsman. That meant the boat was burning about one-thousand gallons of fuel per hour. And given the fourteen-thousand gallons of fuel left in the boat's tanks it was necessary to be careful. The goal was to catch up with a radar blip generally referred to as "Asshole," as in "Look at that asshole run." And the distance was closing.

It was hard to know what kind of target they were onto, other than the fact that it was fast, which suggested a Chinese Type 22 missile boat. They were, according to data retrieved by the CIC, about 140 feet long—making them comparable to the *Arcus* in terms of size.

If the enemy vessel was a Type 22, it was similar in another way as well, because she was armed with eight anti-ship missiles. Three of which had already been fired at the *Arcus* over the last half hour, and lured away by the infrared decoys launched from the hydrofoil's Mark 36 mortars.

The *"Arc"* could have answered with Harpoon missiles, and it might come to that, but Ryson had hopes of something else. He wanted to catch up with the Chinese boat and board it. Because maybe, just maybe, the *Asshole* was carrying intelligence that could help the Allies locate the *Sea Dragon.*

"We're closing," Moy said, and that was true. The *Arcus* was doing 52 knots at that point, while the enemy vessel was making forty. So, the hydrofoil should win. But the Spratly Islands were to the north, as was the Mischief Reef air base.

How long would it be before Chinese fighters arrived? Not long, Ryson reasoned. And that's why the *Arc's* Stinger missile teams were on-deck and prepared to engage.

"Contact!" a lookout shouted. "Off the port bow at ten o'clock!"

Ryson brought his binoculars up for a look. The enemy vessel was stern-on at first. But then it turned and came straight at them. And yes, she was a Type 22. White water curled away from the ship's bow and formed waves.

Ryson lowered the binoculars and turned to Lieutenant Commander Moy. "Destroy the bow gun, but don't sink her unless you have to. The rest is up to you."

That was the right thing to say, even if Ryson was dying to take command. Moy nodded. "Aye, aye, sir. Hang on."

"We are about to engage," Moy announced over the intercom. "We will run straight in, swing to port, and pass within three-thousand feet of the enemy. At that time Stinger 1 will fire on the enemy's bow gun. If that effort fails, Team 2 will take a shot. The objective is to capture the boat, not sink her."

Ryson was impressed. Moy was thinking out of the box. Though intended for airborne targets, there was no reason why the new FIM-92As couldn't be used against surface targets—so long as they had an IR source to home on—and the target was more than 660 feet away.

But what would the infrared seeking missile go for? The bow gun? Or some other part of the boat? Moy was betting on the gun.

Puffs of gray smoke appeared as the autocannon mounted on the missile boat's bow began to fire. Geysers of water leapt into the air as Moy responded in kind. "Keep it high," Moy cautioned. "Above the waterline."

"Standby for a sweeping turn to port," Moy said. "Turn."

What happened next depended on the helmsman. When foil-borne the PHMs "flew" via ACS, or Automatic Control System, which relied on computers, gyros and accelerometers to steer the boat. So, when headed for a specific point, an island for example, it was a simple matter of entering the proper coordinates and letting the ACS do its thing.

But close-quarters combat was different. The helmsman *had* to intervene and there were no coordinates to enter. So as the *Arcus* entered a sweeping turn, and the deck began to tilt, Ryson knew that the petty officer was battling the ACS for control. And successfully too, judging from the smooth ride.

"The gun will cease firing," Moy said. "the Stinger teams will standby. Fire when ready."

The boats were going to pass each other in a few seconds. That meant Team 1's operator would have a very short amount of time in which to react. And, if her missile missed, Team 2 would have to wait their turn. Ryson held his breath, as the boats opened fire on each other with small arms, and the first Stinger took off.

It was impossible to say whether what happened next was the result of luck or skill. The Type 22 fired chaff, the Stinger was drawn off target, and exploded in the air.

Moy was unperturbed. "Give me a turn to starboard. Team 2 will fire when ready."

Ryson felt the *Arcus* skid into the turn. The PHM rounded the Type 22's stern and surged forward. The second Stinger flew straight and true. There was a bright flash as the missile hit the Chinese turret, followed by a loud boom.

The enemy vessel slowed, but didn't stop. Moy gave orders to go hullborne lest the *Arcus* pass the enemy vessel. The hydrofoil lost speed and made a smooth transition, as the helmsman matched speeds. "Well done," Ryson said. "Suppress fire and put us alongside."

The *Arc's* starboard fifty thumped as lighter weapons chattered. Meanwhile the Chief Bosun's Mate gave orders for his people to "Drop fenders, prepare grappling hooks, and get ready to fight."

Commands like that had been common 250 years earlier, but were seldom heard anymore. Ryson's pistol was ready as was the Benelli M4 semi-automatic shotgun. A look of alarm appeared on Moy's face as Ryson prepared to depart the bridge. "Your place is here, sir."

"That's bullshit," Ryson replied. "There's nothing for me to do here. Keep an eye on the sky, Charlie... We're well within range of Mischief Reef, and you know what that means."

The rate of reciprocal fire increased as the distance between the ships decreased. Someone called for a corpsman, and fenders gave, as the vessels made contact.

Ryson was outside by then. Bullets pinged off metal as a Chinese sailor shot at him. There was a prodigious boom when Ryson fired the Benelli. At least half the load of 00 Buck struck the sailor's chest and threw him back. Blood splattered the Type 22's superstructure.

Ryson jumped down onto the main deck where lines and grappling hooks bound the ships together. A Chinese sailor was sawing on a rope with a sheath knife when the *Arc's* XO shot him. "We'll have none of that," she said crossly. "Follow me!" And with that she jumped the gap between the vessels only to be killed by a sailor swinging a fire ax.

Ryson fired another blast, made his way across, and came face-to face with an officer. A blow from the shotgun's butt broke the man's jaw and an American sailor finished the job.

"Find their CIC!" Ryson ordered. "And check the bridge. I want charts, binders, laptops, phones, and the command-and-control computers. Cut the cables. We don't have time to fuck around."

An announcement from Moy served to underline the order. "Two, repeat two, enemy aircraft inbound from the northeast. Prepare to engage."

Ryson was in the Chinese CIC by then. Two sailors were dumping items into bins. What would the Chinese fighter pilots do? Ryson wondered. Would they fire on *both* ships? Or would they hold off? Ryson was hoping for the latter, as he pulled a handful of binders off a shelf, and dumped them into a box.

There were Chinese holdouts in the stern. And Ryson could hear sporadic gunshots, as he slung the shotgun, and carried the box out to the point where willing arms waited to receive it.

The Combat Systems Officer was in charge of document/computer retrieval. His name was Cassidy, and he'd been hit, judging from the bandage on his left arm. "I think we're in good shape, sir. Unless you want us to search the engine room."

"No," Ryson replied. "That won't be necessary. Get your people off. Be sure to count heads."

"Aye, aye sir," Cassidy replied. "Or, we could take the 22 with us."

The thought hadn't occurred to Ryson. But why not? Odds were that the Intel people would love to strip search a Type 22.

"That's a good idea, Lieutenant. Assuming that we are in full control of the boat. Belay the first order, and get me a sitrep."

Jet engines screamed as a Chinese Chengdu J-20 fighter swept over the boats. It didn't fire on them however. And that was a blessing.

Once aboard the *Arcus* Ryson went straight to the bridge. He arrived in time to see a Stinger crew send a missile after the Chengdu. It failed to catch up and had to self-destruct. "Single up the lines," Ryson ordered. "And prepare to break contact. Cassidy is checking the feasibility of taking the 22 with us."

Moy looked surprised. "Yes, sir."

Engines roared as the second Chengdu passed overhead. Then Cassidy spoke in his ear. "This is Seadog Four-Four. Eleven enemy personnel were killed in the fighting. Four are alive. Both engines are operational, and she responds to the helm. Over."

Ryson looked at Moy who shrugged. "This is Six," Ryson replied. "How many personnel do you have? And how many do you need? Over."

"I have six," Cassidy replied. "I have a corpsman. Send me an EN (Engineman) and an ET. I'll put two deckhands back on the *Arcus*. Over."

"Done," Ryson replied. "And I'll send Stinger Team 2 as well. Keep those prisoners under lock and key. Do you read me? Over."

"Five-by-Five sir. Over."

The jets circled as personnel went back and forth between the two vessels. Then the Chief Bosun's mate and a deck ape severed the remaining lines.

That was a good thing and a bad thing. Good, because Moy's crew had what they'd been ordered to get. And bad, because the Chinese fighter pilots had no further reason to withhold fire.

The jets circled wide as they prepared to attack. "Take evasive action," Moy ordered. "Prepare to fire chaff. Prepare to fire missiles."

Ryson figured that, since the jet jockeys didn't know the 22 had been captured, they would leave it alone. For the moment anyway. All he could do was grit his teeth and wait. Moy had done an excellent job so far, and it was his responsibility to defend the boat.

The *Arcus* was on foil by then, "flying" south at top speed, and leaving the 22 to fend for itself. The theory being that the pilots would assume it remained under Chinese control.

Ryson stood with feet spread so he could shift his weight back and forth to accommodate the evasive maneuvers that the helmsman was putting the PHM through. "Fire chaff," Moy said laconically, as a jet chased them. "Fire missiles when ready."

Moy's timing was excellent. The Chengdu fired two missiles. Chaff drew one of them away while the other exploded short of the hydrofoil's stern.

A Stinger missile lanced upwards, found its target, and exploded. Chunks of flaming wreckage cartwheeled through the air. They were still spinning when the second fighter flew through the cloud of debris.

The Chengdu seemed to shudder as a piece of wreckage was sucked into the port engine. Perhaps some fan blades were broken. Or maybe it was something else. But whatever the cause, a trail of black smoke followed the plane as the pilot turned north towards Mischief Reef. A reedy cheer went up. *Luck*, Ryson mused. *So much of war is luck.*

His thoughts were interrupted as one of the ETs spoke over the intercom. "Forward Operating Base Samir is under attack! They're requesting assistance!"

CHAPTER TWELVE

The Ang Nam Ngum Reservoir, Laos

Mickey Fanon was dead. Shot down in the Lucky 7 bar. Which, on reflection, was the worst shit show Kelsey had ever been part of. She and her team had survived untouched. But an opportunity to expand the Allied intelligence network had been lost.

And after stopping at the hotel, the team had gone straight to the plane where the pilots were waiting. The Seastar took off shortly thereafter and made a beeline for Laos. The sun rose two hours later.

Candy Wride turned the Dornier Seastar floatplane south over a broad expanse of sparkling blue water. The vast one hundred and fifty-five square mile Ang Nam Ngum Reservoir was located more than fifty miles north of the capital city of Vientiane. And, because the Vietnamese city of Da Nang was eight hundred and three miles to the east, Wride wanted to refuel.

As Kelsey stared out the window to her left, she saw azure water, green clad islands, and tiny fishing boats. It was all very beautiful. But her mind was focused on a woman in the Vietnamese port city of Da Nang.

According to what she'd been told, Madam Bian Nguyen had been a successful human trafficker prior to the war. Just one of the traffickers who smuggled an estimated eighteen thousand Vietnamese into Europe each year.

However, profitable though the business was, it all but dried up once the war began. But Nguyen was a resourceful woman. So, rather than sit around and bemoan her losses, Nguyen turned to smuggling cigarettes.

It was a well-established profession and a profitable one. Forty-five percent of the Vietnamese population were smokers. And because legal cigarettes were subject to an import tax of more than 100 percent, smokers had every reason to look for less expensive alternatives.

In fact, the black-market cigarette trade was so pervasive, that the government was losing an estimated 360 million Vietnamese dong every year.

Most of the tax-free coffin nails were being smuggled in from the Philippines, which was a net exporter of tobacco products, and only a hop, skip and a jump away. That's where things got interesting.

Kelsey felt a gentle thump as Wride put the plane down, and taxied toward the dilapidated dock where a pink float plane was moored. It had been red at one time. But that was before decades spent baking in the sun. A fuel pump was located near the plane.

As the Seastar got closer Kelsey saw a sign that read: "Joe's Air Tours." Not the fanciest logo—but clear enough. The reservoir was a tourist destination. Or had been prior to the war. And, by hiring a float plane, visitors could sample the best resorts, beaches and scenic vistas in a matter of hours.

Wride brought the plane in next to the floating dock. Brody hopped out to tie up. "I'm going to visit with Joe," Wride announced. "And buy some fuel. I'm guessing he has some overpriced refreshments for sale if you're thirsty."

All of them wanted to stretch their legs, Kelsey included. She followed the pilots to the ramshackle building which clearly served as both a home and office.

A screen door opened into a messy room with no AC other than a fan. It was furnished with mismatched furniture and what appeared to be a brand-new refrigerator.

The man in the swivel chair had thin hair, a red nose, and a noticeable paunch. "Well, well. Will wonders never cease? Candy Wride. A stripper's name if I ever heard one. How 'bout a lap dance?"

"How 'bout some fuel?" Wride replied. "Assuming it's any good."

"I use it," Joe answered, as if that was all she needed to know. "I like your play pretty. What is that? A Dornier?"

"Yes."

"That's a nice one, that is. Where you headed?"

"Hanoi," Wride lied.

"Sure, you are," Joe said cynically. "Well, wherever you're going, be careful. I took a trip east last week, and a Chengdu J-7 buzzed me. The pilot spoke perfect English, and wanted me to provide a clearance code, or land on the nearest pond."

Vietnam was officially neutral but had been forced to let the Chinese air force use its airspace. Kelsey frowned. *"And?"*

Joe swiveled his gaze. "Who's this? She's pretty hot."

"She's my boss," Wride said, as she lit a cigarette.

"Okay then, here's what happened. My passenger, a man who shall remain nameless, gave me a code and the J-7 went away."

Joe riffled through the stuff next to him, found what he was looking for, and gave a slip of paper to Wride. "There you go, sweet buns. Maybe it's still good, and maybe it isn't."

"That's nice of you," Kelsey said. "But *why?*"

"Cynics," Joe replied. "They're everywhere. This may surprise you baby cakes, but I was forty pounds lighter back in the day, and I had all of my hair. Candy and I, well, we ran into each other in Sydney one night—and the rest is history."

Wride blew a column of smoke into the air. "*Old* history."

Joe laughed. "Pump your gas ladies. And no, I don't clean windshields."

They were back in the air forty-five minutes later. Wride was careful to check in with VATM (Vietnam Air Traffic Management) because, with the exception of Chinese planes, which could come and go as they pleased, the Vietnamese kept a tight grip on their airspace.

The sun was up and the weather was clear. But what would have otherwise been an enjoyable trip was marred by the possibility that a Chinese fighter jet would appear out of nowhere and interfere with the flight.

Fortunately, the Seastar was allowed to reach Da Nang unimpeded. And Kelsey felt a sense of relief as the Port of Da Nang appeared. Parker family ships came and went from the harbor all the time. And some had been under her command in years past.

Before the war the port had handled more than 2.7 million tons of cargo. Not counting black market cigarettes that is.

Of course, it was highly unlikely that Madam Nguyen would try to bring her illicit cargos into a port like Da Nang, which was crawling with customs officials. No, with over two thousand miles of coastline available to the smuggler, she would land her cigarettes on deserted beaches, or in tiny fishing villages—where some of the locals were on her payroll.

Merchant ships of every possible description flashed past both sides of the plane as Wride brought it in for a landing. Once on the water Wride had to thread her way between ships, modern junks, and navy vessels to reach the "Happy" seaplane base. It consisted of a floating dock, a barge with a prefab repair facility, and a crane large enough to pluck a plane out of the water.

After being guided into a slip, it was time to tie up and unload. Brody was assigned to stay with the plane. Everyone else carried their bags up two flights of switch backing stairs to a waterfront street where two black SUVs were waiting.

After accepting the keys to both, and tipping the rental car employees, Chaney assigned Smith to drive the second vehicle. Their hotel was located about five miles away, on the west side of the bay, near a marine terminal. And that's where the company's agent was waiting to meet them. His name was Tony Chin. And, in keeping with the Parker family's executive dress code, he was wearing a dark suit and well-polished oxfords.

Kelsey knew him and they shook hands. "Hi Tony, how's the wife? Has she divorced you yet?"

Chin grinned. "Nope. We're still on our honeymoon. It's my mother she wants to divorce."

Kelsey laughed. "I suggest that you side with your wife."

Chin nodded. "I agree."

"So, what's the situation? Are we still locked in with Madam Nguyen?"

"You are," Chin replied. "After the war ends, Nguyen wants to smuggle people again. And she thinks the Parker family could be useful in that regard."

"We don't smuggle people," Kelsey said flatly.

"I know that," Chin replied. "But Madam Nguyen doesn't. And why enlighten her prematurely?" The words were accompanied by a boyish grin.

Kelsey couldn't help but smile in return. "Of course. Why indeed?"

After checking in, and taking a shower, there was barely enough time to get dressed and meet Chaney in the lobby. A single bodyguard. That, according to Chin, was all Madam Nguyen would allow.

But Chin saw no reason for concern. "Nguyen wants to form a positive relationship with you," the agent said. "And violence isn't her style. She pays customs officials. She pays members of the National Assembly. She pays members of the judiciary, and she might pay the Prime Minister for all I know.

"That said, she's often referred to as the Mama Mamba for a reason. By all accounts Nguyen will drop the hammer when she thinks it's necessary."

Cheney was already present when Kelsey arrived in the lobby. The dinner invitation specified "Resort wear. Nothing American."

Kelsey wasn't sure what qualified as "American," but felt sure that Chaney's black bolero jacket and matching pencil pants would make the cut. Kelsey had chosen to wear a wrinkle proof red cocktail dress with matching high heels.

Chin was dressed in the same suit he'd worn earlier. "This is Miss Luu," Chin said, as he introduced a bespectacled young woman in a nondescript business suit. "Miss Luu is Madam Nguyen's secretary."

Luu bowed. Her English was perfect. "It's a pleasure to meet you. Madam Nguyen sends her respects. Dinner will be served aboard the *Water Lilly*. A car is waiting. Please follow me."

The light was fading by then and the city's lights were coming on. The car was a roomy Mercedes S-Class sedan. The interior smelled of leather and the faint scent of water lilies.

A short drive took them to a parking lot and a flight of stairs leading down to a concrete pier and floating dock. There, idling next to dock, was a gleaming Chris Craft.

The boat had a bench style seat upfront, an engine compartment behind that, and another seat in the stern. The exhausts produced the classic burbling sound that Chris Craft owners love.

Chin and Luu sat next to the helmsman, leaving Chaney and Kelsey to occupy the back seat, which was quite comfortable. The soft night air pressed against Kelsey's face as the launch surged out into the harbor.

Ryson came to mind for some reason. What if they were together? What would life with him be like? *Both of us have strong personalities*, Kelsey mused. *But maybe we could work it out.*

Chin shouted something and pointed. And there, up ahead, was a beautiful Chinese junk. The real thing? From days gone by? *No*, Kelsey decided. She was looking at a modern interpretation of the historic boats. The *Water Lily* had three masts. A short mast in the bow, a mainmast forward of the cabin, and a lesser stick in the stern.

Having grown up in a seagoing family, and traveled widely as a child, Kelsey was well acquainted with junks. What made the design unique were lugsails battened with strips of bamboo, and typically supported by a yardarm, roughly two-thirds of the way up whichever mast they served. Bamboo battens kept the sails flat even in high winds, which allowed the ships to tack at angles that surprised Europeans when they first arrived in East Asia.

Furthermore, the design meant that Chinese sailors could climb the battens without resorting to the use of the ratlines found on western sailing ships. And thanks to the shape of their hulls, all but the largest junks could be poled through shallow water, or propelled with oars if necessary.

Nguyen's yacht was moored to a buoy and hung with strings of white lights. A crewman was waiting to help passengers up out of the launch onto a landing stage. Three steps led to the main deck where Madam Nguyen stood waiting.

The smuggler was taller than most Vietnamese women, rail thin, and beautiful in a floral ao dai tunic and pants. Her hair was black with a single streak of white. And thanks to some skillful plastic surgery, plus regular injections of Botox, not a single wrinkle could be seen on her face.

When Nguyen offered her hand, Kelsey felt as though she was holding a bundle of fragile twigs. "Ms. Parker," Nguyen said. "This is an honor. Welcome aboard the *Water Lily.*"

Kelsey bowed. "Thank you for inviting us. The *Water Lily* is stunning. Please accept a small gift from my father and myself."

That was when Chin stepped forward to offer a box. As with so many things, the agent had anticipated the need for a gift, and ordered it a week earlier.

Madam Nguyen opened the box and there, nestled in blue silk, was a beautifully executed model of the *Water Lily*. A look of delight appeared on her face. "It's beautiful! I will keep it on my desk where I will see it every day."

Kelsey glanced at Chin and saw him wink. The evening was off to a good start. Kelsey and Madam Nguyen made small talk as they entered a cabin where a well-set table was waiting.

Once seated the food began to arrive, and there was a lot of it. Ten courses to be exact. Five were served in bowls, like the fried fish belly. And five on plates, like the boiled duck. That was to say nothing of side dishes.

Kelsey ate small quantities of each dish, slurped her noodles, and was careful to eat all her rice. Because, according to Vietnamese tradition, to leave some uneaten would be regarded as wasteful.

Finally, it was time to retire to the lounge, and talk business. "You have a proposal," Madam Nguyen said. "I look forward to hearing it."

The deal that Kelsey put forward was identical to the one made to Milo Eguchi. Ten million dollars for Nguyen, plus a million for whatever employee, or group of employees, spotted the Chinese cruiser *Sea Dragon* and reported her position. "I know you are in the import-export business," Kelsey said tactfully.

"And therefore, employ a small fleet of boats that come and go as needed. Any one of them could provide a nice windfall."

Nguyen sipped her wine. "And if the Chinese find out?"

Kelsey shrugged. "That would be a bad thing. But I assume you choose your crews with care. And have ways to ensure their loyalty. Plus, all they'd have to do is send the coordinates. Nothing more would be expected of them. So, it's very unlikely that the Chinese will be able to intercept such a short transmission, make sense of it, and identify the source."

"You're an excellent saleswoman," Nguyen said. "Let me know if you get tired of working for your father. I will consult with my staff and get back to you."

The business meeting was over. But the get-together lasted for another half hour. Then, after goodbyes had been said, the visitors were taken back to the point where the Mercedes was waiting. Kelsey was dog tired.

After reaching her bed Kelsey expected to crash. But sleep refused to come. Because the most important part of her trip, the part her father cared about more than anything, was still undone. And that was to finalize the arrangements required to rescue her half-sister Rong Parker from a Chinese prison.

***

Aboard the *Arcus*, north of Samir Island, the South China Sea

The PHM *Arcus* was foilborne and going full tilt. Having boarded a Chinese missile boat, and searched the vessel for intelligence, the American crew was faced with an additional crisis.

According to Ryson's XO, Lieutenant Commander Linda Vos, Samir was under attack by Chinese planes and surface vessels. She'd been in touch with the United States Indo-Pacific

Command and they were sending fighters from Manado. The closest naval units were Squadron 7's *Arcus*, which was about an hour away, and the HMAS *Kalbarri* which was two hours out.

That meant Vos and Squadron 7 personnel were on their own for the moment. Ryson was standing in the *"Arc's"* CIC. And, thanks to a drone and satellite link, Ryson could see what was taking place on Samir. It wasn't pretty. An Armindale had been hit, and was on fire. A column of black smoke rose to mark the center of the lagoon.

Half a mile out to sea two Chinese ships were visible. The larger of the two was a corvette. It was bow-on to the island and firing an automatic cannon. Ryson could see geysers of dirt and sand leap into the air as high explosive shells marched across the island.

Ryson felt a wave of guilt. He was the one who had put people on Samir. And the Chinese saw it as a threat. One they were determined to eliminate.

The good news was that both the C-RAM and the Tor missile system were still up and running. Yes, it was obvious that one enemy missile had been able to penetrate the Tor's protective shield, but no defensive system was likely to be 100 percent effective.

As for the threat from above—the air attack had let up. "The Chinese fighters are still here," Vos's radioman volunteered. "But they're flying circles around us just out of range."

Ryson's attention was centered on the corvette. The PHM's Combat Systems Officer Molly Jayson stood next to him. "Let's take the corvette out," he said. "Ask the skipper for permission." The request was little more than a formality and permission was granted.

Jayson gave the order and two Harpoon missiles leaped into the air and flew downrange. The Chinese ship was well within the missiles' one-hundred-and-fifty-mile range, and the weapons were traveling at five hundred mph when they hit the enemy vessel's bow and stern.

What happened next was a sight to see. There were two fiery red explosions. One forward of the superstructure and one aft of it. Then, in what looked like slow motion, the ship broke into three sections. The middle portion of the ship went down first. Quickly followed by the stern. Debris bobbed. And sailors, perhaps a dozen, were thrashing about.

The bow remained partially afloat with the prow pointed at the sky. The stick figure which had been clinging to it splashed into the water. *You can do this Linda*, Ryson thought. *Stop those bastards.*

***

Samir Island, the South China Sea

Lieutenant Commander Linda Vos peered through her binoculars and smiled as the Harpoon missiles hit the corvette. *Thank you, Commander Ryson*, she thought, as most of the warship sank.

Her Armindale, the *Perth*, had been destroyed by an air launched missile. One officer and three Australian sailors were killed. She would grieve for them later. The battle wasn't over.

Vos could see movement through the smoke pouring up from the *Perth*. The Chinese Landing Craft Air Cushion (LCAC) was about to enter the lagoon. It was big, ugly, and shaped like a barge.

The concept was simple. By trapping a cushion of air beneath itself an LCAC could skim the surface of the sea while propeller-like fans drove it forward. And, when once the landing craft hit a beach, it could slide part way up and out of the water. That made LCACs perfect for landing troops and vehicles.

What looked like the front of a modern railroad engine was positioned forward on the vessel's port side. Two bulky gas turbine engines were mounted behind it. A stubby radar mast was located in the stern. It sported a Chinese flag that whipped in the wind.

A boxcar shaped structure occupied the opposite side of the hydrofoil with two additional engines located aft of it. The cargo area between the islands was packed with Chinese soldiers and crates of *what*? Ammo, that's what. Plus, everything they would need for staying on Samir once the battle was won.

LCACs were notoriously noisy as turbine engines roared, spray flew every which way, and windshield wipers slapped back and forth in a futile attempt to keep the craftmaster's viewscreen clear. Top mounted machine guns opened fire on the beach. Vos spoke into her boom mike. "Hold your fire … Wait for my order. Then we'll give them everything we have."

***

Aboard the *Arcus*, north of Samir Island, the South China Sea

Ryson could hear every word Vos said. And though moved by the XO's bravery, he knew the Chinese were going to win. And there wasn't a damned thing he could do about it. Or was there? "Put me through to Commander Vos," Ryson ordered.

"The mike's hot," an ET replied.

The hovercraft was entering the lagoon by then. Vos and her people were firing at it. "Seadog-Six to Seadog-Five. Order the C-RAM and Tor System operators to shut their radars down. *Do it now*! Over."

***

Samir Island, the South China Sea

Vos was taken aback. Ryson's order came out of nowhere, and didn't make any sense. Shut the radars off? What the hell... Chinese planes were circling. And the Tor system was keeping them at bay. Had Ryson lost his mind?

But then it came to her. Harpoon missiles were designed to home in on active radar terminals. And, if *her* radars were off, the only radar the missiles would go for was mounted on the hovercraft! She issued the necessary orders followed by an emphatic, "No questions! Do it. And take cover. Harpoon missiles are inbound. Over."

The sailors barely had time to shut the radars down and take cover before the Harpoons arrived. One would have been enough. But Ryson sent two.

They struck the LCAC like bolts of lightning. The fiery blasts overlapped each other and were followed by secondary explosions—as crates of ammo went off—and chunks of debris were hurled high into the air. Fiery bits and pieces twirled as they fell, each trailing a wisp of smoke, before hissing into the lagoon.

Now two wrecks marked the center of the lagoon. That would make entering the bay more hazardous. But Vos didn't care. She was alive as were most of her sailors. "Turn the radars on," she ordered. "Treat the wounded. And keep an eye peeled for Chinese sailors. I expect some are ashore by now. Over."

***

The *Arcus* arrived half an hour later. Followed by the Type 22 an hour after that.

Tendrils of smoke continued to rise from the wrecks and buildings damaged by cannon fire. Graves were being dug for Allied personnel. Including one for Maggie Farley, Moy's XO. The Chinese bodies were laid side-by-side in a trench. All forty-six of them.

Enemy causalities were higher than that. But the bodies that had gone down with the corvette would never be recovered. Nor would those of troops literally blown to bits. Ryson went ashore in a RIB boat. Vos was waiting. "Welcome back, sir. It's good to see you."

"And *you*," Ryson said. "That was a close call." He looked at the sky. "Where are the Chinese fighters?"

"They went home," Vos replied. "But it isn't over."

"No," Ryson agreed grimly. "It isn't over."

***

Aboard the Parker family plane, south of Hainan, China

After a smooth takeoff from Da Nang, Wride had turned north toward the Chinese island of Hainan, which was home to a very important naval base. And missile batteries that could easily blow the seaplane out of the sky.

To prevent that from happening Wride turned the plane's regular transponder off, and turned the Chinese transponder *on*, thereby making the plane visible to the Chinese air traffic control system.

Then she activated the Chinese army Identification Friend or Foe (IFF) system which should keep enemy fighters from shooting the Seastar down. The system had been effective in the past, and would hopefully work again.

Wride didn't know *why* Kelsey Parker made trips to the Chinese city of Macau. And didn't want to know. Because it didn't take a genius to realize that something shady was taking place. Would a protestation of ignorance be enough to protect Wride, if Allied intelligence landed on the Parker family? No. But not knowing the details made Wride feel better inside. And that, insofar as the pilot could tell, was the way the rest of the team handled the situation as well.

As for *why*, the answer was simple. The Parker family was paying Wride two hundred thou a year, that's why. With most of the money going to her retirement fund.

The interrogatory from the Chinese Air Traffic Control system came seconds later. Wride gave them a code along with the plane's tail number. Five seconds passed, followed by a cheerful, "Roger that. Have a nice day."

***

After a nearly sleepless night Kelsey had boarded the seaplane feeling tired and scared. That was the way she always felt when forced to enter China. Her "handler" was a Ministry of State Security agent named Wei Ching. And if he called, Kelsey had to come running.

Not because she was a turncoat, or a mercenary, but because the Chinese were holding her half-sister prisoner. And, if the Parkers failed to perform the so-called "chores" that Ching gave them, Rong would be executed.

"Rong" was an interesting name. It could be feminine or masculine. And, in keeping with Chinese tradition, "Rong" could connote glory and honor.

On the other hand, the name could also mean "martial." Or warlike. And that was the way Kelsey thought of her sister. As hard, unyielding and combative. Especially where her father was concerned. And that had everything to do with why Rong was a prisoner.

Just prior to the beginning of the war, Rong had announced her intention to move to China, and live with a rock musician she'd met in Hong Kong.

George Parker opposed the plan. He wanted Rong to finish her degree. And, in his opinion, the musician was a slacker and beneath his daughter. His favorite daughter.

The reason for that was plain to see. Rong was the spitting image of Li jing, George Parker's achingly beautiful first wife. The woman he still loved. And the reason why his marriage to Kelsey's mother had failed.

That, Kelsey knew, was the source of the never-ending ache that consumed her. An endless quest for paternal approval that led her to attend the Seattle Maritime Academy and to work tirelessly for her father, eternally striving to please him. But knowing the cause of her affliction had done nothing to cure it.

When the war started, and Rong was trapped in China, it wasn't long before the Chinese government took her into custody—and ran a background check.

Someone in the Chinese hierarchy saw George Parker's company as an asset waiting to be used. And it wasn't long before an emissary arrived in Port Moresby. The proposal he delivered to George Parker was simple: "Do what we tell you to do, or your daughter will die."

Parker dithered for a couple of days but gave in. And the things the family had been forced to do since were shameful. Moving mysterious shipping containers. Hiring employees they didn't need. And, on one occasion, pumping diesel into a Chinese submarine while at sea. All to save a sibling whose first name rhymed with "Wrong."

Now Kelsey was responding to yet another summons. She would, no doubt, receive orders to perform some new form of treachery. Or, and the possibility frightened her, the Chinese had heard about her efforts to help the Allies.

If so, they'd throw her into prison with Rong. Or shoot her. And send a video to her father. Meanwhile Wride, Chaney, and the rest of the team would die too. The possibility made Kelsey feel queasy.

She closed her eyes. There was a ray of hope however. It was a fragile thing, but all she had to cling to. And that was a Chinese criminal named Andrew Soo. A man who, according to one of her contacts, was the Dragon Head (leader) of the Hong Kong-Macao crime triad.

The Hong Kong triad, like other triads, was a transnational organized crime syndicate, with outposts in countries that had large Chinese populations. And, within the closed society of triads, the Hong Kong triad was known as a "black society," rather than a less powerful "dark society." As such it had control over local markets and enjoyed police protection.

Could Soo break Rong out of the detention center in Macau? If so, Rong could be rescued and returned to Port Moresby.

More than that, it would free the Parker family from its ties to Chinese intelligence, and put the months of forced servitude behind them. Kelsey hadn't told her father about the plan. That meant the whole effort was up to her. She felt lonely.

***

Aboard a Chinese Type 22 Missile Boat southeast of Samir Island

It was a beautiful day. The sky was a lighter blue than the sea, which rolled in from the west, and caused the boat to wallow.

But not much, thanks to the missile boat's catamaran style hull. A virtue Ryson hadn't had time to appreciate while the vessel was shooting at the *Arcus.*

But now, as the boat's twin diesels pushed it toward Manado, Ryson had come to appreciate the vessel's virtues. Catamaran hulls were more stable than mono hulls. And while that made for a steady gun platform, and a smoother ride, it also meant they had a wider turning radius.

And, even after the loss of her bow gun, the boat still had teeth. They included six unspent anti-ship missiles, plus a couple of MANPAD (Man portable air-defense) launchers similar to Stingers. Throw in a couple of LMGs and the Type 22 could give a good account of herself—minus the autocannon.

Ryson's crew, some of whom had been wounded during the attack on Samir, were learning how to operate the ship's weapons just in case. But now, thanks to the air cover provided by the planes from Manado, the greater danger was an attack by an Allied jet jockey. That in spite of the alert sent to the local squadron leaders.

Ryson had ordered the boat's chief to stretch American and Australian flags out across the bow—and in the gap just aft of the bridge—but would it be enough? He hoped so. Getting killed by a kid in an F-18 would really piss him off.

Ryson's priorities were to reach Manado quickly, check in with Admiral Nathan, and make sure that the squadron's supply ship departed on time. The people on Samir were running short of everything. That included fuel, food, and ammo. *Every* kind of ammo, especially missiles for the Tor system, which continued to hold the Chinese air force at bay. The latest score was the Tor system 5, and the Chinese pilots 1, after the loss of the *Perth.*

Vos's XO, Lieutenant Andy Tyson, was in command of the Type 22, and clearly enjoying himself. Yes, there was a senior officer on board, but Tyson was in command! That made it a moment to savor. "I'm going below Andy, let me know if you need me."

Tyson said, "Aye, aye sir."

But Ryson knew the young man would do everything possible to avoid rousting him. And, barring at attack, he'd be able to nap undisturbed.

The captain's cabin was not only tiny, but still home to the previous occupant's belongings. As for the man himself, he and the other prisoners were forward, and under guard.

A photo of a pretty Chinese woman sat perched on a fold-down shelf. She watched impassively as Ryson took possession of her husband's bunk, curled into the fetal position, and fell asleep.

**

The city of Macau, China

The light was starting to fade by the time the Seastar landed in the Zhujang River Estuary. The brown water from the Pearl River mixed with the blue water of the South China Sea to create an unappealing brew.

Thanks to the fact that Wride had landed there before, she knew how to best thread her way between small islets, anchored ships, and newly constructed defenses to reach the Macau Seaplane base. The IFF system was sufficient to keep the military off her back. But the civilian authorities wanted more information about the plane and the people aboard. And Brody was in charge of providing it.

The Macau seaplane base was the nicest such facility Wride had ever docked at. And that made sense because the city was a magnet for the richest of the rich. Not to mention the creatures that fed off their leavings.

So now, even as WWIII raged, Macau was awash in cash. And because the Chinese government shared in the profits, the city had been allowed to do business as usual.

The Americans weren't coming any more. Nor were the British, the French and half a dozen other nationalities. But wealthy individuals from Axis countries were quite visible, as were people from neutral states, some of which had subtle ties with China.

Uniformed dock hands rushed to help Brody with the mooring lines, girls in short skirts arrived carrying trays of Champagne, and the dock master helped Brody complete the necessary paperwork.

Once the formalities were complete Kelsey led the team up an aluminum ramp to the street above. Two distinctly different vehicles were waiting at the curb with lights flashing.

One was a retro looking Hongqi L5 luxury sedan. The other was a Mercedes stretch limo. "This is where we part company," Kelsey told them. "The Hongqi is for me. I'll see you at breakfast."

Chaney frowned. "I'll come with you."

"You can't," Kelsey answered. "But thanks. Keep everybody sober just in case."

Then, afraid that she might cry, Kelsey turned to the Chinese car. A man in civilian clothes held a door open for her. An MSS agent? Of course.

They sat opposite each other on the nearly six-foot-wide back seat. Neither of them said a word as the car made its way through the city's streets.

Rather than being blacked out as some European cities were, the lights were on. And at one point Kelsey caught a glimpse of the famous Grand Lisboa Hotel in the distance. It was shaped like an art deco lotus flower and, like the skyscrapers crowded around it, was lit to perfection.

There had been long range bombing attacks against Macau. But damage had been minimal. And, unless that changed, Chinese authorities wanted to keep the city open for business. The lights were part of that.

The hotel disappeared as the car turned and left the downtown area for a parish called Sao Lourenco. That's where the Portuguese-era Macau Government building was located. And where, on previous occasions, Kelsey had been required to meet with an MSS "handler" named Wei Ching.

To protect her identity from prying eyes in orbit, the Hongqi L5 entered an underground parking garage, which was considerably newer than the building above it. From there Kelsey was led up two flights of stairs to a highly polished hallway and a small conference room.

A guard in plainclothes stood with his back to a wall. Ching was present. He stood and bowed. His English was perfect. "Good evening, Ms. Parker. Thank you for accepting our invitation. Please take a seat."

It was more of a command, rather than an "invitation." But in keeping with the Chinese cultural tradition of "face," his approach was intentionally respectful.

"You're welcome," Kelsey said carefully. "What can I do for you?"

Ching was thirty something, had a receding hairline, and was wearing a pair of rimless glasses. He looked more like an accountant than an intelligence agent.

"We have seven suitcase-sized packages which need to be delivered to locations throughout southeast Asia," Ching replied. "It's our expectation that one of your ships will rendezvous with one of our ships—at which time your personnel will accept responsibility for the items in question—and make sure they are delivered."

Kelsey felt nauseous. What would the packages contain? Communications gear? Suitcase sized nukes? The Russians had detonated one such device in the European theatre.

But if she could slow roll the delivery process, and the prison break was successful, maybe she could prevent the packages from reaching their destinations. She forced a smile. "We have a saying. 'The devil is in the details.' An assignment like that will involve some complicated logistics."

The better part of half an hour was spent discussing security, the difficulties involved in the initial transfer, and how deliveries would be made. All of which had to be memorized.

It took all of Kelsey's strength to focus, repeat the instructions Ching gave her, and maintain her composure.

Finally, when the ordeal was over Ching stood. And Kelsey was about to do the same, when he gestured for her to stay. "I have a surprise for you," Ching said. "A reward for good behavior." And with that he gestured to the guard. "Bring her in."

The guard opened the door and Rong entered the room. Despite the lack of makeup, and her drab clothing, Rong was still beautiful. And the resemblance to her mother was striking. Rong's eyes widened. "Kelsey… This *is* a surprise."

Kelsey got up and went over to hug her sister. The embrace felt stiff. "How are you?" Kelsey inquired, as they broke contact.

"How the fuck do you think I am?" Rong demanded. "What's the problem? When are you going to get me out of this shithole?"

"I don't know," Kelsey replied honestly. "At the moment I'm focused on keeping you alive."

Kelsey thought she saw a subtle change of expression in her sister's eyes. She was scared. As she should be. "How long will I be in prison?" Rong inquired anxiously.

"Until they turn you loose," Kelsey said. Part of her wanted to hint at the possibility that Rong would be freed soon. But Kelsey knew that would be a mistake while Ching and the plainclothes guard were present.

"And meanwhile you're going to parties and having a good time," Rong said resentfully.

"That's right," Kelsey replied wearily. "That's all I do."

"Okay," Ching said, as he turned to the guard. "Escort the prisoner out."

"I hate you!" Rong yelled, as she was hustled out of the room.

Ching smiled apologetically. "I'm sure she didn't mean that."

Kelsey knew Rong *did* mean that. But she smiled agreeably. "Of course not."

"Your escorts are waiting in the hall," Ching said. "They will take you to your car."

Kelsey's thoughts were whirling as she returned to the enormous car and took her place next to same man she'd ridden with before. Seeing Rong in person had been a shock. Not just because of what her half-sister had said. But because of what she *hadn't* said. At no time had Rong inquired about her father. He was a given. A figure rather than a person. It would come as a shock to Rong when he died someday.

Kelsey struggled to clear her mind. The night wasn't over. Far from it. She had another meeting to attend. A meeting with Dragon Head Andrew Soo. *How? Where?* Kelsey had no idea. "Soo has people everywhere," the go-between promised. "A person will contact you."

The fact that the driver took Kelsey to her hotel without asking where she was staying spoke volumes. Every move she made was being tracked by the MSS. The Chinese knew about her plane, they knew about her team, and they knew about her hotel.

And, should Kelsey take a walk, she would be tracked by the country's ubiquitous surveillance cameras. Cameras that fed images to facial recognition software that would produce her name in a matter of seconds. So, how did the triads not only survive, but thrive? Kelsey was about to find out.

The car dropped her under the stylish portico that fronted the hotel. Kelsey made her way in, crossed the lobby to the reception desk, and identified herself. "Ah, Ms. Parker," the receptionist said. "Ms. Chaney checked you in. Your bag is in your room. Here's your keycard."

Kelsey thanked him, made her way over to a bank of gleaming elevators, and took the first available lift to the third floor. After walking the length of a long hall Kelsey stopped in front of her door, slipped the card into the reader, and saw a green light appear.

The door opened smoothly. And there, sitting in a chair, was a young woman in a maid's uniform. "Hi," she said brightly. "My name is Mee-Mee. Mr. Soo sent me. Just so you know, this room is free of cameras and listening devices. Please change into the uniform that's lying on the bed. A wig and a pair of glasses are waiting for you in the bathroom. And hurry ... Mr. Soo will be cross if we're late."

Kelsey took the dark blue uniform into the bathroom where she hurried to remove her street clothes and don the one-piece dress. It fit. The wig was black and the bangs were perfect. The fall of hair touched the top of Kelsey's shoulders. And, in a city where most women had black hair, the "look" made sense.

"Good," Mee-Mee said as Kelsey emerged from the bathroom. "Let's go. Help me with the cart."

The cart was loaded with linen, cleaning supplies, and the complimentary items that the hotel provided to guests. The sight of two maids push-pulling it down the hall wouldn't attract the attention of hotel security or MSS personnel if they were watching.

Mee-Mee led Kelsey to a service elevator. Once the cart was aboard Mee-Mee pushed the button for the first floor.

The lift stopped on the second floor to let a real maid board. She looked from face-to-face and turned her back. Nothing had been said, nor did it need to be. The maid knew that Mee-Mee and Kelsey were imposters and was determined to ignore the fact.

Maybe she knew who Mee-Mee was, or maybe she didn't. Either way, ignorance was bliss.

The doors opened onto the first floor. The maid hurried away while Mee-Mee pushed the cart out and into a line of identical conveyances that were lined up against a wall. Then she said, "Follow me."

Mee-Mee led Kelsey through a maze of hallways to a door labeled "Employee Entrance." It opened onto a loading dock where three vans were unloading. Kelsey could see the security cameras and assumed that Mee-Mee could as well. "That's our ride," Mee-Mee said. "The one with a cartoon on the side."

The cartoon figure was that of a plumber, judging from his overalls and the humongous wrench clutched in his right hand. They entered through the back. Kelsey sat on one of the bench seats lining the walls and took a quick look around. There were no tools or fittings to be seen. A shuttle then. Used for moving people around.

The doors slammed shut, the motor started, and the van pulled away. Mee-Mee was checking her phone. That left Kelsey free to think. The visit with her sister had left her shaken. Had Rong always been so mean? No. They'd never been close. The age gap had a lot to do with that. But there had been moments of girlish fun. Outings, pranks, and shared secrets.

Then they'd gradually grown apart. And now, after only rare moments together, Kelsey barely recognized Rong. None of that was apparent to George Parker however. Rong could do no wrong. The pun caused Kelsey to smile.

The van slowed, paused momentarily, and rolled down a slope. "We're about to enter the 1917 Club," Mee-Mee announced. "It caters to Russians. ChiCom apparatchiks (functionaries of the Chinese communist party) aren't allowed. But Mr. Soo is welcome, as are his guests, so you'll be safe."

Kelsey had never considered the Russian presence inside China before. But it made sense. As did some sort of Chinese presence in Russia. However, even though the two countries were allies, it was with the knowledge that they might be enemies in the future.

The van stopped, someone opened the back doors, and Mee-Mee got out. Kelsey followed. They were in an underground parking garage. Overlapping pools of light led the way to retro elevators with scissor-style gates. A plaque with the number "1917" was mounted above them. "Why nineteen-seventeen?" Kelsey inquired.

"Nineteen-seventeen was the year of the Russian revolution," Mee-Mee replied, as they entered. "And that's a big deal." Kelsey was embarrassed. The date *was* a big deal and she should have known.

The elevator rattled loudly as it took them up to the first floor where a security checkpoint was waiting. Both women had to pass through airport-style scanners prior to a pat down by a Russian woman who seemed to relish the process.

Once cleared Kelsey found herself in what had been a hotel lobby but was now a nightclub. Art from the time of the Soviet revolution covered the walls.

Among them were pictures of stylized tanks overcoming obstacles, images of Lenin's jutting profile, paintings of peasants carrying flags, triumphant tractors lowering over well-tilled farmland, and mobs of identical soldiers attacking unseen enemies.

The art, combined with the linen covered tables, gleaming cutlery, and well-groomed patrons made for an elegant atmosphere. A singer crooned. Cigar smoke drifted. And Chinese girls in scanty uniforms waited on tables. "Over there," Mee-Mee said. "Under the chandelier."

The table Mee-Mee referred to was large enough to seat six but was currently occupied by a single person. Mr. Soo? Yes. And as Kelsey neared the table, she was struck by how ordinary the Dragon Head looked. His hair was short and parted on the right. His glasses had black fames. And the nose they sat on was flat, as if broken by a fist many years earlier.

Soo stood and extended a hand. "Ms. Parker … I'm Andrew Soo. It's a pleasure to meet you."

"The pleasure is mutual," Kelsey replied, as they shook hands.

"Please," Soo said. "Have a seat. How did the meeting with Mr. Ching go?"

Kelsey sat down. "As well as it could. You are well informed."

Soo nodded agreeably. "I try. Two of Ching's associates work parttime for me. That's why I can help you." Kelsey liked the no nonsense approach.

A waitress arrived, took Kelsey's order, and left. "So," Kelsey said. "You understand the nature of the task. Tell me how you plan to handle it."

Soo nodded. "The Ministry of State Security is going to move your sister to an inland prison two weeks from now. It's situated hundreds of miles from here, and beyond our reach. That's the bad news. The good news is that the move offers us the perfect opportunity to strike.

"My personnel will intercept the convoy, divide it into sections, and claim what is ours. We'll transport your sister to the fishing village of Coloane. That's where you'll meet her. It's well clear of Macau's harbor defenses."

Kelsey frowned. "I was hoping you would be able to make the transfer at sea."

Soo shook his head. "We aren't sailors, Ms. Parker. There are smugglers though ... I could put you in touch with one of them."

Kelsey's Mojito arrived along with three spring rolls. She took a sip. "That won't be necessary, thank you. I'll put something together. So, Mr. Soo ... How much will this operation cost?"

"Six million U.S.," Soo replied. "With one million down, payable in bitcoin, which must be transferred within forty-eight hours. The balance to be paid within forty-eight hours of delivery."

Kelsey bit into a spring roll. It was delicious. "Four million. Five hundred down. The rest paid on delivery."

Soo shook his head. "No. Five million, one million down, with four on delivery. That's my final offer."

Kelsey nodded. "Done. Let's shake on it." A great deal had been left unsaid. Including the fact that Soo would send assassins to kill the Parkers were they to renege on the deal.

Soo's hand was cool and firm. "Would you like to join me for dinner? The chef is very good."

Mee-Mee had been silent throughout. A testimonial to the trust Soo had in her. Kelsey made eye contact. "Is your last name Soo?"

Mee-Mee nodded. "Mr. Soo is my father."

"Then the three of us will have dinner," Kelsey said. "And I will pick up the tab."

CHAPTER THIRTEEN

Manado Harbor, Indonesia

There were few lights to be seen as the Chinese missile boat, and the American PHM that was acting as its escort, entered Manado Bay. A government ordered blackout was in effect. But isolated rectangles of yellow were visible as were occasional headlights.

A search light mounted on top of the wheelhouse came to life as the 22 neared the unlit warehouse and entered the darkness underneath it. That's where the boats of Squadron 7 were moored. Camera lights came on and Ryson found himself at the center of a media circus.

Seconds after the Type 22 made contact with the dock, Admiral Nathan came aboard followed by a gaggle of reporters and camera people. Ryson was standing on the main deck near the entrance to the bridge. Nathan grabbed his arm. "Here he is!" Nathan proclaimed. "This is Commander Max Ryson, the man who personally captured the warship you're standing on!"

"How did you do it?" a diminutive blond demanded, as she shoved a microphone into Ryson's face. "I *didn't* do it," Ryson insisted. "Lieutenant Commander Moy and the crew of the *Arcus* did it."

"Did you hear that?" Nathan demanded. "The commander is not only brave, he's modest! I spoke with Captain Moy... And according to him, Commander Ryson was armed with a shotgun when he jumped onto this ship and killed the man who tried to stop him! And that, ladies and gentlemen, is what we expect of our naval officers. Where are the prisoners? Let's have a look at them!"

That was just the beginning. The torture continued for the better part of an hour, as Nathan forced Ryson to describe the action from beginning to end. The admiral made no mention of the *Sea Dragon* however. And for that Ryson was grateful, since to do so would alert the Chinese to Squadron 7's central mission, assuming they weren't already aware.

Finally, after the last crew went ashore, Nathan slapped him on the back. "Well done, old sod! It's distasteful, I know that. But people all over the world are hungry for good news. And there's nothing like a tale of derring-do to lift their spirits. Not to mention General Haskell's.

"Lieutenant Tyson can finish up here," Nathan added. "Grab your kit and join me on the launch. I'll buy you a drink on the *Agger.*"

As the launch arrowed across the bay, Nathan kept the conversation light. It wasn't until they were on the liner, and in Nathan's cabin, that the talk turned serious. "Your boat action came just in time," Nathan said, as he poured drinks.

"There's been no sign of the *Sea Dragon* in weeks. And General Haskell wants to know where the bitch is hiding. The NRO doesn't know. The CIA doesn't have a clue. And we sure as hell don't know. But now I have something to push back with. I mean there you were, just short of Mischief Reef, searching a Type 22 for Intel! That should shut Haskell up for a week or so. Here you go, one gin and tonic, with a squeeze of lime."

"Thank you," Ryson said, accepting the glass. "How about Kelsey? And the effort to create ad hoc intelligence networks?"

"That's another success story," Nathan said, as he took a seat. "And another reason for Haskell to be happy. Our girl was able to

recruit the owner of a large fishing fleet *and* a Vietnamese cigarette smuggler. Both of whom stand a good chance of spotting
the *Dragon.*

"There was a bit of a dustup in Yangon however, where Kelsey
and her bodyguards found themselves in the wrong place at the
wrong time, and wound up in a firefight."

Ryson opened his mouth but Nathan interrupted. "No worries. Kelsey and her lot fought their way out. The man they hoped
to meet with wasn't so lucky. He's dead.

"But enough of that," Nathan said dismissively. "Guess where
our girl is now?"

Ryson sipped his drink. The gin was ice cold and felt good on
the back of his throat. "Having her nails done?"

"Of course not," Nathan replied. "She's in China! Macau to
be exact. Don't ask me how she got in. Or made contact with a
triad leader. But she did!

"And here's the best part … It will cost us some money, but
the triad is going to break a man out of prison for her. Not just
any man, but the naval architect generally credited for the *Sea
Dragon's* revolutionary design. Imagine the things *he* could tell
us! Haskell will be over the moon."

"There's a catch though," Nathan added darkly. "The rescue
is slated to take place in two weeks. And Kelsey has to bring her
man out by boat. My first thought was a hydrofoil. But that's
absurd. The Chinese would never allow a PHM to reach the
coast. Never mind survive the return journey."

"You're right, sir," Ryson replied while Nathan sipped his
drink. "And a civilian boat wouldn't have the means to defend
itself. But how 'bout the Type 22?"

Nathan stared. "Oh, my god, that's brilliant! Haskell would
love that!"

"I'm going to need a new bow gun though," Ryson said. "Plus, some Chinese speaking crew members and a submarine. Given how important this man is, it would make sense to get him off the 22 as quickly as possible."

"We'll get cracking in the morning," Nathan said. "Meet me for brekky at 0800."

Once in his cabin Ryson took the kind of long, hot shower that was impossible on a Peg 2, and went to bed. By getting up early he was able to drink half a pot of coffee before the breakfast with Nathan.

To his credit Nathan arrived at breakfast with a crucial piece of information. "The Indonesians use AK-630 automatic cannons on some of their vessels," Nathan announced. "And by promising a certain officer a bottle of rare Orphan Barrel, Muckety-Muck, single-grain Scotch, I managed to secure one. Of course, a gin drinking heathen such as yourself has no idea how special that is."

"True," Ryson agreed, as he ate a bite of bacon. "I assume we're going to inspect the gun before paying the bribe."

"It isn't a bribe," Nathan insisted. "It's a gift."

"Okay," Ryson said. "Let's grab a gunner's mate, and take a look, before delivering the 'gift.'"

With a chief gunner's mate in tow, the officers took a trip across the bay, where an Indonesian kolonel was waiting to greet them. He was clearly curious regarding their need for an AK-630 but knew better than to ask a direct question.

"It's a good system," Kolonel Pra assured them, as they followed a yellow line deeper into the navy supply depot. "It can be used against incoming missiles, aircraft, and enemy ships. We bought ours from Russia."

Once they arrived Ryson saw that the weapon, turret and all, was sitting on a pallet. The next thirty minutes were spent waiting for Chief Wright to inspect the weapon. He finished by saying, "It has some wear, but not much. I think it's good to go."

Nathan opened his briefcase and withdrew a bottle which he handed to Pra. "This is in recognition of your many years of service to the Indonesian navy. Chief Wright and some of his people will return later today."

From the Indonesian base the launch went straight to the hidden moorage under the warehouse. The *Fractus* was in port, which meant commanding officer Lieutenant Mark Conte was as well, and available to take charge of the Type 22.

That involved putting the new 30mm auto cannon in place, rounding up Chinese speaking crew members, and training them. There were multiple mechanical, as well as electronic systems to master, including those associated with the ship's missile launchers. Conte eyed Ryson when the list of to-dos was complete. "Can I command her?"

Ryson grinned. "No. But I'm going to need an XO."

Conte nodded. "I'm in. I'll keep you in the loop."

Once aboard the *Agger* Ryson had no choice but to tackle the stack of paperwork, both electronic and real, which awaited him. And that's where he was, a pot of coffee at his elbow, when a knock came at the door. Maids came and went all the time so Ryson shouted "Come in!" without turning to look. Arms slithered around his neck and a face nuzzled his cheek. Ryson recognized the perfume. He turned to accept a kiss. "Kelsey... How did you get here?"

"I have a plane," Kelsey replied.

Ryson swiveled to face her. "You were in China," he said accusingly.

"Yes," Kelsey said disarmingly.

"How did you get in?"

"My family has been doing business in China for nearly forty years," Kelsey answered. "I sent a request for a meeting to the Chinese Minister of Commerce who agreed to see me."

"And the Australian government said, 'Okay, fine.'"

"No," Kelsey replied. "I forgot to ask them. Why the third degree? The real reason for my visit was to meet with the head of the Hong Kong/Macau triad. Based on information from one of my father's business contacts, I knew that the *Sea Dragon* was the work of a naval architect named Fai Pei.

"But, because he was aligned with ex-president Enlai, Pei wound up in prison. Imagine what he can tell us! All we have to do is get him out of China."

Ryson felt uneasy and wasn't sure why. "That brings us back to the triad," Ryson said. "Aren't they worried about retribution from the government?"

"I asked Mr. Soo about that. He said that the triads were there during the Chinese Revolution in 1949, and they will still be there long after President Lau's death."

"That makes sense," Ryson said. "The Chinese always take the long view."

"So," Kelsey said, "I need help. Mr. Soo agreed to deliver Pei to a fishing village outside of Macau. But we have to take it from there."

"Yes," Ryson acknowledged. "Admiral Nathan mentioned that. We're going to use a Chinese Type 22 missile boat. It's undergoing repairs now."

Kelsey's expression brightened. "Really? How did we get one of those?"

"The *Arcus* managed to capture her," Ryson replied.

"That's wonderful," Kelsey said excitedly. "I have a piece of equipment that could come in handy. And that's the Chinese IFF gear on my plane."

The fact that Kelsey had a Chinese IFF system was almost too good to be true. "And where," Ryson wanted to know, "did you get *that*? On Amazon?"

"No, silly," Kelsey replied. "The Minister of Commerce sent it to my agent in Vietnam. He was afraid my plane would get shot down otherwise."

"Okay," Ryson said. "I'll send someone to get it."

"My mechanic will take care of that," Kelsey assured him. "It will be ready for pickup by five this evening."

"Good," Ryson said. "I guess we're all set then."

"Not quite," Kelsey replied, as she started to unbutton her blouse. "There's one more thing I need help with."

***

With the need to resupply Samir Island, and the repairs to the Type 22 missile boat, the days passed quickly. And suddenly it was time to board the 22 and cast off. The voyage to China was going to cover over 2,600 miles.

Given the boat's top speed of 34 knots, the trip would take at least three days, and require the 22 to refuel 1,300 miles out. That would involve a rendezvous with a so-called "Sea Cow" submarine—a nuclear sub equipped to refuel special ops vessels at sea.

The missile boat had a nickname by then, and was generally referred to as the "*Camo Queen*." A name derived from the "disruptive" blue, gray and black camouflage pattern on the boat's hull.

The effort to find Chinese speaking crew members had been successful. They included: Chief Engineer Ronnie Cheng–a Chinese American raised in Singapore, IT tech Norman Qwan–a member of the Australian navy, and Fire Controlman Mark Simmons–an amateur linguist.

The *Camo Queen* left port at 2000 hours under the cover of darkness, in hopes that she'd be able to cover 320 miles before dawn. That would put the boat a few hundred miles short of the South China Sea, where Type 22s normally prowled.

Ryson hoped the Chinese wouldn't take notice. Allied planes were under strict orders to leave all 22s alone until noon, when the *Camo Queen* would be in enemy waters, and steaming north. As a further protective measure, the boat was equipped with an Allied IFF system, in addition to the Chinese unit obtained from Kelsey.

The night passed peacefully. And that was just as well, since the crewmembers were still in the process of getting to know each other and the ship's systems.

Simmons had a label maker and the task of putting English stickers on every piece of equipment, starting with items related to propulsion, followed by weapons, and then everything else. That included the toilet in the male head, which wore a label that read, "Shitter-Male."

Ryson managed to catch a few hours of sleep before joining Conte on the bridge as the *Queen* passed through the Northwest Danger Shoals. Shortly after sunrise the *Queen* entered the South China Sea, and Conte set a course for the village of Colane.

Regiments of white caps marched in from the north west. But, thanks to her catamaran-style hull, the *Camo Queen* was steadier than a hullborne PHM. And though not subject to sea-sickness, Ryson didn't enjoy being knocked about, as was often the case in monohulls.

The first challenge came less than an hour later when a propeller-driven Chinese Y-9W (GX-10) early warning aircraft appeared out of the haze and circled the boat.

Like its Allied counterparts, the Y-9W was carrying a flying-saucer-shaped radome. And though unarmed Ryson knew the plane was dangerous because of its capacity to summon surface ships *and* jet fighters. He was quick to grab a mike. "If you don't look Chinese stay below. If you *do* look Chinese go out and wave. You can bet that they're taking pictures."

"Contact," Qwan said, laconically. "Switching to Mandarin."

Since Ryson didn't speak Chinese he had to trust Qwan to get the job done without triggering suspicions. Thanks to the Type 22's code books, plus a crash course on Chinese radio procedure from an Australian ham radio operator, Qwan was mostly prepared for the job.

Two or three minutes of gabble ensued. Once it was over the Chinese plane waggled its wings and banked to the north. Qwan was quick to report. "The Chinese IFF system was a big help, sir. They wanted to know why our hull number wasn't on their list.

"I told them that our boat is undergoing sea trials, and the hull number hasn't been posted yet. They bought it."

"That was quick thinking," Ryson said. "Well done. Was there anything else?"

"No, sir."

"Good. Carry on."

With the exception of hazy ships in the far distance, and a seagull that decided to follow the missile boat, there was nothing to see for the next couple of hours.

Then a fleet of fishing boats appeared. Kelsey was on the bridge, and eyed the boats through a pair of binoculars. "See the white over green paint? Those boats are part of the Dyak Fishing company's fleet," she said. "They belong to Mr. Milo Eguchi. And they're on the lookout for the *Sea Dragon*."

Ryson accepted the binoculars and brought them up to his eyes. He was impressed. What Kelsey had been able to accomplish was nothing short of amazing.

After spotting the warship, the fleet split in two with boats veering port and starboard. Was that based on experience? Did Chinese warships plow through the middle of such flotillas rather than alter course? Ryson thought they did. Even though vessels that did so risked fouling their propellers in nets.

Fortunately, the *Camo Queen* was equipped with waterjets. That meant there were no propellers to foul. It also meant the boat was less likely to be detected by submarines. So, with an open lane in front of him, the helmsman saw no reason to alter course.

As before, Ryson took no chances. "All non-Chinese personnel will go below. Chinese personnel will make an appearance. No waving this time. There's bound to be a Chinese spy or two in that fleet. And it seems unlikely that Chinese sailors wave to lowly fishermen."

Some of the fishing boats were so close that Ryson could make out individual faces as the *Camo Queen* passed through the fleet. What were the fishermen thinking? According to Kelsey they were from Borneo, which was theoretically neutral. But surely, with the exception of a tiny minority, they didn't like the Chinese or their warships.

The afternoon passed without incident. As the sun sank into the western sky the tension on the bridge continued to increase. The *Queen* was running low on fuel. And, if something prevented the supply submarine *North Dakota* from making the rendezvous at 2100 hours, the missile boat would be dead in the water before long.

The *North Dakota* had been one of the first Ohio class nuclear powered, ballistic missile submarines to be commissioned. And when newer boats came along, the *Dakota* was converted for use as an undersea tanker, and special ops troop transport.

That was the good news. The bad news was that Chinese attack submarines "owned" the South China sea, and were constantly searching for Allied boats of any size or purpose. So, if the *North Dakota* had been sunk, the men and women on the Type 22 were truly SOL.

Time seemed to slow. Finally, after what seemed like an eternity, 2030 rolled around. And that was the moment when the transport was supposed to deploy a floating wire antenna and establish radio contact.

Seconds ticked away. And then, just as Ryson was beginning to worry, Qwan spoke. "I have the *Dakota* on the horn, sir … They're running on time, and giving away freshly baked cookies with each tank of diesel."

Ryson grinned. "Tell them we could definitely use the cookies. And some diesel too."

Once in position it was time for the *Queen* to cut power and wait. Stars glittered, and waves passed under the twin hulls, as the missile boat rose and fell.

Then came a disturbance off to starboard. Bubbles broke the surface and the water churned when a black conning tower appeared. Seawater ran off the sub's oblong hull as it rose above the waves. Fenders were dropped into place, and Ryson felt a gentle thud as hulls met.

A line was passed and used to pull a hose across the intervening gap. An adapter was installed on the hose. Fuel began to flow moments later. Both Ryson and the sub's CO had reason to worry. The vessels were nearly helpless while refueling was underway.

Radar would detect incoming planes and ships in time to break contact. But, if an attack sub was stalking the duo, and managed to evade the *Dakota's* sonar, both vessels would be destroyed.

However, it wouldn't do any good to dwell on that and Ryson didn't. He made a point of discussing baseball with Conte while sipping coffee.

Even though it felt like hours. the entire process took less than forty-five minutes. Once the hose was withdrawn, a container of warm cookies was passed across, and the missile boat was ready for the next leg of its journey. "A message from the *North Dakota*," Qwan said. "'We'll see you on the flip side. Good hunting.'"

With full tanks and empty screens Ryson thought it would be safe to grab some sleep. "You have it," he told Conte. "I'll relieve you in four."

After getting a ham and cheese and a bottle of water from the galley, Ryson retreated to the captain's cabin, where he ate half the sandwich—and drank nearly all the water. Ryson was fully dressed as he pulled a blanket up over his chest. *Kelsey*, he thought. *She spends most of her time in her cabin. I wonder why?* Sleep pulled him down.

Trouble arrived, as trouble often did, shortly after dawn. It took the shape of a sleek Type 055 guided-missile destroyer. That was how the Chinese classified their ship.

But by U.S. standards the Type 055s qualified as cruisers because of their size, multi-mission capabilities, and on-board flag facilities. All of which meant the "destroyer" could crush the *Queen* like an ant should it have a reason to do so.

"It'll pass us by," Conte predicted when the ship appeared on the horizon. And there were plenty of reasons to believe that would be the case. Why, after all, would the tin can's CO want to hassle a pissant Type 22?

But the bastard did. As became apparent when the destroyer was about a mile away. "She's the *Yinchuan*," Qwan said. "And she wants to know what we're doing here. More than that, her captain ordered us to heave to, and wait for a boarding party to come across."

Ryson's mind was racing. Shit, shit, shit. He couldn't fight and he couldn't refuse. But a boarding party would be disastrous. What he needed was a believable excuse.

"Tell them that we would welcome a boarding party," Ryson said. "Including three or four medical personnel. Tell them to take precautions however, because all but two of our crewmembers have coughs, high fevers and are suffering from diarrhea."

Five long minutes passed. "They changed their minds," Qwan said. "We are to proceed at top speed for Hainan, and seek medical attention there."

"Tell them we will comply," Ryson said.

A white bow wave appeared as the *Yinchuan* began to increase power and angled away. No fucking way was the CO about to expose his crew to a communicable disease. "That was close," Conte said. "Too close."

"Yeah," Ryson agreed. "It's going to be a long day."

Timing was critical. The *Queen* was supposed to arrive in the Chinese village of Coloane at 2000 that evening. And Ryson planned to be on time. Not early, because the missile boat might attract attention, and not late or else the triad might fade.

So Ryson worked with Conte to calculate the precise speed, which combined with the prevailing sea state, would put the *Camo Queen* in Coloane at precisely 2000.

The hours dragged by. Darkness fell. And unlike Manado harbor in Indonesia, Macau's lights were on. A no-no during WWII.

But now, in the age of computer guided weapons, it didn't really matter. Missiles and smart bombs didn't care if the lights were on or off. They would hit their targets regardless. That's what the Chinese believed. Although other countries were more conservative.

"We're running fifteen minutes ahead of schedule," Conte cautioned.

"Throttle back a bit," Ryson ordered. "It would be rude to arrive at the party early. How 'bout that Kelsey? Have you heard anything from Mr. Soo?"

Kesey had spent most of the time in her cabin up until then. But now, with the lights of Macau glittering ahead, she was like a race horse at the starting gate. She was fidgety, talkative, and given to bouts of awkward laughter.

Kelsey's sat phone was their link to triad leader Soo, and she was holding it in her hand. "Nothing yet," she replied as she eyed her watch. "But there wouldn't be. The prisoner transfer is scheduled for 1830. The snatch is supposed to take place at approximately 1930, followed by a handoff at 2000."

Ryson had heard it all before of course. And hoped that Kelsey's confidence was justified. He tried to imagine how it would go down. A car, maybe two, leaving the detention center in Macau. There would be traffic, but not much due to gas rationing.

At some point a triad vehicle would cut in front of the police car. And, if Ryson was running the operation, another would pull up from behind. Then the first car would brake, forcing the transfer vehicle to slow.

In the case of two vehicles, odds were that the escort car would lead rather than follow. And as a motorcycle pulled up beside it, a passenger would shoot the car's driver, causing his vehicle to crash or stop.

Meanwhile the second car, the one containing Mr. Pei, would come to a stop. Perhaps the driver and guard would offer to surrender. It wouldn't make any difference. By killing the policemen, Mr. Soo's thugs would slow the official response.

At that point Mr. Pei would be extracted from the transfer vehicle, loaded into a rescue car, and spirited away. Assuming everything went well, the triad cars would disappear into traffic. But if something went wrong there would be a gigundo shit show. Perhaps in Coloane.

With that possibility in mind, Ryson gave orders for the *Queen* to dock bow-on to the village, so the 30mm cannon could be brought to bear. He hoped it wouldn't be necessary to fire. There would be lots of collateral damage if the autocannon let loose.

The missile boat cut through the water, the lights grew brighter, and time passed. Kelsey was just outside the wheelhouse where her sat phone could "see" the satellite above.

She was antsy as 1930 came and went. Then, at 1942, a call came in. Kelsey thumbed a button and said, "Go." She listened. "Got it. We'll be there."

Kelsey stepped into the wheelhouse. The look of relief on her face was plain to see. "They have him," she said. "And they're on the way. But some sort of celebration is underway. And there's more traffic than usual. They might be a few minutes late."

Ryson nodded. "Okay, thanks." The village was straight ahead. In order to reach the public pier, the Type 22 had to avoid the fishing boats which were moored to buoys.

Colored lights reflected off the dark oily water. Beyond the dock, and the street that served it, rectangles of buttery yellow light were visible. Ryson could imagine families getting ready for bed, unaware of the drama about to take place outside. Then the drone arrived.

It was a quadcopter drone with a rounded camera pod on its belly. Red and blue lights flashed as a voice barked words in Mandarin. Chief Engineer Cheng was on the bridge. He was dressed in a Chinese uniform. "It's the police," he said. "They want our harbor access code."

"What the hell is *that?*"

Cheng shook his head. "I don't know. It must be some sort of security measure."

"Go out and tell the drone that we're having engine trouble and going to dock."

Cheng did as he was told. But the drone continued to circle the *Queen,* even as sirens stuttered, screeched and wailed in the distance. Flashing lights appeared on the street.

Ryson spoke into a mike. "The bastards are onto us," he said grimly. "Prepare to fire on targets of opportunity. It looks like we'll be forced to depart without our passenger."

"No!" Kelsey said emphatically. "Not yet ... Give them five minutes. She'll be here by then."

"Standby," Ryson said over the intercom. "We're holding. But be ready."

That was when the drone flew in through the open door. Cheng threw his arms around the device and carried it to the deck. Muzzle flashes appeared as a machine gun began to chatter, and was quickly joined by a second weapon, as bullets pinged the hull. "We're pulling out," Ryson announced. "Half astern. Open fire."

A tongue of fire appeared as the 30mm rotary cannon began to fire short bursts. The shells destroyed the shack at the end of the pier. Then, as Gunner's Mate Wes Cory swept the outgoing fire from left to right, a police car exploded—and a storefront was destroyed moments later.

Meanwhile, Cheng was smashing the drone into the deck, even as a disembodied voice ordered him to surrender. Kelsey had been outside with the sat phone to her ear. She entered the wheelhouse. "Stop!" she shouted. "She's here! In a skiff! Off the stern."

Ryson thumbed the switch. "Deck crew to the stern. Our passenger is in a small boat. Get him aboard."

"I can see the boat," a lookout said. "We're on it."

The small arms fire had died away, only to be supplanted by the rhythmic thud, thud, thud of a heavy machine gun, as a six-wheeled armored personnel carrier appeared on the scene. The *Queen* shuddered as large caliber shells pounded her hull.

Cory didn't like that and brought the 30 to bear on the vehicle. Dozens of high explosive shells struck the vehicle's turret and blew it off. A fountain of fire shot up into the air, and secondary explosions rocked the APC, as reserve ammo bins began to cook off.

"That's right motherfuckers," Cory declared. "Your fucking pea shooter is a fucking piece of fucking shit!"

"Belay that bullshit," Conte ordered. "And learn a new word."

"We have a girl," the Chief announced. "But there's no sign of a man."

"Secure her," Ryson ordered. "Full speed astern. We're out of here. All hands will prepare for a running fight. I'm looking at you, Fire Control ... We're going to need those anti-ship missiles. All eight of them. Get the Stingers on deck."

The Type 22 had been carrying six anti-ship missiles when captured. And, once the boat was approved for the trip to China, Ryson put in a request for two TL-10 Sky Dragons to fill the empty tubes.

There was only one country other than China that used them and that was Axis member Iran. But as luck would have it, thirty-six TL-10s had been aboard a ship bound for Iran, and were intercepted in the Arabian Sea. Two were flown in. So, the *Queen* had teeth. But only eight of them.

Water churned white as the *Camo Queen* backed out, turned to the southeast, and Ryson ordered "Full speed ahead." Then he turned to Conte. "Get ahold of the operations folks at INDOPACCOM. Give them a sitrep. Tell them we're going to need a full-on extraction by the *North Dakota*. And the sooner the better. The Chinese are going to come after us with everything they have. Oh, and the *North Dakota* is going to need backup. Do you read me?"

"Five-by-five," Conte replied. "I'm on it."

Confident that things were at least momentarily under control Ryson hurried aft. A *girl*? Instead of a man? Was that intentional? Or had an innocent fisherwoman been kidnapped?

Ryson ran into the Chief Bosun's Mate by the missile array. "Where's Kelsey? Have you seen her?"

"She took the girl and went below," the chief replied. "Permission to speak freely?"

"Of course."

"Both were crying. They know each other."

That was completely unexpected. What the hell? "Thanks, Chief. Make the rounds. You know what to say."

Chief Bossert had been in the navy for seventeen years. He nodded. "Yes, sir. I know what to say. There ain't nothin' to worry about."

Ryson grinned. "Exactly."

Ryson went below, made his way to Kelsey's cabin, and rapped on the hatch. It was Kelsey who opened it. But it was the other woman who claimed Ryson's attention. *Li jing*. He was looking at a Eurasian version of George Parker's first wife.

Ryson looked from the woman in the blue prison outfit to Kelsey. "Your sister?"

Kelsey bit her lower lip. "Yes."

"So, the Mr. Pei story was a lie."

"He exists," Kelsey said miserably. "And he's in prison. But yes, I lied. Rong is my sister. My half-sister. The Chinese were using her to blackmail my family. They forced us to do terrible things."

Ryson was filled with rage. His fists were clenched. The Parkers were double agents. His voice was tight. "I'm no lawyer. Maybe this is treason. Or maybe it's something else. But you are going to prison. If it was up to me, you'd be taken out and shot. In fact, I'd be happy to do the job myself."

Tears trickled down Kelsey's cheeks. Her eyes beseeched him. "Please, Max... Please forgive me."

"Never," Ryson replied. "And, if one person on this boat dies his, or her, blood will be on your hands."

Ryson took hold of a wrist, towed Kelsey out into the passageway, and bellowed. "Find Chief Bossert!"

Bossert arrived thirty seconds later. "Sir?"

"Take Ms. Parker into custody. Chain her to something. The other woman is her sister. Restrain her as well. Do you understand?"

Bossert was understandably confused, but nodded his head. Orders were orders. "Yes, sir."

"Good. I'll be on the bridge."

Ryson arrived in the wheelhouse to find that more bad news was waiting for him. "The *North Dakota* is supposed to check in with INDOPACCOM every hour on the hour," Conte told him. "And the next contact is thirty-six minutes away."

Ryson swore. There was no way to make radio contact with a sub unless it deployed an antenna. And it would be necessary for thirty-six minutes to pass before the sub could receive new orders.

How far away would the *North Dakota* be when that occurred? It would be a matter of luck. Meanwhile, as the *Camo*

Queen ran for her life, at least half of the Chinese navy would be in hot pursuit.

The first indication of this came as new blips appeared on the CIC's radar screens. The boat's CSO (Combat Systems Officer) was a lieutenant named Kady Willke. She was generally referred to as "the Loot" by her subordinates, a nickname she treasured. "We have one, two, *three* planes inbound from the west," Willke announced. "Tracking. Over."

Ryson was wearing a headset in order to communicate with crew members who couldn't hear the ship's speakers. "Stinger crews will stand by to repel aircraft. Three from the west. Fire Control will prepare to fire chaff. Over."

A Mark 36 Chaff and Decoy Launching System had been fitted to the *Camo Queen* to replace the Chinese version. Ryson turned to the helmsman. "Commence evasive maneuvers."

"Evasive maneuvers. Aye, aye, sir."

"Five surface targets," Willke said. "In from the west. Fire Control is ready. Tracking."

"Wait for it," Ryson replied. "We need clean hits. One missile per target. If the targets sink, then good. But our main goal is to stop or delay them."

"Incoming missiles," Willke reported.

"Fire chaff," Ryson ordered.

The Mark 36 system consisted of two arrays of six mortars each. One array to port, and one to starboard. Three tubes in each cluster were set at a different angles to ensure an effective spread. Each mortar produced a soft thud followed by a puff of gray smoke as an infrared decoy shot up to explode and scatter chaff.

"Targets optimal," Willke said.

"Fire missiles," Ryson ordered.

The Type 22 lurched as the Sky Dragon missiles left their tubes, and raced into the night. Would they hit their targets? And if so, how many? Ryson waited to learn his fate.

***

Aboard the United States submarine SSTN *North Dakota* in the South China Sea

The coordinates for the original rendezvous with the Type 22 missile boat were hundreds of miles to the south. But the *North Dakota* had been sent north to refuel one of the navy's new, less expensive diesel submarines. And that put the sub in the wrong place at the wrong time. Or the right place, depending on one's perspective.

Commander Les Bonner experienced a sinking feeling as he received new orders from INDOPACCOM. The Chinese missile boat and its Allied crew were in trouble. He was to make all possible speed to their location, surface, and pick them up.

A suicide mission if there ever was one. First, because the missile boat was going to lead Chinese vessels to his sub. And second, because the "*Gas Can,*" as his sailors called it, would be vulnerable while on the surface. *Very* vulnerable.

It was funny in a way. Bonner had been judged smart enough to be accepted at Annapolis, smart enough to graduate at the middle of his class, and smart enough to be selected for the elite Naval Nuclear Power School in Charleston.

But not smart enough to command a ballistic missile sub or an attack boat. But a sea going gas station? Yes. The brass thought he could handle that.

And after years of internal struggle Bonner had come to accept his lot. And to look forward to retirement. Who knew?

Maybe they'd buck him up to 06 just before he went ashore for the last time.

Now, having been found wanting, he was about to be thrust into what was shaping up to be a sea going Alamo. And would almost certainly leave his wife crying over an empty grave. A lump formed in Bonner's throat. "Roger that, sir … Out."

Bonner was in the sub's high tech control room. That's where the *North Dakota's* pilot and copilot were located, along with his XO, Lieutenant Commander Nicole Hardy, and Chief of the boat, Miles Ford.

Non verbals were important. Bonner knew that. That's why Bonner had a smile on his face when he turned to face them. "We have new orders … We're going to head west, rendezvous with the missile boat, and take the crew aboard."

Hardy frowned. "They're in trouble, aren't they?"

"You could say that," Bonner allowed.

"And the Chinese navy is after them? Including attack subs?"

"We don't have Intel on any attack subs, but yeah," Bonner admitted.

"So, we're going to surface in the middle of a shit show," Chief Ford added.

"Pretty much," Bonner agreed. "But here's the good news. Two of our attack boats are on their way to provide support."

"And the ETA for the first one is?" Hardy inquired.

"Three hours give or take."

"And the ETA for the rendezvous is?"

"An hour or so."

The control room was silent as everyone took the information in. "So, I have time for a nap," Ford said. All of them laughed.

Bonner felt grateful as he issued orders. Ford was the boat's beating heart. And if he was confident, the crew would be as well. He felt the deck tilt as the *North Dakota* turned onto a new course. The *Gas Can* was going to war.

***

Aboard the *Camo Queen*, east of Macau, China

One of the incoming missiles detected a target, went for it, and exploded hundreds of feet above the missile boat. A second weapon came closer but met the same fate.

Smoking confetti twirled out of the sky as the *Camo Queen* continued to race east in a desperate attempt to reach the *North Dakota* before the Chinese caught up with her.

"One target is dead in the water," Willkie observed, as the 22's missiles fell. "The other targets are still in the hunt."

An hour, Ryson thought. *We have to survive for an hour. And four ships are chasing us.*

"We have a new target to the east," Willkie added. "And it's coming our way."

"Get operations on the horn," Ryson ordered. "Maybe they can tell us what it is. This is unlikely, but request air support. Maybe we'll luck out."

They didn't luck out. The blip, according to orbital Intel, was a Chinese destroyer. And the *Camo Queen* was too far away from the nearest carrier group to receive air support.

"Two of the four western targets are pulling ahead of the others," Willkie reported. "That suggests that they are smaller and faster."

Ryson was reminded of the C 14 missile boat that Atworthy's Armindale had done battle with. The catamarans were small, armed with short range missiles, and capable of speeds up to 50 knots. That meant they were faster than the *Queen*. He eyed his watch. Forty-five minutes to go.

Then the planes arrived. They circled like vultures over a dying animal. The first one dived. "Fire chaff," Conte ordered. "Engage with missiles. Fire when ready."

Stinger Team 1 fired. But their missile went after a flare and exploded.

Team 2 was ready with a follow-up. Their Stinger found its target. There was an explosion as the missile hit an engine, followed by a second explosion, and a third—as the Sukhoi Su-27 disintegrated.

The second and third planes attacked in quick succession. Missiles flashed off wings, sought targets, and blew up as the SRBOC mortars continued to chug.

How many decoys did the *Queen* have? Ryson couldn't remember. He hoped it was enough.

Then one of the Chinese jet jockeys made a mistake. Previous runs had been made from the west, toward the missile boat's stern, but this pilot decided to tackle the *Queen* head on. And more than that, to come in low *under* the chaff, skimming the wave tops.

And since missiles weren't getting through, the pilot decided to use the plane's secondary weapons. His 30mm GSh-30-1 autocannon was loaded with a hundred and fifty rounds, half of which splashed into the sea before he got close, leaving him with only seventy-five shells to put on the target.

What the pilot hadn't considered was the fact that the *Camo Queen's* bow gun could elevate high enough to engage planes, and that Gunner's Mate Wes Cory was itching to bag a jet. "Come on motherfucker! Eat lead!"

And the Sukhoi *did* eat lead. A lot of it, even as rockets flared off the airplane's wings, seeking the enemy. One went astray while the other struck the bridge. The force of the explosion destroyed the windscreen, killed Conte, and took the helmsman's head clean off.

Blood flew everywhere, and the deck was slick with it, as Ryson stepped in to take control of the wheel. Wind buffeted his face as the bow cannon roared. The jet seemed to hesitate, and a wing dipped into the water. Ryson turned the boat to port to avoid the wreckage, while Cory screamed. "*Yes! Yes! Fuck yes!* That's for my brother, you goddamned mother fucker!"

"Willkie," Ryson said. "Conte's down. So's the quartermaster. Both are dead. What's our status?"

"We took a hit aft of the radar mast, starboard side," Willkie replied. "Both members of Stinger Team 2 were wounded. One is still on the job."

"The fast movers are closing from the west. They're visible from the stern. And the target incoming from the east can be seen on the horizon."

Ryson looked to his left. And sure enough, a ship *was* visible in the distance. A destroyer? Yes. Or a frigate. "What about the sub? Any news?"

"None so far."

This sucks, Ryson thought, as the third plane attacked. *I'll join the army next time.*

***

Aboard the United States submarine SSTN *North Dakota* in the South China Sea

Tim Hassan had been a sonar operator for only three months. But it was an easy call to make. "We have high speed screws in from the east. Plus, active sonar."

Bonner swore. He had two choices. Surface and die. Or run and hide, leaving the men and women on the missile boat to perish. But that was unacceptable. "*Palpate et moriar.*" (Touch me and die.) That was the boat's motto. A leftover from its previous incarnation as a ballistic missile sub. *Before* it was reduced to a tanker.

But the *Dakota* had four torpedo tubes. Each loaded with a Mk-48 torpedo. The weapons could be wire guided. Or, thanks to onboard AI, the fish could locate targets on their own. And that was the mode Bonner chose. The orders startled everyone.

"Bring the boat up to photonics depth. Standby to fire torpedoes. Program them to run independently."

A sailor said, "This shit is getting real."

"Belay that," Ford ordered. "And see me when this is over."

The deck tilted slightly as the *North Dakota* rose, the photonics package broke the surface, and Bonner hurried to take a look. It was a tin can alright, a Type 052D guided-missile destroyer, according to the data on the screen.

A quick pivot revealed the Type 22 boat as well, black smoke boiling up from midships, dead in the water. Why was she still afloat? The tin can could have destroyed the boat from a long way off. Maybe the enemy warship had orders to capture Allied personnel if they could. What a propaganda coup that would be! "I think they made us," Hardy said. "They're in range."

It was a suggestion disguised as a comment. And Bonner knew the XO was correct. A Mk-48 could travel for more than twenty miles and still strike its target. And the tin can was only ten miles away. He didn't have time to play cat and mouse. So, the best strategy was to fire everything he had, and hope that at least one of his weapons hit the target. "Stand by to fire tubes 1, 2, 3, and 4," Bonner said. "Fire!"

Normally Bonner would monitor the torpedoes while taking steps to avoid whatever reprisal the destroyer might be capable of. But he had a different priority, and that was to rescue the people on the missile boat. "We have a job to do. Give me flank speed."

CHAPTER FOURTEEN

Aboard the *Camo Queen*, in the South China Sea

The missile boat was out of decoys by the time the third plane swooped in to fire a missile. The weapon struck just aft of the superstructure. Hot gasses and flying shrapnel penetrated the space below. "Doc" Crayton and an operations specialist were killed. "We have three missiles left," Ryson said. "Kill the C 14 missile boats."

"Yes, sir," Willkie replied. "Firing 1, firing 2, and firing 3. Tracking."

"Prepare to abandon ship," Ryson announced. "Don PFDs and launch rafts."

"Hits!" Willkie announced. "One C 14 destroyed, and one damaged."

That made Ryson feel slightly better, but not much. "Well done. Get on deck, Lieutenant. And I mean *now*. We're taking water."

Ryson stepped out of the wheelhouse and onto the main deck. Distant thumps were heard. Two of them. "Look!" a sailor yelled, as he pointed east.

Ryson had to squint into the light reflecting off the sea. Something was wrong with the Chinese destroyer. Smoke was billowing up from a fire below deck and the ship had taken on a pronounced list. But *why?* There weren't any Allied planes in the sky—and Allied surface vessels were nowhere to be seen.

Then it came to him. *The North Dakota!* It seemed that the submarine still had a set of torpedo tubes. And a captain who knew how to use them. "Clear the ship!" Ryson yelled. "Get clear!"

An eight-person raft was bobbing two yards away. Chief Bossert waved. "Jump Skipper!"

Ryson remained where he was. "Is everyone accounted for?"

"Yes, sir!" Bossert replied. "We had to leave the dead behind."

That, unfortunately, was a fact of life. Or death.

Ryson jumped, landed in the water, and surfaced to discover hands reaching for him. Strong arms pulled him up and over the side. And there, sitting no more than a foot away, was Kelsey. Her sister was slumped in the stern.

Ryson pointed a finger at Kelsey. "Throw the bitch overboard."

Kelsey blanched and tried to pull away. "Sorry, sir," Bossert replied. "No can do."

Ryson was about to give the order a second time when the sea started to boil, and a conning tower appeared. "Paddle!" Chief Bossert ordered. "Paddle hard!"

The remaining jet had been circling. Now, upon spotting the sub, it attacked.

***

Aboard the United States submarine SSTN *North Dakota* in the South China Sea

Orders flew as the submarine *North Dakota* surfaced. "Missile teams, on deck! Rescue teams, on deck! Prepare to take personnel aboard. Some could be wounded."

Sailors boiled up out of the conning tower and descended to the deck. The Stinger teams were the first to arrive with launchers loaded. Ford was in charge. "Here they come! Acquire targets! Fire when ready!"

The fighter was already diving on the sub. So there were only seconds in which to aim and fire. The missiles leapt out of their tubes, seemed to pause for a second, and took off trailing spirals of gray smoke behind them. "Reload!" Ford ordered. "Prepare to fire!"

But there was no need. Both Stingers hit the jet. There was a flash of light followed by a resonant boom as the Sukhoi ceased to exist.

Meanwhile the first raft came alongside. It wasn't easy to bring people up and over the sub's rounded hull. But ropes were thrown. And except for the wounded, the incoming sailors managed to pull themselves up, shoes slipping as they fought for traction.

Two of Ryson's crewmembers weren't in any condition to do that. Fortunately, Chief Bossert was there to expertly rope each casualty, so the sub's crew could pull the casualties up and carry them below.

As the second raft arrived, a missile fell on what remained of the missile boat. Chinese warships were arriving from the west with orders to finish the *Camo Queen* off. There was a thump, followed by a muted boom, and the Type 22 was gone.

Strangely, Ryson felt badly about that. The *Camo Queen* had been *his* boat. For a while anyway, and he'd been fond of her.

The surviving members of Ryson's crew were below deck by that time, and the sub was beginning to submerge. The *Dakota* was designed to carry up to sixty special forces personnel. That meant there was plenty of space for the survivors.

Ryson was sitting on the edge of a bunk, wrapped in a blanket, and staring at the deck under his bare feet. The mission had been a lie, precious lives had been lost, and the *Sea Dragon* continued to prowl the seas. It was the worst moment of his life. Depression pulled him down.

***

The mood in the *Dakota's* control room was different. "The destroyer is on her side," Hardy said exultantly. "She'll sink soon."

"Wonderful," Bonner said. "Did you take pictures?"

"Of course," his XO replied. "Why?"

"Because no one will believe us if you didn't." Bonner answered.

Hardy laughed. "The fast attack submarine, *Gas Can*. We rock."

***

Aboard the semi-submersible cruiser *Sea Dragon,* off Sumatra

Captain Ko eyed the most recent weather report. A storm was brewing. And a good thing too, since it would be critical to a successful attack on Bangkok, Thailand's capitol.

The mission came as a surprise to Ko because the PRC had been friendly with Thailand since 1975, and been regarded as a regional ally until the month before.

The country was governed by a military junta, a prime minister and, to a lesser extent, a king. All of which worked well from a Chinese perspective. But when Rama X died unexpectedly, and his son Rama XI inherited the throne, everything changed.

The young King Yingluck Chulaloke had been educated in the west, was demonstrably empathetic to his subjects, and therefore popular. So popular, that the majority of Thai citizens supported Chulaloke's decision to join the Alliance, despite the dangers that posed.

It was a bet really, a bet that the Allies would win the war, thereby placing Thailand on the right side of history. And a gamble that China wouldn't invade.

Much to everyone's surprise the ruling junta backed Chulaloke's plan. After all, they reasoned, if China sent troops to Thailand—they'd have to pass through either Myanmar or Laos. And if the invasion went poorly the Allies might attack China from the south.

But President Lau wasn't about to sit still for that sort of thing, and summoned Vice Admiral Chao who, as the architect of the attack on Okinawa, was something of a favorite.

After explaining the strategic situation, Lau made his pitch. "Since a land invasion might fail, what about an attack from the sea? The sort of attack that would turn the populace against Chulaloke and, if properly planned, might even result in his death?"

Chao had a tendency to like all of Lau's ideas, especially those that could help him make full admiral.

Ko saw Chao as a version of Abraham Maslow's man with a hammer, meaning a person to whom everything looks like a nail. And the *Sea Dragon* was that nail.

And so the order came down. "Take the *Sea Dragon*, attack Bangkok, and use information supplied by MSS to kill Rama XI."

It was a stupid plan. Because in order to reach the Gulf of Thailand and launch missiles, the *Sea Dragon* would have to round the Cambodian coast, and pass through the part of the South China Sea dominated by the Allies. All of whom were searching for Ko's ship.

That's where the storm came in. According to the government meteorologists a tropical storm was brewing. And not just any tropical storm, but one that might produce cyclones. A fact that would send most, if not all, of the Alliance surface ships scurrying for a safe port. Meanwhile, thanks to her low center of gravity and submarine-like design, the *Sea Dragon* would slip through unnoticed.

That was the plan. And, after Ko made his way up into Conning Tower 1, there was every indication that the storm had arrived. The light was starting to fade, the wind was blowing the tops off waves, and cold spume was flying through the air.

In spite of her enormous size, the semi-submersible was pitching forward and back, as if bowing to Goddess Tianfei who would protect them. And that was just as well, since no one else could.

***

The sour stench of vomit hung in the air as Lieutenant Jev Jing was thrown sideways into a steel hatch. Then the *Sea Dragon* dipped into the trough between a couple of waves, causing unsecured equipment and litter to cascade down the main passageway. Jing battled to keep his footing and barely managed to do so. He was on his way to the Operations Compartment where he was scheduled to relieve the communications officer on duty.

The shit show on Tonaki Island seemed like ancient history at that point. After killing Lieutenant Ma, who'd been intent on murdering a Japanese family, Jing had assumed he would be punished. But, when the time came for Jing to face a disciplinary panel—consisting of Captain Ko, Chief Engineer Hong, and a marine captain named Ho—he was surprised by the way it turned out. After telling the story of how the landing went, and how the sound of gunfire summoned him to the village, he discovered that one of Ma's men had been beheaded with a samurai sword.

The murderer was already dead at that point, and Ma was inside a house, preparing to slaughter the killer's family, when

Jing entered. "I shot Lieutenant Ma," Jing confessed. "The murderer was dead. And I feared that killing his family would trigger a general uprising. And, well, killing civilians is wrong."

The last argument was the weakest. That's the way many military men would see it. But it was true. And, fortunately for Jing, the panel agreed. No charges were filed.

In the report submitted to higher authorities Ma was listed as having been killed in action. That being a simple way to paper everything over, and avoid needless pain for Ma's family.

As a result, Jing's status had risen. "How about Jing?" he overheard a sailor say. "He killed an officer and got away with it!"

Jing managed to grab a railing as the ship heaved, made use of it to drag himself along, and stumbled into the com compartment. A chair offered a welcome landing spot. A tech was barfing into a waste basket. The watch had begun.

***

It was completely dark and a 34-knot wind was blowing from the south. The *Sea Dragon* was pitching, but thanks to the fact that most of her hull was partially submerged, the wind didn't have much superstructure to push against. Visibility was zero. And everything of importance could be seen on radar. So, Ko sent his sailors below, and followed them down.

The main threat, other than the storm, were enemy submarines. Weather conditions were meaningless to them. But with an attack sub scouting the way for the *Sea Dragon,* it was very unlikely that the cruiser would be subject to a surprise attack.

The second most important threat was psychological. And had to do with morale which, in Ko's opinion, was too good. A strange situation to be sure. But real nevertheless.

Ko put out a request for his department heads to gather in the wardroom. The officers who met there represented the deck, operations, weapons, engineering, communications, medical and intelligence departments. Only two of them were visibly seasick.

Once the officers were seated, a sailor served tea, and placed dishes of peanuts on the table. Ko knew the sailor was listening. And would share what he heard with shipmates, who would tell their friends, and so forth. An informal process that would help to spread Ko's message.

"There is," Ko told them from his position at the end of the table, "a proverb about pride: 'Modesty benefits, arrogance hurts—and the modest receive benefit, while the conceited reap failure.' And we, my friends, are both overconfident and conceited."

Most of the officers at the table saw Ko as brilliant but eccentric. The altar to Tianfei being an obvious example of that. And here was yet another one of Captain Ko's quirks.

After three amazing victories, with only a few casualties, the *Sea Dragon* was a powerful emblem of China's martial prowess and limitless future. That was a good thing.

It was, nevertheless, necessary to maintain a *Wu biaoqing de lian* (expressionless face). Most of the department heads were thinking about sex, money, or power as Ko delivered a ten-minute sermon on the merits of humility. Ko closed with a quote from Confucius: "Humility is the solid foundation of all virtues."

Once dismissed the officers hurried away. The single exception was Chief Engineer Hong. He stood. "They hear, but don't understand."

"That's true," Ko agreed. "But it was necessary to try. They don't seem to grasp the difficulty of what lies ahead."

Hong nodded. "We will get in. But will we get out?"

"Exactly," Ko replied. "The answer is up to Tianfei."

"And the Allies."

Ko grinned. "*And* the Allies.'"

***

The storm raged for hours. But finally, around 0300, the maelstrom began to abate. The *Sea Dragon's* crew was exhausted by then. Physical injuries included a broken arm, a lacerated forehead, a concussion, two sprains, and a case of dehydration so severe than an IV drip was required.

Those on duty struggled to maintain focus. And those who were off duty found it hard to sleep. Fortunately, there were no emergencies to contend with. And, from Ko's point of view, the discomfort had been worth it as the *Sea Dragon* approached the Gulf of Thailand.

The ship rounded Ca Mau Cape off of Cambodia at 0546. The next leg of the journey involved steaming north through the Gulf of Thailand to the Bight of Bangkok. That would put the capitol city inside the seventy-five-mile range of the cruiser's YJ-91 missiles. Hong's words echoed in Ko's head. "We will get in. But will we get out?"

Four hundred and fifty miles to go, Ko thought. The latest weather report was calling for three-to-four-foot waves, force winds of two-to-six, plus heavy rain and reduced visibility. That, Ko believed, combined with the *Sea Dragon's* low radar cross section, would allow the ship to proceed undetected.

The trip lasted all day and into the evening. That at least was a good thing, since it would permit the *Sea Dragon* to withdraw under the cover of darkness. Glimmers of light could be seen at times, but had a tendency to appear and disappear, as squalls passed through the area.

The ship's complement of two hundred missiles had been divided in half, with one hundred earmarked for the attack, and a hundred reserved for the return trip.

Fully half of those launchers were loaded with antiair weapons. As in the past Ko planned to rely on his submarine escort to defend the *Sea Dragon* from Allied attack subs. Although, rather than the two escorts assigned to Ko previously, there was only one. "Attack subs are in short supply," Chao told him. "Sorry. But that's how it is."

Most of the *Dragon's* ship-to-ship, or in this case ship-to-shore, missiles had been loaded with targeting information provided by MSS and military intelligence.

Ten weapons had been set aside for his highness King Yingluck Chulaloke. Because, once *he* was dead, the political situation would revert to what China viewed as normal, and the possibility of a southern front would be foreclosed.

But, unlike the government buildings slated for destruction, Rama XI was a moving target. So spies had been assigned to track the royal's movements, and upload his location just prior to the attack at 1800.

And sure enough, the necessary coordinates were downloaded at 1745, which gave the *Sea Dragon's* operations people fifteen minutes to program the YJ-91s.

Ko didn't care where Chulaloke was, so long as the King was within range, which was the case. So, when the time came, all Ko had to do was give two simple orders: "Prepare to fire missiles ... *Fire!*" The *Sea Dragon* shuddered as missiles left their tubes at a rate of one every eight seconds.

Once the last YJ-91 was in the air, the Chinese cruiser turned south. Damage assessments would be conducted by spies and satellites in space.

Home. That was the only thing Ko cared about.

There was no counterattack by Thailand's government, which lacked the capability to sort the *Sea Dragon* out of the clutter on their radar screens, or to launch retaliatory missile strikes.

But Allies had the means to not only search for the attacker but to rain hell down on it. And Ko knew the search had begun. His exit strategy was brutally simple. Kill everything that got in the way. And that was why he'd been careful to keep the ship's sometimes cantankerous railgun in reserve. Ko was counting on it, plus the one hundred missiles waiting in the ship's tubes, to clear a path.

The weather continued to improve, as the semisubmersible made a beeline for the Ca Mau Cape, and the South China Sea beyond. The cloak of darkness was like an old friend.

But it was only a matter of time before the eastern sky began to lighten and the sun rose. Though partially submerged, the *Sea Dragon's* conning towers were exposed.

But when the attack came, it was from beneath the surface of the sea, rather than from above. The Australian Collins-class sub, HMAS *Danson*, managed to fire all of her torpedo tubes, before being attacked by the *Sea Dragon's* underwater escort.

Five of the *Danson's* six torpedoes were drawn off target by the *Sea Dragon's* decoys. But one of the Mark 48 torpedoes scored a hit.

***

Lieutenant Jev Jing felt the impact. Alarms went off. Compartments were sealed. And Jing felt a stab of fear. No! It couldn't be. The *Sea Dragon* was invulnerable to enemy fire!

Captain Ko delivered the news via the ship's intercom. "The ship was struck by a single torpedo. Three compartments were flooded. But since those spaces house empty missile launchers our capacity to maneuver and fight remains undiminished. The enemy submarine was destroyed. Carry on."

The truth was slightly different. The additional weight in the flooded compartments had a negative effect on the semisubmersible's buoyancy. And there was the possibility that it would generate noise that enemy sonar could detect.

But Ko saw no reason to disclose that information. Nor did he mention the fact that, if the Allied sub had been able to get a message off, then the Allies knew where the *Sea Dragon* was. And they would respond accordingly. An assumption that was proven to be accurate only minutes later. Suddenly, according to a high priority message from naval headquarters in Beijing— the lead elements of an American carrier group had left Japan—and were steaming south.

But Admiral Chao was ready for such a move, and countered by sending a Chinese carrier group north. A move which would theoretically give the damaged cruiser a chance to reach its home port unopposed. And would finally provide the Chinese navy an opportunity to lay waste to the *xia Riben guizi* (little Japanese devils).

Many Chinese officers assumed that their ships would win such a contest. Ko wasn't one of them. But he could hardly complain since the *Sea Dragon* was likely to be the chief beneficiary of Chao's initiative. And for the better part of six suspenseful hours, it appeared that all available American ships *were* headed for the impending battle, like iron filings drawn to a magnet.

But shortly after the *Dragon* entered the South China Sea two blips appeared on radar. And thanks to video being streamed to the cruiser from a GJ-2 UAV, Ko learned that the blips were American destroyers, presumably in company with an attack sub.

Within seconds it became clear that the Americans could "see" the Chinese cruiser. The *Arleigh Burke* class destroyers were armed with a wide variety of weapons. But it was the enemy's ship-to-ship missiles that Ko feared most, four of which were in the air, and headed his way.

As luck would have it, Ko was in Operations 1 when the enemy ships were spotted and the Harpoons were fired. Even so, there was a momentary time lag as the fire control computer requested permission to fire anti-air missiles, and the duty officer turned to Ko seeking permission. He said, "Yes!" but it was too late. The sea-skimming missiles were traveling at more than five hundred mph, and were halfway to the *Sea Dragon* by then.

Mortars burped decoys into the air and three of the American weapons exploded harmlessly. But the fourth struck the hull forward of Conning Tower 1. The warhead was packing 488 pounds of HE and blew a hole through the hull, killing three crewmembers.

Because most of the cruiser's hull was awash, water poured in through the hole, causing automatic systems to seal the flooded compartment.

The *Sea Dragon* was fighting for her life. Anti-air missiles sleeted into the air, as more Harpoons were launched, and Chinese YJ-91 anti-ship missiles skimmed the waves.

Both American vessels mounted SRBOC launchers which did an effective job of luring the Chinese weapons away. In addition, both destroyers were equipped with Mk 53 Nulka hovering decoys, each of which produced a ship-like radar signature.

Meanwhile, below the surface of the sea, the American boats were towing AN/SLQ-25A Nixie torpedo decoys. The crew on the Chinese attack sub wasn't fooled however.

They knew the first sonic signatures they heard would be from decoys, and were happy to expend two torpedoes on the Nixies.

But in doing so, the subs revealed themselves to the men and women aboard the *USS Waco*, the attack sub sent to protect the American destroyers. A spread of Mark 48 torpedoes began to search for the Chinese attack boat and found it.

There was a brief moment of celebration aboard the *Waco* as two underwater explosions were heard, followed by the distinctive sounds of a ship breaking up.

But just as the Chinese boat revealed itself to the *Waco*, the American boat became electronically "visible" to the *Sea Dragon*, which was armed with two anti-sub rocket launchers. Each rocket released a torpedo. And both of them went looking for a submarine. One of them scored a hit.

Meanwhile, as the surface combatants continued to close with each other, the battle became even more intense. Ko was desperate to break contact and run. His ship had sustained two serious wounds and he feared that the Americans would win the war of attrition.

So, despite the fact that Ko had been hoping to keep the popup railgun in reserve, he had no choice but to use it.

Thanks to the ship's radar, the overhead drone, and a downlink from a Chinese satellite, all of the ship's interlocking fire control systems were updated at five second intervals. That made the process of firing the railgun easy: Raise the weapon from below deck, run an automated systems check, and issue orders.

The destroyers were about ten miles apart and coming toward the *Sea Dragon* at approximately 34 knots per hour. The ship to port, as seen from the *Sea Dragon*, had been labeled as "Target 1." And the one to the right was "Target 2."

Ko gave the orders. "Prepare to fire on Target 1. *Fire!* Prepare to fire on Target 2. *Fire!*" Sixty seconds elapsed before the second shell departed.

The smart shells raced down range at five thousand mph. They weren't packing explosive charges. Nor did they need to. Kinetic energy alone was enough to penetrate Target 1's main deck, the deck below, *and* the engine room—where the projectile shattered. Shrapnel flew in every direction. Jagged pieces of steel punctured the hull, water poured in, and alarms sounded. The order to abandon ship was given three minutes later.

Target 2 fared no better. The speeding railgun shell fell on its superstructure, destroyed the bridge, plunged through the main deck—and punched a hole in the hull.

Like its sister ship, the tin can sank within fifteen minutes. Life boats and rafts were left bobbing where it had been.

Ko had no interest in taking prisoners. His submarine escort had been destroyed, and he had three flooded compartments to contend with. All he wanted to do was reach the safety of the sub pens in the Yulin navy base. And do so as quickly as possible. The *Sea Dragon* limped north.

***

On the island of Samir, in the South China Sea

Commander Max Ryson was lying on his back, staring at the sky. It was blue with white striations. There were no contrails to be seen. Not a single one. And Ryson thought he knew why. Hundreds of miles north of Samir, and west of Taiwan, enormous fleets were about to clash. And that, Ryson felt sure, was where the semisubmersible cruiser was. If so, the Chinese would have a huge advantage.

The thought made him even more depressed. The trip to the village of Coloane had been nothing short of a disaster, both personally and professionally.

The full extent of Kelsey's treachery had shaken Ryson to the core, leaving him unsure of his judgement, and his ability to lead. *I was thinking with my dick*, Ryson decided. *And people died as a result.*

After a relatively short trip aboard the *Dakota*, the survivors had been transferred to an Indonesian destroyer, which took them to Manado—where members of the Australian Federal Police took both Parker women into custody.

"Kelsey's in serious trouble," Admiral Nathan said. "And the Feds want to get a deposition from Rong. Mr. Soo will get paid by the way. The ASIS (Australia's Secret Intelligence Collection Agency) blokes think the Hong Kong-Macau triad could come in handy.

"As for George, well, he's in Sydney by now. And all the money he has won't be enough to get him out of the kind of trouble he's in. Don't blame yourself, Max. There's no way you could have known."

Ryson *did* blame himself. But all he could do was return to work. And he was aboard the supply ship *Alcona* when she returned to Samir Island. Soon followed by a tanker which had orders to remain on station for two weeks. And that was a good thing, because the entire squadron was anchored around Samir, or out on patrol.

The sun was warm. The sand was soft. And a gentle breeze ruffled the surface of the lagoon. Sleep brought a welcome escape. Then a female voice said, "Wake up, Skipper ... We have work to do."

Kelsey? Ryson opened his eyes. Lieutenant Commander Linda Vos was standing over him. What was that in her eyes? Concern? Or pity?

Ryson sat up. "Work? What kind of work?"

"The *Sea Dragon* attacked Bangkok," Vos told him. "It looks as though the Chinese were trying to assassinate King Ramos XI. Fortunately, they failed.

"Then, on the way home an Australian sub managed to torpedo, but not sink, the *Dragon*. I knew the skipper," she added. "He was a nice man."

Vos's use of the past tense spoke volumes. "I'm sorry," Ryson said, as he stood. "Very sorry."

"Thanks," Vos replied. "According to the folks at INDOPACCOM the *Dragon* was still running for home when it was intercepted by two American destroyers."

Ryson winced. "And?"

"And, one of the tin cans scored a hit. But the *Sea Dragon's* railgun sank them both. One shell each. A submarine named the *USS Waco* is missing as well."

Ryson shook his head sadly. "Then the *Sea Dragon* ran."

"Exactly," Vos said. "And, because most of the Chinese fleet was focused on the battle up north, the *Dragon* was on her own. Then a layer of clouds moved in. That's when the satellite nerds lost track of her."

All of Ryson's PHMs were named after cloud formations. Was it an omen? His brain began to race. "So, they want us to find her?"

"No," Vos replied. "Thanks to a tip from one of Kelsey Parker's cigarette smugglers, we know where the *Sea Dragon* is."

"Which is?"

"Mischief Reef. The Intel people think she was forced to take refuge there in order to make temporary repairs. The Chinese have four fighters stationed on the atoll.

"And," Voss added, "based on what happened to our submarines, we can assume that at least one attack boat is lurking in the area too.

"Our orders are to get there as quickly as we can and keep the *Sea Dragon* bottled up, until the heavy hitters can arrive from the north."

Assuming they win the big battle, Ryson thought. *And how long will that take?* He pushed the thought away. "Is the squadron ready for sea?"

"The *Nimbus* and *Fractus* are taking on fuel. The rest are cranking up."

"And air support?"

"I tried. But all I could get was a Global Hawk drone. It doesn't have any weapons, but will arrive on station within the hour, and can loiter for twenty-five hours—not counting travel time."

Ryson grinned. "Thanks, Linda. You're not bad for an Aussie."

"And you're okay for a Yank," she replied.

Both officers grinned. "I'll board the *Arcus*," Ryson said. "You'll be on the *Cumulus*. The Armindales will bring up the rear. I realize you would prefer to be on one of the Aussie boats. But, if something happens to me, you'll need to be up front where the PHMs are."

Vos knew the American boats were faster than the remaining Armindale and would arrive first. Barkley wouldn't like having the squadron's XO looking over her shoulder. But Vos planned to remain in the background and pray that nothing happened to Ryson.

What ensued was a scramble to board boats, prepare for combat, and get underway. Mischief Reef was more than three hours away for the PHMs. But all of them, officers and enlisted alike, had been looking for the Chinese ghost ship for a month by then, and were eager to close with the enemy. Consequences be damned.

It was a risk. But Ryson gave orders for the tanker to follow. The boats would be sucking max fuel, and there was no way to know how long the mission would last.

Once foilborne, the *Arcus* led the way, with the other hydrofoils following in a column behind. It was a sight of the sort not seen since WWII when PT boats ventured out to battle the Japanese.

Ryson was filled with a heady mix of excitement, anticipation, and gut-churning fear. He knew, based on previous experience, that the fear could be controlled. And that the adrenaline would clear his mind.

The *Sea Dragon* had advantages, the most important of which was the damned railgun. A weapon with a range of at least 124 miles, judging from what had happened to the *USS Concord*.

The Chinese cruiser was armed with missiles as well. As many as two hundred of them. But some had been expended during the attack on Bangkok. So how many were left? It seemed safe to assume that at least 25 percent of the ship's weapons had been fired. Probably more.

As for efficacy, Chinese anti-air missiles had proven to be quite accurate, and were likely to intercept at least some of the squadron's Harpoons.

But the cruiser's ship-to-ship YJ-91 missiles had a range of seventy-five miles. That was significantly less than the squadron's capacity to strike targets one hundred and fifty miles away.

So, what did all this suggest? *We'll fire our missiles while we're beyond the range of both the railgun and the YJ-91 missiles*, Ryson concluded. *All of them. From every boat.*

Ryson made use of a secure channel to communicate his plan to the rest of the boats. "So, that's it," he said. "Any questions?"

All the commanding officers were wondering the same thing: "What if we fail to destroy the *Sea Dragon* with missiles? What then?"

But, none of them gave voice to their doubts. And that was fortunate. Because Ryson lacked any answers.

***

Mischief Reef, the South China Sea

The *Sea Dragon* was inside the lagoon at Mischief Reef, the tide was falling, and she would soon be aground. Not by accident, but on purpose.

There had been a time, hundreds of years earlier, when a process called "careening" was used to ground sailing vessels at high tide and expose one side of the ship's hull. Then, before the water returned, repairs could be made.

And Captain Ko was well aware of the practice. That's why the cruiser was anchored at the shallow end of the lagoon, not far from the airstrip and the equipment associated with it.

That included a considerable pile of junk and plenty of welding equipment. "This is what we need," Chief Engineer Hong said, as he tapped a rusty boiler. "Look at that! Curved steel. What more could you want? Cut this section out."

Hong used a can of white spray paint to outline the rectangle of metal he wanted. Members of his team went to work with cutting torches minutes later.

Meanwhile Lieutenant Jev Jing was waist deep in the lagoon. He was supervising the team of sailors tasked with building a platform for the welders to stand on when the metal "patch" arrived on site.

A jagged hole marked the spot where the Allied torpedo had hit. And, because of two open hatches, the seawater had gushed through the opening, filling three compartments.

The internal hatches separating the compartments should have been closed while the crew was at battle stations. And later, once the cruiser arrived in Yulin, some careless bastard was going to pay.

But that was in the future. In the meantime, a temporary repair was required to prevent more water from leaking out of the flooded compartments and into conduits that led to other parts of the ship.

That's where the patch came in. But in order to install it, Hong's crew had to stand on something. And rather than wade around in the lagoon themselves, Jing's superiors assigned him the task. Jing lacked any relevant experience, and was planning to build a structure made of wood, when a petty officer pointed out that wood floats. And the metal staging used to repair airplanes would constitute a better solution. Jing was thrilled to receive some useful advice and was quick to make the switch.

But to execute the plan it was necessary to take the staging apart, carry it out into the lagoon by hand, and reassemble it with rusty nuts and bolts. Fortunately, the local jet mechanics had a plentiful supply of American WD40 which, when applied to recalcitrant parts, made a huge difference.

So, by the time Hong and twenty sweating sailors lugged the curved piece of metal out to the Sea Dragon, the platform was in place. Hong took a look at it, turned to Jing, and said: "Good job." It was one of the happiest moments in the young man's life.

***

Captain Ko was standing in the *Sea Dragon's* CIC when the hull shifted under his feet. Metal groaned. That was to be expected.

The hole was located on the port side of the hull. To access the gash, the crew would have to roll the ship to starboard.

What would have been an impossible job on a more traditional ship, was made easy by the fact that Hong's people could pump water from the port to starboard ballast tanks, thereby shifting enough weight to expose the jagged opening. The *Sea Dragon's* decks were slanted as a result which made it difficult to move around inside the hull.

Ko was scanning the latest Intel report. There were no threats inbound from the north, and wouldn't be, until the battle of Taiwan came to its bloody conclusion.

Then, if the Allies won, they would send units south. But, if China's fleet was victorious, they would chase the *Yemen ren* (barbarians) all the way to Japan.

Meanwhile, according to satellite and drone surveillance, nine radar blips were headed for Mischief Reef from the south. Fortunately, based on video from the drone, the blips were patrol boats rather than major warships. It appeared that six were armed with missiles and three weren't. *That's like sending ants to kill an elephant*, Ko mused.

Ego, Ko thought. *The greatest enemy of all.*

***

Aboard the *USS Arcus*, northbound in the South China Sea

Sunlight glittered on the surface of the sea as the PHM *Arcus* led Squadron 7 north. The boat was foilborne and "flying" along at nearly 52 knots. Ryson consulted his watch. The moment was upon them.

Between them the Pegasus 2 patrol boats could launch forty-eight Harpoon missiles. Ryson knew, or thought he knew, that

Chinese anti-air weapons would intercept many of them. Others would be drawn off target by mortar launched decoys. But that was the nature of things. All he could do was try. And, by launching all the Harpoons at one time, the total number of incoming weapons might be enough to overwhelm the *Sea Dragon's* defenses.

There was another reason as well. A calculation so cold that Ryson was hesitant to admit it to himself. And that was the need to use the Harpoons while he could. Because the destruction of a single PHM would result in the loss of eight offensive weapons. And, according to the techs in the CIC, jet fighters were in bound from the north. That meant there was a good chance that one or more of his vessels would be sunk within the hour.

Ryson thumbed a mike. "This is Six. All PHMs will prepare to fire *all* missiles on the count of 3. One, 2, 3, *fire!*" Ryson felt a series of jolts as Moy's crew fired every Harpoon the *Arcus* had. The other hydrofoils did likewise. Death flew through the air.

***

Aboard the Chinese semisubmersible cruiser *Sea Dragon*, in the Mischief Reef lagoon

Ko could see the incoming blips. All he could do was grit his teeth, because the ships which launched the missiles were still too far away to strike back at.

There was another problem too. Or could be. And that was the way the ship was listing to port. Would that have a negative effect on the *Sea Dragon's* anti-air missiles? Causing them to miss their targets?

Not according to the man in charge of the ship's missiles. "Ships roll," Lieutenant Commander Yoo pointed out. "And our missiles were designed to compensate for that."

Once the incoming Harpoons were sufficiently close, the anti-air weapons raced off to intercept them. That wasn't all. The Mischief Reef base had SAM launchers of its own. And those missiles joined the fray.

One by one the Harpoons were intercepted and destroyed. But the sheer number of them was more than the Mischief Reef's combined defenses could handle. And three of the forty-eight weapons made it through.

One scored a direct hit on the airstrip's radome, destroying the antenna inside, and blinded the base. Another struck a SAM site where it caused a series of explosions. The third nailed the *Sea Dragon*.

Conning Tower 2 was badly mangled. In fact, the access hatch was open to the sky, and couldn't be closed. But, because the opening was well above the waterline, it wouldn't matter unless it rained. And at that point a mop and a bucket would be enough to handle the problem. Conning Tower 1 was untouched.

That was bad. But Chief Engineer Hong's patch was in place and the tide was rising. *My turn is coming*, Ko thought. *And the Yemen ren will be sorry.*

CHAPTER FIFTEEN

Aboard the *USS Arcus*, northbound in the South China Sea

Each PHM, and each Armindale, had two Stinger teams—which meant the squadron could fire eighteen missiles at once. Then, as the anti-air teams hurried to reload, the fire would become more sporadic. So Ryson wanted to make the most of the initial broadside.

"This is Six," Ryson said. "Odds are that the enemy planes will attack one at a time. Let's give their flight leader a warm welcome. Lock onto the bastard, and ignore the rest of the bastards for the moment. And when I say, 'Fire,' let him have it. Maybe we can kill their leader. Over."

The Chinese attacked exactly the way Ryson anticipated they would—in a line, like beads on a string. He made the call as missiles flared from the lead plane's wings. "Fire!"

Stingers spiraled up into the sky, all searching for heat. The first Chengdu J-20 fighter fired chaff and three Stingers fell for it. Each exploded in turn.

But as those missiles were transformed into gray puffs of smoke, the rest of the Stingers zeroed in. And the combined explosions turned the J-20 into confetti. Now the assistant flight leader was in charge. And, Ryson assumed, was scared shitless.

All the boats were firing chaff. White wakes twisted, turned and crossed each other as the boats took evasive action. "Call your targets," Ryson ordered. "Coordinate your fire. Over."

That was when two Chinese missiles hit the *Contrail*, exploded, and caused the boat to slew around. Lieutenant Dan Torres and his bridge crew were killed instantly. Then the 30mm ammo bin blew, destroying what remained of the hydrofoil.

There was a steady stream of chatter from the Stinger teams. "Targeting the plane to the south. Firing."

"Bandit in from the north. Tracking, tracking, tracking … Firing!"

A fireball marked the spot where the Chengdu had been. *Two down*, Ryson thought, *two to go*.

"Target to the west," a sailor said. "Let's gangbang him. Prepare to fire."

That was followed by a chorus of "Rogers." Then came the order to fire, not from an officer, but the E4 who had taken charge. Explosions bracketed the plane. A wing sheared off. And, like a seed pod falling from a maple tree, the remains of the enemy plane twirled into the ocean. "Nice job," Ryson said. "Keep it up. Over."

One plane remained. And the boats were running out of Stingers. But that, as it turned out, didn't matter. The remaining pilot loosed all his remaining missiles and rockets on *Kalbarri*, failed to score a hit, and performed a gun run on an empty patch of water. Then he turned, and flew north.

Ryson could imagine what the pilot would tell the people at his base. "They had missiles, lots of them, and the other guys went down! I destroyed one of their ships though … But, after I ran out of ordinance, I was forced to return."

The fact that the survivor's racks were empty would serve to support the lies. A medal would follow. But Ryson didn't care. He was all for it. The way was open now … And the *Sea Dragon* was waiting.

***

Aboard the Chinese semisubmersible cruiser *Sea Dragon*, in the Mischief Reef lagoon

Captain Ko was in Operations 1. The *Sea Dragon* was afloat, but just barely, as the tide continued to rise. Ko was determined to destroy the Allied boats before they could inflict further damage on his ship. They were well within range by that time. And the remaining ship-to-ship missiles were ready. "Prepare to fire," Ko ordered. *"Fire!"*

Every ship-to-ship missile the cruiser had shot into the air. All forty-eight of them. They arced to the south, spent a minute in flight, and fell like thunderbolts.

***

A Chinese missile went straight for a decoy fired by the *Cumulus*, hit it only ten feet above the launcher, and exploded. The blast bored a hole down to the engine room where it destroyed the boat's gas turbine engine. At that point the *Cumulus* might be able to proceed hullborne, but appeared to dead in the water.

First, the *Contrail*, and now this. Ryson felt a gigantic hole open up in the pit of his stomach. Vos. What about Vos? Grief threatened to overwhelm him. *Not now*, Ryson thought, *not now. Focus.*

Then, as quickly as it began, the barrage was over. And when a minute passed without another barrage, Ryson concluded that the *Sea Dragon*'s launchers were empty.

Suddenly, and unbidden, the song *Highway to Hell by AC/DC* began to blast over the squadron's radios. Moy looked at Ryson as if to say, "Kill it?"

Ryson shook his head. He could see the low-lying smudge ahead. "We're going in!" Ryson shouted over the music. "Into the lagoon! Engage with guns!"

That was when a shell from the *Sea Dragon's* railgun hit the *HMAS Kalbarri*, and broke the Australian boat in half. Ryson swore, as the *Arcus* led the *Fractus,* the *Stratus,* and the *Nimbus* in through one of two passageways which provided access to the lagoon.

All of the PHMs were foilborne and began to fire the moment the *Sea Dragon* came into view. The *HMAS Rockhampton,* meanwhile, was still to the south and trying to catch up.

Ryson watched in horror as the *Sea Dragon's* bow turned toward what he thought of as Passageway Number 1, while the cruiser's railgun began to track the *Fractus.*

A single shot was all it took to kill the PHM. The rock and roll music stopped.

Slowly, but surely, the *Sea Dragon* was gaining speed. And Ryson's orders were to keep her bottled up. That was the moment when an artillery shell hit the *Arcus* in the stern. *Artillery,* Ryson thought. *The possibility never occurred to me. I'm a fucking idiot.*

"The steering's gone!" the helmsman shouted, as the PHM roared toward a sandy beach. "We're going in!"

The words were followed by a jolt as the foils hit the bottom, held for a moment, and collapsed. Water flew up all around as the hydrofoil came down twenty feet short of the beach. Ryson was thrown forwards, hit his head, and fell to the deck.

His head hurt, and Ryson felt dizzy, as he stumbled out of the wheelhouse. The *Nimbus* was still in it, and turning a wide circle, as commanding officer Marie Moreno went at the Chinese cruiser with her gun blazing. Ryson saw hits all over the deck and around the remaining conning tower. But the shells had little effect.

Ryson felt his heart sink as shore batteries fired, waterspouts rose all around the hydrofoil, and a shell fell on the boat. The resulting explosion sent a blast wave surging across the lagoon. Ryson felt the warm air collide with his face. *It's over*, he thought bitterly. *Dozens of lives lost for nothing.*

Then the *HMAS Rockhampton* roared into the Lagoon with a bone in her teeth. Ryson wanted to order skipper Lieutenant Mike Christian to break it off, to save his crew, when he saw the boat's starboard torpedo launcher. "Oh, my God," Ryson shouted. "Mike's going to do it! He's going to take a shot at the bitch!"

As Ryson watched, a Mark 48 torpedo shot out of the launcher and splashed into the water. A trail could be seen as the long, sleek weapon sought its target.

Ryson couldn't see the *Rockhampton's* port side from where he was, but assumed that the other torpedo was racing toward the *Sea Dragon* as well, and traveling at 52 knots.

Taken together the weapons were packing 2,000 pounds worth of explosive. And the range was so short that it would be almost impossible to miss. And Mike didn't.

The Mark 48s slammed into the Chinese cruiser about half way down its 667-foot length, going off within seconds of each other. Ryson cheered as the blast wave from overlapping explosions sent waves rippling across the lagoon.

Pillars of fire jetted up through two of the hatches through which missiles were launched; the enemy ship shook as if palsied, and uttered what sounded like a groan. Then the cruiser broke in half.

The *Sea Dragon* couldn't sink. The water wasn't deep enough for that. So, she came to rest on the bottom, as ant-like crewmen poured up and out of Conning Tower 1.

Ryson was still celebrating when an artillery round went off one hundred feet away and tiny bits of shrapnel peppered his body. Moy was there to grab and drag him away. "Come with me, sir … Mike will pick us up from the other side of the reef."

There were Chinese installations a thousand yards to the left, and an equal distance to the right. Moy was careful to split the distance between them. Small arms fire threw up geysers of sand as Chinese soldiers advanced from both directions.

But the *Rockhampton* was bow-on to the beach by then. And the Armindale's port and starboard fifty-caliber machines guns were more than sufficient to keep the Chinese soldiers at bay.

Ryson stood by as Moy urged his sailors into the surf and took a count to make sure that all of them were accounted for. Only then did the officers follow. The water was blood warm.

RIB boats arrived to pluck the *Arc's* crew out of the water and carry them to the *Rockhampton.* Once everyone was aboard, and RIBs were stowed, the Armindale backed away—guns firing.

Ryson made his way to the bridge. Lieutenant Mike Christian had a huge grin on his face. "You were right, sir … Torpedoes work."

Ryson laughed. "And you made the most of them, Mike … I've never seen a finer sight. Your entry into the lagoon, and the run that followed, is worthy of a painting.

"I suspect the Australian government is going to hang medals all over your body. Now, if you could put me with a radio tech, I have some calls to make. I hope the *Cumulus* is still afloat."

***

Lieutenant Jev Jing and about thirty members of the Sea Dragon's bedraggled crew were sitting on the beach waiting for someone to give orders. No one did.

An Allied patrol boat was speeding south, and getting smaller with each passing moment. *How?* How was such a thing possible?

"Look," a sailor said, "It's Chief Engineer Hong!" And it *was* Hong who marched up out of the water with a body cradled in his arms.

And as Hong came closer Jing saw that the body was that of Captain Ko. The man who loved his ship. And his crew. Would the functionaries in Beijing blame Ko for losing the *Sea Dragon*? Of course, they would. A suitable proverb came to mind: "He who blames others has a long way to go on his journey. He who blames himself is halfway there. He who blames no one has arrived."

***

Aboard the Allied transport *Agger*, in Manado Harbor, Indonesia

Two weeks had passed since the Allied victory at the Battle of Taiwan. A conflict that raged for three days, and resulted in the sinking of ships on both sides, but most tellingly the loss of the nuclear-powered carrier *Zhongguo Liming* (Chinese Dawn).

That, plus the much-publicized destruction of the raider *Sea Dragon*, lifted spirits all around the world. And did something to offset losses in Europe and the Middle East.

Ryson's time had been spent writing letters, dozens of them, to the families of crew members lost. He tried to make each one special, and evocative of the man or woman who had died, but it was difficult. The effort often called for multiple drafts. He was working on one for Sub Lieutenant Lewis when a knock came at the door.

Ryson said, "Enter!" and turned to see Lieutenant Commander, soon to be Commander, Linda Vos RAN (Royal Australian Navy) enter the room.

RED TIDE

After a short search, the *Rockhampton* had been able to join company with the tanker which had the *Cumulus* in tow. Fortunately, Vos had survived uninjured. "Linda! Come in, and congratulations! I hear you're getting a bump to commander, plus a ship."

Vos sat on the neighboring couch. She looked very professional in her summer whites. "Yes, thanks to you."

Ryson shook his head. "Not so. I wrote you up, that's for sure ... But you earned it. So, when do you leave? Is there time for a dinner ashore?"

"There is," Vos assured him. "And I would enjoy that. I'm taking a bit of leave before I report to my command. I hear you've been summoned to Washington D.C."

"True," Ryson replied. "I was. But I asked them to put the medal in the mail. The squadron needs to be rebuilt from the bottom up. And I don't care for D.C."

"What about leave?" Vos inquired. "Surely you have some on the books."

"I do," Ryson admitted. "But where would I go?"

Vos smiled. "Can you ride a horse?"

"Absolutely not."

"Would you like to learn?"

Ryson looked at her. Vos was a pretty woman. The kind that doesn't think of herself that way but is. The lines around her eyes had been earned while staring into the sea-glare. And her mouth was *what?* Kissable? Yes. "I would like to learn," Ryson told her. "Theoretically anyway."

Vos laughed. "I own a cattle station back home. A neighbor runs it for me. We could spend a couple of weeks there."

Ryson liked the look in her eyes. "Would the beer be cold?"

"Ice cold."

"Would people shoot at me?"

"No."

"Then I'm in."

"Good," Vos said as she stood. "I'll make a dinner reservation for tonight. We can discuss the details then." The door clicked behind her.

Ryson stared at it for a moment before returning to work. He felt better than he had in months. The war would continue. But something good was about to happen.

AUTHOR'S NOTE

As usual, I played fast and loose with some things, and was factual about others.

The *Sea Dragon* doesn't exist. But the possibility of such a ship does. If you run a search using the terms "Arsenal Ship," "Semi-submersible naval vessel," and "Railgun" you'll come up with some very interesting articles. The *Sea Dragon* qualifies as both an arsenal ship and a semisubmersible. Plus, she's armed with a railgun.

Chinese politics are pretty opaque, but tensions between China's top two leaders do exist, and could be a problem. Read the *Wall Street Journal* article "Discord Between China's Top Two Leaders Spills into the Open" to get an inkling of what's possible.

The Yulin Naval Base is very real, and capable of handling twenty nuclear submarines.

The Chinese list their surnames first. But, to avoid confusion for my western readers, I chose to put given names first.

The Russian Black Sea Fleet controls the Black Sea for all practical purposes, and occasionally sends ships into the Mediterranean.

In the sort of WWIII scenario imagined in my Winds of War books, the Allies would have no choice but to attack the Russian Fleet in order to protect countries like Bulgaria, Romania and Ukraine.

Plus, even though Turkey is a member of NATO, some people feel their present government can't be trusted. I'm one of them. But I hope things will improve someday. I've been to Turkey and like the country.

Pegasus class hydrofoils were employed by the U.S. Navy from 1977 through 1993. The PHMs (Patrol, Hydrofoil, Missile) boats featured in this book are "next generation" PHMs as conceived of by me and the team of *Pegasus* experts listed under "Acknowledgements."

As a group we had fun imagining what "Peg 2s" would be like, which is to say very similar to the originals—but with some improvements regarding size, speed, and technology.

I'm of the opinion that the United States should bring this class of vessel back for a wide variety of missions including those depicted in this book.

Samir island is a product of my imagination, but is similar in many ways to the very real atoll called Mischief Reef, which is presently occupied by the Chinese—and fictionally located north of Samir. (See map.)

Should you care to "visit" Mischief Reef, fire up Google Earth, and enter "Mischief Reef." Once you "arrive," you'll see a lagoon with Chinese ships in it, plus a very serviceable airstrip—which wasn't built to accommodate tourism.

Chinese Triads exist. They're ranked as portrayed in the book, and there's one in Hong Kong–Macao. And yes, they've been around for a long, long time.

I thought that "Sea Cow" submarines, like the fictional *North Dakota* were my invention until I Googled the name, and discovered that the Germans had Type XIV U-boats (modified Type IXDs), which were designed to resupply other U-boats. They were nicknamed "*Milchkuh/Milchkühe*" (milk cows).

Do such vessels exist now? Hmm. I wonder. Two of our ballistic missile subs were retrofitted to carry up to 66 special operations troops, so why not some diesel fuel too?

And yes, for any reader who may have questioned it, WD40 is available in China. I found it on the internet.

ABOUT THE WINDS OF WAR SERIES

I n **RED SANDS**, volume six of the Winds of War series, WIII continues to rage as the Allies launch multiple raids deep into Iran looking for finished nuclear weapons that they believe exist.

RED SANDS is the story of Strike Team 3, a combined arms unit consisting of mechanized infantry Strykers and Tanks. Their objective is to seize control of the hardened Fuel Enrichment Plant at Natanz and search it. The facility is located twenty-six feet underground, and protected by a concrete wall that's eight feet thick.

In February of 2003 General Mohamed El Baradei visited the site and reported that 160 centrifuges were complete, and ready for operation, with 1,000 more under construction. The site has been cloaked in secrecy ever since.

In order for Major Sean Finn and his troops to accomplish their mission, they will have to cope with the self-absorbed Saudi Prince (attached to the unit for political reasons), a company of Russian tanks that's rolling south from the Caspian Sea, Iranian armor sent to kill them, and the Kavir desert.

And ultimately Strike Team 3 will have to deal with another enemy as well. A man so barbarous that he's called the "Butcher of Kom," and for good reason.

"It is," in the words of the *New York Times* reporter embedded with Strike Team 3, "the definition of a suicide mission."

ABOUT WILLIAM C. DIETZ

For more about **William C. Dietz** and his fiction, please visit williamcdietz.com.

You can find Bill on Facebook at: www.facebook.com/williamcdietz.

Printed in Great Britain
by Amazon

61946236R00210